BORN IN BLOOD

BORN IN BLOOD

The SEAL Saga: Book 2

MEGAN MICHELLE

ISBN: 9798988886112

Trigger Warnings:

- Child death
- Human trafficking
- Reference to abortion
- Reference to miscarriage
- Reference to sexual assault including sexual assault of a minor
- Rough sex
- Suicide bombs
- Violence against children

Please note this is not an exhaustive list and only includes things that would not be expected given the context of the plot.

Your mental health is important and should be prioritized.

PART I:

ENDINGS

Chapter 1

SEPTEMBER 2020

COUNTING HER BREATHS, RACHEL Ryker ducked low and sprinted across the street. She crouched down under the cover of the windowsill, her legs shaking from the adrenaline and her spine sweating from the morning heat. She could be any other civilian, clad in jeans and a t-shirt, except for the black scarf she had slung around her neck. She'd bought it from a market in Afghanistan, years ago, and she always wore it when she was deployed. Now, she pulled the scarf over her recognizable blonde hair, thankful for whatever instinct had urged her to wear it this morning, as her eyes tracked her target.

"What the fuck is he doing here?" she muttered to herself. Her eyes darted up and down the street, assessing for threats—a residual habit from her time in combat—until finally fixating on a bald man with a greying beard, dressed in a faded Navy sweatshirt.

She didn't entirely trust herself that it was him. She'd never actually seen the man out of uniform, but she'd recognize his smug disposition anywhere.

Rachel and her boyfriend, Christopher Williams, had only been living in D.C. for a few weeks. It had been a calm, peaceful few weeks until right this moment when retired Admiral Richard Leftwich, also known as the asshole who'd gotten Rachel pulled out of combat and put on a desk, appeared at her favorite coffee shop, Cardigan Coffee. Why the man felt the need to get his coffee from a Taylor Swift themed coffee shop, she had no idea. She'd had enough conversations with the man over the past decade to know he was most definitely not a Swiftie, and he was most definitely very out of place.

Logical or not, Rachel immediately reached the conclusion that he was somewhere he wouldn't run into anyone he knew on purpose. She'd suspected he was up to some shady shit for months now, ever since she'd gotten the intel report back from Matt showing that Leftwich had made several phone calls to an unknown number in Syria. Each of those phone calls had been placed just hours before Rachel's SEAL team had hit a compound to recover a USB with a malware code that had been stolen from the U.S. government—from her father's house, to be more specific. The man was conspiring with known terrorists and therefore guilty of treason. Not that anyone seemed to believe her.

How dare he interrupt her peace, interrupt her treating herself. She rarely consumed sugar, but on days she knew would be awful, caffeinated chocolate in the form of a mocha was the solution, the bribe, to get her to engage in the day with a smile, however fake. Awful came in many forms, but the agenda for today was downright dreadful. Today was the day she got to sit in front of a panel of senators and convince them that yes, she did in fact know how to do the job she'd been assigned to do. Dealing with politicians was her least favorite thing to do. The idea of convincing other people she was qualified to do something she'd been doing for years made her want to rip her own fingernails off.

A boom rattled the windows, and Rachel dared a glance over the windowsill.

No bombs, no gunfire. Just a delivery driver setting down a rather large coffee shipment.

Rachel stared through the coffee shop window, her eyes tracking the caffeine deprived civilians as she looked for her target. She glanced over her shoulder, then back through the window. *There.* In the back corner. Leftwich.

Her eyes darted around, looking for anyone else she recognized, anyone he could be meeting with. She pulled her phone out of her back pocket, ready to take pictures. She hadn't been planning to do reconnaissance this morning and knew the camera on her three-year-old phone was hardly adequate. Just as she lifted the phone to snap a picture through the window, it buzzed. She cursed then nearly dropped the phone, promptly looking down to read the notification.

Yashfa to Skylark: *Call me. I need help!*

Yashfa was one of four girls Rachel had befriended a few years ago while on deployment in Khost, Afghanistan. Yashfa and her sister Yamna were sweet, despite their father, Khalid Khan, being a notorious Al-Qaeda leader. She'd hardly contacted Rachel over the past year, and the fact that she was texting Rachel now must really mean there was an emergency.

Rachel stood, her back pressed against the exterior wall of the coffee shop, then tapped Yashfa's name in her contact list. Yashfa picked up immediately.

"What's wrong?" Rachel asked in Pashto, Yashfa's native language.

Without hesitating, Yashfa said, "Kamal is missing."

Rachel furrowed her brow. "Who?"

"Yamna's son. He is thirteen. Our father took him," Yashfa said, rushing to get out the words.

"Took him where?" Rachel asked, unhappy that a known terrorist had kidnapped her friend's son.

"We do not know." Yashfa let out an audible sigh. "Our father came to Khost, showed up at Yamna's door— I don't know what he is planning, what he is doing . . ."

"Shit!" Rachel peeked her head over the windowsill again, scanning the coffee shop. Leftwich was still sitting by himself, tapping his fingers on a manila envelope. Rachel's eyes narrowed on the envelope. *Where the fuck did that come from?*

"Rachel? Rachel, did you hear me? Are you in Afghanistan? Can you help?"

Rachel let out a dejected sigh. "Yes, I'm here. I heard you." *What the hell is in that envelope?* "I'm not in Afghanistan . . . I'm . . . I can't tell you where I am, but I'm not coming back to Afghanistan. I've been reassigned." Rachel explained all about how she'd been injured on her last SEAL mission with her team in Syria—how she'd been stabbed with a knife, had her uterus removed as a result, and been permanently pulled from combat. "I sit at a desk at a command center now. Or I will, once my transfer and promotion are official."

"This is very urgent, Rachel," Yashfa stressed.

"I agree." Rachel winced, not entirely sure what she was agreeing to since she'd been more focused on Leftwich than Yashfa. "Your father just showed up, though? Yashfa, neither of you have spoken to your father in years!"

"He appeared on Yamna's doorstep, came inside and said, 'Kamal is old enough to learn to be a man, he must come with me.' Yamna said no, which our father doesn't like being told *no*. He told Kamal to get in the car. Kamal just sat there. We all just sat there. Me and Yamna and our husbands and all of our children. Our father repeated again, 'Kamal needed to go learn to be a man.' I don't even know what that means, but Yamna started protesting. You know Yamna. She's quiet and shy and barely says anything ever—"

Rachel saw movement in the corner of her eye. Leftwich was opening the envelope. If she could just get close enough—

"Do you think you could get him back? Kamal?" Yashfa asked.

Rachel knew getting a kid back from their grandfather was a bit outside her teams' typical responsibilities, no matter who the kid or the grandfather was. She would need to pull a lot of strings to get this done. "Yashfa, I—"

"That man you've been hunting, Samir Al-Abadi . . . My father will be meeting with him."

Rachel rolled her back into the wall, her attention snapping fully onto Yashfa. "That can't be right." Samir had pissed off Khalid years ago, when Samir broke off from Al-Qaeda to join ISIS.

"I heard my father speak his name, and I remembered instantly that you had been looking for him after you left Khost. It's why you went to help Veeda. I thought it was odd too because my father has never said his name before, but it was while he was on the phone, and I don't think he knew I was listening because it was right after he hit Yamna—"

"Wait, wait, wait," Rachel said, trying to keep up. "He hit Yamna?"

"Yes, when he took Kamal. Listen, Rachel! This is important. I heard him say that he's meeting Samir in three days."

"I can't get there in three days." No, Rachel couldn't get there at all.

"I know," Yashfa said dejectedly. "But Zarah can."

"Zarah?" Rachel asked, surprised.

"I texted Zarah after everything happened, and she volunteered to follow my father. He does not know her, and she is less conspicuous than me or Yamna, so he will not notice her."

"Where are they even meeting?"

"We do not know."

Rachel rubbed her temples, thinking through this plan. Zarah was ballsy for a woman of her station, and Rachel had no doubt she knew what she was doing. After all, Zarah had employed a couple of assholes to beat the shit out of Rachel so that she could prove her loyalty. But even if Zarah was qualified to do this, Rachel still hated the fact that she couldn't be there to do the recon herself. Especially since Samir was involved. She knew more than anyone just how lethal Samir's vengeance would be if Zarah got caught.

"I . . ." Rachel pinched the bridge of her nose and looked down.

She had a lot going on, and getting Kamal back from his grandfather would require more than a few favors and a lot of convincing that this was a mission worth pursuing. A missing kid might not warrant SEAL attention. But if Khalid was meeting with Samir . . .

Rachel had wanted Samir on his knees, right in front of her, staring down the barrel of her gun, for over a decade. With Zarah, Yashfa, and Yamna all following Khalid and listening for information, this could be her chance to finally catch Samir—and Khalid in the process. Like a two for one special.

She couldn't help but chuckle. "Okay, but I need you and Yamna and Zarah to report back to me anything you hear about Samir. Anything he and your father are planning, where they are. I want to know every last detail. If you promise to do that, I will call in every favor I can to get Kamal back to Yamna as quickly as possible."

"Yes," Yashfa agreed. "Yamna wants Kamal back immediately."

Rachel hesitated, knowing full well that *immediately* wasn't possible, and certainly not until her promotion and official appointment to HQ came through. "It's going to take a while, Yashfa. Technically, getting a kid back from his grandfather isn't something the U.S. military does. Since we're friends, since I promised to get rid of your father for you, and because Samir Al-Abadi is clearly involved, I can pull some strings and try to get this prioritized. I need to be honest though. It won't be easy."

"Just . . . please help, Rachel. Yamna, she's not herself. She's frantic. I'm worried about her. I'm worried about Kamal. He's young, and we've done our best not to let our father's ideas influence our children, but . . ."

"Where is Yamna?"

"In her bedroom with her husband."

"Where are you?"

"In their living room. My husband took our children home, but given Yamna's mental state, I'm staying here to watch her other children."

"Do they know you're calling me?"

"No. I'll tell Yamna once she calms down, but our husbands don't need to know."

"Okay," Rachel said. "Okay. I'll send a team out to Khost as soon as I can. And I'm contacting Zarah to make sure everything goes smoothly. I'm busy for most of the day today, but I'll call her as soon as I can."

"Thank you, Rachel. You know I wouldn't have contacted you unless I was desperate."

"I know," Rachel said before hanging up.

Her head was spinning. Khalid and Samir. Working together. Not to mention Khalid had abducted Yamna's son. She didn't know what those two were up to, but she'd be damned if she wasn't going to find out.

This new partnership must have been the result of Veeda's marriage to Samir's nephew. Yashfa's friend had been traded, used as a bartering chip in a larger scheme. An image flashed behind Rachel's eyes—of Veeda dead on the ground, and Rachel's teammate, Aiden, dead beside her. There were too many points in time she wished she could change, and all of them led right to where she was now.

Rachel scrubbed her hands over her face. She needed to focus. Leftwich being at the same coffee shop as her was an unwelcome surprise that may well turn out to be convenient later, once she had more time to follow him. If she followed him now, she'd surely be late to her Senate confirmation hearing scheduled for that morning. But if she could get even a hint of what he was up to, it might be worth it. Khalid taking Yamna's son . . .

It had been an intense seven minutes since she'd parked Christopher's truck. She peered through the window again. Leftwich was flipping through a stack of documents, nodding to himself. Rachel's eyes started tracking again, studying the other patrons. She didn't recognize anyone. She looked to Leftwich again. He was shoving everything back into the folder, as if he'd gotten what he came for.

Rachel sighed at her boots.

The coffee shop had a back door.

If someone had handed off that envelope to Leftwich, they were long gone by now. This was why she hated reconnaissance so damned much. It was tedious, boring, and took forever to get any results, and if you even blinked—

She glanced at the time on her phone just as a splitting headache from caffeine withdrawal kicked in. She couldn't risk going into the coffee shop since Leftwich was still camped out at his table. But caffeine infused chocolate was the only way she'd get through the litany of questions the Senate was sure to barrage her with later that morning.

After grumbling a string of curses to herself, she took a deep breath and focused on finding a solution. Another deep breath later, and she heard the *click clack* of high heels on pavement. Perfect!

She waved to the woman approaching the front door of the coffee shop, signaling her to stop. "Hey, sorry to bother you," Rachel said, the lie already on her tongue. "I was going to go in and get a mocha, but my ex-boyfriend is in there, and I really can't deal."

The woman smiled and nodded. "I got you, girl." She accepted a ten-dollar bill from Rachel, took her order, and headed inside.

Well, that was one problem solved. On to the next.

Rachel typed out a text to Zarah.

Skylark to Zarah: *All good?*

No response.

A few minutes later, mocha in hand thanks to the helpful stranger, Rachel checked her phone again. Still nothing from Zarah. She walked back to Christopher's truck, got in, and drove home, certain that Zarah would text her back soon.

Chapter 2:

SEPTEMBER 2020

RACHEL STORMED INTO THE living room, kicking over a box labeled *fragile* as she went. She was satisfied by the sound of glass rattling in return.

"Hey, I was just about to unpack that," Christopher said from the couch, looking up from the book he was reading.

"Yeah, that's what it looks like," Rachel huffed.

"Coffee first." Christopher winked and held up the mug of black coffee in his hand. "You got your mocha. Why are you still in a mood?"

"Stupid box shouldn't have been in my way," Rachel grumbled, balling her hand on her hip. They were almost done unpacking. Well, Christopher was. Rachel and Christopher had bought a house together in the Kalorama neighborhood—a beautiful three-story embassy style built out of white painted brick. Finding the house had been a fairly quick process, and even though Rachel hated living in D.C., the house was perfect. They'd shipped their respective belongings from Florida and Texas, and Rachel, bored within the first hour of unpacking, had let Christopher have this project.

"Right, it's the box's fault," Christopher teased, taking a sip of his coffee. "Besides the box, what happened while you were getting coffee?"

Rachel's fingers tightened around the paper mug in her hand. "Coffee turned into recon. I hate recon." *And a missing persons case.* How the fuck was she going to find Kamal when she was stuck in D.C.?

"Explain," Christopher urged.

"It's tedious and boring."

"No, I know why you hate recon." Christopher chuckled. "How did getting a mocha turn into a reconnaissance mission?"

Rachel scowled. "Guess who else gets coffee there? You'll never guess. I swear, all the gods hate me. It's awful here, Christopher. I'm constantly surrounded by all the people I despise."

Christopher pursed his lips, waiting for her to get to the point and start naming names.

Rachel went on. "It's bad enough the asshole gets me pulled and stuck on a fucking desk. Then he has the audacity to get coffee where I get coffee, and someone dropped an envelope on his table."

"Did I miss the day where you bought Cardigan Coffee, or is it still a public place?" Christopher teased.

"Be serious!" Rachel yelled.

"Baby, people are allowed to get coffee wherever they want. Why Dick Leftwich wants to hang out at a Taylor Swift themed coffee shop, I don't know, but—"

"He's up to something."

"Uh-huh." Christopher agreed noncommittally before turning his attention back to the book in his hand.

"You don't care about this at all!" Rachel pouted.

"I care but I can't do anything about it," Christopher noted. "I, like Leftwich, am retired. That means neither of us has the power, authority, or resources to do much of anything that you'd be interested in investigating."

Rachel let out a growl through her teeth. She'd been irritated since she first saw Leftwich outside the coffee shop, and Christopher's unwillingness to indulge her theories about Leftwich just frustrated her even more. She kicked the box she'd tripped on coming in. "Fix this."

"Yes, ma'am. I'll get right on it as soon as I finish reading this chapter."

"What are you reading?" she asked, trying to temper her frustration. They both knew she wasn't mad at the box, or the book, or Christopher.

Christopher held up the book for her to see.

"The feminist bible, good," Rachel joked, happy to see he was reading *Women Who Run with Wolves* by Clarissa Pinkola Estés.

"What is all the yelling about down here?" Rachel jumped, startled by her father's voice as he jogged down the stairs. "You remember your hearing is today?" Admiral Thomas Ryker said, all business.

"Yes, Daddy." Rachel rolled her eyes. That was the other layer of irritation. Her father had insisted on coming to her confirmation hearing, and Christopher had insisted her parents stay with them.

"Maybe stop bitching about things and go get ready?" Tom suggested.

Rachel's brow furrowed as she checked the time on her phone. "My hearing isn't for three hours."

"Tom, it'll take her about seven minutes to get dressed. She's fine," Christopher intervened.

"Your mother told me you need to wash and dry your hair . . . She had a list." Tom shook his head. "Go get ready while Chris and I sort out breakfast."

Rachel's nose wrinkled. Listening to her mother lecture her about various beauty rituals was hardly something she wanted to do. Her eyes darted around the room, looking for anything she could use as an excuse, before finally landing on the box she'd tripped over coming into the house. "I need to finish unpacking some stuff first. I promised Christopher I'd get it done."

Christopher, still lounging on the couch, coughed to cover his laughter. "That box is full of kitchen things, Rache."

Rachel cocked her head to the side, understanding perfectly well that he didn't want her doing anything in the kitchen since he was the one who cooked. "Yes, I can read the label." She smiled, picked up the box, and carried it to the kitchen.

It didn't take long for her to get bored. She'd unpacked the box. Technically. Everything was out of the box and spread out on the kitchen table. She didn't know what half the items were, so she really had no idea where they should go. Hence why Christopher had been put in charge of unpacking it.

She did know what knives were for though.

"Are you going to repaint that wall?" Christopher asked after coming into the kitchen. He placed his empty coffee mug in the sink then turned to face her, arms crossed over his chest as he leaned against the counter.

"What would even be the point?" Rachel asked as she leaned back in her chair and flung one of the steak knives skillfully through the air. It lodged itself into the wall right next to the other knives she'd been targeting with.

"Right." Christopher looked at his feet and shook his head. "Why don't you go get ready then if you're going to wash your hair?"

"But you need help with this."

"You're going to sit there and watch me put these things away?" Christopher raised an eyebrow at her.

"Yeah. Teamwork." Rachel flashed him a bright grin.

"You don't think I can do this myself?"

"Well, you haven't so far, and I've been tripping over that box for days."

"Because I've been unpacking the rest of the house. The things we needed more urgently. I promise I can put all of this away without being supervised." His voice held a slight twinge of annoyance.

Rachel raised a skeptical eyebrow and pursed her lips. "Are you sure?"

"I said I'd do it while you're in the shower. Don't you trust me?"

"With my life." Rachel nodded.

"But not with unpacking?" He shook his head. "Baby, you don't care where anything is in the kitchen, so just relinquish control a little bit and trust me to handle it while you get ready for your hearing." He looked her up and down. "Not to be mean, but you probably should wash your hair. And your dad wanted to go through a list of questions to practice with you again."

Rachel stared at him, wide-eyed. He'd been begging her for help with unpacking for weeks. "But you need help," she insisted.

"What I needed help unpacking was your clothes and all ten thousand books you own because I didn't know how you wanted them organized. The kitchen I can handle."

"But what if you need help deciding where something should go?"

Christopher gave her a skeptical look and held up a metal object. "If you can tell me what this is, I'll let you help."

Rachel scrunched up her face, not quite ready to admit he'd won. "It's a metal kitchen thingy."

"What does it do?"

"Food related things?"

"It's a potato masher. It's used to mash potatoes."

"How the hell would I know that?" Rachel asked.

"My point exactly. Now stop micromanaging and go get ready. I promise, I have the kitchen under control. You have more important things to do."

Rachel pursed her lips and nodded, seeming to agree, but she didn't leave her chair until Christopher had found a home for every item that had been in the box.

Chapter 3

SEPTEMBER 2020

SCHOOLING HER FACE INTO stoic submission was getting more difficult by the second. Dressed in her service khakis with her hair twisted into a low chignon, Rachel balled her hand into a fist, letting her nails dig into her palm as her father checked her uniform and straightened her pins for what she was sure was the hundredth time. They were camped out in a back hallway of the Senate building, waiting for her confirmation hearing to start.

"Daddy, I know how to dress myself," Rachel complained, her eyes darting up and down the hallway.

"We're at the Senate, Rachel, and you aren't even in proper uniform," Tom chided her, as though she could forget where they were or why they were there.

"I'm fairly certain the senators don't know shit about uniform code. Besides, Christopher already checked," Rachel countered. She caught sight of Christopher in her periphery, scratching the back of his head and staring at his feet, doing his best to not get involved. Retired or not, he wasn't about to disagree with an admiral.

"You're about to get promoted to rear admiral, Rachel. It's a big deal. You need to take this seriously and respect the process and the tradition. I know you have more ribbons than this, and you should be wearing your medals."

"I'm as in uniform as I feel is appropriate. I have my top three ribbons as required. I do not need any shiny trinkets, any mementos of melancholy decorating my uniform to prove myself to the senate. My record speaks for itself," Rachel insisted.

Tom finally stopped fussing over her moments later when they were called inside.

Rachel sat at a long table facing a panel of senators, her heart pounding in her ears. Despite all of the shit talking, she was secretly nervous but hoped it didn't show. She knew she had a bad habit of running her mouth and insulting politicians, either by directly stating or simply implying that they were stupid. Now though, with her career in the palm of their hands, she didn't feel so mouthy.

She dared a quick glance behind her to the audience, catching Christopher's blue eyes for just a second. He winked playfully at her, and it was all she needed. Rachel turned back in her seat, folded her hands on the table, and plastered on a friendly smile as Senator Darrold Erhart, Chairman of the Committee, started the hearing.

"Thank you, Captain Ryker, for your service, dedication, and willingness to take on this important role. SEAL Command Headquarters is the primary point for planning, coordinating, and overseeing all SEAL missions of a highly covert and classified nature. This is an important position integral to the safety of this nation." Senator Erhart adjusted the angle of his microphone.

"SEAL Command HQ's uniformed workforce is known to have the highest level of credibility, competence, and professionalism. It will be your responsibility to maintain that high degree of integrity while supporting the SEALs operating under your command, as well as their families, with the aim of ensuring all missions are completed and all SEALs can return home safely. You may be required to work around the clock to ensure the teams have the support they need to achieve mission complete status. I, again, thank you for your willingness to take on this important role and look forward to hearing your testimony. I now recognize Ranking Member Saltzman," Senator Erhart concluded.

"Thank you, Mr. Chairman." Senator Saltzman looked at Rachel. "Captain Ryker, welcome and thank you for your many years of service and dedication to this country. You may proceed with your opening statement."

Rachel sat straight in her chair and made eye contact with each member of the committee. "Thank you, Chairman Erhart, Ranking Member Saltzman, and distinguished members of the committee," Rachel started. "It is an honor and a privilege to appear before you today as a nominee for the rank of rear admiral to serve as Mission Commander at SEAL Command Headquarters in the Middle East Special Projects Division. I am very grateful to the president, secretary of defense, and the chairman of the joint chiefs of staff, as well as Admiral Paul Eastwood, Master Mission Commander at SEAL Command Headquarters, for placing their faith and trust in me."

Truthfully, she wasn't grateful at all. This whole thing was a nightmare.

"My family is here, and I thank them sincerely for their support. I would especially like to thank my partner, Christopher, who has stood by my side in several capacities over the past eleven years." Rachel couldn't help but smile, knowing that Chairman Erhart and several of the committee members were aware of her and Christopher's history.

"Not here today are family, friends, and fellow SEALs whom we have lost, least of whom, my grandfather, Major General Jackson Ryker, of the United States Army 101st Airborne Division. His stories about his time in France inspired my own love of jumping out of airplanes and helicopters, much to my father's dismay since he wanted me to be a pilot." She paused and steadied herself, wishing she'd ignored protocol and skipped over the thanking people part of her opening statement. The Senate was no place for emotions. "I would also like to take a moment to remember and honor Commander Henry Tull and Petty Officer Second Class Aiden Bennet, both of whom were amazing teammates and friends and were both killed in action. Their commitment and sacrifice keep me going and remind me daily of the importance and severity of my work. Lastly, I would like to thank the men and women at SEAL Command Headquarters, regional commands, all of our trainers and coordinators, as well as every single doctor, nurse, and medic for their service and for saving my life, and the lives of countless others, over and over again. We all know that I wouldn't be here without them.

"As this committee knows, I have served as a SEAL for the past ten years, mainly on missions and operations which fell under the purview of a joint task force. As squadron leader for the Middle East Special Projects Division, I have had the honor, privilege, and pleasure of establishing and building working relationships with officers and enlisted personnel in all branches of the military, as well as analysts and operatives at the NSA, the CIA, and Homeland Security. I fully intend to maintain, and when necessary, leverage those relationships to best serve the missions assigned to my squadron, always putting national interests ahead of politics and inter-agency disputes. Furthermore, I intend to rely upon my recent time in combat, knowing that it is my greatest asset when it comes to planning missions, as my boots-on-the-ground knowledge provides me with a level of expertise that is difficult to gain through intelligence reports. I am already fully briefed and up-to-date on the most highly sought after targets and assets for each agency that collaborates with the SEAL teams in my division, and I know the strengths and weaknesses of each SEAL team and each individual SEAL who will be under my command, as I have fought right alongside them for the past decade. I fully commit to preserving the integrity of this position at all costs while defending this nation. Chairman Erhart, Ranking Member Saltzman, and distinguished members of the committee, it is truly an honor to be considered for this position," Rachel concluded.

"Thank you very much, Captain Ryker," Chairman Erhart responded. "I have a series of questions that are standard for nominees. You may respond appropriately."

Rachel replied *yes* and *no* to the questions that followed, careful not to show her boredom. Too many questions about integrity and conflicts of interest. It *was* Washington. She presumed other people may need clear definitions regarding ethics and morality. She composed her face and did her best to act interested in what Erhart was saying, suspecting, based on his tone and clenched jaw, that he was just as bored as she was.

The last question seemed a bit more relevant. "Do you agree, when asked before this committee, to give your personal views, even if your views differ from the Administration?" Erhart looked her right in the eye as he asked the question.

Rachel nodded, managing to suppress her smirk. She was never one to tow the party line. "I do." *Bless your hearts, I really fucking do.*

"Thank you, Captain Ryker. Senator Peters, you may proceed with questioning," Chairman Erhart said, turning to a young woman further down the panel.

"Captain Ryker, you are, to this committee's knowledge, the only female SEAL. How has that affected your ability to serve and your ability to lead?" Senator Isabel Peters asked.

"Thank you, Senator," Rachel began, slightly irritated that a woman would ask that. She smiled as warmly as she could manage and looked Isabel Peters, a woman only two years her senior, in the eye. "As a woman in a position of power yourself, I'm sure you are aware that being a woman can be our greatest asset, though it also comes with challenges." She paused, trying to ensure her tone wasn't too condescending. "While overseas with my team, we did sometimes encounter challenges due to the laws governing women's behavior, which are prevalent in the countries we were most frequently sent to. However, my team had my back, just like I had theirs. We are all well versed in the local laws and regulations wherever we go, so that we can ensure everyone's safety. At the same time, my sex allows me to speak with female sources to gather intelligence in a way that the men on my team cannot. It allows me to go partly undetected, as I'm frequently underestimated. That being said, I outperformed, and continue to outperform, most of the men on most of the training exercises we were given, including hand-to-hand combat and military strategy."

Rachel paused, letting that bit of information echo throughout the room.

"With regards to how being a woman affects my ability to lead," she continued, "I will admit it was challenging in the beginning to gain the respect of certain men. But as I said, it was difficult for them to question my leadership once they saw me fight. I lead my team differently than my predecessor. I'm more focused on listening and observing than yelling at people, although I am quite good at that too. I have implemented several initiatives to ensure that my men and their families are supported in every way possible, specifically with regards to mental health and team building. I fully intend, if confirmed to this position, to implement those initiatives with all the teams under my command." She thought back to the last Share and Care session she'd had with Indigo. If only she'd known it was going to be the last one, she would've listened more.

"Thank you, Captain Ryker," Senator Peters replied. "I have no more questions for you at this time. Senator Kane, you may proceed."

"Thank you, Senator Peters," Senator Kane, the next senator down the line, said. "Captain Ryker, at this time, which organization is a bigger threat to U.S. interests: Al-Qaeda or ISIS?"

"That is a fantastic question, Senator Kane. Thank you." *Finally a worthwhile question.* "They are both threats to the U.S. but in different ways and for different reasons. Al-Qaeda seems intent on destroying the West, planning terrorist attacks on our home soil and in European countries. In that way, I would say they pose a greater threat to the American people. However, ISIS is much more hostile and brutal with their tactics and are more likely to attack foreigners on their soil. In the past, Al-Qaeda has cooperated with Western journalists and aid-workers. ISIS does not. They are taking people—Westerners—hostage. Not for ransom but because they can. They are trying to show the world that they can. It's making it difficult for NGOs and humanitarian aid organizations to operate. What's worse is that they are using these tactics on the people in the territories they are trying to take over. Public executions, beheadings, rape. I'm fairly sure that if all U.S. troops pulled out of the Middle East—which we aren't going to do—that ISIS would more or less leave us alone and not care that we existed. But we care that they exist, so we'll be staying over there for the foreseeable future."

God help us all if they start combining ISIS tactics with Al-Qaeda's Western targets.

"What do you mean they would leave us alone if we left them alone?"

Senator Kane pressed.

Rachel thought she had been clear, but she'd known Senator Kane a long time and had always found him a bit slow. "I mean, they are trying to form a state that can be governed under Islamic Law, or at least their interpretation of Islamic Law. If they succeeded in that and had whatever land or territory or level of dominance they found adequate, then they wouldn't have anyone left to fight. They wouldn't have, as they put it, infidels and puppet governments in their way. Their supposed enemies wouldn't exist anymore. I've had several long discussions with ISIS members about this, and that is what they all tell me. They would love to carve out a section of the Middle East just for themselves, sort of like Israel. But whose land are they going to get? First of all, no one wants them forming an Islamic State. Not with the way they're interpreting Islamic Law. Not with the amount of violence they're purporting on their own people in order to control them. We can't just take someone else's country, someone else's home, and hand it over to them. Besides, if we did that, they'd probably just ask for more. They are using social media and propaganda to recruit and essentially indoctrinate young people, seeing as that's primarily who's on social media. Furthermore, ISIS is gaining a following in other countries like Nigeria, Somalia, and the Philippines, so I guess our Africa and Asia Pacific teams will be pretty busy as well. So, to answer your question, both ISIS and Al-Qaeda are equal threats for different reasons and in different regions. We need to be targeting both groups, which I assure you, we are."

Senator Kane leaned in closer, challenging her. "If you had to pick one though?"

I will argue with you until you give me enough funding so we don't have to pick you incompetent dickwad. She forced her mouth to remain shut, knowing better than to voice her actual thoughts on the matter. But then she realized she knew something no one else knew—Al-Qaeda and ISIS were working together. Khalid Khan was teaming up with Samir Al-Abadi. For the first time, both of her enemies were working under the same wing, pursuing the same unknown goal. Khalid was a pain in the ass but not as organized or ambitious as Samir. Not as much of a leader. So, while she did need the SEALS to search for Khalid Khan in order to find Kamal, she would have better luck if she could convince the politicians that Samir was the larger threat here.

"ISIS is carrying out brutal attacks targeting civilians and security forces, and a few months ago, attacked a prison to free several of their members. We—or I should say SEAL Command, since technically I'm not working currently—are tracking all known members of ISIS to the best of our ability. Unfortunately, that's easier said than done with our limited resources."

"Limited resources?" Senator Kane said, taking the bait. He rifled through the papers on his desk, as if he'd find a complete inventory report on all the supplies they'd ever allotted to the SEALs. "Last I checked, your division had a budget of—"

"I know what the budget is," Rachel interrupted. "It has nothing to do with a budget. Not really. It has to do with the fact that there are more members of ISIS than my teams can track at once. They're not all hanging around at a country club together playing golf." Rachel heard a forced cough in the audience and knew Christopher was signaling her to reign it in. "Senator Kane, I currently have seven teams of twelve SEALs. That is not enough. As difficult as this is to understand, I'm a complete workaholic, let's be clear about that. I'd move over to the Middle East and track these—" *What the hell is a professional word for misogynistic shithead?* "—people, all day and all night every day of the year. But my men have families and need breaks. Didn't *you* just take a sixty-day vacation to some resort in the Bahamas?" She cocked her head to the side and stared him down.

"Yes . . ." Senator Kane confirmed.

"So, my guys can't be over there three hundred and sixty-five days a year every year for the next decade. We're already operational a minimum of two hundred days out of each year. It's too much. They have to be allowed to come home at some point to recuperate. Then we have the issue of people getting injured or sometimes even killed. I do not currently have enough SEALs to track every single one of our targets in the Middle East. Does that clarify what I meant by lack of resources?"

"That clarifies your point." Senator Kane nodded. "Thank you, Captain Ryker. Senator Scott, you may proceed."

"Thank you, Senator Kane." The senator to Kane's right spoke. He leaned forward, his face more open, less stern, than the others. "Captain Ryker, could you give us a summary of the current situation in the Middle East? I understand you can't tell us everything. I'm sure some things are classified at this point, but a summary."

Rachel kept a perfectly straight face as she leaned towards the microphone in front of her, even though she wanted to laugh at the absurdity of his question. "Yes, Senator Scott. In summary, the current state of the Middle East is chaos." She could tell by the look on his face that he expected more and proceeded to give the senators a run down—country by country—of everything going on in the Middle East.

"*Does* Iran have nuclear weapons?" Senator Scott interrupted her update to ask.

Probably. "Not to my knowledge, but it's not like they're going to be truthful about that when we ask." It was getting exceedingly difficult not to roll her eyes at him.

"Perhaps we should have someone look into that . . ." he mused.

"Get me more teams and I'd be happy to." Rachel smiled. She had no intention of wasting the SEAL's time doing any such thing.

"Thank you, Captain Ryker. I'd like to go back to something you said earlier when you answered Senator Kane's questions. You said you had conversations with several ISIS members?" Senator Scott asked.

"That is correct," Rachel confirmed.

"Why?"

"Because you have to get to know your enemy in order to beat them." Rachel studied the faces of the committee members and quickly determined that wasn't an acceptable answer. "Occasionally, we detain members of terrorist organizations in an attempt to get information from them. Other times, we may deliver them to the CIA for whatever reason the CIA wants them for." *To interrogate them using techniques y'all have outlawed.* "So, I ask them questions." *Then break their bones when they lie to me.* "I want to understand their motives. Sometimes it can be a very long car or helicopter ride." She shrugged.

Senator Scott nodded and pursed his lips. "I have no further questions for Captain Ryker at this time. Senator Reed, you may proceed."

"Thank you." Senator Reed had a glint in his eye as he tapped his pen repeatedly on the desk. "Captain Ryker, you mentioned that you know who the top targets are for each branch of the military and each agency your teams partner with."

"Correct," Rachel grit her teeth, annoyed by his erratic pen tapping.

"Who are *your* top targets? Who do *you* feel we should be prioritizing?"

Rachel couldn't help but smile. "Samir Al-Abadi." *Whom Zarah will hopefully find soon.* "Samir has always been at the top of my list, Senator. He's moved up the ranks in ISIS after leaving Al-Qaeda in 2014."

"I have a folder full of profiles of top-level targets." Senator Reed held up a stack of papers. "Why Samir Al-Abadi?"

"As I'm sure you know, he's the puppet master behind countless attacks. He excels at securing funding. He's influential and can get people to do things with minimal effort. He dreams big but has no problem hitting us, or our allies, with small terrorist attacks to keep everyone on edge. No matter what we do, he's always a half step ahead of us. He's responsible for the deaths of several SEALs and countless intelligence assets over the span of a decade."

Senator Reed pursed his lips. "So, you have a personal vendetta and are out for revenge? Is that how you make strategy decisions?"

"No." Rachel's jaw clenched. *Hell fucking yes.*

He asked her question after question about ISIS and Samir, and Rachel continued to give the same cut and paste answers she'd practiced a hundred times. Yes, Samir was dangerous. Yes, he should be the U.S.'s number one target. She didn't mention the new information about Samir meeting Khalid in Al-Qaeda territory. She still didn't know what that meant or what game he was trying to play, but she sure as hell didn't want to share it with the Senate before she figured it out. Which she knew she couldn't do until she spoke with Zarah. If these Senators could just hurry up with their questions . . .

Smile. Men are much more manageable when women smile. If you ever want this to end, you have to put them at ease.

Rachel brushed her hand over the side of her head, smoothing her already perfect hair, then relaxed her face into a soft smile and adjusted her tone to sound more eager and helpful, rather than expressing the condescension she so acutely felt. "Would you like Samir Al-Abadi's full resume? Would you like to know how many innocent people he's killed? How many people he's indoctrinated to join his cause? How many buildings and villages he's torched with people inside their homes, asleep, because they refused to join him?"

"Do you have those actual numbers?" Senator Reed shifted uncomfortably as he flipped through the papers in front of him.

If I smile at him, he gets nervous. Rachel tucked that bit of information away. "Of course I do. I can send over a written report if you'd like."

"Already have it." Senator Reed shuffled through the mess of documents in front of him, grinned, and held up a file. "Senator Warrant, you may continue."

"Thank you, Senator Reed." Warrant sounded bored. "Captain Ryker, you—"

Rachel barely heard what he said over the faint sound of a door opening and closing. This was supposed to be a closed hearing. No one should be coming in or out. She turned her head just slightly so she could get a peripheral view of the back of the room. Her eyes followed a blur of movement as a few men in suits filtered in, tailing a man with dark hair and a face that screamed *punch me*.

President Frank Verity.

He slipped into a chair along the back wall, his guard dogs posting up at their stations near all the exits. Rachel balled her fists, her nails digging into her skin. What the fuck was he doing here? Presidents didn't come to this sort of thing. And by the smug smirk plastered on his face, Rachel figured he knew just how unwanted his presence was.

"Captain Ryker?" Senator Warrant's tone darkened with impatience.

Rachel inched her head back toward the senator. "Yes?"

"Should I repeat the question?" And now patronizing.

"Um," Rachel said, unsure. "Y-yes."

Warrant's mouth drew firm. "You recently came under personal scrutiny for potential misconduct. Please explain how that exemplifies your integrity and ability to lead."

Rachel's brow creased. Hadn't she already been through this line of questioning? Her eyes cut back toward Frank. This hearing had gone very sour, very fast. She drew herself up straighter and lifted her chin, determined to turn this around. "As you and the other members of this committee know, I was falsely accused of fraternization after bringing a high-ranking admiral up on charges of gender discrimination. All the charges against me were dropped, as there was no evidence—"

"However, you are now cohabitating with the person in question, are you not?"

"Senator, as I said, I was cleared of all charges. Nothing happened until after—"

"The investigation into you relied heavily, if not solely, on the testimony of your own close friends and fellow SEAL team members. Did it not?"

"Yes . . ." Rachel answered.

She had thought it was strange that she'd been called to a confirmation hearing for a promotion. Admiral Eastwood had found it strange as well since, typically, recommendations were made, and the Senate voted. Now they knew why a hearing had been deemed necessary.

"And we are supposed to believe everything they said to defend you?"

"Senator, it is my understanding that everyone who testified did so under oath. Are you questioning the integrity of over fifty U.S. Navy SEALs, myself included, as well as all the Navy and civilian personnel involved in that preliminary hearing?"

"Answer the question, Captain," Senator Warrant insisted.

What the actual fuck? She knew Senator Warrant had a tendency to be a class-A jerk, but this was a whole new level. "Senator, I believe I *have* answered your question, but to clarify, I believe in the integrity of the justice system. No evidence was found against myself or Captain, then Commander, Williams. What has happened since Captain Williams retired was fully above board. You can check with Navy Human Resources. I'm sure they would love to go through all one hundred forms and documents that I had to submit to them before anything could happen between myself and Captain Williams, which, frankly sir, is not under the purview of this committee," Rachel answered as calmly as she could.

"Captain Ryker, everything is under the purview of this committee," Senator Warrant said. "I would also like to point out that you sued the Navy for gender discrimination. I believe that calls your loyalty into question."

These questions about her gender and personal life were ridiculous, as though she couldn't destroy every single senator on that committee with the secrets she knew about them. But maybe they didn't all realize just how much she knew.

"Thank you, Senator, for clarifying the issue. If I recall correctly, Chairman Erhart asked a few hours ago if I agreed, when asked before this committee, to give my personal views, even if those views differ from the Administration. That is how the question was phrased, if I recall correctly?" Rachel asked.

"Yes, that was the question, and you replied that you would," Chairman Erhart confirmed.

"Well, in that case, Senator Warrant, I believe standing up for myself, standing up for all women in the armed forces, and calling out high-ranking officials for their misconduct would be a fantastic example of my dedication to giving my personal views, even when they differ from the administration, or in this case, SEAL Command. I'm sure that you could ask anyone who knows me, and they will tell you that I do not keep my opinions to myself and that I am entirely steadfast in my pursuit of equality, freedom, liberty, and justice for all. Furthermore, these traits are precisely what make me *overqualified* for the position of Mission Commander at SEAL Command HQ. I was already assigned to mission and operation planning and strategy as a junior officer and never once shied away from telling a more senior officer that he was wrong. And I say *he* because, let's face it, most of the people at SEAL Command are men, and if I am confirmed to the rank of rear admiral, I will be the highest-ranking woman at Command HQ and one of the few people there who can still pass the SEAL fitness test for entrance to the training, let alone assignment to a team." Rachel was burning with fury but forced herself to maintain her composure.

"If I may also point out," she continued, "these sorts of conferments—promotion of rank, that is—are typically voted upon in the Senate and do not even require this type of hearing. It is therefore *my opinion*, Senator Warrant, that you have chosen to question my confirmation to rear admiral and assignment to HQ based on some sort of witch hunt or personal vendetta that you may have against me."

"Enough," Chairman Erhart ordered. "Senator Warrant, you are entirely out of line. It is certainly not up to this committee to scrutinize the criminal justice system. There is nothing in Captain Ryker's service record that should block her from this promotion or assignment, and if this is the line of questioning you will continue with, rather than asking her about her military and leadership expertise, then I will need to remove you from this hearing. Now, are there any more questions for Captain Ryker that actually pertain to her experience or her leadership strategy for when she is officially appointed to SEAL Command?" The entire room went silent. The senators all looked back and forth between one another, shocked. "Well, if there are no other questions, then I would like to thank Captain Ryker for her testimony here today and say that on behalf of this committee, we look forward to continuing to work with you. We will come back with our decision as promptly as possible following the committee vote and the full Senate vote."

"Thank you, Chairman Erhart, Ranking Member Saltzman, and all the distinguished members of this committee for allowing me to answer your questions," Rachel said as gracefully as she could manage. She couldn't believe Senator Warrant had convinced the rest of the committee a hearing was necessary based on, what? A personal vendetta? Or maybe he hated all women—she wasn't sure. It was clear, however, that for all the progress made in the war in the Middle East, for every terrorist she'd hunted down and executed, it seemed to make no difference in the global war on women.

She stood and made her way for the exit. Christopher was by her side within seconds.

"Just breathe. We'll be out of here soon enough," he assured her. He pulled her phone out of his pocket and handed it to her.

Rachel hurriedly clicked though her notifications. Still no response from Zarah. Nothing from Yashfa, or Yamna either.

Rachel typed out a text to Zarah.

Skylark to Zarah: *How's it going?*

No response. Rachel sighed and shoved the phone back into her pocket. Maybe she didn't have any service. She was sure Zarah would get back to her soon.

"All good?" Christopher asked, noting her nervousness.

Rachel nodded. *Just a missing kid and an unresponsive intelligence asset. No big deal.* Deciding to turn her attention to a different problem, she scanned the crowd for her father. "Fucking hell," she said under her breath.

Christopher followed her line of sight. "Is that—"

Rachel nodded. The tall man with nearly black hair—clearly dyed to cover the grey she knew was there—was unmistakable.

"I guess it makes sense your father would know the president. Perks of being an admiral, I guess."

Rachel shook her head. "They're old buddies. College roommates. Frank Verity is my godfather, actually . . . not that he's qualified to teach anyone about God or morality or being a decent human being." She grimaced then turned, looking for an alternate escape route.

"Cool." Christopher grinned.

Rachel rolled her eyes. "He's a misogynistic jackass. Don't get too excited." Christopher was, and always had been, a political science nerd. The only thing he enjoyed talking about more than political theory was maps and navigation.

"Can you introduce me?" He clearly wasn't getting the point.

"No, because then I'd have to speak to him."

"For about two minutes, then you can make an excuse and go hide in the bathroom or something."

"Haven't I been through enough?" Rachel whined. "I will do literally anything you want except converse with Frank, no matter how brief that conversation would be."

Christopher chuckled and leaned down to whisper in her ear. "When do you not agree to do whatever I want?"

Her face flushed momentarily. "We are at the Senate!"

Christopher smirked. "We have to wait for your parents anyway. We may as well go over there and say hi." He placed his hand on the small of her back and nudged her in her father's direction.

"I was wondering how long you were going to stand over there and ignore me, Rear Admiral Ryker!" President Verity pulled her into a non-consensual hug as soon as she was standing within his reach.

"Hi Frank," she mumbled as he pressed her face into his chest.

"Do you need to go home and change first, or?" Frank's dark eyes scanned Rachel's body, lingering a bit too long for her liking.

"Not sure what you think is happening." Rachel grimaced.

"We're having lunch at the White House," Tom informed her. "And no, we aren't going home to change, no matter how much your mother insists you need to. I'm hungry, and after all that bullshit I just listened to, I need a drink."

"Which bullshit?" Rachel glanced in her father's direction. "My bullshit or—"

"Senator Warrant's bullshit. Honey, your bullshit was flawless."

Chapter 4:

SEPTEMBER 2020

THEY ARRIVED AT THE White House promptly at 1325 and were escorted into a formal dining room where President Frank Verity and his wife, Trischa, were already waiting.

"Rachel, sweetheart, it's so lovely to see you! And I'm so happy you're in D.C. now," Trischa gushed, pulling Rachel in for a hug. "I'm thrilled we could finally put this together, and what luck that your parents are in town too!"

"It's such a shame Bryant and Jameson couldn't join us," Frank chimed in.

"Oh yes, quite a shame," Rachel agreed sarcastically. Bryant Verity and her brother were two of her least favorite people.

"And Christopher," Trischa continued, turning to him, "it sure is great to meet the man who's finally caught Rachel's interest."

"Great to meet you, Mrs. Verity," Christopher said, shaking her hand.

"Oh, call me Trischa, I insist. Anna-Beth tells me you're a retired SEAL. I guess Rachel had something to do with your retirement?"

"Yes, ma'am," Christopher answered.

"Well, it makes sense. Hopefully, you can keep up with her." Frank winked.

Trischa's eyes scanned Rachel's uniform. "Isn't there a skirt that goes with that outfit? Such a travesty the military is always trying to turn women into men." She shook her head disapprovingly.

"Yes." Anna-Beth glared at Rachel. "For some reason, Rachel doesn't seem to own the skirts that go with any of her uniforms."

"Not sure I own any skirts or dresses, since I hate wearing them," Rachel grumbled.

Frank gave her a sideways glance and smirked. "Aren't you always going on about all that feminist non-sense and body positivity? Surly you know you look great in a skirt."

"Really not the issue." Rachel forced herself to stop talking before she blurted out, *your eyes on my legs would be the issue.* "Anyway." Rachel changed the subject before Frank's comments could get more inappropriate. "What's for lunch?"

"Rachel, we haven't even had drinks yet." Trischa laughed.

"It's the middle of the day . . ." Rachel said, checking the time on her phone.

"Hey, it's five o'clock somewhere, right?" Frank joked. "What can we get you both?"

"Whiskey," Rachel answered.

Anna-Beth gave her a disapproving look. "It's lunch Rachel."

"I can't have whiskey at lunch?" Rachel asked. "Why do they get to have whiskey at lunch?" Rachel asked, pointing to Frank, Tom, and Christopher, who were engrossed in conversation by the drink cart on the other side of the room.

Trischa darted across the room, graceful and demure as ever, and returned with a tall glass in her hand. "Here you go, Rachel." The ice clinked against the glass as Trischa handed her the drink. "A compromise," she said, looking at Anna-Beth.

"Thank you, Trischa." Rachel forced a smile and sipped Trischa's version of a whiskey and lemonade through the bright pink straw. It was about ninety-five percent lemonade and whatever combination of ice and whiskey Trischa believed would pacify her.

Christopher walked over to her then. "What are you drinking?" he asked, eyeing her glass.

Rachel forced her face to remain neutral. "A gender appropriate beverage." She shoved her drink in his face.

Christopher's eyes widened as he took a sip through the straw.

"So, Rachel," Frank said, following Christopher to where the women were standing, "when are you starting at SEAL Command?"

"Sometime after the Senate votes and makes it official?" She gave him a quizzical stare. If anyone knew how this worked, shouldn't it be the president?

"Well, that's just a formality, really." Frank waved off her comment.

"Pretty sure I just swore before the senate that I had not and would not do anything to presuppose the outcome of the hearing," Rachel reminded him.

"Oh Rachel, no one ever takes that seriously! Nothing would get done if anyone did!" Frank laughed.

Tom put one arm around Rachel's shoulders and pulled her to his side for a reassuring squeeze. "Come on, Frank! You know she's still got integrity. Give her some time to acclimate to D.C.," Tom joked.

"Where no one has integrity?" Rachel raised an eyebrow, agreeing with her father's implication but surprised he had said it out loud, even in jest.

Anna-Beth glared at her.

Trischa interjected with an excited clap of her hands. "Rachel, I was hoping you would want to help me with my new project! You know the First Lady is always expected to have a project, and you would be perfect for this!"

"Trischa, I'm not sure I'm going to have much time for projects," Rachel said tentatively.

"Now, you said you haven't started working yet, and you really would be the perfect spokesperson. You're young—relatively speaking—beautiful, confident, and so accomplished. You've worked extensively in the Middle East, doing whatever it is you do—"

"I'm a Navy SEAL," Rachel cut her off.

Trischa waved off her comment. "You even speak all the languages they speak over there."

Rachel raised an eyebrow. "How many languages do you imagine I speak?"

"Frank tells me you're fluent in Arabic and . . . some other language . . ."

Trischa shrugged.

"Arabic and Pashto. Do you have any idea how many languages are actually spoken in the Middle East?" Rachel cocked her head to the side.

"Not the point. I think you would be the perfect face of my campaign to raise awareness for the disproportionate number of children who are displaced because of all the unrest over there," Trischa explained.

Rachel took a deep breath, trying to remain calm. "What do you mean by *displaced?*"

"You know, these children. Their homes are bombed, their parents die, poor things. They are forced to traverse the globe, looking for someplace to live—"

"Asylum seekers and refugees?" Christopher's brow knit together. He was doing as good of a job hiding his distaste for Trischa's comments as Rachel was.

"Yes." Trischa nodded. "We need to do something to help all these children."

"Tell your husband to have fewer wars," Rachel tried.

"I did not start any of these wars, Rachel. I've only been president for a few months. It's not my fault the former president had a heart attack and died."

"No, of course not." Rachel rolled her eyes. Frank was more than capable of killing someone, and highly likely to do it, if it meant he got more power. Poisoning someone to induce a heart attack? She knew he knew how to do that. She'd taught him how. "What are you wanting to do about this problem, exactly?" she asked Trischa.

"Raise awareness. I don't think most people realize that some of these children are very young."

"I'm aware." Rachel's jaw clenched.

"I'm planning a fundraiser," Trischa added. "You know, the First Lady is expected to do this sort of thing."

"For which organization?" Rachel asked.

"I haven't decided yet," Trischa admitted. "I was hoping you could just handle this for me."

Why would the First Lady plan her own event? "Sorry, I don't have time." Rachel took a sip of her drink, thoroughly frustrated that it wasn't stronger.

"Well, honey, think about it and let me know if you can find the time. It would be great to have you on the team!" Trischa said.

"Yes, I will definitely think about it," Rachel said, convincing everyone except Christopher that she actually would.

"Rachel, it would be great if you could help," Frank interjected. "You know so much about these issues, and it would make me and my administration look a hell of a lot better, you know? A bit of anti-war, save the kids messaging is always appreciated by the public."

Rachel blinked twice. "Maybe just actually be anti-war and pro-child?"

"No, Rachel, sweetheart, you aren't getting it." Frank shook his head. "We need to have this event. Let the American people know innocent children are being harmed by these horrible terrorists. Make them *think* we're all anti-war, pro-peace, but in actuality, they'll be so upset by all this that they'll *want* to increase the defense budget and really go after these guys."

"I'm not sure I'm following." Christopher frowned.

Rachel's stomach churned, and she could feel the bile rising in her throat. "No, Christopher, of course you aren't following because that's the dumbest thing I've ever heard. You're just too polite to tell him that!"

"Rachel!" Anna-Beth scolded her.

"Yeah, I won't be helping with any sort of superficial, propaganda-filled, trick-the-American-people bullshit fundraiser to get more money into the pockets of your defense contractor buddies. Thanks anyway."

"I'll change your mind." Frank winked at her.

"Not if you never get around to feeding me. I've been up since 0430, and I was promised lunch, not dinner. It's after 1400."

"Rachel, don't be rude!" Anna-Beth seemed visibly horrified by Rachel's tone.

"It's fine, Anna-Beth," Frank assured her. "We all know Rachel gets moody when she's hungry. Besides, I can assure you, it's far from the worst thing she's ever said to me."

"Not only when she's hungry," Tom teased.

"No, she came out of the womb in a mood." Anna-Beth shook her head.

"Wasn't Frank there when I was born?" Rachel asked.

"Yes. Your father was traveling for work, so Trischa stayed with Jamie and Bryant, and Frank took me to the hospital," Anna-Beth explained.

"Seems like Frank is the common denominator," Rachel noted.

Tom raised a skeptical eyebrow. "Hardly."

"You sure?" Rachel glared at Frank.

"I have several examples of you being extremely moody and irritable that do not involve Frank," Tom said.

"Such as?" Rachel wanted to get a few jabs in at Frank and test what sort of anecdotes her father could actually come up with.

"Such as the time you stole my Mercedes when you were fourteen, then lied and said you needed to buy tampons, but when I got home, you were sitting on the roof drinking a bottle of very expensive scotch."

Rachel's entire body tensed. She knew where this story was going, and it certainly wasn't anywhere pleasant. She wanted to run.

"If you didn't see her driving, how'd you find out she took your car?" Christopher asked.

"We lived on base. Everyone knew my car. I had about twenty different people call to tell me they saw Rachel driving my car. How she got past the guard gate, I have no idea."

Rachel's jaw clenched. "You let me fly a plane. Why the hell couldn't I drive the car?"

"I let you co-pilot with me," Tom clarified. "Really not the same thing as a fourteen-year-old who had no idea how to operate a motor vehicle driving around by herself in traffic."

"I wasn't by myself," Rachel blurted out before she thought the better of it.

Tom leaned towards her, eyes narrowed. "Who were you with?"

"Probably one of the Marines." Frank winked at Rachel and pointed to a doorway on the opposite side of the room. "Food's in there."

They finally sat down to eat, and Christopher and Rachel listened as Anna-Beth and Trischa exchanged gossip about their mutual friends while Tom and Frank discussed golf and fishing. They offered comments occasionally, agreeing about the nice weather or that they enjoyed visiting Paris too. Rachel glanced at her phone every few minutes, willing the time to go faster. Just as she lifted her fork to her mouth, one of the Secret Service agents peeled himself from his post on the wall, coming to Frank's side to whisper something in his ear. Rachel caught the words *Eastwood* and *situation room*.

Frank pushed back his chair and stood. "If you'll excuse me," he said.

Rachel dropped her fork and jumped up as well. As she moved to follow him, a line of agents rushed forward, blocking her. "Move," Rachel demanded, glaring at the nearest agent.

"Ms. Ryker, this matter does not concern you," the agent said.

"It's Captain Ryker, and anything regarding Eastwood concerns me," she challenged.

"Rachel, you're on leave," Tom chimed in.

"It's alright," Frank conceded, waving her through. "On leave or not, no one knows more about the situation in the Middle East than your daughter." He turned to Tom. "Come on, you might as well both come in with me."

Rachel saw Christopher's jaw clench and his knuckles go white as he gripped his fork. "Told you not to retire." She winked, blew him a kiss, and ran after Frank.

"I assume you want your malware code back," the man on the screen said.

Rachel, Tom, and Frank were clustered around a large screen that was split into two, showing both sides of a video call. Admiral Paul Eastwood, Rachel's boss, was on one side of the screen. On the other side was the man who was speaking. He had a rich complexion and a long dark beard and was about Rachel's age. He had a purple and black checkered keffiyeh scarf draped around his neck, mocking her. Rachel instantly recognized the man as Samir Al-Abadi.

"I'll trade you for it," Samir continued.

"What would be the point? You clearly already have it," Eastwood pointed out. The creases around his eyes were visible, his white hair neatly cropped. Rachel couldn't tell where he was. Some boring secure room at HQ, she presumed. She knew Eastwood was about ten years younger than her father, but he looked so much older. Combat aged you, no matter your role. But pilots were mandated a certain number of hours of sleep while SEALs were not.

"Shit," Rachel muttered to herself, knowing the men on the call couldn't hear her or see her. They were granted enough access so that they could view the call, though neither Eastwood nor Samir could see them monitoring. Eastwood had Frank in his ear, but otherwise, they were bystanders to the call.

In all of the chaos of Yamna's son being taken, and Samir meeting with Khalid, Rachel had forgotten about the stupid malware code that Samir had stolen—a code originally developed to target Iran's nuclear program—from her parent's house two years ago. Rachel had lost two friends and a uterus trying to get it back from him. Now the fucker was flaunting it like a bargaining chip.

"My programmer found the flaw in your code and fixed the problem for you. You know I hate Iran as much as you do, as much as Israel does. If you want this back, corrected, so it will work, I'll give it back to you. I just want something in exchange." Samir paused, a smile spreading across his face. "Or someone, I should say."

"Who?" Eastwood asked.

"Is anyone trying to trace this call?" Tom asked.

Frank nodded.

"You have an operative. She goes by *Skylark*." Samir's eyes went cold, as if he could see her through the screen, to her. "I want her. You can have this code in exchange."

Tom's head whipped around, his eyes locking on Rachel.

"No," Eastwood said definitively.

"Why the fuck not?" Rachel grumbled, knowing that if she got in the same room as Samir, she could easily take him out.

"Really? I have her friend here." Samir moved the camera, and Rachel's breath caught in her throat. Zarah was on the screen, bound and gagged and covered in bruises, though she had a defiant look in her eye. "She wouldn't offer her life for her friend?"

"Make the trade," Rachel said, clutching the table in front of her, knowing full well that Eastwood couldn't hear her.

"You can't have Skylark, Samir. You can't have anything. The United States does not negotiate with terrorists," Eastwood said harshly.

Samir's hand was over his heart, a look of shock spreading across his face. Rachel knew it was fake, but it looked genuine enough. "You misunderstand. I am not a terrorist. I'm a politician."

"Why do you want Skylark?" Eastwood redirected.

"She's committed numerous crimes in my country that have gone unpunished." Samir shrugged as though it should be obvious. "Give me Skylark or tell me where she is, or else this woman dies."

"I don't even know who the woman you have with you is," Eastwood admitted.

"She knows Skylark." Samir held up Zarah's phone so that the screen with Rachel's contact information was showing. "Thirty seconds." Samir got a knife and put it to Zarah's throat.

"Frank, tell him to make the trade!" Rachel demanded. Her eyes darted to a slight movement at the bottom of the screen. It was Zarah's fingers, twitching and moving at odd angles against her bindings. Rachel focused in on them. Her finger moved into the shape of a hook. Then up, down, slashing across the middle . . . almost like the letters J and A. Then her finger moved down again.

Was she spelling something?

"Zoom in," Rachel ordered.

"The United States does not negotiate with terrorists," Frank said, ignoring her. Eastwood echoed the same words again.

Zarah's fingers started moving in the same rhythm again.

J.

A.

L.

Samir yanked Zarah up by the hair then slid a knife along her throat, killing her instantly, as a long deep cut spilled dark red blood down her chest and onto the floor. Her body slumped over in a heap of flesh just as the call ended.

"What the fuck happened?" Frank asked.

Rachel slammed her fist on the table. "I just lost one of my best intelligence assets, is what happened!"

"Assets?" Tom's tone was stern as he raised an eyebrow at her.

"Yes, I have intelligence assets in the Middle East. What the fuck do you think I'm over there doing?" Rachel couldn't control her tone or the volume of her voice.

"Assets, plural?" Tom asked.

"Yes!" Rachel was enraged. "And now I have one less, thanks to y'all refusing to make smart decisions."

"How would trading you for her have been smart?" Frank asked.

Rachel rolled her eyes. Frank had been in politics for decades, but he'd just taken over as president a few months prior. She crossed her arms over her chest and turned to him. "I know you're new to being Commander in Chief, but in case you aren't all the way caught up, getting me into a room with Samir Al-Abadi, or any terrorist for that matter, would result in there being one less terrorist in the world for my teams to deal with. You just missed a fantastic opportunity to take out Samir, and you got an innocent woman killed in the process!"

"Assets are expendable. *You* are not," Tom argued.

"Because I'm your daughter?" Rachel made a tight fist, pressing her nails into her palm as hard as she could.

"Rachel, do you understand how much money the U.S. Navy spent training you?" Tom asked.

Her jaw clenched. "I know the exact dollar amount that the United States has spent on training me, yes." Rachel glared at him as she calculated the amount that both the CIA and the Navy had spent training her, down to the exact penny. "I also know that I took a vow to protect the innocent, to exchange my life for even one innocent life, which apparently is a vow I won't be keeping since I'll be stuck on a desk for the rest of my career!"

"Why are you reacting like you just watched your friend die?" Tom challenged. "Assets are assets. They are expendable. They die."

"I watch my friends die all the time, Daddy. Assets too. Sorry I'm still human and not completely numb to it." The sarcasm in her apology was impossible to miss. "Someone please tell me you were able to trace that call!"

"He called over WIFI using a VPN. We have no idea where he is," an agent sitting on the other side of the room explained.

"I don't expect you to be numb to it, but—" Tom was cut off by Rachel throwing a chair across the room.

"Still have that temper, I see," Frank teased.

Rachel looked Frank in the eye. "Block my appointment to HQ and send me back to the Middle East."

"Can't do that. The Senate is voting right now, and the Navy already determined that you're needed at HQ." Frank shook his head.

"You aren't going back, Rachel," Tom added.

"I could help more if I was there," Rachel argued.

Tom crossed his arms over his chest and leaned against a table. "You were an intelligence officer before you were a SEAL."

"Yes . . ."

"Surely she isn't the first asset you've lost." Tom pointed towards the now-black screen.

Rachel winced at her feet, then stared longingly at the screen as memories flooded her brain. "No. *She* is not the first asset I've lost."

"Well, you're sort of acting like she is." Tom's eyes narrowed at her. "Paul Eastwood isn't going to work forever, Rachel. He's got to retire at some point."

"He's younger than you," Rachel noted.

"He is. I also have people below me whom I'm getting ready so they can take over for me one day. Paul chose you, Rachel. As much as I hate it—as much as I hate that you spent so much time in combat, in danger—you're safe now, and the Navy needs you at HQ. You need to be fully up to speed there so that when the day comes, you can take over."

"I can already do Eastwood's job." Not that she wanted to. She wanted her rifle back. She wanted to be on the ground hunting terrorists with her team. Dying in combat had always been the plan. This bureaucratic bullshit? Not so much.

"You can plan and run missions, sure," Tom agreed. "The other stuff, leadership and politics and prioritizing . . . You know, things like not throwing a chair across the room when someone dies. That's what you need to learn before you can take over."

"I assumed throwing a chair was preferable to punching Frank." Rachel couldn't help but smirk.

"I appreciate that." Frank winced and rubbed his jaw. It wouldn't have been the first time Rachel punched him.

"Baby girl." Tom shook his head. "You can't lead effectively if you're this emotionally reactive. You've got to separate your personal relationships from your professional ones, or you'll never be able to make the tough calls."

"I make tough calls and send my friends into danger all the time. But usually I'm there backing them up . . . or they're backing me up." *Or ignoring me and running straight into a firefight.*

"Not anymore." Tom shook his head.

Rachel bit the inside of her cheek as too many memories flooded her brain. That horrific internal film reel of tragedy after tragedy: Henry Tull getting shot in the head right in front of her, Aiden Bennet running straight into a line of heavy fire, Veeda's body crumpled on the ground in the middle of a dark courtyard . . . The list of lives—friends—lost went on and on.

"Did Christopher know your asset too?" Tom asked.

"Her name is Zarah, and of course he did."

"You know you can't tell him about this, right?"

She stared at her feet. "I know." There wasn't a lot she kept from Christopher. A few specific secrets, sure. But not telling him about this? The thought of lying to Christopher about something that had so recently involved him—about the woman who had given them so much intel—was hard to swallow. She'd feel like it was a betrayal, but he'd been involved with this shit long enough that hopefully he'd understand. The only lies she'd ever told Christopher were about her past. Though they weren't lies, really. Just lies by omission. Just not opening up about something he'd never think to ask about. *This* lie by omission, however, gutted her.

"Smile," Tom ordered.

Rachel forced the corners of her mouth upwards.

"Do better."

"Why? Christopher will know it's fake regardless. He's well aware the situation room isn't for happy phone calls." She was exhausted from pretending everything was fine—that she was fine. She'd been smiling and keeping her opinions to herself ever since her parents arrived at her house. If anyone knew how much she forced her smiles, she'd win a fucking Oscar. But this . . . watching Samir kill Zarah was too much. She couldn't fake her way through this.

"We don't need Trischa and Anna-Beth worrying," Frank explained.

Rachel nodded, knowing that "upsetting the women" was a cardinal sin. She forced her face and body to relax before following her father and Frank back to lunch.

CHAPTER 5:

SEPTEMBER 2020

THE SECOND THEY GOT home Rachel went upstairs to change into a sports bra and shorts before racing down to the basement. She needed to hit something. She turned up the music as loud as it would go and went to work on the punching bag hanging from the ceiling, determined to unleash all of her frustration and rage. The punching bag wasn't doing it for her though. She still felt terrible and needed something more extreme to get her feelings to go away. She walked over to the other side of the room and grinned as her bare fist collided with the exposed brick wall.

"What the fuck, Rachel?" she heard Christopher yell as his arms wrapped around her, pulling her away to restrain her. It was no use. She put all her weight against Christopher and spun them around, slamming him into the wall. He pulled her into him even tighter as he whispered in her ear, "Babe, deep breath, okay? I know you're mad but—"

"I'm not mad," Rachel answered. "Mad doesn't even come close." She jabbed Christopher in the ribs with her elbow, forcing him to let go of her. She started pacing back and forth, hyperventilating. Her eyes blazed with hatred and fury. It was the same way she felt after Aiden's death, when she'd sought out Carter. She hadn't felt like this in so long, not since she'd started dating Christopher, but that impulsive need was rearing its ugly head.

Rachel knew there was no way Christopher would stand idly by and watch her hurt herself. She was going to have to get him to do it. She wanted to hurt someone badly, to inflict some serious harm on someone—anyone—which always made her feel like a terrible person. Self-loathing and self-deprecation took over. She hated the world and everyone in it almost as much as she hated herself. But she knew Christopher wasn't easily provoked to violence, and she knew he could restrain her if he really wanted to. She would have to get creative.

Christopher took a few steps towards Rachel, maintaining eye contact with her the whole time. She took a poorly aimed swing at his head with her right fist, missing on purpose. He grabbed her arm and spun her around, pinning it behind her back.

"Are you looking for a fight?" he asked her. She said nothing. "Rachel?"

She shifted her weight backward and then forward, causing Christopher to lose his balance so she could throw him over her shoulder and onto the ground. He swiftly swung his leg around, sweeping her legs out from underneath her so she landed on the floor right beside him. She had made her intentions crystal clear. He rolled over and got on top of her, pinning her to the ground.

Rachel raised her knee and jammed it into Christopher's stomach in response to his ridiculous question. He adjusted his grip on her wrists so that he could hold both of her arms down with one hand, then put his other hand on her throat, twisting her neck just enough to make it harder for her to breathe without inflicting any actual harm.

She laughed. "I know you can do it harder than that!"

He pressed against her throat a little harder, refusing to actually choke her. She wrapped her leg around his hips and pulled him in to her. He kissed her on the neck, close to where his hand was.

"Harder," she demanded, whispering in his ear seductively.

He kissed her again, trying to get her to think about something else.

Rachel flipped him over and slapped him hard across the face with the back of her hand. She was straddling him now, but he still had a hold of one of her wrists. Christopher flipped her onto her back then kissed her again, this time, a deep kiss on the lips.

"If that's what you want, you're going to have to take it," Rachel challenged with a twinkle in her eye.

Christopher raised an eyebrow. "Just to be clear, what I think you're saying is—"

Rachel flipped him over again and stood up before he could finish his sentence. "If you fight me and win, then you get whatever you want. But if I win . . ." She knew she was going to let him take her right there on the floor, regardless of who won.

Christopher got up. "If it's a fight you want, then that's what you'll get." He slammed her against the wall. She lifted her knee to his stomach. He took a step back, causing her knee to miss his solar plexus, then hesitated a moment, staring into her eyes.

Rachel knew her eyes were wide and her breathing was heavy. She needed to feel something—anything—before panic took over. Christopher was smart, but he wasn't catching on fast enough to be helpful. Pain was the best way to regulate the guilt she felt. She knew Christopher hated seeing her in pain, knew showing him just how unhinged she could be was a risk. But she was desperate. She stared straight into his eyes, tucked her chin to her chest, then slammed her head backwards into the brick wall.

Christopher's eyes went wide with a mix of shock and fury. He pulled her away from the wall and spun her into the middle of the room. "Don't do that!" he yelled at her.

She laughed viciously. "What are you going to do about it?" she challenged.

He picked her up and threw her on the floor before getting on top of her and holding her down so she couldn't hurt herself again.

"What the fuck, Rachel! You don't get to do dumb shit like that." Christopher studied her face.

"Make me stop. Make me think about something else," Rachel pleaded. Between the Senate hearing, Zarah dying, and trying to sort out how to find Kamal when she couldn't go looking for him herself, she'd lost control. Her mind was a mess of trauma, guilt, and fear. Her rage and desire for blood only made her hate herself, made her feel guilty. She craved punishment, craved pain, and wished Christopher had left her alone in the basement so he wouldn't have to see her like this. She'd managed to keep it together for a couple months of living together. To act mentally stable . . . or stable enough, at least.

Christopher kissed her again. He held her hands over her head and used his knee to slide her leg to the side, using his weight to hold it at a ninety-degree angle. She let him kiss her over and over again, just enough to let him know she wanted him, before she continued fighting back. She flipped him over and gave him a quick jab to the ribs before she stood up. He got up too and slammed her against the wall again so it would be harder for her to attack. She kissed him, and her tongue was in his mouth for just a few moments before she pushed him away again.

Rachel was happy to see that Christopher was finally catching on. Every time he did what she wanted, she rewarded him with a kiss. He went at her again, trying to force her up against the wall. She dodged and ducked under his arm, spinning around to switch places and hold him against the wall instead. Her left forearm was on his throat and her right hand was on his belt, slowly sliding into his waistband, just enough to get him thinking the way she wanted him to. She pressed up against him and kissed him, feeling him get hard against her. His hands slid down her body to her waist, pulling her tighter against him.

Christopher gave her a sly smile, taking the hint, and grabbed her. He spun her so that her face was up against the wall, then pinned her arms above her head. He slid his other hand inside her shorts and started touching her, teasing her, testing her.

Rachel bit her lip. God, he was a fast learner. She let him touch her, reveling in the pleasure for a moment before she got one arm loose and jabbed him in the ribs again, forcing him off of her so that she could turn around and face him. She gave him a look, daring him to take her. He took the bait. Christopher tore down her shorts and underwear, then undid his pants, before lifting her up against the wall, his hands cupping her ass, and thrusting into her deep and hard, kissing her neck as she called out with passionate lust, begging him to fuck her harder. She had won. She had gotten exactly what she wanted. She let him take her, be deep inside of her for a few minutes, before pushing him off. He turned her around again, more forcefully this time, so that she was face up against the wall and kicked her foot out into a wide stance so that she couldn't fight back as easily. He took her from behind, pressing into her, consumed by his own desire, his own need for her, ignoring her needs completely, taking her for himself, exactly as she had intended. She got one of her arms free and moved it down, touching herself as he fucked her. Semi-selfish self-indulgence? It's not like he was about to complain. It didn't take long for her to bring herself to orgasm. She'd been so turned on throughout the whole fight. Every hit, every time he threw her against the wall—it helped to quench her thirst for punishment and increased her hunger for him. It was the perfect mix of pain and pleasure as she came around him, her muscles contracting in bursts of satisfaction until he finished.

Christopher tenderly kissed her neck and wrapped one arm around her waist. His other hand leaned on the wall above Rachel's head. He took a minute, kissing her softly. She made little noises of pleasure and grasped his arm tighter around her waist with both of her hands.

"Hey," he whispered in her ear, "you good?"

"Mmm" was all she said before she turned around and kissed him sweetly on the lips, circling her arms around his neck. "Thank you," she said, kissing him again.

Christopher let out a small laugh that was barely audible. "I should have guessed you'd like it rough," he said. Rachel smiled sweetly, pretending she didn't know what he was talking about. "It's really just a mix of your two favorite activities, isn't it?" he teased.

Rachel laughed and kissed him again. "You know me too well," she said. That had gone much better than expected. Christopher didn't seem horrified or irritated at all. Carter always hated when she made him do that to her. But Christopher was definitely not Carter.

"Let me see the back of your head. You hit it pretty hard," Christopher ordered. She obliged. There wasn't any blood. "You aren't actually hurt, right?"

"I'm fine," Rachel said, giving him another kiss. She felt fantastic actually. Better than she had in a long time.

His eyes darted to her hand as she pulled away. "Ice."

"Don't worry about my hand. Are you okay?" Rachel asked, grazing her thumb over his cheek.

"Yeah. Just a bruised rib, probably, thanks to your elbow!" They both burst out laughing. This was nothing new, really. They'd been sparring and fighting with each other for eleven years, after all. They knew what they could take and what they couldn't. He kissed her tenderly on the lips and brushed a strand of hair behind her ear before gazing into her eyes. "Seriously though, are you okay?"

Rachel shook her head, biting her lip to stop from crying.

"Tell me," Christopher said gently, taking her hand.

"Back there . . . in the situation room." She took a deep breath. "Zarah's dead."

Christopher squeezed her hand. "How?"

"Christopher," she sounded pained, "you know I can't tell you."

"Screw the Navy. This isn't about the Navy. This is about you and what you're feeling. And I can tell this is killing you."

Rachel looked away, not disagreeing. That's why she needed the pain, why she always needed the pain. To stop feeling. But it was too much. How many people would she have to lose before she would finally break?

Christopher sighed, pulling away slightly so he could fully look at her. "Look, I don't know what happened in there, but I know you. I know you probably feel responsible for what happened to her, but you're not."

"But—"

"But if you had been there, then you could've stopped it? You'd have gotten the job done better, more efficiently? I know." Christopher kissed Rachel on the forehead.

"Khalid Khan kidnapped Yamna's son." Her voice was barely above a whisper.

"You're looking for a missing kid?"

"No, apparently, *I'm* not. I'm here, but I need to be there if I'm going to be able to do anything about any of this."

"Baby, I'm sorry, but you're not going back over there. I'm not going back either. It sucks, but it is what it is. We both have to settle in here, learn to chill the fuck out, and in the meantime, you need to learn to delegate your responsibilities to other people."

"I don't trust other people!"

"You trust Luke, and Ryan, and Matt."

"They're on leave. What can they do?"

"Their job," Christopher said seriously. "Trust your teams. Relinquish some control, okay?"

"Okay." Rachel nodded. Christopher let go of her hands and turned to grab her shirt off the floor. "Christopher?" He turned back, his eyes full of love and understanding. That act alone made her crumble. "Why does everyone I try to protect end up dead?"

"Baby," he said, coming back over to wrap his arms around her again.

"It's not just Zarah. It's Aiden and Veeda and Emma . . ."

"Who's Emma?"

Rachel took a deep breath and dug her nails into Christopher's back, pulling herself into him. "Remember when my dad was telling the story about the car? How I took it when I was fourteen?"

"I remember," Christopher assured her. "You stole his car to go buy tampons off base for whatever reason."

Rachel nodded as best she could with her forehead pressed into Christopher. "I had to take Emma to a doctor's appointment, because . . . Ugh, I guess that's not the beginning. The beginning is before that." Christopher chuckled and gave her another kiss on the top of her head. She had a bad habit of telling stories out of chronological order.

"I guess the beginning was a year before when I was at her house. She was my best friend, not counting Carter, but that's really not the same thing. No, Emma Baker was my best friend since before I can remember. We did cheer together and rodeo. We were thirteen, and it was after a football game. It was late and her house was closer than going back to base, so I decided to sleep over. We did it most weekends that there were night games. So, I spent the night at her house one night. I woke up and went downstairs to get some water and I saw . . . Well, her mom had been dating this guy for a while, and he'd moved in. I don't know how long before that. A while. I didn't really know what was happening. They were just there on the floor. I mean, I thought I knew, but . . . I was thirteen, almost fourteen. It was the week before my birthday. Emma was fourteen. Her birthday is . . . was . . . in the summer. I had some idea . . . I was pretty sure I knew what I was seeing, but it was so . . . unthinkable . . . I didn't trust myself. Now I know . . . Anyway, after I saw them, I went back to her room and went back to sleep, trying not to think about it. Then later, when she came to me and said she wasn't feeling well, I made her take a test, you know. And that's why I had to take the car and drive her so she could . . . fix it."

Christopher's jaw clenched. "Her mom's boyfriend got her pregnant?" he asked to confirm. Rachel nodded. "And you drove her to get an abortion?"

She nodded again. "And my dad was so mad about me taking his car, but I couldn't tell him why. So I told him I had to go buy tampons 'cause I knew he'd get uncomfortable and stop asking." Tears started streaming down Rachel's face.

"I should have said something to someone, but who was I gonna tell? What was I gonna tell? I tried to ask the counselor at school, you know, how to help a friend if she was having a hard time, but that wasn't particularly useful. And then . . . then when they called me in and told me . . . It was six months after—" She sniffled. "After I took the car. And they called me to the office at school and asked me who she'd been sleeping with and told me she was dead. She'd gotten pregnant again, and the first time . . . God, those places, and all the protesters calling her a whore and a slut and yelling at her that she was going to hell . . . No wonder she didn't want to go back. So she tried to do it herself. And I guess, technically, she succeeded. She just killed herself in the process too."

Rachel took a gulp of air. "They lied and told everyone it had been a suicide. That she'd slit her wrists, but that's not what happened, and I didn't know what to say. I didn't want to get her in trouble, so I told them I didn't know who it was. It had been so long since I took her, and since I saw them.

It could have been someone else, I don't know. They let me call home to have one of my parents come get me, but my mom was off somewhere, and my dad was busy as usual, so they let me take the bus home. But I didn't go home. Not right away. I went to the commissary and got a bottle of whiskey, then went up on the roof of our house. Then my dad found me later and was mad that I was drunk. I guess he should've been. Then, when he found out later that Emma had died, he wasn't so mad anymore. But he still thinks she killed herself, like they said. If I'd just said something, told someone what I thought was going on . . ."

Christopher pulled Rachel in as tight as he could while she cried. "Have you ever told anyone any of this?" he asked after a few minutes.

"No, only you."

"Well, thank you for trusting me," he said, kissing her on the top of her head again. He let her cry for a minute before continuing. "Baby, it's not your fault," Christopher started soothingly. "I know you think it is, and it probably feels that way, but the only person to blame, the only one at fault, is the asshole who abused her."

"I know. In my head, I know that. But if I had said something . . . But I didn't know what to say. I still don't."

Christopher pulled her in tight to him. "Remember the first time you came to the ranch, and we were in my old room? When you asked me what the bad part was? What I was trying to forget, what it was that had made me so crazy and reckless? You said you'd been the same way, but you knew why you'd been like that. You mentioned taking your father's car. So now I guess I know what you meant by 'battle scars from being a girl in a patriarchal society.'"

"And you said, 'show me yours and I'll show you mine,'" she said, wiping the tears from her eyes and looking up at him.

Christopher chuckled. "Don't you think we've shared enough war stories for one day?"

Rachel grunted in dissent.

Christopher pulled her closer. "I think we should consider the idea of counseling . . . for you, I mean."

"Why? I'm—"

"Fine. Yes, I know, you're always fine," Christopher finished. "But you barely eat or sleep. You're going to get pulled over for speeding and likely arrested for reckless endangerment considering how fast you drive, and you just found out Zarah died. It might be worth considering, is all."

"I don't think it's gonna help."

"Why not?"

Rachel shrugged. "I'm not the problem. D.C. is the problem. They need to have smaller stores and less annoying people."

"Right, I agree with you on that. But the fact of the matter is, your job is here, so once you actually start work, you have to be here. So maybe go to counseling and see if they can help you find a better way of relating to D.C.," Christopher explained. "Just go and try it. It's fun, you'll see."

"If you think counseling is so fun, why don't you go?"

"Maybe I will," Christopher said.

Rachel rolled her eyes. "Fine, I'll go. What am I going to do about Samir and Khalid, though?"

"Tonight? Nothing." Christopher smiled down at her. "The world will still need saving tomorrow."

CHAPTER 6:

SEPTEMBER 2020

RACHEL WAS SITTING IN the counselor's office a few days later, not sure what to say or do. Even though she absolutely hated therapy, she knew Christopher was right. She needed to find a way to tolerate living in D.C. She explained everything about why she had moved, how she had gotten injured, the gender discrimination case she had filed and won against Admiral Leftwich after he had decided she was no longer fit to serve in combat, and her reassignment to a desk here in D.C. The counselor, Catherine, listened, occasionally asking questions to clarify or get more information.

"Do you have any friends in D.C.?" Catherine asked.

"No, well, what do you mean by friends? I know a lot of people, but I don't particularly like them." *What is a friend?* Rachel couldn't believe she was asking that. *God, I must really be screwed up!*

"What do you normally do all day since you haven't started work yet?"

Haven't officially started working. Still need to find Kamal, though. "I hang out with Christopher." Rachel shrugged.

"And what do you and Christopher normally do?"

Rachel winked and smiled at the floor.

"Do you have any *female* friends here in D.C.?" Catherine redirected.

"I don't have very many female friends at all . . ." Rachel pulled back a bit, her face screwing up at the admission. *Where exactly am I supposed to meet women to be friends with when I'm constantly surrounded by men?* "I have Christopher's sisters, but they live in Texas. Charlene lives in Kentucky. She's married to my friend, Matt, who is my team's medic . . . Not *my* team." She frowned at the floor. "Then I have Kristen, who was my lawyer when I sued the Navy, but I outrank her so that gets complicated. All my friends are guys. SEALs . . . and they don't live in D.C."

"That makes sense since that's who you've been surrounded by for the past decade. Why did you wince at the question, though?" Catherine asked.

"What do you mean? Rachel's brow furrowed.

"When you said you don't have very many female friends at all, you winced like it was painful to talk about."

Rachel immediately schooled her face into a neutral expression. "I have no idea what you mean."

"Well . . ." Catherine cocked her head to the side and gave Rachel a quizzical stare. "I asked if you had female friends here. You said you don't have very many female friends at all, which implies that you *do* have *some* female friends, but they don't live here. You mentioned Christopher's sisters and your friend Charlene and colleague Kristen. Do you have any other female friends that you didn't tell me about?"

"Classified," Rachel whispered almost to herself.

"Doctor-patient confidentiality," Catherine reminded her.

Rachel winced again. "They're sort of intelligence assets, I guess. I don't know. They keep dying."

Catherine waited quietly for her to continue.

Rachel let out a frustrated huff. Clearly, Catherine wasn't going to let this go. "I started my naval career as an intelligence officer . . . Human intelligence."

"Can you explain what that is?" Catherine requested.

Rachel nodded. "I would find people, and the people working under me would find people—locals from wherever we were deployed—to recruit to be intelligence assets, to give us information, basically. I have a bad habit of getting too close to them, and they have a bad habit of dying."

"I suppose it would be pretty risky to be an intelligence asset for the U.S. military."

Rachel nodded again. "My friend Veeda died. Her husband found out she was helping us, and they killed her. My friend, my teammate, Aiden . . . He was in love with her. He died trying to save her."

"Where were you when that happened?"

"Running across a courtyard, taking heavy fire, trying to get to ten American aid workers who were being held hostage," she said nonchalantly.

"Did you watch them die?"

"I saw enough." Rachel's jaw clenched. "I made a call. Allegedly the right call, but two of my friends died as a result."

Catherine nodded. "You said before '*they* are intelligence assets.' Which of your assets died other than Veeda?"

Do you want them in chronological order, starting from the beginning or most recent? Rachel pressed her lips into a tight line. Her mouth and body language kept betraying her. "Maybe this was a mistake."

"Let me ask this instead. How long ago did Veeda and Aiden die?"

"April 2019."

"Did you go to therapy after that?"

"Hell no." Rachel chuckled. "I'm only here now because Christopher told me I had to."

"Because something happened?" Catherine guessed. "One of your other assets died?"

Rachel nodded slowly. This chick was good. "Because I couldn't be there. She was trying to follow someone . . . Because I was stuck here and couldn't go myself. Now she's dead."

"So, you feel her death is your fault?"

"No. It's the Navy's fault for sticking me here, for not being willing to negotiate with terrorists in order to save an innocent woman's life," Rachel blurted out.

Catherine's brow furrowed. "Tell me more about that."

Rachel wrinkled her nose and scratched behind her ear. "Can you explain the confidentiality thing again?"

Catherine gave her a warm smile. "Rachel, I am legally bound to not tell anyone anything you say unless you have a specific plan to harm yourself, or someone else, not counting a U.S. Military sanctioned mission, that is. I get things are classified, but I'm sure you can tell me what's going on without getting into too many specifics. If I'm going to help you, you need to trust me."

Rachel's eyebrows shot up. "Trust." She chuckled. "People keep telling me to trust them. Relinquish control. Delegate."

"You don't want to?" Catherine guessed. "Or you don't know how?"

Rachel's nose twitched. Admitting she didn't know how to do something was something she didn't know how to do, so she forced herself to try to trust Catherine. "This guy . . . this . . . well, I've been hunting him for as long as I can remember. He's a terrorist." Rachel winced again as her head flooded with memories. "Zarah was following him for me. My friend. Asset," she corrected. "Zarah was trying to find out what he was up to. He caught her, figured out she knows me . . . My phone number was in her phone under my call sign. He knows my call sign. Hell, he knows *me* . . . Anyway, somehow, he got in touch with my C.O.—don't ask me how—and he offered to make a trade. Me for Zarah. I've been dying to get into a room with the man for over a decade. So I could kill him, you know?" Rachel couldn't help but smirk, then she froze. "That would be one of those officially sanctioned SEAL missions, not a danger to others, or whatever," she clarified.

"I understand." Catherine nodded. "Your job is to capture or kill terrorists, Rachel. This is still covered under doctor-patient confidentiality."

Rachel nodded, choosing to believe Catherine. "My idiot boss just kept saying 'the U.S. does not negotiate with terrorists.' Like that's at all helpful." She sighed. "If I'd been in Afghanistan instead of here, I would have been following him myself. I would have killed him, and Zarah would still be alive. Win-win, if you ask me. A terrorist is dead, I get to have some fun, and Zarah gets to live. Instead, he's still doing God knows what awful thing, and she's dead, and I'm stuck here with no power, no authority, on leave, wasting time, with nothing to do but talk to you."

"That's a lot to deal with." Catherine glanced at the clock. "I want to talk about that more, but—"

"I don't," Rachel interrupted, crossing her arms over her chest and slumping back into her chair.

"You don't have to talk about it anymore. Not today, at least, since we're almost out of time. We're going to talk about trust and control more too. For homework until our next session—"

"This shit comes with homework?" Rachel wrinkled her nose.

Another reassuring smile from Catherine. "It seems like most of your friends are friends of convenience?"

"What?" Rachel scrunched up her face, having no idea what that meant.

"Christopher's sisters, your teammate's wife, your lawyer, other SEALs, intelligence assets. These people are all your friends because of your job. The relationships aren't based on mutual interests, hobbies, that sort of thing. You may have hobbies or interests in common with them, but I'd guess the relationships center mostly around work."

"I suppose they might," Rachel bit out the words.

"Where else could you make friends?"

"I dunno."

"Think about it for a minute."

Rachel shook her head. "I'm not here to take tests, Catherine. Just tell me the right answer."

Catherine chuckled. "Well, most people make friends through activities or hobbies. Maybe at the gym or some sort of class or a sports team. The friendship is based on a mutual interest, such as liking the same music or books, going to the same types of museums. That sort of thing. It's also common to make friends through other friends."

"No, that wouldn't work at all." Rachel shook her head. "If I'm already standing next to the person sharing an activity or whatever, when would I run a background check on them?"

Catherine blinked rapidly, trying to process what Rachel was saying. "Also, most people don't run background checks on their friends . . ."

"Well, I can't let just anyone into my life." Rachel frowned.

"Okay, what about making friends through the friends you already have?"

"Tell me more."

"Would you feel more comfortable making new friends who are male or female?"

"It's been a while since I did girl stuff," Rachel admitted. "But I definitely have a harder time trusting men. I haven't had the best experiences with men . . . Sort of want to kick most of them in the balls most of the time."

"Right. Do you trust your friend . . ." Catherine glanced down at her notepad. "Kristen, is the one who lives here, right?"

"Yes. Kristen lives here. But she's a work friend."

"Do you trust her judgement? Would you trust other women that she's friends with?"

"Umm, not like, with my life or anything. She's a lawyer. I mean, I'm sure the Navy taught her to shoot a gun at some point." Rachel wasn't understanding.

"Right. That's another thing. Most of the people you're friends with, you're responsible for protecting. The other SEALs, they have your back and you have theirs. But you're their boss, so you're ultimately responsible, right? Same with your intelligence assets."

Rachel tensed and glanced over at the clock, willing this conversation to end as quickly as possible before she was forced to take too hard of a look at herself. "Cut to the chase, Catherine."

"What would you think about inviting your friend Kristen out for a drink or dinner or something? See if she has other friends she could invite. Have some girl time?"

Rachel nodded slowly. "I can do that." *Girl time* sounded awful, but whatever. Rachel sent a quick text to Kristen and received a prompt response that she had plans with her friends Saturday night and that Rachel was more than welcome to join. She turned her screen towards Catherine, showing her the text. "Done."

"Without investigating her friends before you meet them."

Rachel pursed her lips, not liking that caveat at all. "Fine. Can I run a background check on them after I meet them?"

"Why would you need to do that?" Catherine asked seriously. She held up a hand, stopping Rachel from arguing. "I mean very seriously, why. These are women your friend Kristen knows. You trust her, and she trusts them. You are having drinks with them once, not at your home. You aren't inviting them to be a major part of your life. They don't know what your job is. It's just one night out together. So, why would you need to investigate them at all, either before or after meeting them?"

"I . . ." Rachel blinked. "Umm."

"You're trying really hard to come up with a valid reason, aren't you?"

"But what if something happens?" Rachel's brow furrowed.

"Like what?" Catherine glanced at the clock.

"If someone dies or something."

"From having drinks with you?" Catherine cocked her head to the side. "I think you know that's not likely."

"But—"

Catherine shook her head. "Think about why you feel compelled to investigate every single human you interact with. I suspect your reasons will come back to trust and control, but evaluate your thought process on this. Hang out with Kristen, and we'll talk more at our next session."

Chapter 7:

SEPTEMBER 2020

RACHEL DESPERATELY NEEDED A treat after that therapy session and decided to swing by Cardigan Coffee on her way home. Trusting people in situations she didn't have control over sounded like an absolute nightmare, and as much as she liked Kristen, making new friends Catherine's way sounded horrifically stressful. She'd spent most of her life investigating people, keeping track of their secrets, both to keep them safe but also so she had ammunition to use against them if she ever needed it. She'd always needed to know everything about everyone while also ensuring that they didn't know any more about her than they absolutely needed to. She'd been like that ever since she was a kid, but as a CIA operative turned SEAL, secret keeping was an absolute necessity for survival.

She was just about to open the door to Cardigan Coffee when she suddenly stopped dead in her tracks, pulling back like a wolf observing its newfound prey.

"Fucking hell," Rachel muttered to herself. She turned her back, pulled up the hood of her sweatshirt, and took three steps away from the door just in time for Leftwich to step out onto the sidewalk. She pulled her phone out of her pocket and pretended to read something on it, all the while aiming the camera over her shoulder so that she could capture Leftwich.

He got into his car and glanced over his shoulder. Rachel looked down again, hoping he wouldn't notice her. As soon as he pulled away from the curb, she raced back to Christopher's truck and pulled out into traffic a few cars behind Leftwich. He was about to turn at the upcoming traffic light, so Rachel merged into the right lane, following just close enough to where she could still see him. Another mile later, he pulled into a parking lot and got out at a picnic area in the middle of Rock Creek Park.

"Well, isn't this fucking interesting," Rachel said to herself. She snapped several photos of Admiral Richard Leftwich and Joe Petchill, Director of Operations at the CIA, thanks to Frank's recent appointment. The two of them were having what looked like a heated debate as Petchill handed Leftwich a thick file. Rachel jumped out of the truck and snuck over to hide in the bushes along the path where she could hear them—mostly—but still be out of their sight.

Leftwich hated the CIA and Petchill, specifically. She'd heard him call Petchill every name in the book—before turning to her and calling her a few of the same. Manipulative, conniving, deranged, immoral. Those were some of the nicer things that Leftwich had had to say. As much as Rachel hated agreeing with Leftwich, he'd had a point about Petchill. His hatred for Rachel? Well, she'd never sussed out if that was because of her connection to the CIA or simply because she was a woman. Likely both, she'd always presumed.

She got as close as she could and started filming, knowing the sound quality would be atrocious, but it was better than nothing.

"Frank wants your opinion," Petchill said.

"Fucking Frank. What is it this time?" Leftwich grumbled.

"He wants your opinion on the Iran situation. We've confirmed who has the USB. He's considering a deal."

Rachel wrinkled her nose as the two men mumbled and grumbled their way through an argument she couldn't quite hear. Leftwich looked irate. Petchill was calm cool and collected.

"—target?" Rachel barley caught the end of Leftwich's question.

"Iran," Petchill affirmed.

"That could work. Who has the code though?"

"Sam. He has the kids too."

"Are the kids ready to go? Ready to work?"

"I think so." Petchill sounded as though he didn't actually care.

"How much does Frank know about *that*?"

"Enough to be useful. But after that, he's sort of outgrown his usefulness, hasn't he?"

"Fine. I'll get back to you with an opinion."

Rachel heard the groan of wood and the shuffle of leaves, then the slam of a car door. After a few heartbeats, she parted the shrubs just enough to see Leftwich drive away, Petchill cautiously following behind.

Rachel stayed hidden until Petchill left as well, then she scrambled out from the bushes. She stared at the bench that they'd been sitting on, filtering through their conversation. It wasn't making a lot of sense: *Sam has the code. Iran is the target. Frank wants an opinion. Are the kids ready to work?*

Unfortunately, there were a lot of people named Sam and Frank, and a lot of different codes circulating around. Rachel already suspected—had *accused*—Leftwich of stealing a malware code from her father and giving it to Samir Al-Abadi. Frank Verity knew Samir had that code. It had just been confirmed the other day when Samir had killed Zarah. Was Frank in on this act of treason too? On top of all this—whatever *it* actually was—she still had no idea how to go about finding Kamal. The poor kid could be anywhere by now.

Rachel glanced down at her phone and noted the time. Christopher would be wondering where she was.

Chapter 8:

SEPTEMBER 2020

"YOU WERE GONE A while?" Christopher said, more of a question than a statement. "What's the mileage on the truck?" He pulled out his phone and opened the spreadsheet he used to keep track of the truck's mileage.

Rachel showed him the photo she'd taken of the dashboard, having anticipated the question. "You know that truck isn't Navy property, right? You don't have to track the mileage."

"Knowing the current mileage is essential for proper vehicle maintenance." Rachel rolled her eyes, but it didn't stop him from giving her the full lecture on *why* proper vehicle maintenance was so essential.

"Babe, it's just a truck. You have to chill!"

Christopher crossed his arms over his chest. Rachel didn't yell often, and certainly not at him. Something else was happening here, and he figured therapy maybe hadn't been too much fun for her. He tried a different tactic. "Where else did you go?"

"Why?"

"I'm just curious." He shrugged. "Don't want to be left out of anything fun."

"I just went to therapy and back," she insisted.

He smiled, opened Google Maps, and zoomed in on their neighborhood. "I know the roads here are really confusing, especially if you have Taylor Swift turned all the way up and are more focused on singing than navigating, but to get to your therapist, you go—"

"I know where to go!"

"I'd love to believe you, but you put twice as many miles on the truck as you should have. Gas is expensive. Car maintenance is expensive. I'm just trying to help so you don't get lost. I want you to be safe, to feel safe. Not end up in some sketchy neighborhood or something." She'd nearly died in his arms not so many months ago, and the thought of losing her was unbearable. The thought of anything happening to her . . . He could hardly stand to let her out of his sight, as irrational as that was. She was a SEAL for fuck's sake and could more than handle herself. But still, some primal, horrifically un-feminist part of him desperately needed to protect her. He knew it was best to keep *that* to himself though.

"What are you gonna do, Christopher, track my location and call me every time you think I made a wrong turn?"

"No." It wasn't the worst idea. *How do I explain this without getting a lecture on gender norms and feminism?* "I can drive you from now on and wait for you. It's not like I'm doing anything anyways, and that way we don't waste gas or put more miles than necessary on the truck." *Good. Make it about protecting the truck, not protecting her.*

"Whatever." Rachel rolled her eyes. "You're gonna have to drive me to girls' night on Saturday."

"What?" Christopher was confused. As far as he knew, Rachel didn't have any friends to have a girls' night with.

"My therapy homework is to get drunk with Kristen and her friends. They're going out on Saturday, which is in three days."

"That doesn't sound like therapy homework." Christopher had done plenty of therapy. He'd gone after every single deployment, and no therapist had ever told him to get drunk. The opposite, in fact, had been the typical recommendation.

"I'm supposed to be making friends and learning to trust people," Rachel clarified.

That makes more sense. "Where are you meeting them?"

Rachel showed him the text from Kristen with the address to the wine bar.

"Oh, you can take the metro then. You just take the red line to the silver line, so if you walk towards . . ."

Rachel gave Christopher a blank stare as he rattled off his instructions. She knew he'd repeat himself a thousand times and that she could check Google Maps when the time came. Worst case scenario, she'd get a rideshare. Christopher's obsessive memorization of streets and traffic patterns and the D.C. metro were entirely unnecessary. But he enjoyed it. More importantly, his damned spreadsheet had given her an idea. She pulled her phone out of her back pocket and started typing as she nodded along with his instructions. He smiled, likely assuming she was typing the directions he was rattling off. She wasn't.

Skylark to Yamna: *Check the mileage on your father's car to see how far he drives when he leaves. That way we can narrow down where he goes.*

Yamna to Skylark: *You want me to check his car? I don't know anything about cars.*

Skylark to Yamna: *Find someone who does and have them help you.*

Chapter 9:

OCTOBER 2020

AFTER NAVIGATING THE D.C. metro with ease, thanks to Christopher's explicit instructions on which train to take, Rachel walked into a small wine bar close to the Capitol Building. Christopher had typed the directions into a note on her phone, pulled it up on Google Maps for her, and called her six times to check she hadn't gotten lost.

Her eyes darted around nervously until she spotted Kristen at a table in the back corner with two other women. Rachel paused, shifting her weight to her left foot. Her right ankle itched where her tactical knife usually was. Christopher had somehow convinced her that wearing heels was more normal than combat boots. He had even called their friend Charlene and his sisters to confirm. Rachel bent her knee and kicked her foot up to where she could reach, then scratched the spot where she usually hid her knife. She was uncomfortable and edgy and was quickly realizing that her tactical knife may be more like a security blanket.

You don't need your knife. You can kill people with your bare hands. Suck it up and get in there.

She took a deep breath, hoping she remembered how to act in normal social situations. She wasn't particularly confident that she did, but was determined to succeed at this anyway. Ten long paces later and she was at Kristen's table.

"Hey! You found it!" Kristen exclaimed. She jumped up to hug Rachel. "This is Julie, and this is Ashley." She waved to the two women sitting at the table, then motioned for Rachel to sit down. "We were just discussing what we wanted to order. If we want to split a bottle, assuming we can agree on something, or if we're going with individual glasses."

"Well, I'm good with anything," Rachel said. "If I had to choose, I prefer red, but white is fine too."

"Red's good with me," Julie said, "but these two are more partial to white." She pointed to Kristen and Ashley.

"Why don't we get a bottle of red and a bottle of white? That's a little more than two glasses per person," Rachel pointed out. Supplies, logistics, and alcohol were things she *did* know how to do.

"Genius!" Kristen said. "Ashley and I can get a bottle of chardonnay, and you two can figure out what you want."

"Pinot okay with you?" Julie asked Rachel.

"Perfect!" Rachel answered. She'd drink anything at this point.

They ordered, and the waiter returned promptly with their bottles and glasses. Julie and Kristen tasted and approved, and the waiter poured them each a glass.

"So, how do you two know each other?" Julie asked Rachel and Kristen.

Kristen caught Rachel's eye and gave her a reassuring nod before filling Ashley and Julie in on how they'd met. Next, Rachel told them about her move to D.C. with Christopher, which prompted both Julie and Ashley to demand photos of Christopher and of the house. Rachel was unsure. She'd spent over a decade protecting Christopher's identity just as much as she'd protected her own. She winced and gave Kristen a sideways glance.

"Christopher is retired," Kristen whispered. "I think you can show them a picture."

Rachel pressed her lips into a tight line as she fought all of her instincts. Relenting, she unlocked her phone and found a photo of Christopher standing in front of their house.

"I don't know which is more beautiful, your boyfriend or your house!" Julie gushed.

"Are all the guys in the Navy this hot?" Ashley asked. "If so, I need to know where they hang out."

"All the ones under Rachel's command are," Kristen blurted out. She looked quickly at Rachel and blushed.

Ashley cocked her head to the side. "What's your actual job, Rachel?"

Rachel scratched the back of her head, her lips pursed and eyes on the table.

Kristen sighed. "My client pleads the fifth. Stop asking."

Julie gave Kristen an admonishing stare. "Rachel, give each of us a dollar, and then everything is covered under attorney-client privilege."

"National security?" Rachel looked to Kristen for guidance.

"You scanned the room when you came in, right?" Kristen whispered to Rachel, her eyes darting around the room. "You recognize anyone you need to worry about?"

"I worry about everyone, including these two," Rachel whispered back through gritted teeth.

Kristen sighed and looked first to Julie, then to Ashley. She leaned across the table and lowered her voice. "I'm not worried about you two knowing anything because I know I can trust you, but anyone in this place could overhear something."

"Classified military secrets?" Julie rubbed her palms together and grinned.

Kristen turned her attention to Rachel next. "You *do* realize that sitting here and acting suspicious is just drawing more attention to the issue?"

Rachel blinked twice then cocked her head to the side, looking at Kristen. "Guess when the last time I hung out with anyone who wasn't in the military was."

Kristen burst out laughing. "Didn't you grow up on a base somewhere?"

"Yes." Rachel nodded.

"Then I'd guess never!"

Rachel dipped her head, confirming Kristen was correct.

"Well, I've known these two for forever, and I wouldn't have let them meet you if they couldn't be trusted. Do you trust me?"

This question again. "I suppose." Rachel pursed her lips.

The corner of Kristen's mouth curled, and she huffed out a quiet laugh. "Rachel commands a combat squadron and spent quite a bit of time in combat herself. That's how she met Christopher."

Ashley's eyes went wide.

"That is so fucking badass!" Julie's jaw was practically on the floor.

"Weren't you terrified?" Ashley asked.

"What's there to be afraid of?" Rachel's brow furrowed. "Either you live or you die, and if you die, then you're dead."

"Wow. You *really* suck at being normal." Kristen grimaced.

Rachel narrowed her eyes at Kristen.

Kristen bowed her head and clenched her jaw. "Apologies, ma'am."

"I'm not mad at your insubordination." Rachel slapped her lightly on the arm. "That was just plain mean!"

Kristen chuckled. "It was true though."

"Just plain mean." Rachel forced her lips into a pout, doing her best to act sullen.

"Shut up and drink your wine." Kristen giggled.

"Now that Kristen's told you too much about me," Rachel glared at her, "time for reciprocity. How do you two know Kristen?"

"Julie and I went to law school together. Ashley and I were college roommates," Kristen explained.

"And what do they do now?" Rachel's eyes bore into Kristen. She was exceedingly frustrated and had concluded that this was the dumbest way to get information from people. Background checks were much more efficient, and enhanced interrogation was much more fun.

"I work with employment contracts and represent people who are accusing their company of discrimination, wrongful termination, sexual harassment, or who have been accused of breeching a contract. Like violating a nondisclosure or noncompete clause. Things like that," Julie explained.

"Good. Fight the patriarchy!" Rachel grinned.

"More like corporate greed." Julie nodded.

"I run a nonprofit that works to increase mental health resources in schools," Ashley chimed in.

Rachel was immediately fascinated. "What are the main resources that you're lobbying for? Or are you trying to get laws changed?" Rachel asked.

"A bit of both, actually. We want to get a federal law passed that ensures students have access to full-time counselors, starting in elementary school, but it's tricky with all the state laws. We're also working on getting more general awareness for mental health issues out to the public and hoping that, at some point, the Department of Health and Human Services will get onboard. But D.C. is so full of bureaucracy and red tape, it's ridiculous."

"Precisely why I wish I wasn't living here. You can't go anywhere in this city without running into at least one politician . . ."

As if she'd somehow summoned one such politician, Rachel noticed a finely-dressed man pull open the big oak doors across the bar. She grumbled under her breath, instantly recognizing him as her brother's best friend and college roommate, Senator Hunter Adams.

Hunter locked eyes with her and made his way across the bar and to their table. "Hey Rache! What are you doing in D.C?"

Rachel wrinkled her nose at him. "Ladies," she said, turning in toward the girls and *away* from him, "this is Senator Hunter Adams of New Hampshire." She tried to sound respectful, though she felt anything but. "Who are you here with?"

"You know." Hunter shrugged.

"Right, well, nice to see you again," Rachel said politely, hoping he would get the hint and leave.

"Why are you so mad?" Hunter almost looked sad. If she didn't know him better, she'd even say heartbroken.

"Because, Hunter, you know why!" She didn't want to get into decades of drama with Hunter in front of Kristen and her friends.

"How can I make it up to you?" He leaned in, bracing his forearm on the table, and stuck out his lower lip.

Rachel rolled her eyes. "Ashley, what forms of payment does your non-profit take for donations?"

Ashley pulled up the website on her phone, and Rachel handed it to

Hunter.

"Make a generous contribution or go away," Rachel insisted.

Hunter skimmed through the website and then pulled it up on his own phone to fill in the donation form. He showed it to Rachel before pushing *submit*, then he grabbed a chair and joined them. He immediately picked up Rachel's glass and took a sip.

Rachel glared at him. "Senator Adams went to college with my brother," she explained. "I'm assuming his wife is out of town and he's bored."

"Come on, I'm sure I'll figure out a way to entertain myself. Give me a minute. I just got here!" Hunter chuckled as he glanced around the bar. "Assuming you aren't available."

"I am never available, Hunter."

"Well, not *never* . . ." Hunter smirked.

"Never again!" Rachel rolled her eyes. One drunken night with Hunter had been enough regret for a lifetime.

"Fine. At least give me some help then."

"It's a wine bar, Hunter. Girls come here in groups to hang out with their friends. Not to be harassed by idiots like you." At least she knew that much.

"I'm very sure that you're right, Rachel, but that doesn't mean I'm not up to the challenge."

"Where *is* Claire?" Rachel asked him, assuming he was still married.

"In New York, probably doing the same thing I'm doing here." Hunter shrugged. "We'd get divorced, but it looks bad. And it's an election year so we can't have that, now can we?"

"In what universe is adultery better than divorce?" Rachel didn't bother to mask her irritation.

"It's more fun and less expensive."

Julie and Kristen laughed. "He's not wrong," Julie said.

"Do you swear that Claire is cheating on you too?" Rachel asked Hunter.

"Yes, I promise!"

"And when we send someone from Ashley's nonprofit to start bossing you around about how to vote—"

"From what I just read on the website, it's a great organization." Hunter smiled at Ashley. "You're welcome to discuss policy with me or my staff anytime."

"She is also not available. Not to you anyway." Rachel glared at him, suddenly feeling very protective of Ashley.

"Actually." Hunter playfully pressed his palm against Rachel's mouth, trying to get her to shut up so he could talk to Ashley. "Do you ever work with immigrant kids or refugees?"

Rachel cocked her head to the side and pushed his hand away from her face. "Since when do you give a shit about immigrants, refugees, or kids?"

"Since Trischa talked me into planning an event for her."

"Dear Lord." Rachel chuckled. "She tried to get me to help with that too!"

Hunter's brows knit together. "When did you talk to Trischa?"

"When I was forced to have lunch with her and Frank."

Hunter burst out laughing. "Sucks to be you! Trischa Verity is always a chore."

"Trischa Verity?" Ashley's eyes went wide. "As in, the First Lady?"

"Yup." Hunter nodded. "I went to college with her son, and she's been a pain in my ass ever since. The title and presumed power are going to her head though. She seems to genuinely believe that First Lady is the same thing as being queen." He grimaced. "In all seriousness, Ashley, I do need some sort of nonprofit to partner with or else we'll be raising money for nothing."

"I'm sure we can come up with something. Training school counselors to help refugee kids integrate into schools, something like that?" Ashley suggested.

"I honestly don't care what you do with the money. I plan on raising a lot of money and need someone to give the money to. You seem reputable. Lots of organizations aren't. If Rachel trusts you—" He looked at Rachel.

"I just met her tonight. I don't know much about her or her organization," Rachel told Hunter.

"You don't actually think I give a shit, do you?" Hunter chuckled. "Seriously, Rachel. I want to stay in Frank's good graces, which means I have to play nice with Trischa. If it looks like I'm helping kids in the process . . ." He shrugged. "It's all about optics. You know that."

"It's a legitimate organization, Rachel," Kristen assured her. "They actually use the money they raise for what they say they'll use it for. I've known Ashley since before she started the organization and even helped her with some of the paperwork to get their nonprofit 501(c) status."

Rachel nodded. Trust and lack of control sure were coming into play with this one. "I will endorse this on three conditions." Rachel glared at Hunter. "You two will not sleep together. You will treat her with respect and professionalism, meaning no hitting on her. And you keep your eyes on her eyes and nowhere else."

Hunter rolled his eyes. "Shockingly, I do know how to do that."

"If I find out you didn't comply with that, if Ashley or anyone she works with has any complaints about you—"

"You'll spill all of my secrets and make it so I can never get elected to office again. I know."

Rachel nodded and flashed him a ferocious grin just as her phone beeped.

Hawk to Skylark: *I'm at the sports bar down the street from you. Let me know when you're ready to leave and I'll come get you.*

"This fucking man, I swear!" she grumbled to herself.

"Problem?" Kristen's brow furrowed.

Rachel showed her the text from Christopher. "He's convinced I can't find my way home. He called me six times on my way here."

"Who is this?" Hunter asked.

"My boyfriend or whatever." Rachel sighed, still slightly uncomfortable calling him that.

"Why does he think you'll get lost?" Kristen asked.

"A few reasons." Rachel bit the inside of her cheek. "One, he's a navigator, so he has maps of everywhere he's ever been memorized. He's obsessed. Two, I got drunk and lost while we were on leave once, *maybe* twice, and he had to come find me. Which he doesn't mind doing, but he was sort of in the middle of something at the time and wasn't particularly happy I interrupted his fun."

"Have him come here." Kristen grabbed Rachel's phone out of her hand and texted Christopher back to let him know his presence at girls' night was suddenly mandatory.

"You seriously have a boyfriend?" Hunter was stunned.

"Play nice or I'll kill you. Or he will," Rachel threatened.

Christopher got the text from Rachel requesting that he join her at the wine bar. He downed his beer, left a wad of cash on the bar, and headed down the block. He walked into the wine bar and found Rachel glaring at a man who was likely a few years older than her. Kristen sat beside her, laughing along with two other women. Christopher slid between the tables, pausing to kiss Rachel on the top of her head before taking up the chair next to her. "What's so funny?" he asked, looking around at everyone.

"Nothing." Rachel mumbled.

The man started, "I was just telling everyone about the time—"

Rachel picked up the cheese knife that was at her place setting and pointed it at the man. "Hunter, I swear, if you don't shut the fuck up—"

"You behave, or I'll call your mother." Hunter shoved her hand away from him.

"You know her mother?" Christopher gave Hunter a sideways glance.

"You're the boyfriend, I presume?" Hunter raised an eyebrow.

Christopher nodded and placed his hand on Rachel's thigh under the table. He tapped out C.A.L.M. in morse code with his index finger. Her eyebrows shot up, then she turned her angry stare on him.

"Seriously?" Rachel sighed.

Christopher chuckled. "It's rare I see you this angry. Normally when you get pissed off, you get calmer."

"Normally when I get pissed off, I can handle it in a very different way than I'm sure I'm allowed to here!" she hissed.

Christopher rolled his eyes and turned his attention to Kristen. "Care to translate, Campbell?"

"Senator Adams was sharing some funny yet embarrassing anecdotes from when Rachel was a teenager."

Christopher's brow furrowed.

"He's friends with Jamie," Rachel explained.

"Oh!" That made more sense.

"I'll stop now though because Rachel was right. You probably could kill me." Hunter smiled.

"Smart move, Hunter." Kristen winked. "I'm confident Chris would be more than happy to cause you immense pain."

"Babe, is this yours?" Christopher reached for her wine glass.

"Yes, but Hunter drank out of it, and given that so many diseases can be passed through saliva . . . well . . . I'm not sure where his dick has been lately. Best not share with him." She cringed and slid the glass towards Hunter, then motioned for the server to come over and ordered two more bottles and two new glasses.

"That was rude," Hunter complained.

"It was true," Rachel noted.

"What do you do, Christopher?" Hunter leaned his elbow on the table, turning his body so he could talk across Rachel.

"I just retired from the Navy."

"Makes sense." Hunter nudged Rachel. "I'm sure your father is ecstatic."

"Why would he be?" Rachel had never looked so confused.

"I dunno, last I checked Admiral Ryker was sort of obsessed with the Navy."

"That's true. I'm not sure what it has to do with my dating life, though." She turned her attention back to Christopher. "Guess who got roped into helping Frank and Trischa with their bullshit fundraiser?" She nodded with her head towards Hunter.

Christopher burst out laughing. "Sucks to be you, Hunter. One lunch with Trischa made it plenty evident that that event will be a nightmare."

"Not if people help me." Hunter's whine morphed into a wide grin as his eyes slid across the table. "Ashley is going to help me."

"No, I said I'd take whatever money you raise. I said nothing about actually planning an event," Ashley corrected.

"Please?" Hunter's sad puppy eyes and pursed lips made everyone laugh.

"Fine! I'll help." Ashley giggled.

"Thank you!" Hunter pressed his palms together like he was praying and bowed his head towards her in appreciation. His eyes slid back to Rachel. "Any other volunteers? Perhaps someone who speaks whatever language these kids speak?"

"God, you're worse than Trischa and Frank!" Rachel complained.

Hunter leaned across her to talk to Christopher again. "Did the Navy teach *you* any useful languages?"

Christopher took a slow sip of his wine. "They may have."

"What else did they teach you?"

"How to kill obnoxious men, mostly." Rachel nearly choked on her wine as she said it, laughing.

"Hilarious, Rache," Hunter chided her.

"Wasn't really kidding, but okay." She shrugged.

"You, stop." Hunter leaned across her so he could talk to Christopher easier. "What did you do in the Navy?"

"I was a surface warfare officer." There was no way Christopher was going to tell this idiot he'd been a SEAL. Senator or not. Besides, he had been a surface warfare officer for two years before becoming a SEAL.

"Catchy title. What the fuck does it mean?" Hunter swatted at Rachel's hands as she tried to push him away from her.

"You're a senator. Shouldn't you know that?" Rachel wrinkled her nose at him.

"I'm not on the Armed Services Committee, and if I ever have to know anything about the military, I call Jamie and he tells me what to say or do."

"God help us all," Rachel grumbled. Christopher knew her brother was the biggest slacker there ever was.

Christopher redirected, finally answering Hunter's question. "I made sure troops and supplies got from point A to point B."

Hunter perked up at that. "Can you make sure refugee kids and supplies get from point A to point B?"

"I could, but I'm not sure I want to."

"Rachel," Hunter stared at her wide-eyed. "Convince Chris to help me!"

Rachel rolled her head lazily towards Christopher. "I'm sure you're bored, and Hunter does throw good parties."

"Besides, you can be the sexual harassment police and make sure Hunter follows Rachel's no flirting and no touching rules. You're familiar with those," Kristen teased.

"Who are you not allowed to flirt with?" Christopher looked at Hunter.

"Ashley or anyone she works with or is friends with or probably anyone Rachel is remotely fond of."

"Seriously?" Christopher gave Rachel a sideways glance.

"Yes. He's remarkably unprofessional, and the only person he should be flirting with is his wife."

Christopher considered for a moment before deciding he really didn't want to help with the clean up after Rachel killed Hunter for cheating on his wife. He also didn't want to have to bail her out of jail for assaulting a senator. He switched to Arabic, assuming no one else at the table would understand. "You seriously want me to chaperone them?"

Rachel nodded and switched to Arabic as well. "A certain someone else is bound to be involved, especially if you're meeting at their home . . ."

Christopher gave her a quizzical stare and listened carefully as she tapped out F.R.A.N.K. in morse code on the table.

Chapter 10

OCTOBER 2020

A FEW DAYS WENT by, and Rachel was feeling bored and restless. She needed Yashfa and Yamna to move faster so she could start tracking Khalid Khan. She needed the Senate to vote on her promotion faster so she could get a team to Khost to really start looking for Kamal. Christopher was actively trying to keep her entertained like a little kid having to stay inside on a snow day. Their latest activity: adding books to Rachel's Amazon cart. Just as Christopher was explaining, for the hundredth time, the benefits of e-books versus paperbacks, Rachel got a text.

Yamna to Skylark: *834km*

Rachel instantly jumped up in search of a map, a ruler, and a pencil.

"Umm, hello?" Christopher called from his spot on the couch. "Babe, we aren't done! Where are you going?"

Ignoring him, Rachel carried all of her supplies into her home office and spread out a map of the Middle East on the floor. She easily located Khost then checked the scale in the bottom corner. She really hated maps, and she'd been spoiled having Christopher handle anything maps or geography related over the past decade. She wrinkled her nose and put her hands on her hips, contemplating how best to complete this task.

She wandered out to the kitchen, ruler in hand, and started going through all the drawers. Since she didn't cook, she had no idea where anything was in the kitchen. That was entirely Christopher's domain.

"What are you doing?" Christopher asked, following her into the kitchen. He watched her with an amused expression on his face.

"I need to make a circle."

"Why?"

"To draw on a map." She started measuring the diameter of various cups and bowls.

Christopher raised an eyebrow and chuckled. "Can I please help you?"

"Did you magically get your security clearance back?" Rachel's voice was hopeful.

"No, but I'm guessing you want your map to be accurate."

Rachel rolled her eyes. "I know how to do it."

"I know you do, but . . ." He grimaced at the wine glass in her right hand and the ruler in her left.

"But what?" Rachel huffed. She didn't want to admit that he was better at maps than she was or that her confidence was lacking, even if both were true.

"But nothing." He watched as she put down the wine glass and picked up a bowl to measure instead. "I just miss drawing on maps."

"No, you were going to say 'but you suck at geography and are going to screw it up.'"

A low chuckle escaped Christopher's lips, and his eyes darted to the floor. "That's not what I was going to say."

"Really?" Rachel glared at him.

"I was going to be more diplomatic and kind about it."

Rachel rolled her eyes. "I need to know what is in a four hundred seventeen kilometer radius from Khost."

"That's a pretty big area, and a bowl is definitely not the best way to draw a circle on a map," Christopher noted as he quickly found a compass and held it up for Rachel to see.

"I didn't know we had one of those."

"*We* don't. I, however, have several." He walked into Rachel's office and knelt on the floor next to the map. Within seconds, he had a perfect circle drawn around Khost.

"Shit." Rachel sighed when she saw how big the circle Christopher had drawn actually was. "Well, that doesn't narrow things down much . . . and Pakistan is inside that circle."

"Yes, ma'am, it is." Christopher nodded.

"If they drove across the border . . ." She chewed on her bottom lip.

"It would be a logistical nightmare full of red tape to get any kidnapped children back?" Christopher looked up at her.

Rachel nodded, ignoring the part where he knew too much about what was going on for someone who no longer had clearance. She considered for a minute, wishing she could discuss her theories with Christopher, but she couldn't. She stared at the map silently instead.

Just because he drove 834km doesn't mean he drove to one location and back. It also doesn't mean he drove in a straight line.

The radius at least told her where Khalid Khan *hadn't* gone, but it was still too big of an area for one SEAL team to cover, and she highly doubted Eastwood would give her more than one team.

"These are mountains." Rachel looked at Christopher for confirmation as she pointed to a few areas inside the circle on the map.

"Correct." He nodded. "And this blue part over here is water," he teased, pointing to an area very far outside the circle.

Rachel sighed and put her hands on her hips. His teasing was not appreciated. "You know I think better out loud, but I'm not allowed to tell you stuff, so I don't know how to figure this out!"

"I see." The corner of Christopher's lip tugged up.

"I . . . *we* have had a very efficient way of working for over a decade. I can't do things that way anymore because you got this dumb idea in your head to retire." Rachel scolded him.

"It was an excellent idea." Christopher smirked.

Rachel glared at him. "In this particular situation, it is highly inconvenient, and I cannot discuss this with you."

Christopher laughed and looked up at the ceiling. "Baby, I'm not stupid. I know you're trying to figure out what Khalid Khan is up to, and I'm guessing he's driving to someplace inside the circle you just had me draw."

"I can neither confirm nor deny—"

"Uh-huh." Christopher's smirk was back. "Focus on inside the circle and see if you remember anything Yashfa or Yamna may have mentioned."

Rachel pressed her lips in a tight line as a reminder to stay quiet and not share too much with Christopher. She scanned the town names—Kabul, Aryob Zazi, Hesarak—until her attention finally snagged on one.

Jalalabad.

Why did that feel so familiar?

She sorted through all of the information she'd learned over the past few weeks, and suddenly it came to her.

Zarah.

Right before Samir had killed her, she'd been trying to send Rachel a message. Spelling out letters with her fingers. She had spelled J-A-L. Could she have been trying to communicate the name of a town? Had she followed Khalid to Jalalabad?

There was only one way to be certain. She needed eyes and ears in Jalalabad.

"Leave please," Rachel ordered Christopher.

"Yes, ma'am." He gave her a salute then winked, closing the door behind him.

Christopher went back out to the kitchen to put away the cups and bowls Rachel had gotten out. Her idea to find a circular object with the correct diameter and trace it was adorable, if also horrific. Arts and crafts was high on the list of things not to delegate to Rachel, right along with maps, geography, basic navigation, cooking, and technology.

He realized for the first time since retiring that he was sad. He missed working, missed being useful. He didn't regret it for a second, but sitting at home all day was getting old. At some point, he'd need a project or a job. Something to occupy his time while Rachel was working, which was more or less always. As much as he was looking forward to helping Hunter and Ashley with their fundraiser—whatever hell *that* was going to entail—it was far from a permanent solution.

He had no idea where to start though. He'd spent high school playing football and helping out on his family's ranch. College had been busy with more football and going to class often enough to not lose his scholarship. Then he'd joined the Navy, gone to Officer Candidate School, and more or less been assigned things to do. He was smart, capable, driven, but had no idea how to operate in the real world. His only two friends not in the military, his two childhood best friends, had gotten jobs straight out of college too, and while he was certain they would try to help if he asked them for help, he was equally certain he didn't want to be a general contractor or county sheriff.

His future was a problem for another day. Helping Rachel find Kamal was priority number one. He couldn't help though. Not legally, anyway. Making phone calls to old friends, however, was not illegal. He knew Rachel would be occupied for a while, pondering Khalid Khan's motives and next moves. He glanced down the hall to make sure her office door was still closed before he picked up his cell phone and placed a call.

"Hawk?" The voice on the other end sounded tense.

"Viper, I need some help," Christopher started. *Viper* was Army Delta Force. In other words, the second most elite group the United States military had, right behind the SEALs. Not that they'd admit it. Viper, like Christopher, was a navigation expert. They'd run into each other several times over the years at various trainings and had, on occasion, exchanged intel with each other.

"Yeah, you SEALs usually do." Viper chuckled.

"Remind me again, who saved whose life last time I saw you?" Christopher teased.

"You pulling me out of the hotel pool after I got drunk and fell in is hardly saving my life," Viper argued. "It's not like you saved me from drowning at sea or something."

"No, you'd have to be able to find the ocean for me to do that!" Christopher jabbed.

"What do you need, Hawk?"

"I need intel coming out of Afghanistan, potentially Pakistan too." After seeing the area Khalid Khan was likely to be in, he knew they needed to consider Pakistan as part of the equation.

"As I'm sure you've figured out, since I answered my phone, I'm stateside currently. If you can be more specific though, I can check in with another team and get back to you."

"Yeah, anything about missing kids."

"There's always missing kids," Viper grumbled.

"Khalid Khan and missing kids," Christopher amended.

Viper huffed out a laugh. "You want a slide deck or the full report?"

"Shit," Christopher muttered. "You know something."

"We had a general briefing last week. Our intel shows Khalid Khan is likely working with Aquib Faizan, which means—"

"Human trafficking," Christopher finished for him. "Send me everything you have."

A courier arrived at the house a few hours later with a thick envelope containing a file from Viper. Christopher settled in at the kitchen table, reading and annotating, highlighting and flagging every bit of information Rachel would find important. Army intelligence had noted a decrease in the number of children attending schools in every major metropolitan area of Afghanistan, specifically a decrease in the number of *boys* attending schools. They'd investigated, of course, and had reached the conclusion that ten thousand boys between the ages of seven and seventeen had simply vanished.

Aquib Faizan was noted as a person of interest, but it wasn't his usual MO. Christoper and Rachel had been tracking the man for decades, and he'd always been much more interested in trafficking women and girls. The man more or less had the sex trafficking market cornered in the Middle East.

There weren't too many players in the region who didn't report to Aquib Faizan. It didn't make sense. Christopher pulled out his phone and placed another call to Viper.

"They're trafficking *boys*?" Christopher cut right to the chase.

"Yeah, we don't get it either. Not as much profit as trafficking women and girls since the market is smaller, but who the fuck knows? He is working with Khalid Khan though. That we have confirmed. Or at least we have photos of them meeting."

"Shit," Christopher mumbled as he flipped through the photos included in the file. "This is not good, but it's also helpful."

"Good." Viper paused. "Well, I'm deploying in a few weeks. So this is all I can get you."

"Thanks. Stay safe."

"Always." Viper chuckled before hanging up.

Christopher went through the report one last time before typing up a summary on his laptop and pressing *Print*. He tucked the documents back into the file and walked into Rachel's home office just as his summary sheet was done printing. "I got you a present," he said.

"I love you, but I'm very busy." Rachel didn't bother to glance up at him.

Christopher smirked. "I love you too, but I'm not the present. This is." He dropped the file on her desk then swiped the summary sheet off the printer and put it on top of the file. "Aquib Faizan and Khalid Khan are working together. Trafficking boys between the ages of seven and seventeen, as far as Delta can tell."

"Do your Delta buddies know you're retired?" Rachel raised an eyebrow.

"Didn't come up."

The corner of Rachel's lip curled up, then she started skimming the summary sheet and her face fell. "This makes no sense. I mean . . . there's always been a market for trafficking boys. Pedophiles and all that . . ." Rachel grimaced. "But Aquib usually specializes in *very* beautiful women."

"My thoughts exactly." Christopher nodded.

Rachel flipped through the file, her jaw tense. "How do ten thousand boys just disappear? Seriously, what is Army intelligence doing? Is anyone looking for these kids?"

"Unclear," Christopher admitted. "Viper said they had a general briefing, but he's about to deploy so . . ."

Rachel had both elbows on her desk, head in her hands, and started massaging her temples. "I need to take this to HQ."

Chapter 11

OCTOBER 2020

RACHEL SHOWED THE GUARD her military ID and emptied her pockets onto the conveyor belt. She wasn't technically working, but they couldn't exactly keep her out of SEAL HQ either. She hadn't had much time to ponder Christopher's delightful updates from the Army and wasn't looking forward to telling her boss how she'd gotten the intel either. Her main focus had been on putting the puzzle pieces together—something she was still doing.

What she did know was that a whole bunch of boys, including Kamal, had gone missing in Afghanistan. Khalid Khan was working with Aquib Faizan. He was also working with Samir Al-Abadi. Her mind flashed back to the conversation she'd overheard at Rock Creek Park a few days before. *Sam has the kids.*

Her mind was spinning with information and hypotheticals as she tried to rule out some of the crazier theories her mind had come up with. What she'd landed on was that the six men she hated most in the world—Admiral Richard Leftwich, Director Joe Petchill, Samir Al-Abadi, Aquib Faizan, Khalid Khan, and President Frank Verity—were potentially all involved in trafficking these boys. And the other missing piece: that damned malware code and Iran.

She knew it didn't make sense. Not yet, anyway. But she had enough information that she had to inform her boss and at least pretend to play by the rules.

The elevator pinged to announce its arrival in the lobby. Rachel made her way to the top floor and meandered into Admiral Eastwood's office.

"Did you miss me?" Rachel asked. The door to his office was open, and she casually leaned against the doorframe, crossing her arms over her chest.

"What in God's name are you doing here, Ryker?" Eastwood grumbled.

Rachel chuckled. "Which god are you consulting? They may be inclined to give you different answers."

"Allow me to rephrase. Captain Ryker, why the fuck are you in my office when you are supposed to be on leave?"

"Khalid Khan has been abducting children, one of which is his grandson. My intelligence asset Yamna's, son."

"Rachel, the U.S. government cannot send out an amber alert for every kid that goes missing in the Middle East. This has nothing to do with us."

Rachel grumbled. Why couldn't Eastwood see the dots here? "It does if Leftwich and Petchill are talking about it." She handed him her phone, playing the video she'd taken in Rock Creek Park.

Eastwood threw up his hands and leaned back in his chair. "Look, I passed along the evidence you provided for me back in July. There is an official investigation into Leftwich happening now. Your off-the-books recon will interfere with that. At the same time, it's putting you in a position where you're likely to catch Petchill's interest, seeing as he's clearly involved in whatever Leftwich is up to." He gestured to Rachel's phone and the video showing Petchill and Leftwich together. "Petchill hates you as much as Leftwich does. The difference is that Petchill has the means to kill you, and believe me, if you give him the chance, he will. He does not give a shit that the CIA isn't supposed to operate on U.S. soil."

"What the fuck are you talking about?" Rachel leaned forward.

"Cut the crap. You know damned well what I'm talking about. This goes back further than I'm sure either of us would like to think about."

Rachel winced, very much preferring to not think about the past.

"You and I both made decisions a long time ago. We have to live with the consequences of those decisions. Unfortunately, Petchill has power and influence now, and he knows enough that if he put any effort into it, if he connected the few pieces of information that he already has, he could destroy both of us. Now that Frank is president . . . Frank has all the information, all the dots connected. He likes you but isn't smart enough to know he can't trust Petchill, hence why Petchill still has his job."

"I'll just kill Petchill before he can kill me." Rachel shrugged.

"Not the time, Ryker. Trust me. This is not the time for *that*. I promise you will get to all your targets, even the personal ones. When the time is right, I will let you take out Petchill and a whole host of other people. But *now* is not the time for *that*."

Rachel's eyes were wide as she tried to temper her frustration. "But I really think Petchill and Leftwich and Frank are working with Samir!"

"This video is your evidence?" Eastwood gave her a neutral stare.

"Yes, and my instincts."

"Convenient that your instinct is telling you the four people you hate most in the world are all working together to do something terrible." He sighed. "This video is not evidence of anything. I can see how your mind filled in the blanks the way it did, but it's not enough to act on. I'll pass it along to the people investigating Leftwich though."

"But—" Rachel started to protest but, in her periphery, she saw a man with defined cheekbones and a square jaw, topped off with perfectly cropped blond hair. Out of uniform, the man was a near-perfect replica of the Ken doll her mother had been certain she'd wanted to play with as a kid. Here at HQ, in uniform, he was fucking G.I. Joe in the flesh. "Lux!" she yelled down the hall to her good friend, Commander Luke Hall. "What are you doing here?"

"Strategy meeting. You?" His brow furrowed as he took several long strides towards her.

"Good, come strategize about this." She moved aside so he could enter Eastwood's office, then closed the door behind him. "Sir, the *six* men I hate most in the world are working together," Rachel corrected Eastwood. She proceeded to fill in Luke and Eastwood on the full situation in Afghanistan, including the intel report—obtained by questionable means—from Army intelligence.

"Khalid Khan, Aquib Faizan, and Samir Al-Abadi are working together and abducting *children*?" Luke's bright blue eyes were wide.

"Allegedly." Eastwood sighed.

Luke looked at Rachel.

"My intelligence asset, who happens to be Khalid Khan's daughter, told me, and that file from the Army confirms it."

"Your asset told you?" Luke glared at Eastwood. "I'd say that's pretty solid intel, sir."

Eastwood rested his elbows on the desk and planted his face in his palms, clearly exasperated with both of them. "The report from the Army provides some numbers and context. It's not actually that helpful."

"But—" Rachel started protesting again.

Eastwood held up a hand to stop her. "Ryker, you want to escalate things with Khalid Khan? Fine. Work your contacts and get me more information about what he's doing, but you back off from Leftwich and Petchill. I mean it. You drop it."

Rachel scrunched up her face but decided to take the partial win. She was fairly certain that Khalid Khan would eventually lead to Samir, and Samir would eventually lead to Petchill and Leftwich, whether anyone believed her or not. "What sort of information?"

"Proof Khalid Khan is doing what you say he's doing." Eastwood sighed.

"If you can narrow down where he is, get me GPS coordinates, then Onyx can deploy and do some recon," Luke told her.

"Onyx isn't set to deploy for quite a while, Lux," Eastwood reminded him.

"I think I can speak for every man on my team when I say that if there are kids who need saving, we're going. Ryker, get me coordinates and transport, and we'll head over there."

"He's somewhere near Jalalabad."

"Specific," Luke grumbled.

"I will find a way to get you coordinates ASAP." She smiled at Luke then turned her attention back to Eastwood.

"You're supposed to be on leave," Eastwood reminded her.

Luke chuckled. "She's allergic to relaxation, sir. I thought you knew!"

"Please stop encouraging her," Eastwood grumbled. "Williams colluding with her is enough of a headache, and I don't even want to think about what sort of mischief they're concocting now that they're living together."

Luke burst out laughing and gave Rachel a nudge with his elbow. "I've been on leave with them. I'm sure I can imagine just fine what they're up to, based on what I've heard through hotel room walls!"

"Not at all what I meant, Hall!" Eastwood bellowed. "Ryker, you are supposed to be on leave. You are supposed to be relaxing and waiting for your promotion to be official. You are not supposed to be working, and that includes tracking a terrorist and getting GPS coordinates for where he's camped out!"

"I think rescuing these kids is much more important than Ryker's vacation," Luke argued.

Eastwood's eyes bore into Luke. "Seriously? Your insubordination is getting to be as bad as hers!" He gestured towards Rachel.

Luke shrugged, practically daring Eastwood to do something about it.

After a frustrated sigh, Eastwood turned his attention back to Rachel. "Can you please take a vacation or something? Somewhere within the continental United States."

"Why?" Rachel scrunched up her nose.

"Because you are annoying me with your crazy theories, and I'd like a break. Do I need to call Williams and order him to pack you up in his truck and take you someplace you won't be able to work on this?"

"I dunno, sir. Williams is usually better at finding people than kidnapping people," Luke teased.

Eastwood's jaw clenched. "I'm sure he can manage to restrain her if he tries hard enough."

Luke forced a cough, trying to stifle his laughter, and shot Rachel a knowing look.

"Fine." Rachel rolled her eyes. She knew she needed to agree before Luke told Eastwood too much about her private life. "I'll go on a trip with my boyfriend."

"Cool. Are we done?" Luke looked back and forth between Rachel and Eastwood.

"I suppose." Rachel sighed.

"Yes, get the fuck out of my office. Both of you," Eastwood ordered.

Rachel turned the doorknob and shoved the door open, waiting for Luke to go out first, then gave Eastwood a withering stare. "I will contemplate how to solve this from Florida, but I'm taking my laptop with me."

"Fine. Go." Eastwood gestured towards the door.

Rachel turned and ran down the hallway after Luke. "Lux!"

"Say hi to Chris. I gotta go," Luke replied as he pressed the button for the elevator.

"You don't want to hang out?" She frowned, already irritated he hadn't told her he was in town.

"As much as I love you, I think I'll have a better time with the girl I met this morning getting coffee."

"Yes. You probably will," Rachel agreed. "How long are you in town?"

"I have a flight back to Portland at 0500 tomorrow."

"Well . . . thanks for postponing your date a bit to help with this. I'll get you coordinates somehow."

"I know you will. You always find a way to get shit done. I really am late though, if I'm gonna go back to my hotel and change."

"Why are you gonna change?" Rachel eyed Luke's uniform.

"I should go on this date in uniform?"

"You're trying to sleep with her, not actually talk and get to know her, right?"

Luke's jaw tightened. "Are you going to hit me if I say yes?" The elevator doors opened, and they both got on.

Rachel gave Luke a sideways glance as she pressed the button for the lobby. "No. I know you're emotionally damaged, and I love you in spite of that. Just go in uniform and make sure you run by the store and buy condoms on your way. Seriously, people are disgusting, and you can't go to Afghanistan to save these kids if you get chlamydia or something."

Luke smirked then reached into his pocket and pulled out a condom. "Always prepared."

Chapter 12

OCTOBER 2020

CHRISTOPHER WAS SITTING ON a blue velvet sofa in the drawing room of the White House, Ashley sitting ram-rod straight beside him. Hunter Adams, clearly more comfortable in this setting, leaned back in an armchair to his left. They were all waiting for instruction, but Trischa Verity seemed more concerned with heckling the staff about iced tea and lemonade than she was planning her own event.

"Okay, so we have fifteen kids coming from . . . somewhere . . ." Hunter's face scrunched up as he handed a paper to Christopher.

"Kabul?" Christopher read off the paper.

"Whatever." Hunter shrugged.

"Kabul is in Afghanistan," Christopher explained.

"I believe you." Hunter grinned.

"How are they getting here?" Ashley asked.

Christopher scanned the paper, reading as quickly as he could. "It looks like they've been at a refugee camp run by Eros Aid, just outside of Kabul. They'll be on a flight from there—" Christopher paused as President Verity came into the room.

Frank's eyes darted around, taking everything in. "How are things going?"

"Just discussing logistics for getting the kids here," Christopher filled him in.

"You." Frank pointed at Ashley. "I haven't met you yet."

Ashley stood and shook his hand. "Pleasure to meet you, Mr. President."

"She runs the nonprofit we're giving the money to," Hunter explained.

"Oh, well, if you have time, I'd love to hear more about your organization." Frank smiled. "Have you seen the Oval Office yet?"

"If you have time for her to tell you about it in the Oval Office, then you have time to sit with us and listen." Christopher locked eyes with Frank. "She was about to fill Trischa in on everything anyway."

"Oh, I," Frank glanced over at his wife, who was still overseeing the pouring of beverages in the corner of the room.

"She's friends with Rachel." Christopher nodded towards Ashley.

"How good of friends?" Frank asked.

"Based on the threats I received . . ." Hunter winked at Frank.

Christopher gestured toward an empty chair. "Mr. President."

"I told you, Chris, call me Frank. You're likely to marry my goddaughter, for Christ's sake."

Hunter scoffed. "Right, like Rachel will ever settle down."

"If anyone has a shot, it's him." Frank motioned towards Christopher.

"I had a shot!" Hunter was clearly offended.

"No, you *took* a shot, you didn't *have* a shot," Frank corrected with a chuckle. "Like you could keep up with her anyway. You'd be exhausted."

The way Frank said it made Christopher's insides twist into knots.

"I promise, I can keep up with Rachel just fine." Hunter smirked.

The implication was evident and somewhat horrifying, though not surprising. Hunter had known Rachel a long time. Christopher decided to reframe everything and direct the conversation away from Rachel's sexual history. "Really, Hunter? You enjoy getting up at four a.m. to run ten miles?"

"No." Hunter grimaced. "Who in their right mind would do that?"

"Rachel. Although, I've convinced her to push it back to 0500." Christopher smiled.

"Like I said. Who in their right mind? We all know Rachel's a little nuts."

"Well, it sure does keep things interesting." Frank winked at Hunter.

"Anyway." Christopher glanced over at Ashley, then looked back at Frank. "Eros Aid will be transporting these kids here. We'll need someone to pick them up and get them here from the airport. Since they'll be coming to the White House, I assume the Secret Service will need to be involved?"

"Correct." Frank's eyes landed on Ashley. "We're having a silent auction as part of this event, right?"

"Yes," Trischa confirmed from across the room. She had moved on from the drink cart and was now picking at the arrangement of snacks, wielding a bag of chips in an angry gesture toward the waiter who'd been following her around.

Christopher turned back around just in time to catch Frank lifting his hand toward Ashley's shoulder. "Ashley, I'd love your opinion on something," Frank said. "I have an early edition of *Grimms' Fairy Tales* that I was thinking of donating to the auction. I'd love for you to take a look. The books are in my office. I can show you while we wait for Trischa."

Christopher angled his body so that he was closer to Ashley, catching Frank off guard. "Why don't you bring them here?" Christopher suggested, raising an eyebrow.

"They are rather delicate—" Frank insisted.

"I would love to take a look," Hunter interjected, glancing meaningfully over at Christopher. "I *did* minor in English after all. I'm sure that makes me some sort of book expert," he joked. "What you *should* donate is that Civil War rifle you have."

"That *I* want to see!" Christopher lit up. "Ashley, why don't you see if you can get Trischa to focus on the meeting by the time we get back."

"Sure, Chris." Ashley's brow furrowed.

"Fine." Frank stalked off and led Hunter out of the room.

Christopher leaned down and whispered in Ashley's ear. "Do not ever let yourself be alone with Frank."

Ashley gave him a look of realization.

Christopher nodded. "Remember how Rachel was joking that I needed to chaperone Hunter?"

Ashley nodded.

"She told me to keep you safe from Frank too. She's known them both most of her life. If she doesn't trust them with you, neither do I." He paused. "I'm sure you've already noticed Frank is—"

"Creepy as fuck?" Ashley whispered back.

Christopher pressed his lips into a tight line and gave her a curt nod. "Stay with Trischa. Do not leave her side until I'm back."

"Thank you, Chris." Ashley gave him an appreciative smile then crossed the room to help Trischa with the snack fiasco.

Christopher easily caught up with Frank and Hunter and followed them into a small room at the end of the hallway, locked with a code on the door.

Frank typed in the code and shoved the door open. "This is where I keep my collection of, well, very rare and expensive things."

"Does this door lock from the inside?" Christopher asked.

"No."

"Good." Christopher pulled it shut behind him and crossed his arms over his chest, staring Frank down and blocking the exit. "If Rachel threatened to kill Hunter if he flirted with Ashley, I wonder what she'll do to you."

Hunter chuckled. "She's just being dramatic so I'll take her seriously. She wouldn't actually hurt me. Just maybe share some secrets that could ruin my next campaign. Besides, she knows she doesn't really have to worry about me. Sure, I'll flirt and I'll try, but if a girl says no, it's a no and I move on."

Christopher raised an eyebrow. "Frank, do you share Hunter's opinion, or are you smarter than he is?"

Frank sneered. "Rachel wouldn't kill me."

"Are you sure? Because I already signed up to help burry your body if anything happens to Ashley."

Hunter's eyes went wide. "Dude, did you just threaten the President of the United States?"

"Yes, he did." Frank chuckled. "Is Rachel capable of killing me? Yes. Will she? No, she won't, because what you fail to realize is that I'm much more valuable to her alive than dead."

"Why is that?"

"Because, my dear boy, for every one of my secrets she keeps, I keep one of hers. *Quid pro quo*. Unlike Hunter here, who doesn't know any of her secrets and therefore can't defend himself against her."

"Sounds like I got a bad deal," Hunter mumbled.

"That's because you were too busy staring at her ass to negotiate." Frank smacked him on the back of the head. "And, because of that, you're no longer allowed to fuck any of her friends."

"Neither are you." Christopher pointed at Frank. "You keep your hands and your dick to yourself."

"You and Rachel are really willing to go to jail just to keep me from having a bit of fun?" Frank challenged.

Christopher smirked. "No one's going to jail, Frank. Check our service records if you don't believe me."

Frank gulped as sweat started beading on his brow.

"I think I'm missing something." Hunter's nose wrinkled.

"You aren't missing anything, Hunter. You just don't respect Rachel enough to listen when she speaks."

"What?" Hunter was getting more confused by the second.

"Didn't she tell you my job in the Navy was to kill obnoxious men?"

"Pretty sure your job was to find them, and her job was to kill them," Frank noted.

Christopher raised an eyebrow at him. "Well, Frank, target fucking acquired."

"If anything happens to me, my people already know Rachel's the number one suspect."

"She has that much dirt on you?"

"She has that much dirt on *everyone*. The girl is diabolical."

"Rachel *kills* people?" Hunter was clearly struggling to catch up.

"Yes, Hunter. She's a goddamned assassin!" Frank shouted.

Christopher pursed his lips "Never heard anyone call her that." He shrugged. "Can't really say it's inaccurate though."

"Jamie's a fucking liar! He told me she was some sort of secretary!" Hunter complained.

"Reasons why we don't allow Senator Adams to be on the Armed Services Committee," Frank teased.

"I really thought she was just saying that colloquially so I'd know she really didn't want me flirting with Ashley. Which I won't. She didn't have to threaten me, just tell me. She knows I wouldn't actually hurt anyone or force anyone." Hunter's eyes darted to Frank.

"Are you two done thinking with your dicks so we can get back to planning this ridiculous event?" Christopher looked each of them in the eye.

"Yes." Hunter nodded.

"I suppose," Frank conceded.

"Get the books you wanted to show Ashley," Christopher ordered.

Frank wrinkled his nose, clearly unhappy to be taking orders from anyone, then turned and grabbed a book of the shelf closest to him.

"The binding on that is beautiful!" Hunter snatched the book out of Frank's hands and followed Christopher back to the sitting room where Ashley and Trischa were waiting.

Chapter 13

OCTOBER 2020

RACHEL HAD OPENED UP about Zarah's death and Kamal's kidnapping, but Christopher suspected something else had happened since then. She couldn't tell him what it was, and he hadn't pushed, but it had made her grumpier than usual. When she had packed her duffel, she kept muttering curses under her breath like "stupid Eastwood" or "two-timing shady bastard." Her thoughts were clearly somewhere else, and when she'd brought up the idea to spend a few days down in Florida, Christopher had been all too happy to get her mind off of whatever was stressing her out in D.C. Maybe the fresh ocean air was just what she needed to calm her nerves.

Hell, he could probably use the distraction himself. Things hadn't been particularly exciting these past few weeks since moving to D.C. He'd had chores to do around the house, like unboxing their stuff and trimming the lawn and painting the porch railings, but he was still adjusting to this new domestic lifestyle, just like Rachel was. He just seemed to be adjusting better to it than she was. At least that's what he was telling himself. But to tell the truth, he was itching to get back out there just as badly as Rachel was. The whole missing-kids thing was really bothering him. While he considered himself to be a fairly humble person, he also knew no one could track someone down like he could. He felt guilty for retiring, like he'd abandoned all the kids in need all over the world.

Not being able to help Rachel find Kamal was turning his stomach in knots, but he could tell his distress was a burden Rachel wouldn't be able to bear on top of everything else she was dealing with, so he shoved it down and focused on Rachel. Christopher agreed they both needed a change of scenery and had been more than willing to drive the nine hundred twenty-six miles to Rachel's apartment in Clearwater Beach, Florida. He spent most of the drive teasing her about how much mileage she was racking up on his truck since they'd moved in together. He watched as the odometer ticked up and up, and he made sure to comment on it every hundred miles or so, hoping to make the point that her 'quick trip to the beach' was much farther than she actually realized.

He pulled the truck up outside of Rachel's apartment, easily finding parking. As usual, she'd been no help with actual directions despite claiming they didn't need the GPS since, according to her, she knew where they were going. Rachel's directions were as spontaneous as she was, suddenly exclaiming "oh, you should turn at the pink house" with no clarification as to whether it should be a right or left turn. Christopher was used to it, of course, but as an expert navigator, he found this to be one of Rachel's few truly annoying traits.

Before the engine was off, she was already out of the truck and grabbing her bag from the back, keys to the apartment in hand. He grabbed his bag and followed her down the sandstone path and up two flights of stairs.

Rachel unlocked the door, her beige Navy issue duffle bag slung over her left shoulder. Christopher was right behind her with his own bag. She went inside and stopped abruptly in the entryway. There was a tall brunette woman standing in her kitchen.

"Who the hell are you?" Rachel shouted just as she heard Carter, her legal husband, call from another room, "Hey Jess, how's dinner coming along?"

Carter rounded the corner from the guest bedroom, stopping mid-stride as he spotted Rachel and Christopher in the doorway. Rachel, obviously annoyed, gestured to the young woman in Rachel's kitchen. "Who's this?"

"That's my girlfriend, Jessica," Carter replied.

"And what, may I ask, are y'all doing here?" Rachel continued, arms crossed over her chest.

"Last I checked, this was joint property, and you were deployed," Carter clarified.

Rachel laughed, but it wasn't her usual sweet laugh. This laugh was full of fury. "Isn't it so like you to try to get off on a technicality, Carter? I mean, really. You're fucking lucky I didn't have a gun in my hand." She turned to Jessica, who had backed away toward the stove, looking confused. "Jessica, sweetheart, how old are you?" Rachel asked in a callous tone.

Christopher's eyes scanned Jessica's face and body. It was unlike Rachel to question a woman's age—to question a woman at all, really—but a quick examination of Jessica's face had him questioning, too. Her chocolatey doe eyes and flawless skin made her look like she was barely eighteen.

"I'm twenty-five," Jessica replied hesitantly.

"And do you have some sort of job?" Rachel asked.

Christopher's brow furrowed, trying to figure out where Rachel was going with this.

"Yeah . . . I'm an elementary school teacher. Third grade."

"And you're dating Carter?" Rachel asked in disbelief. She gestured to Carter, who was standing defensively beside Jessica in the kitchen.

Christopher choked down a laugh, amused that Rachel would be shocked that someone as pretty as Jessica would date Carter. Rachel had dated and married Carter. She really wasn't in a position to judge. Not that there was anything wrong with Carter, other than his personality.

"Um, yeah. We've been dating for a while now. Like almost a year, I guess," Jessica replied.

"What are *you* doing here?" Carter interjected.

"Excuse me? What am I doing in my own home? *My* home that *I* bought with *my* money before we got married that *I* pay the bills for?" Rachel, outraged, turned back to Jessica. "He did tell you he's married, didn't he?"

"Also a technicality, I believe," Carter stated.

Christopher couldn't help but laugh at that one. There were very few people sharp enough to even come close to winning an argument with Rachel, and Carter had always been one of them. "Hey, he's got you on that one, babe," Christopher said.

He saw Rachel's body tense. Her right hand balled into a fist, and he put a hand on her shoulder before she got the bright idea to punch Carter.

"*Babe*? Well now, who's the one keeping secrets?" Carter smirked.

Christopher looked back and forth between them. "I'd say both of you, apparently."

"So, you just bring people here now?" Rachel wasn't at all done yelling at Carter.

Christopher scratched the back of his head and looked at his feet, then gave Jessica an apologetic look.

"Yeah," Carter replied.

"What the hell are you thinking? I could have classified documents lying around. Fuck, good thing my gun's packed and I didn't shoot you!"

"When have you ever left anything lying around? You're a paranoid, obsessive compulsive control freak!" Carter laughed.

Christopher pressed his lips into a tight line and looked down. *Truer words have never been spoken.*

Rachel narrowed her eyes and pulled Christopher by the sleeve of his t-shirt to her bedroom.

Once the door was closed and they were alone, Christopher whirled on her. "Seriously Rachel, when's the last time you two talked?" He was trying not to be irritated with her or at the situation, but clearly she hadn't spoken to Carter since they'd gotten back from Syria.

"I don't know. Didn't one of you call him after? He's my legal next of kin, so I assumed someone talked to him."

"I didn't," Christopher stated. "We didn't exactly have time to call him and involve him in making medical decisions. You were sort of dying. I told you that! We had a whole conversation about who made the decision, remember?"

"Well, stop agreeing with him about shit. You're supposed to have my back." She slapped him on the chest.

He caught her wrist and held her arm. "I'm agreeing with whoever's right," Christopher explained.

"Why?" Her eyes narrowed.

"For the sake of civility and peace." Christopher pulled her into him and kissed her forehead before letting go of her wrist and going out to the kitchen. He knew there was no way Rachel was going to initiate a serious conversation with Carter when she was already mad at him. He tracked her as she stomped out of the bedroom and out onto the balcony. Carter was watching her too, his arms crossed and lips tight.

"Carter, when's the last time you two talked?" Christopher asked, hoping to get a straight answer.

Carter shrugged. "Don't know. It's been a while. Maybe a year and a half? You know, that time she was at my place freaking out, and I called you. I guess that was probably the last time. It had been a while since we spoke when I met Jessica."

"You two have got to be fucking kidding me with this shit!" Christopher threw up his hands. Turning toward the balcony, he yelled, "Babe, you haven't talked to Carter since Aiden and Veeda died?"

"You can all go fuck yourselves as far as I'm concerned," Rachel called back.

Christopher sighed, knowing she was mad at the situation and not at him specifically. "Get your ass out there and talk to her, Carter." When Carter didn't budge, Christopher pointed at the balcony. "I'm serious. Right now!" At least if Carter went out there, Rachel would be cornered and forced to talk. He turned to Jessica, who was sitting further down the counter, out of the crossfire. Smart girl. "Nice to meet you, by the way. I'm Christopher and that's Rachel," he said, pointing to the balcony. "She will not actually shoot you, but she probably will run a background check on you."

"Yeah, I'm a teacher, so I'm not allowed to have a criminal record . . ." Jessica said.

"Oh, that's definitely not what she's checking for." Christopher laughed and walked over to the fridge, took out two beers, and handed them both to Carter. "Go. *Now*. Talk!"

"I don't get it." Jessica's face scrunched up. "What would she be checking for?"

"If you know anyone who knows anyone who may potentially be linked in any minuscule way to any terrorists. If you've liked anything on social media that a potential terrorist also liked, for example." Carter rolled his eyes as he headed for the balcony, ignoring Jessica's shocked expression.

Chapter 14

OCTOBER 2020

RACHEL DIDN'T WANT TO deal with Carter and Jessica. She wanted to breathe in the ocean air and relax. That's why they were there. To relax. Carter being at her apartment was annoying enough. He had no reason and no right to be at her apartment. Him being there with his girlfriend—his twenty-five-year-old, sweet, bubbly girlfriend with her perfectly curled brown hair and perfect skin—was downright obnoxious. She trusted Carter, mostly. But bringing someone she'd never met before, someone she knew nothing about, someone Carter may not know much about? It was unacceptable.

"For fuck's sake," Rachel grumbled to herself as she heard footsteps behind her. She turned to find Carter.

"Peace offering," he said, handing Rachel a beer.

She accepted the beer from Carter and popped it open on the balcony railing, then took a long sip as she stared out over the sun setting on the ocean. "Seriously Carter, what the fuck? You just come to my apartment whenever you want?"

"Yeah, like I said, you're never here. I'd think you would appreciate it if I made sure it's still standing and hasn't gotten damaged in a hurricane or something," Carter remarked.

Rachel rolled her eyes and took another sip of her beer.

"When did the Navy change their no-dating policy?" he asked calmly.

"He's retired."

"How long?"

"A few months."

"And now you're dating? Or just hooking up?"

Rachel shrugged.

"God Rache, give me something! Chris insisted I come out here and talk to you, and he seemed pretty pissed it had been so long since we spoke. So, what's going on? Why are you here and not running around in the Middle East somewhere? I know you wouldn't be here if you could be there."

"I can't be there," Rachel said sadly, tears welling up in her eyes.

"Fuck," Carter muttered. "Rachel, what the hell happened?"

"Injured in combat." She choked on the words.

"Yeah, that's not new. Must have been pretty serious if you aren't going back." Carter looked at the ground, shifting his weight uncomfortably.

Rachel nodded her head. "Yup. Apparently, it's very serious." She chugged the beer and went inside to find a bottle of whiskey. When she found one, she immediately put it to her lips and took a long swallow as she walked back outside. She didn't want to talk to Carter about what had happened in Syria. She didn't want to talk to anyone about it, but she knew she had to.

"Still can't share your feelings without being drunk, can you?" Carter asserted.

"Feelings and war stories aren't exactly the same thing," Rachel clarified.

Carter closed the balcony door, giving them some privacy. "Talk, Ryker."

Rachel turned to face him, pulling her shirt up and her waistband down just enough for him to see her scar.

"Looks like you had a C-section. Didn't know they did those in combat zones," Carter joked.

"Yeah well, shit happens." She leaned back against the balcony railing, looking at the ground.

"Rache, I'm going to need more information. Technicality or not, I am your husband. If you have a kid running around somewhere, I should probably know about it."

Rachel laughed through her tears, and after a deep breath in, clarified. "No Carter. No kid, sorry. Not gonna be a kid either."

"I can keep guessing, Rachel, but I have a feeling I'm not going to figure this one out." The frustration was evident in his voice.

"Aren't you a detective or something?" Rachel mocked.

"Deputy sheriff," he corrected her. "Tell me what happened."

Rachel took another sip of whiskey before letting out a sigh. "We were on a mission collecting intel. The compound was supposed to be empty, but it wasn't. I went upstairs and got stabbed with a ten-inch blade that was then twisted. But it's okay 'cause I broke the guy's neck and threw him down the stairs after he stabbed me. Or as he stabbed me. The timeline's a little fuzzy." She scratched the back of her head and wrinkled her nose.

Carter had to laugh at the last part. "Of course you did!"

Rachel smiled, proud she'd managed to kill the guy, and passed Carter the whiskey bottle.

"Peace offering," she said, mimicking Carter's earlier joke.

He took a sip. "Organ damage?"

"Hysterectomy," she confirmed.

"That's why you said no babies, I guess."

Rachel nodded, an empty look on her face. She'd never been particularly interested in kids. She had always assumed, maybe even planned to die in combat doing what she loved most. "They had to remove my uterus to save my life, and apparently the Navy considers that to be vital organ damage, thereby permanently removing me from combat."

"Since when is a uterus a vital organ?"

"Precisely the point I made in court-martial when I sued the Navy for gender discrimination," Rachel said.

"Oh fuck. Rachel, how serious is this? Do you still have a job?" Carter asked uneasily. "Is that why Christopher is with you? To monitor your . . . mental stability, I guess I could call it?"

Rachel sighed at the implication. Carter and her mother both constantly questioned her mental health. "No, he's here because we are having a romantic beach weekend together with you and Jessica, apparently." They both laughed out loud at the absurdity of it all. Once their laughter subsided, she sighed and looked at her feet. "I still have a job, Carter. Just not the one I want." Her voice was full of sadness and dejection.

"What's the new job, then?" Carter asked.

"Mission Commander at SEAL HQ in D.C."

"Fuck that's cool."

"They're promoting me to rear admiral. Pending Senate approval, of course."

"Shit. So, you and Chris?"

"Madly in love." Rachel laughed drunkenly.

"Seriously? You're a little tipsy, so I want to be sure."

"Seriously." She studied Carter's face for a minute, knowing what she was about to say was going to hurt him. "I'm really happy, Carter. I'm truly, genuinely happy. We sort of bought a house together in D.C."

Carter nodded, looking straight ahead, unable to look at her while she was saying these things. Rachel was sitting with her hand on her stomach, staring longingly at the sliding glass door where she could see Christopher in the kitchen making dinner with Jessica.

"You're worried he wants kids, aren't you?" Carter asked.

"He says no, but I know he does. He forgets I've been listening to him dream out loud about what happens after the Navy for the past eleven years," she answered.

"You still have the embryos if you need them. Use a surrogate," Carter suggested.

Rachel looked at him incredulously. "Carter, isn't that a little weird? I mean—"

"Rachel, that was always the deal, and you know it. I always hoped it would be me and you, but we agreed you could use them with someone else if something happened and the unfertilized eggs you froze weren't viable. I'm not going back on my word on that."

"Thank you," Rachel said timidly. "But we're really not there yet."

They sat in silence for several minutes. "You want a divorce?" Carter asked bluntly.

Rachel shrugged. "Probably a good idea." The truth was that she urgently needed a divorce before she got court-martialed for adultery or conduct unbecoming of an officer. But she knew Carter would drag his feet and make it more difficult if he sensed she was desperate.

"Yeah, I guess you don't really need me anymore."

"Need you?"

"Paperwork. Chris is retired, you're living together, and you're not going back into combat apparently, so you no longer need my name on a call sheet or any sort of HR paperwork."

"Right." She winced. "Just divorce me so we can both have a shot in hell at being happy, okay?"

"I am happy. With Jessica I mean. You—" He paused. "Do you even know how to be happy?"

"What the fuck does that mean?" Rachel scrunched up her face then took another sip of whiskey.

Carter raised an eyebrow. "The stoicism, the self-harm, the risk taking?" He counted off on his fingers. "You've got so many walls up, you're bound to self-sabotage."

"I do not do that!" Rachel protested.

"Are you sure? Wandering the desert together is one thing. Living together and having an actual relationship with real feelings and problems and conflict resolution is a whole other thing. Solving problems with your words, not with your fists."

"You have no idea what you're talking about!" Rachel yelled.

"Oh, come on! Chris is normal and rational. Mostly. He's going to get sick of all your manic-depressive nonsense really quick if he's stuck with you in D.C. and figures out it's not all combat related and that it's just who you are. You're restless and selfish and manipulative, Rachel. You always have been." Carter's voice was raised now.

Rachel raised hers to match. "He hasn't gotten sick of me yet!" Besides, Christopher always called her self*less,* caring, and kind. Of course he didn't know her like Carter knew her. He only knew her when she'd been happy, doing what she loved to do. Maybe a few months of being chained to a desk *would* force Christopher to see what Carter saw.

"Have you made him hit you with a belt? Maybe try that and see what happens before you get too confident. Maybe see how long you can actually be monogamous. Not sure he's gonna appreciate you cheating on him any more than I did."

"I never did that! Except when we were married, but that was the agreement."

"In high school, Rachel!"

"We were broken up then."

"Well, no one told me!"

"Not my fault you can't listen and comprehend information when I speak."

Carter shook his head. "I am not the problem, Rachel. You are. You test people and push them away to see if they'll come back. You play with their feelings, their hearts, like it's a game. It's sick."

"Fuck you, Carter. Are you taking care of the divorce, or do I have to?" She was close to hitting him. He knew exactly what to say to destabilize her and trigger her anxiety and self-doubt.

Carter took a deep breath to calm down and steady his voice. "Alright, I'll handle it." He nodded. "But can I still borrow this place when you're not here? Since we are still friends."

"Fine, but you have to tell me when you'll be here," she conceded knowing she'd need to placate him and give him something. "I'll even let you keep your house." She teased. She'd bought the house in Alabama that Carter was currently living in. He hadn't paid a dime. But given what he could get if they actually got lawyers involved- She didn't want a house in fucking Alabama anyway.

"Agreed! Now, should we go in and see if there's any food?" Carter asked her as he stood up.

"You go in," Rachel said, her eyes fixed to the ground. "I need a minute."

Chapter 15:

OCTOBER 2020

RACHEL SAT ON THE balcony, trying to calm herself down. Emotional regulation was far from her top skill. Her impulse to run kicked in, so she stood up and rushed inside. She was mad. Mad at Carter, mad at the Navy, and mad at herself for getting stabbed in the first place. She knew she was being unfair to Christopher since she was actually mad at Carter but couldn't bring herself to apologize. Her mind was spinning, contemplating everything Carter had said. The accusations and insults weren't new. She'd been hearing them for years from Carter and from her mother. None of it was true though . . . Not really. She just got restless when she felt confined, when she felt like she was losing control to someone or something else. Christopher loved her. She knew he'd never leave her, or at least she thought so, but Carter's words had sent her mind spiraling, and she was suddenly unsure. She knew she was about to lose it. Hit Carter or hurt herself. She needed to get out of there and made a beeline for the front door. She sprinted for the ocean—the gulf, she knew Christopher would correct her—and dove under the waves, swimming away from shore as quickly as she could before submerging herself in the dark water.

She'd barely been under when two hands, two arms, wrapped around her and forced her to the surface. Rachel took a huge gasp when she came up for air, then looked at Christopher dismayed. "Why did you do that?" she demanded, irritated.

"Um, so you wouldn't die?" Christopher replied.

"You don't trust me?" Rachel asked, a hint of sadness in her voice now.

"I trust you implicitly," Christopher said.

"Then don't do that again," Rachel demanded before submerging herself again in the dark, choppy water. Minutes ticked by before he pulled her up again. "What the fuck Christopher?" she screamed once she'd taken a breath.

"I will not let you drown yourself! Eight minutes is too long," he insisted.

She glared at him, knowing she'd only been under for seven minutes and forty-three seconds. It wasn't like him to exaggerate. He was panicking but she didn't understand why. "No, over ten is too long."

"When have you ever held your breath for ten minutes?" Christopher asked doubtfully.

"I do it all the time," Rachel said.

"I've been training with you for eleven years and I've never seen you hold your breath for ten minutes," Christopher contested.

"Just because I don't want to make the rest of you feel bad," she shot back. "You said you trust me, so show me you trust me. If I don't come up by ten minutes and seven seconds, you can pull me up, drag me to the beach, and kick my ass if you want to."

Christopher had to laugh at that. "Fine. Ten minutes and seven seconds, but you hold my wrist the entire time." He set a timer on his watch so he could be exact, then they each wrapped a hand around each other's wrists. "Go on my count," he ordered. "Three, two, one."

Christopher started the timer, and Rachel was under the water. The minutes ticked down from ten, to seven, to five. She sang to herself in her head, knowing exactly how long each song was. She winced and gripped his wrist tighter. She had ninety seconds left.

She knew why he had insisted on holding hands. Not to be cute but to monitor her pulse. Well, that had backfired. She was fine, and his pulse was racing.

He was terrified.

She didn't care.

Probably for the first time ever, she put her own wellbeing before his. Maybe she was selfish like Carter thought. It wasn't like she had planned to run out of the apartment like that, and she certainly hadn't intended for Christopher to follow her. Carter's accusations and insinuations had thrown her for a loop, just like they always did. She was still adjusting to being back stateside, let alone adjusting to the idea of never going back to combat. Things with Christopher were good. Very good. If they could just stay together, just the two of them, and block out the rest of the world, everything would be fine and maybe, just maybe, she might stop feeling the urge to run.

Christopher started worrying when there were only ninety seconds left, fully prepared to reach in and pull Rachel up. It was the longest ninety seconds of his life. He could feel his heart pounding in his chest as every memory, every moment with her, flashed before his eyes. She gripped his wrist tighter, and it took all his mental strength to trust her and let her stay under.

Just as the timer ticked down to two seconds, Rachel surfaced, taking in a huge gulp of air and breathing heavily.

"How much time did I have left?" she asked as she heard the alarm ring on Christopher's watch.

"Two seconds," he answered. "Ten minutes and five seconds down in the open ocean." He didn't know whether to be impressed or horrified.

Rachel nodded. "I'm not going to drown myself, Christopher," she stated definitively. "I would never do that. And if for some insane reason I did, do you really think I'd let you watch? I just needed a break from everything, that's all."

"Ten minutes is a pretty long break," Christopher said, still concerned.

Rachel was silent.

"Please say something." He was desperate to know how she was feeling.

"One more."

"You're going again?" he asked skeptically.

"Yes, I'm going again," she insisted impatiently. "Set your stupid watch timer if you must."

Christopher set the timer again and counted her down. Three, two, one, and she was underwater. He waited more patiently this time for her to come up, realizing that she knew what she was doing. The timer ticked down, minutes and seconds passing by more slowly than they normally would. At ten minutes and seven seconds exactly, Rachel came up for air.

"Good?" Christopher asked her, certain his frustration was evident.

"All good," she assured him.

They swam back to the beach, perfectly in sync with each other. Christopher could tell she was much calmer now. He was sure there must be a safer way for her to regulate her emotions, but he didn't have any suggestions off the top of his head. "You know it's dangerous to go that long without oxygen, right?" Christopher asked as they walked from the shoreline back to the apartment. He knew she knew that. They'd had the same training, after all.

"I could stand to lose a few brain cells," she scoffed.

"I don't think you get to pick which one's you lose." Christopher's voice was calm, but inside, he felt like he was dying. The thought of losing her terrified him. He had almost lost her in Syria, and watching her, holding her, feeling her pulse calm and steady under the water, had reminded him of just how close she'd come to dying. How close he'd been to losing the one person he could always rely on, always trust. The one person he could never live without. He followed her up the stairs and into the apartment in silence. The tension and frustration between them was palpable. In their eleven years of friendship, they'd barely argued, rarely been mad at each other. They'd been irritated and disagreed with each other plenty, and they were both reckless, but this was the first time either of them had done something the other had explicitly asked them not to do.

Rachel opened the door to the apartment. Carter and Jessica were watching TV. Rachel wrinkled her nose then looked over her shoulder at Christopher. His jaw was clenched. She knew she'd fucked up. He was mad or angry or disappointed. At her. *Because* of her. He'd practically begged her not to stay underwater so long. She should have come up the second she felt his heart rate go up. But she hadn't. She considered for a moment what she would have done if Christopher hadn't been there. It's not like it would have been the first time she'd hurt herself on purpose. He knew that. She knew that. And she knew he hated it every time she did. There was nowhere for them to fight it out, to release their frustration. Certainly not without Carter and Jessica having a front row seat, and she sure as fuck was not about to give Carter the satisfaction of being right about her self-sabotaging nature.

She gave Christopher a small wave of the hand, indicating that he should follow her. She led him to the bathroom, closing the door behind them. She turned on the shower and got in, still fully clothed, keeping eye contact with him the entire time. She saw the irritation and fury in his eyes. The fear he was pretending not to feel. It wasn't often he showed his fear, but over a decade of friendship had taught her the subtle signs—the hazy look in his eye masked by anger, the way his muscles tensed, frozen in place, and the very specific set of his jaw when the muscles in his neck and throat tightened. She didn't know how to apologize. Not with words, anyway. Words were tricky, subtle things. She glanced down at her feet then back up at him through her lashes. The most submissive glance she'd ever given him, hoping he'd get the point. Hoping he sensed her guilt. She tugged on his hand, pulling him into the shower, under the water with her. She laced her fingers though his then tucked both of their hands behind her back, signaling to him that he was in control, he could have his way.

He pressed his forehead to hers, his warm breath mingling with hers as the hot water poured over them. He released one of her hands then rubbed his thumb over her lips before running his hand down the side of her body to her waist, his eyes tracing her curves like he was plotting out where to start, how to destroy her, decimate her, dominate her. She loved it when he got like this. Hot, frustrated. Not quite angry, but certainly agitated. He was so giving, so gentle with her most of the time that she had to push him almost to the breaking point for him to allow himself any sort of self-indulgence. This was his reward for tolerating her instability.

Christopher pressed his pelvis into Rachel's, pinning her against the shower wall. He was hard, and the look she was giving him . . . Damn that look. He couldn't take it. He had to have her, and he couldn't wait. He pulled her shirt off over her head, threw it out of the shower and onto the bathroom floor, and looked at her standing in front of him in wet jeans and a black bra, her wrists crossed demurely behind her back. There was nothing demure about Rachel Ryker, not usually. She knew he was mad. He knew she was using sex to distract him, to force him to forgive her without having to formulate an apology. He could tell she felt bad, felt guilty, and knew that with Rachel, actions always meant more than words.

He yanked her hand towards him, placing it on his waistband, knowing she'd understand his instructions just fine. He tugged off his t-shirt while she went to work on his jeans. He kissed the top of her head while reaching around to skillfully unhook her bra. She had his pants off in seconds, kissing him and licking him as she knelt down, sliding his jeans and boxers down with her. He stepped out of his pants, and she threw them on the floor before taking him deep in her mouth. He waited a few minutes, running his fingers through her wet, tangled hair as she knelt in front of him, then pulled her up to him. He kissed her and moved her against the wall of the shower as he went to work unbuttoning her jeans, tugging them off. Once they were out of the way, he picked her up, pressing her harder against the wall, and kissed her deeply. She arched into him and wrapped her legs around his waist as he sunk into her.

Rachel let out a deep moan as Christopher thrust into her, fucking her forcefully against the shower wall. It was decadent. She kissed his neck and ran her fingers through his hair as he thrust into her over and over again, forcefully and with such vigor that she couldn't help but let out another loud moan as she tightened around him. Christopher was fully aware that Carter was in the next room and was certain that the running water wasn't loud enough to cover the noise. Christopher put his lips over hers, keeping his tongue in Rachel's mouth to stifle her moans as he pounded into her over and over, deeper and harder. He took out his frustration, his turmoil, pounding into her like his life depended on it.

Rachel bit her lip as he came. She held him tight with her legs, refusing to let him put her down. She combed her fingers through his hair, looking at him blissfully as she kissed him on the lips again, softer now than she had before, full of love and devotion.

"I'm sorry," Rachel said, her palm on his cheek. "I shouldn't have done that."

"Shouldn't have done what?" Christopher mumbled, kissing her neck. He was so enamored with her, so caught up in what they were doing, that he'd forgotten how they'd gotten there and why he'd been upset with her in the first place. He slowly put her down, never breaking the kiss, and moved his hands towards her waist, feeling her breasts as he went, his fingers sliding, lightly grazing her nipples, unable to get enough, unwilling to stop.

She took his head in her hands, breaking his concentration as she forced him to look her in the eye, bringing him back to reality, back to real feelings and problems and conversations. Back from their fortified bubble of love and passion where nothing existed but the two of them, where the world could disappear without them noticing.

"I'm sorry, Christopher," she stared deep into his eyes. "I shouldn't have scared you like that. I promise though, I was in control the entire time. I was safe." She paused before choking out the next part. "I knew you were scared, and I did what I wanted anyway. It was selfish and stupid and I hope you still love me."

Christopher pulled away from her slightly, suddenly remembering what had happened, realizing what she was apologizing for. "Thank you," he said, sincerely. He looked at her, worry washing over his face again as he saw the tears welling in her eyes. "I've told you hundreds, if not thousands of times . . ." He was having a hard time finding the words. His mind was filled with images of her in the water, images of her in the shower crying out in passion, images of her on their last mission, bleeding, dying in the helicopter. Everything was blurring together—Skylark and Rachel, one in the same. The most amazing, beautiful, magnificently powerful, and intelligent woman he'd ever known. "I'm not going anywhere, Rachel," he said. "I'm here, with you, forever. However long that gets to be. Whatever you need."

It took about five minutes before Rachel spoke. The water from the shower poured over them both, helping to wash away all their negative emotions. "I'm not mad at you, Christopher."

"I already know that," he said calmly.

"I'm just mad at a lot of other things."

"What did Carter say that pissed you off so much?" Christopher had spent enough time with Rachel and Carter over the years—in person and listening to Rachel's end of countless phone calls—to know what had happened.

"He said I was going to self-sabotage and drive you away and that I could never be happy."

"You know I love you." He put his hand under her chin and tipped her face up, forcing her to meet his gaze.

"Yes."

"You know I already know these things about you?"

Her brow furrowed. "You think I self-sabotage and drive people away and can't be happy?"

"I watched you do that last spring and all summer." Christopher smiled.

"Right." Rachel nodded.

"Rachel, you choose everyone else over yourself. I know you do. You'd give up anything to make someone else feel better, to make their life the tiniest bit better. You can be happy if you choose to be. If you take down all the walls and let me in."

"I think you were just in." She winked.

"Rachel, I'm being serious."

"Can it just be me and you and we can forget about everything and everyone else for a while?" She stared up at him, her eyes shining brightly with hope.

"It's always me and you," Christopher assured her, grazing his thumb across her lips.

"I don't know how to do this." Rachel looked down at her feet, the water rushing over her. "I don't know how to do the whole settling down thing. I'll try my best, though. I know I lose it sometimes, worry you by being reckless. I just get . . ." She trailed off, trying to find the right word.

Christopher pressed his forehead against hers. "I know," was all he answered. She was staring at her feet, trying to make sense of her own thoughts, trying to find the right way to explain herself.

"I know I can be difficult," she continued, with a hint of remorse in her voice. Rachel turned her head to look at Christopher, ready to admit to him what she could barely admit to herself. "I'm yours, Christopher Williams. From this day until the day I die, I'm yours entirely. Body, mind, and soul, I belong to you."

Christopher looked at her, surprised. For all her ranting about needing to dismantle the patriarchy and liberate women from global subjugation, he had never expected her to say anything like that. He was shocked by her sincerity, how heartfelt and honest she was being with him. He knew it must be difficult to say those words out loud. He took her hand and pulled it to his lips, kissing it lovingly.

"I will cherish you, love you, and honor you always," he said. "You are by far the most amazing human being I have ever met, Rachel Ryker. I promise you I'm not going anywhere. I know you. Don't forget that. I know who you are to your core, and that may scare you, but it doesn't scare me." He paused, watching her face, and carefully gauged her reaction to his words.

"I'm here for you," he continued. "You give my life meaning. Loving you is the only thing I want to do for the rest of my life. Wherever we live, wherever we work. None of that matters to me because I know that no matter what you're doing, you will be doing something to make the world a better place. I know you'll be putting everyone else before yourself, ignoring your own wants, always staying focused on the greater good. So while you do that, while you take care of everyone else, my one and only job will be to take care of you, however you need me to do that."

Chapter 16

OCTOBER 2020

AFTER SPENDING A FEW more days down in Florida—not so much the romantic vacation she'd hoped for—Rachel and Christopher had finally come back to D.C. She'd been spared another lecture about how she'd almost drowned herself on the promise that she go back to therapy. Which was what she was doing here, back in Catherine's office. Trying to keep her promise to Christopher. She had a lot of promises to keep. Find Kamal and get GPS coordinates for Luke. At least she was keeping this one.

Rachel slid down in her chair, crossing her arms, and tried to convince Catherine that getting injured in combat wasn't as horrific and traumatizing as it sounded. Catherine put her through the entire diagnostic interview to assess her for PTSD. Rachel had memorized all the questions and the correct answers to avoid a diagnosis, but she elected to be truthful this time. She wasn't having flashbacks or nightmares—not lately anyway. She *was* impulsive and didn't sleep, sure, but she'd always been like that. Her main issue was feeling stuck. She didn't know how to explain the sense of overwhelming dread she sometimes felt. Not fear or panic exactly. Not really depression either. She imagined it was how wild animals felt after being confined. Losing their independence, their freedom, their control. Not that Christopher was at all controlling. She'd just always had a phobia of getting stuck. She had to keep moving, keep doing something to feel alive. It wasn't just the idea of living in one house, in one place, or being with just one person. It was something bigger. An insatiable hunger for adventure, for purpose and meaning.

"In what way is D.C. confining? It's a huge city and you aren't working, so you can do whatever you want," Catherine asked. Rachel sighed. Catherine was *not g*etting it.

"I feel like I'm being watched. When I'm in the field with my team," Rachel smirked, "then I can do whatever the hell I want. Mostly. Here . . . I don't know how to *be* here. How to act . . ."

Catherine raised an eyebrow, urging Rachel to continue.

"I feel a lot of pressure. People expect me to be someone I'm not. Someone I don't want to be. I've avoided D.C. my entire life for many reasons. Social politics. Actual politics." She shook her head. "My father is an admiral. My mother is an heiress. I was raised to be a proper socialite. Join the right clubs, raise money for the right organizations, smile pretty and flirt with the right men. I hate it. I rebelled against it, a few awful debutant balls notwithstanding."

"I can't really see you in a ballgown," Catherine agreed.

"It happens on occasion." Rachel grimaced. "Growing up on base, I saw a different world. I considered enlisting, skipping college all together, but my father wouldn't hear of it. And what do you know? I have some fucked up desire to please him, get his approval." She shrugged. "Women weren't allowed to serve in combat then, anyway, and that's all I ever wanted to do. So, I went to college and used my family's connections, trying to get the rules changed. They eventually did, but not before—" Rachel's jaw clenched, and she looked out the window.

Catherine waited patiently for Rachel to continue, clearly having already figured out that pressing her wasn't the way to get her to talk.

"All I ever wanted was to be useful. To live up to my family's legacy of service. I made decisions when I was younger. Got into bed with the wrong people, both figuratively and quite literally. Some of those decisions had consequences that I'm still dealing with now."

"And that's part of why you feel stuck, confined here?"

"How am I supposed to save the world from a desk?" Rachel's eyes welled up. "Before, I could get on a plane and go handle shit. I saw a problem, I devised a plan, and then executed." She smiled to herself. "Executed the plan and the terrorist involved." Her eyes darted up to Catherine's. "Maybe it's bad to admit I enjoy killing people. But it's what I'm best at, and I've been doing it a long time."

"Since you became a SEAL." Catherine nodded.

"Longer than that." Rachel let out a sharp exhale, the air catching momentarily in her throat. "I was in intelligence before I was a SEAL," she reminded Catherine. "You work in D.C. You keep people's secrets. So I can only imagine you have a better idea of what that means than a lot of other people do."

"Navy intelligence or . . ." Catherine pried.

Rachel chuckled. "A lot of agencies seem to think they own me. It's fine. I don't care who's paying me as long as I can keep people safe. I've lost enough friends. Watched enough soldiers die—civilians, too. Now I'm here, and I'll be stuck at HQ watching it all unfold on a giant screen right in front of me with no agency, no ability to intervene other than giving my teams orders. Orders they may or may not hear or understand or be able to actually follow. If comms go out . . ." She shook her head. "I have too much blood on my hands already."

"That makes sense. It would be harder to execute a terrorist from here than if you were standing right in front of them." Catherine nodded. "The teams you'll be overseeing, they're capable?"

"Yes."

"You trust them to do their jobs?"

"Of course."

"So, is it because you miss the action or because you can't relinquish control over the op?"

"Failure is not an option, Catherine."

"I'm not an expert, but from what I understand, Navy SEALs don't tend to fail at things."

"Depends on your definition of failure. I have remarkably high standards."

"Tell me more."

"A lot of people . . . My father was yelling at me about this," She rolled her eyes. "People expect soldiers, SEALs, to die. They expect intelligence assets, informants, to die. It's dangerous."

Catherine nodded.

"I find that unacceptable. Furthermore, it reflects poorly on me. Aiden, for example. I told him to stay put, but he ran to save Veeda anyway. I was standing right next to him, and I couldn't stop him. If something like that happens again . . . I know very well the guys will switch off their earpieces if they don't like what I'm telling them. They'll lie and say they couldn't hear me. I know because we all do it. Because there is no way some asshole at command has a better understanding of the situation we're standing in—trying to solve, trying to survive—than we do. I'm that asshole now. I'm the stuck up prick in the clean, freshly pressed uniform with my hair perfect and boots shiny, yelling at the guys covered in blood fighting for their lives, risking everything as if I'm somehow better than they are." She paused to catch her breath. "And, to make things worse, if they make a bad call, whether they were ignoring me or not, I get shit. If I make a bad call, I still get shit."

"Being a leader is always hard," Catherine noted.

Rachel rolled her eyes. "I worked really hard to get the men to respect me. My teams do. My boss does. But—" She shook her head. "The accusations of sleeping my way to the top, using my dad's name to get ahead." She scoffed. "He didn't even know what I was doing. And the other thing, sleeping your way to the top just means some asshole wouldn't promote you unless you put out. It has nothing to do with your actual competence or ability to perform the job. It's flat out blatant sexual harassment and sexual abuse, if not assault."

"Sounds like you're speaking from experience."

Rachel glanced at the clock. She'd said a lot in a short time. Much more than she ever intended to. "I'm doing my best to accept the fact that I'll be chained to a desk for the rest of my career. What I cannot accept is the fact that I'll have to take a backseat, sit back with my feet up on my desk, watching everything go down. Watching things crumble around me, which they will."

"That all sounds terrifying." Catherine frowned. "Having to plan things for other people, hoping they can do what needs to be done, and having to hold your breath and watch while they try their best."

Rachel nodded.

"But that's the job," Catherine reminded her. "What are the other parts of the job? The other aspects of leadership that you *do* have control over?"

"What do you mean?"

"A lot of research has been done lately on the difference in how women and men lead. Rachel, you aren't the first military officer I've had as a patient. I've had several, actually. You are, however, the first *female* officer I've treated."

Rachel's nose wrinkled.

"Cut to the chase, I know." Catherine chuckled. "A lot of research shows that women are more effective leaders than men."

"Obviously." Rachel rolled her eyes.

"The reason for that is at least partially because women lead with empathy. They are more likely to think about others, about the big picture and the greater good, rather than serving their own egos. In the two times we've talked, it's been very evident that that is how you lead. Sure, you're worried about how your teams' performance reflects on you, but you have to be worried about your career. Mostly, though, you've focused on protecting your teams, the people under you."

Rachel nodded.

"Are there ways to do that other than jumping in front of them, taking a bullet for them?"

"Like what?"

"Making sure they have the best equipment, keeping them focused, emotionally safe, mentally stable? You know firsthand how hard their jobs are, what they're up against. What can you give them from here that would have helped you when you were running an op in-country?"

"Making sure they have enough food. And I'm constantly arguing for better safety gear . . ."

"And now you're in D.C., surrounded by politicians and defense contractors and the people who decide the budgets," Catherine pointed out. "When you get promoted at any job in any industry, the responsibilities change. The tasks and ways you help change. Sometimes, promotions mean you're losing the fun parts, the parts of your job you enjoyed. But more responsibility, or different responsibility, often means making a difference in a bigger way. So, instead of obsessing over how you can prevent someone from getting shot—I have a feeling someone will whether you're there or not—"

Rachel chuckled. "Getting shot is fine. Dying is not."

"You're not a medic or a nurse or a doctor."

"No, I'm not."

"So, let the medics do their jobs."

Rachel grunted and slumped down in her chair.

"Your job, your new job, is to have big picture operational oversight. To use your connections and influence to affect change on a larger scale. Not micromanaging and arguing with your teams about which door to a compound they're going to breach."

"If someone else dies . . . it might break me."

"It's okay to feel, to fall apart. That's how we grow. That's how we learn to plan better for the next time. So, what are some big picture things you can do to help your teams from here?"

Chapter 17:

OCTOBER 2020

RACHEL MADE HER WAY home and plopped herself in her chair behind her desk, entirely frustrated with her day. *Big picture things to help,* Catherine had said. *Using my connections and influence to affect large-scale change.* Rachel considered what she would do if she were in Afghanistan. She needed to know where Khalid Khan was going so that she could send a team to follow him and figure out what he was doing. She tapped her fingers on her desk. Maybe they could get a drone up in Khost, over Yamna's house, and follow his car from there? That sounded like a huge budgetary *no* though. But following his car? There was no way Yashfa and Yamna would get away with that. Zarah had already tried and failed. Rachel couldn't put anyone else's life in danger like that. Besides, women weren't supposed to be driving in Afghanistan, so how could they?

"I need some sort of techy thing," she muttered to herself. This was another problem Christopher usually solved for her. Technology sure was a pain in the ass, but utilizing it often saved lives. The next problem was getting the tech to someone who could set it up to monitor Khalid and his car.

Luke needed GPS coordinates. She didn't need eyes and ears, per say.

She needed numbers. Digits on a screen. All she needed to do was track his car. Yamna had already proven she had access to the car when she'd checked the mileage. That meant she could put a tracking device on the car too. *If* Rachel could find a safe way to get a tracking device to her. But she couldn't.

She couldn't.

But maybe a young blonde, semi-trustworthy, somewhat skilled, CIA analyst could?

Paige Larsson had managed to get Pari out of Afghanistan when Rachel needed her help. Paige, while young, inexperienced, and highly distractible, *was* capable. And if she got caught, if she died? Well, Rachel didn't like her that much anyway. It was an awful thing to think, but she'd rather risk Paige's life than Yashfa or Yamna's. Not just because she liked Yashfa and Yamna better, but because they provided more valuable information. She needed them long term. She needed Paige for as long as it took to find a tracking device at the CIA office in Khost and get it to Yashfa and Yamna.

The fact that Paige was CIA and not Navy, and therefore not obligated to take orders from her, was another perk. Rachel couldn't get in trouble, not too much anyway, for this off-the-books op. Even if it went wrong, even if Paige insisted it was all Rachel's idea, Paige would technically be acting alone of her own free will. She'd still feel awful if anything actually did happen to Paige. But still, if it went well, Rachel would be praised for her skill at interagency collaboration and for thinking outside the box. Plus, she'd be one step closer to finding Khalid, Samir, and Kamal.

Paige Larsson was sitting at her desk inside the CIA building in Khost, Afghanistan, leaning back in her chair with her feet propped up. Her head hurt from staring at too many tiny boxes on her screen. Being an intelligence analyst wasn't as thrilling as she'd hoped it would be when she'd joined the CIA, but it was certainly better than a lot of other jobs. She took a deep breath, massaging her temples as she did, and exhaled slowly. She couldn't make sense of the data in the spreadsheet she'd been staring at all morning.

Her phone pinged with a new message, and she reached over to grab it, eager for the distraction.

Skylark to Paige: *Still in Khost? Need help!*

Paige's eyes lit up. She would never admit it out loud, but Rachel Ryker was secretly her idol, her role model, the person she wished she could be, but being a field agent was likely not in Paige's future.

Paige to Skylark: *Yes, how can I help?*

Within seconds, Paige's phone rang. She picked up instantly.

"You remember Yashfa and Yamna, my intelligence assets in Khost?" Rachel started, not even bothering to say hello. "I need you to get a tracking device to either of them. The kind you can attach to a car. Then y'all need to install it."

"Okay . . ." Paige said, trying to catch up.

"Do not fuck this up, Paige!" Rachel's voice was harsh.

"I'm not a field agent, Rachel."

"You're a woman. And as a woman living in Afghanistan, you have a unique ability to go undetected, which means you have a unique ability to get shit done. I'm not there, so that means I have to rely on you. Get the tracking device from whomever at the CIA handles that sort of thing, put on a burqa, and get the device to either Yashfa or Yamna with instructions for how to set it up."

"But I—"

"No buts," Rachel cut her off.

Paige had a lot of *buts*, a lot of reasons to say no to Rachel. *It's not my job. I don't know how. I'm not authorized to do this.* All of which could be followed up with a thousand questions, least of which was is *Rachel* even authorized to do this? It seemed she was, and Paige had been looking for an opportunity to prove herself. She'd been in the same role for years, sitting at the same desk, being talked down to by her male colleagues, listening to them tell her she was 'just an analyst.' As if they could do anything without her analyzing the intel they were collecting. This was it. This was her shot, potentially the only chance she'd have for upward momentum on her career trajectory. She had no idea how to install a tracker on a car, but how hard could it be? Surely the thing came with an instruction manual. "Yes, ma'am. I'll do my best."

"Your best is all you *can* do," Rachel said before hanging up.

Paige was shocked. She had been fairly certain that the few times she'd met Rachel in person, Rachel had hated her. Apparently, she'd been wrong. Apparently, Rachel trusted her and had faith in her skills and ability to get things done. She popped out of her chair and headed down the hallway to see a man about a tracking device.

Paige waited in a dark alley, watching Yamna's house carefully. The sun was setting, and Khalid Khan would be leaving his daughter's house to go to the mosque any minute. Paige was wearing a burqa, as instructed, and had the tracking device tucked away. This was her chance to prove herself. She didn't want to let Rachel down. Her heart rate was high. She was nervous. After a few deep breaths and a silent pep talk, she peered around the corner. Sure enough, two men were leaving Yamna's house on foot. She snapped a photo on her phone, zoomed in, and confirmed one of the men was Khalid Khan.

She waited for the men to walk down the street and around the corner before she slowly crept out of the alley and knocked on Yamna's door.

A petite woman opened the door, her large eyes looking over Paige warily. "Paige?"

Paige nodded, then said in Pashto, "I'll call Rachel."

A second woman approached the door. Yamna gestured toward her. "My sister, Yashfa."

Paige smiled, then remembered they couldn't see her face. "Nice to meet you both." She hoped her voice wasn't shaking too badly.

The phone call connected, and Paige put the audio on speaker just as Rachel's voice came through. "What is happening?" she demanded.

"Rachel, I'm here with the thing . . ." Paige hesitated saying the word *tracker* aloud.

"Why do you sound terrified?" Rachel switched to English. "Get it together. If you seem scared, they will be too."

"Right," Paige replied in English before switching back to Pashto. "We need to put this tracker on the car. I'm reading the instructions, and I asked the tech guys—"

"I have the instructions pulled up here as well," Rachel assured her.

"Rachel, what do we do?" Yashfa asked.

"You turn on the tracker and stick it under the car somewhere," Rachel replied. "Then I'll push some buttons on my end, and we should be able to see where the car is."

Paige, Yashfa, and Yamna all looked at each other.

"You have done this before?" Yashfa asked Paige.

"Um . . ." Paige had no fucking clue what she was doing but really didn't' want to admit that.

"She knows what she's doing," Rachel lied. "Go over to the car and get to work. We don't have that much time."

Paige followed Yashfa and Yamna to a late 1980s sedan. She knelt on the ground and felt under the car's rear bumper. "There's a ledge sort of . . . I think this is a good spot." She was trying to remember every detail the technicians had told her. She pulled the device out of her pocket and held down the button for five seconds, until a green light started flashing. "It should be on now." She read off the serial number to Rachel.

"Hang on," Rachel instructed.

Paige waited several minutes while a slew of curse words flew out of Rachel's mouth. "What color is the light, Paige?"

"Flashing green."

"Flashing? Like blinking?"

"Yes ma'am."

Rachel groaned, and Paige could envision her rolling her eyes. "It shouldn't be blinking. Hold down the *on* button until the light stops blinking."

Paige did as she was told. "It's off now, I think."

"Good. I'm trying to fix it. Give me a few minutes," Rachel told her.

"We don't have minutes," Paige reminded her.

"Calm down!" Rachel ordered, then was silent for a few minutes. "Try turning it on again. Hold the button down until you get a solid green light on the device."

Paige held her breath and tried restarting the tracking device. Seconds later, she had a green light. "We're good. It's green," she clipped into the phone.

"Find a place where it won't be visible and it will stay secure. Think about the fact that a lot of the roads are uneven and bumpy, and it could fall off. Tape it on if necessary."

"Right. That's why you said to bring duct tape," Paige said quietly.

"Tell me you didn't forget the tape."

"No ma'am," Paige assured Rachel quickly. She waved her hand out for Yamna to pass her the tape, then pushed herself down to the ground with her head under the rear bumper. "Is there such a thing as too much tape?" Paige asked.

"As long as it isn't visible, you're good," Rachel told her.

Paige ripped off a strip of tape with her teeth then secured the device to the bottom of the car, repeating the process until she was certain it wouldn't fall off. She was about to give the all clear when she suddenly saw a pool of light down the road.

"Shit," she said. "There's a car."

"Don't let it see you," Rachel commanded from the other end of the phone.

Yashfa and Yamna jumped to hide behind the side of the car that wasn't facing the street, their small frames hunched into balls. Paige crawled forward so that her whole body was under the car, her knees and elbows scraping against the gravel.

The car slowed as it crept by the sedan. Paige counted the seconds. One. Two. Three. Four.

Paige's heart jumped into her throat. The car was nearly parallel to the sedan, its tires close enough for Paige to touch. But just when the car seemed like it might come to a complete stop, the tires kicked up dust again and it was barreling back down the street. She waited until she couldn't see the light anymore then whispered, "Is it gone?"

"Yes, it's gone," Yashfa whispered back.

"Let's get out of here," Paige said, crawling back out from under the car.

Two hours later, Rachel was still sitting at her desk, staring at her laptop and waiting for Khalid Khan's car to move. Her head snapped up at the sound of Christopher's voice.

Christopher flashed her a quizzical glance. "Baby, you've been hiding in here for hours. What are you up to?"

"Not a damned thing." She forced herself to frown and shook her head.

"Really?" He reached for her laptop, turning it quickly so he could see her screen. "Installing tracking devices?" She still had the technical manual pulled up.

"Just some light reading." Rachel tried to force her voice into nonchalance.

Christopher burst out laughing. "I'm sure! Does Eastwood know you're stalking people?"

"I am doing no such thing!"

"Then why do you have the tracking app open in this other window?" He had her laptop in his hand and was clicking between windows. "Happy to see you managed to activate a tracker without my help." He smirked.

"I'm not *that* bad at technology." Rachel rolled her eyes.

"Good job, baby. Did you also figure out how to get notifications sent to your phone any time his car moves?"

"What?" Rachel had no idea what he was talking about.

Christopher shook his head before proceeding to type something into the search bar on the app. Rachel's phone buzzed moments later.

"'Satellite connected,'" Rachel read out loud. "How did you do that?"

A wide grin spread over Christopher's face. "I vividly recall the day during BUD/s when we learned this. You were staring out the window, making a list of flaws you had noted amongst our classmates, along with notes on what you disliked about our instructors."

Rachel scrunched up her face. "That does sort of sound like something I would do."

Christopher shook his head, then bent down and kissed her forehead. "Time to eat."

Rachel grumbled, "Time for this asshole to get in his car and drive somewhere."

"I set it to record so you can go back and rewatch where he goes. You don't have to watch it every single second."

Rachel pursed her lips, unconvinced.

"Food," Christopher ordered, pointing towards the kitchen. "Besides, you got mail. Something from the Butler County Court?"

"My divorce papers!" Rachel's eyebrows shot up. "You're sure this is good?" She pointed at her laptop.

Christopher rolled his eyes, picked up her laptop, and carried it to the kitchen. "I guess we're watching this while we eat."

Rachel raced to the kitchen, quickly finding the envelope containing her divorce papers, and ripped it open. Her eyes narrowed. "I have a court date. November twentieth."

"I can make Alabama on the way to Texas if you want to go to the ranch for Thanksgiving."

"Yes!" Rachel's eyes lit up.

"Should we invite your parents too?"

"To my court date?"

"To Thanksgiving. Might help make some peace?"

Rachel scrunched up her face again.

"My mom will be in a mood because, Josh," Christopher reasoned, "Your parents can distract her from that, and she can distract them from you. We come out looking like we give a shit about Thanksgiving."

Rachel grinned. "Genius."

Chapter 18

NOVEMBER 2020

RACHEL TAPPED HER FINGERS impatiently on the center console as Christopher pulled the truck up in front of Carter's house—*Rachel's* house, if they were being technical about it. She hadn't been there in over a year and a half and hadn't been there sober in even longer. She got out of the truck and stared at the front porch as so many memories came flooding back. "Well, here goes nothing," she said to herself. She got out of the truck, took two steps towards the porch, and froze. Her mind flashed back to the first time, the only time, she had been there with Christopher. They had just gotten back from their first deployment as SEALs. Rachel had thought she'd seen horrible things, all the horrible things possible to see, in her two years as an intelligence officer. But she'd been wrong.

She'd come back from that deployment changed. Something had broken inside her, like she'd lost a piece of her soul. She remembered flying into Tampa, going home to her apartment, but then somehow, she'd ended up here, standing outside of Carter's house—their house—drunk. More drunk than she'd ever been prior or since. It hadn't been the happy, fun, looking-for-sex kind of drunk she usually was when she ended up at Carter's. This had been a panicked, paranoid rage. She'd been full of terror and sadness, trying desperately to forget the things she'd seen, and trying even harder to forget the things she'd done.

Rachel walked around to the side of the house and grabbed on to the porch railing, looking up. She remembered trying to climb up here to get on the roof, but she'd fallen. And she could see why. This was a terrible place to get up to the roof from, plus it had been pouring down rain that night. She hadn't had her keys with her, and Carter hadn't had a spare key hidden that she'd known of, so she'd had to break in through a window. Given that she was so drunk, she hadn't been quiet about it.

That's when Carter had woken up. He'd come to the window, pistol in hand. He was a deputy sheriff, after all. She'd reacted on instinct and disarmed him immediately, knocking him to the floor and standing over him, gun to his head. He'd started screaming at her to put the gun down, but it had taken awhile for her to realize what she was doing, where she was. Once she did, she'd felt guilty about that too, adding it to the long list of other things. She'd put Carter's pistol to her own head, wanting everything to be over, wanting to find some peace.

Somehow, Carter had gotten Rachel's phone and gone through her recent call log. He'd seen that Christopher's number had been dialed most frequently and called him. Christopher had been staying with a friend in Georgia only two hours away and had driven as fast as he could to get to her. She'd been on the front porch screaming at Carter, alternating putting the gun to her head and to his when Christopher had arrived. He had easily disarmed her since she was drunk. He'd kicked the gun away from her and Carter and had wrapped his arms tightly around Rachel's, restraining her until she stopped yelling, stopped fighting back, and finally collapsed into wailing sobs of trauma and fear. They had never talked about it. There wasn't anything to say. He knew why she'd been like that. He knew exactly why.

"Fucking Viakaou," Rachel said out loud, mostly to herself, but Christopher heard her. Christopher understood her. He knew exactly what she was thinking about. A blind spot. A blip on a map. GPS coordinates to a place the SEALs had dubbed Viakaou. Short for Violence and Chaos. Literal hell on earth, according to anyone who had been there and managed to make it back.

"You good, babe?"

"I haven't been here since. Not sober anyway," Rachel explained.

Christopher nodded, knowing exactly what she was referring to, and walked over to stand behind her, carefully wrapping both arms around her and resting his chin on the top of her head. "Take a minute," he told her. "There's a lot going on. Married or just technically married, this can't be easy. There's bound to be a lot of memories, a lot of feelings. Just stay in it. Stay present." He kissed the top of her head and pulled her even closer to him.

Rachel hugged Christopher's arms to her. She always felt better in his arms. It was the only place in the world she felt truly safe and whole. "Okay," she said after a minute. Christopher let go, and she walked up the steps, onto the porch, and slid her key into the lock of the front door.

"Hey! You do have a key!" Carter teased as she came into the house.

Christopher didn't understand the joke. "How do you usually get in when you come here?" he asked Rachel.

"Oh, she's very creative," Carter said. "If she can't find where I hid the spare key within a few minutes, she usually breaks in through a window or just stands outside screaming. One time, she pulled out a gun and shot the lock off. That was fun to fix." Rachel rolled her eyes. "What?" Carter asked. "I didn't say what kind of gun you used."

"Not a small caliber pistol then, I'm guessing," Christopher said.

"Nope. That shotgun was promptly confiscated once she was inside."

Christopher laughed and shook his head. "Rachel, you know how to pick a lock. Why did you blast it off with a shotgun?"

"I was in a hurry." She shrugged as though it were a perfectly legitimate reason.

"I think the more important question is why she had a shotgun with her in the first place," Carter pointed out.

Rachel shrugged again. "It was after—" Realizing she couldn't say where they had been in front of Carter, she gave the name of the operation they had been working on instead. "It was after *High Tide*."

"Oh, yeah, that makes more sense. I was so tired when we got back, I got a hotel next to the airport instead of going home."

"It's good you two have each other," Carter said ironically.

"There's no need to be facetious, Carter!" Rachel yelled.

"There's no need to use such big words, Rachel," Carter jabbed back.

"It means don't be an ass," Rachel clarified. "God, try reading a book or something."

Carter rolled his eyes.

"Where's Jessica? Oh my god, you are still dating her, right? Or did you fuck that up?"

"She's at work. Some sort of open house thing at the school. She sort of has to be there to interact with the parents and kids."

Christopher tried not to laugh. They bickered more like siblings than soon-to-be exes.

"Do you have luggage? You are going to be here for multiple days?" Carter asked.

"Yeah, it's in the truck," Christopher said. Carter nodded and showed him around the house.

Rachel wandered into the living room and sat on the floor, laughing to herself, thinking about the last time she had been there eighteen months ago, after Aiden and Veeda had been killed. She had been drunk and angry and out of her mind with grief.

"Are you having a psychotic break or something?" Carter asked her as he came back into the living room. Rachel looked at him and raised her eyebrows, still laughing. "Oh, for fuck's sake Rachel. That wasn't funny then, and it isn't funny now."

"It was fun."

"I swear to fucking God, Rachel," Carter muttered under his breath.

"What? It was fun!" She giggled.

"Something is seriously wrong with your brain. Now get your shit together, or I'm going to have to start telling secrets," Carter threatened.

"What secrets?" Rachel asked. Carter pointed to the spot on the floor where she was sitting. "I don't think you want to start that game, Carter. I've got just as much I could tell—"

Christopher walked into the room and saw Rachel sitting on the floor. "Rachel," Christopher interjected, "whatever you're doing right now, you need to stop."

"I'm not doing anything," Rachel said innocently. "I'm just sitting on the floor in *my* living room."

"I don't know exactly why Carter is annoyed that you're sitting there, and I don't think I want to know the specifics, but just get up and try to be civil."

"Fine." Rachel rolled her eyes and waited for Christopher to leave. "Carter, I apologize for making you think about that. Would you like to tell me where else I can't sit?" Her apology wasn't the least bit heartfelt.

"Seriously? I don't think you can sit anywhere in this house without it making me think of something. When you aren't here, it's fine. I don't think about you. Not like that, anyway. Sometimes, like when I'm watching the news, I think about you, hoping that you're safe wherever you are. But I guess you're in D.C. permanently now . . . You being here, it's like being visited by a ghost or something."

"Yeah," Rachel said. "Why do you think I'm always drunk when I come here?"

Carter nodded. "It's a lot."

"Yup. Twenty-six years of memories," Rachel agreed.

"We haven't had the house for twenty-six years."

"Not just the house. I mean everything," Rachel clarified.

Carter nodded. "You know I'd never actually tell Chris—"

"Oh, I know you wouldn't 'cause you don't have a death wish," Rachel said. "I won't say anything to Jessica. Not anything bad anyway," Rachel assured him.

Carter shook his head. "God, please don't tell her about that! That's entirely your drama and has nothing to do with me or her."

"I know. I'll keep it to myself. It'll be our little secret." Rachel winked. "Besides, I'm not sure Christopher would be particularly shocked if you did tell him."

Carter didn't try to hide his annoyance. "Of course not—"

Rachel's phone beeped, cutting Carter off. "Shit!" she shouted as she stared at the screen.

"Problem?" Carter's brow furrowed.

"HVT on the move!"

Carter wrinkled his nose. "Aren't you on leave?"

Rachel chuckled in response.

"If you're on leave, why are you tracking high value targets? I'm assuming that's still what HVT means?"

"Christopher!" Rachel yelled. "Where the hell does this road go?"

Christopher wandered in and took her phone, studying the map on the screen. "He's driving on Kabul Highway."

"I asked where the road goes, not what it's called!" Rachel huffed.

"Babe, it's called Kabul Highway. Where the fuck do you think it goes?"

Rachel rolled her eyes. "I think he's going to Jalalabad. So Kabul would not confirm my theory."

"He'd have to drive through Kabul to get to Jalalabad, assuming he was leaving from Khost."

"So, I'm not wrong?"

Christopher shrugged. "Not yet, you aren't. Wait and see where he actually stops."

Rachel turned her attention back to her phone, staring intently at the tiny red dot that indicated the location of Khalid Khan's car.

"It's going to take him four hours and thirty-seven minutes to get to Kabul," Christopher noted. "I don't think you need to stare at your screen for that entire time."

"It's fine. It'll give her something to do while we watch the game." Carter smiled.

"Game?" Rachel asked, half interested.

"The L.A. Rams are playing Tampa Bay in about fifteen minutes," Carter explained.

"Football?" Rachel's brow furrowed.

"Yes," Carter and Christopher answered simultaneously.

"I'm assuming you'd prefer to watch the game rather than listen to Rachel comment on where her target is driving?" Carter asked Christopher.

"I'm sure I'll be multitasking. She's bound to have geography questions."

Several hours later, the guys were each several beers in. Rachel was still on the floor staring intently at her phone.

"Where is he going now?" Rachel mused. Khalid Khan's car had veered off the main road and stopped.

Christopher glanced over at her. "It's the fourth quarter, babe. Game's almost over. I can look after that."

"Fuck!" Carter yelled.

"What happened?" Christopher asked, sounding irritated.

"Interception."

"I take my eyes off the screen for one second—"

"Calm down. It's football. They'll show you a hundred replays." Rachel rolled her eyes then shoved her phone in Christopher's face. "This road goes to Jalalabad."

"Are you asking me or telling me?" Christopher didn't take his eyes off the TV.

"I would like confirmation please."

"Sure, in a minute." Christopher pushed her phone out of his face.

Rachel sat on the floor, pouting. "Christopher, this is much more important than football."

"Baby, if he's driving to Jalalabad, he'll still be driving to Jalalabad when the game's over."

"Sports are stupid," Rachel complained.

Christopher ignored her until the next commercial came on, then took her phone. Khalid's car was back on the highway and moving quickly. "Yes, that road goes to Jalalabad. Drive time is two hours and fifty minutes, meaning that I will be asleep before he gets there, assuming that *is* where he's going."

"Why did he stop here?" She pointed at the location on the screen where the car had stopped earlier.

Christopher's brows knit together. "To get gas?"

Rachel couldn't tell if he was guessing or telling her.

"He'd have to stop for gas at some point. I don't know what car he's driving, so I don't know how many miles to gallon he's getting or how full his gas tank was when he left Khost, but my assumption would be he stopped at a gas station."

That made perfect sense, and Rachel felt a little dumb for not having thought of it herself. "Thank you!" She grinned then set an alarm for the time Khalid Khan should arrive in Jalalabad, assuming that was where he was going.

Two hours and fifty minutes later, Rachel's alarm rang. She rolled over in bed, switched it off, and opened the app for the tracking software. Sure enough, Khalid Khan's car was stopped in the mountains north of Jalalabad. She quickly took a screenshot of the GPS coordinates and texted it to Luke and Eastwood.

Chapter 19

NOVEMBER 2020

THE NEXT EVENING, RACHEL was beyond intoxicated. She'd spent the afternoon at the courthouse with Carter signing divorce papers and had insisted on celebrating with a bottle of champagne. Or whatever cheap shit she'd gotten from the gas station by Carter's house. Christopher took her outside to the front porch so she could get some air. She started dancing and singing "Call It What You Want" and "King of My Heart" by Taylor Swift, clearly directing every word of each song to him.

"Are we going to have a repeat of New York?" Christopher pulled her hips into him.

"No, because Ryan isn't here to stop me." Rachel's lips were mere inches from his.

The last time they had been in New York together had been when they were both on active duty. Before she'd been injured, before Christopher had retired, before either of them had been ready to admit their feelings for each other. Despite the Navy's strict no fraternization policy, Rachel had gotten incredibly drunk and spent the entire night shamelessly flirting with Christopher. The only thing that kept either of them from acting on the sexual tension they had both felt was the fact that Ryan had been there to intervene.

Christopher laughed. "Ryan may not be here, but Carter is. Maybe try to consider his feelings?"

"It's fine!" Rachel insisted.

"We both know you can't be quiet, Rachel."

"I *can* be quiet. I just figure you appreciate my verbal feedback." She giggled.

"I definitely do, but that's not my point." He grinned. "How would you feel if you had to listen to him with Jessica?"

Rachel shrugged. "It honestly wouldn't bother me at all. Besides, it's not like I haven't . . . Well, no, I promised to be nice, so I shouldn't tell you."

"Tell me what?"

"Well, in high school, we may have gone to prom together, but he definitely spent most of the night with Amy Martin in a hotel room and not me. And I know that because I had the other key to the room, and I went to check on him because he was so drunk, and there he was with Amy Martin. Carter pretends he doesn't remember that, even though I know for a fact that he does remember."

"Are you sure he remembers?"

"Yes. He did it because he, again, while very drunk, decided it would be a good idea to ask me to marry him. I said no because one, we were seventeen, and two, he was drunk as shit and there was no way he was serious. But then he got mad and ran off with Amy, and the next day when I explained to him that maybe he had been a bit drunk and immature, he said it was my fault he slept with Amy because I said I wouldn't marry him. And so, to your earlier point, he can fuck Jessica as loudly as he wants, and I would not care."

"He seriously got drunk and proposed to you at prom?" Christopher asked.

"Yup!"

"Did he have a ring?"

"Nope."

"And when you said no, he ran off with another girl?"

"Exactly."

"Wow, that's—"

"That's Carter. And everyone says *I'm* the problem." She pointed clumsily at herself.

"What lies are you out here telling, Rache?" Carter asked as he and Jessica came outside to join them.

"No lies, just truthful stories," Rachel assured him.

"Or some convoluted version of a semi-truthful story." Carter glared at her. "I thought we said no sharing secrets."

"I said I wouldn't tell *Jessica* any secrets. Or at least not that particular one. I didn't say anything about not telling Christopher your secrets. And before you get some stupid idea to start talking now, remember that you come off way worse in that story than I do. Hell, technically you could have gone to jail if . . ." Rachel looked at Jessica.

Jessica raised both eyebrows, clearly wanting to hear the rest of the story.

"If you'd lied," Carter finished for her. "But you know you can't get away with that shit here."

Rachel tensed, her jaw clenched, and her hand curled into a tight fist.

"Hey! Remember how you two were getting along and had decided to be friends?" Jessica jumped in. "Let's go back to that."

"It's very difficult to be friends with someone who likes to make up stories and spread lies about you," Carter said, glaring at Rachel.

"I agree," Rachel said, staring at him with hatred in her eyes. How many times had he told her mother lies in an attempt to control her, keep her, force her to do what he wanted? Carter shook his head and smirked. "I'd get ahold of my anger if I were you. Assaulting a police officer is taken very seriously around here. Hell," he chuckled, "you'd probably get dishonorably discharged."

"Carter." She uttered his name as a final warning and took a step towards him.

"Maybe I should call your mom and tell her you've lost your mind again? Get you put on a seventy-two-hour psychiatric hold? Or would it be more effective to tell the sheriff about the time—"

He was baiting her, and she was too drunk to stop herself. She shifted forward, ready to strike, but Christopher was there, calm as always, and wrapped his arms around her. He lifted her up over his shoulder, restraining her, and looped one arm tightly around her legs as she struggled to get away, then carried her to bed kicking and screaming and cursing Carter the entire way.

Christopher was beyond exhausted, and it was only 1900. Somehow Carter managed to bring out the worst in Rachel. Every. Single. Time. He knew exactly how to get a rise out of her. How to make it look like she was out of control. The way Carter was carrying on, he'd almost knocked him out for her. He dropped Rachel on the bed in Carter's guest room and let out a sharp exhale. "I dunno what he was referring to—"

"It doesn't matter. He always manages to leave enough truth in his stories so everyone believes him."

Christopher watched as she dug her fingernails into her wrist. "Alright, enough of that." He nudged her hands apart. "Forget about him. You're legally divorced. You never have to see him again if you don't want to. I'd suggest we leave now, but neither of us are sober enough to drive."

"I can't forget."

"Really?" Christopher smirked. "I have a feeling I can help with that." He'd stopped caring about what Carter thought. He wanted to get back at Carter just as much as Rachel did—but psychological warfare was much more effective than throwing a few punches.

Christopher grabbed a Bluetooth speaker out of his bag, connected his phone, and played Nine Inch Nails as loudly as the speaker would go. He pulled Rachel up off the bed and slammed her up against the wall hard enough to distract her from her thoughts, then kissed her deeply and tugged at her clothes.

"Don't be nice," she whispered in his ear as he kissed her neck. He looked at her hesitantly. "Please," she begged.

Christopher smiled and shook his head, knowing he needed to do whatever it took to distract her from Carter. He'd seen the look in her eye out on the porch, and he'd seen that same look in her eye plenty of times before. It always resulted in a slow and painful death for the person on the receiving end. While Carter was a pain in the ass, he didn't deserve to die, but Rachel was likely too drunk to realize that.

After moving her back to the bed, he made his way down. Kissing her, licking her, while his hand gripped her thigh. She put her hand on his and forced him to squeeze harder. He looked up at her and saw how much she was enjoying it. He kept going, his other hand touching her softly, getting her ready for him. She had her fingers in his hair, pulling, urging him up to her. He moved up to kiss her lips.

Christopher remembered when they had been in the basement, and he'd had his hand on her throat. She had kept begging him to do it harder. He decided to test something, already knowing she could take it and suspecting she'd like it. Suspecting she'd love it, actually. He kissed her neck and then applied pressure to just the right spot, knowing she'd lose consciousness if he held his hand there too hard or for too long. He watched as she struggled to take a breath.

"Harder. It's okay, I trust you," she managed to say.

He pressed harder, keeping a careful eye on her breathing and two fingers on the other side of her neck to monitor her pulse. He saw her face relax, and he let go.

"Again," she begged, staring deep into his eyes, telling him exactly what she wanted. He felt her one last time, checking that she was still ready, and then thrust into her. She let out a cry of pleasure and arched her back.

"Do it again," she requested.

Christopher pushed into her over and over, kissing her neck and applying pressure with his hand again. She closed her eyes and inhaled sharply as he pressed down on the side of her neck. The whole time he was sliding in and out of her. He couldn't believe how aroused she was getting. He couldn't believe how aroused he was, either. Her muscles convulsed around him as she climaxed repeatedly beneath him. She had slipped into a serene euphoria, content and entirely at peace.

He thrust into her harder before sliding her leg over his shoulder so he could go deeper, wanting to get at her very core. He gripped her leg tightly with one hand and her opposite wrist with the other as he held her down.

She moved his hand back to her throat.

Christopher tried to slow down. He wanted to savor the experience. It was transcendent, and she was boundless, wanting more, needing more, craving him endlessly, as much as he was craving her. He tried to focus on her pulse, her breathing, knowing that he couldn't let himself get carried away, no matter how much she was begging him to do it harder, longer, more.

He pressed down on her neck one more time while thrusting in and out of her, pounding into her deep and hard. She came again, even more powerfully than before. Her back arched and she let out a muted moan, not able to get enough air for it to be audible. He let himself spill into her, pushing himself in deeper and deeper as he finished. She kissed him as he pulled out of her, then held his face and kissed him again, sweetly expressing her gratitude for her newly found tranquility. He'd never seen her so calm in the entire eleven years that he'd known her. He rolled to the side of her and laid down, pulling her into his arms and kissing her forehead.

"More," she breathed.

Christopher turned his head to look at her and smirked. He couldn't say no to that.

When Rachel woke up, she was calm. Calmer than she'd been in years, maybe ever. She was a bit out of it, feeling spacey and almost high. The endorphins rushing through her body were intoxicating. She was disoriented and wasn't sure where she was, but moments from the night before flashed through her mind. Christopher on top of her, holding her down. Christopher inside of her, the feel of him throbbing, taking her hard and with force, claiming possession of her. She remembered his hands on her thighs, on her wrists, on her hips and waist and felt his hand on her throat. She smiled to herself as she remembered him coming inside her, kissing her, holding her, then starting again.

She got up and put on the underwear, jeans, and tank top scattered on the floor and then wandered out of the room. She recognized where she was but was having a hard time integrating what she was seeing with what she was feeling. It wasn't making sense. She wandered to the bathroom and found a hair tie. They weren't the ones she usually bought though. She picked one up anyway and wandered out to the kitchen, brushing her hair off her neck and twisting it into a bun as she did.

"For fuck's sake, Rachel!" Carter's voice startled her out of her dreamlike state. She looked at him, not understanding what he was saying, not comprehending why he was there.

"What happened?" she asked.

Carter looked at Christopher, who was sitting on the couch with a cup of coffee, and then back at Rachel. Neither of them understood what he was getting at. Carter walked over to Rachel and turned her so that Christopher could see the bruise on her neck. Rachel still didn't understand, so he poked it hard to make sure she would feel it.

"Oops." She giggled, then winked at Jessica who was sitting at the kitchen table reading something on her phone.

"Seriously?" Carter asked. "And look how fucking happy you are. Completely pleased with yourself, aren't you?" He looked her over, checking for, and finding, more bruises. "God, you're even more fucked up than I thought."

Rachel watched Christopher the whole time Carter prodded her, inspected her, a serene smile on her face. She wasn't going to let Carter take away her peace and euphoria. This felt too good. She gently pushed him away from her and walked over to the couch to sit next to Christopher. She curled up into him, tucking her knees into her chest. He put his arm around her shoulders, pulling her close so he could kiss the top of her head.

"You slept for eight hours," Christopher told her, tipping her face up to his so he could look into her eyes.

"I don't think I've ever done that before," Rachel stated a bit absently.

"No, I don't think you have," Christopher said, kissing her tenderly on the lips. He seemed as far gone as she was.

"I kept wondering if you were dead in there," Carter said bitterly. "Apparently I was right to wonder."

"Mind your own business, Carter," Rachel said calmly, still staring deep into Christopher's eyes. She pulled Christopher's face closer to her to kiss him again, not caring at all that Carter and Jessica were watching them. Christopher had apparently stopped caring too. He put his hand under her chin and kissed her again and again, softly, tenderly. Their kisses were full of devotion, sincerity—perfectly intimate and pure.

"Carter," Jessica's tone was stern.

"You want *me* to apologize?" Carter was incensed.

"Well, I didn't do anything." Rachel shrugged. "You're the one who implemented a stop-and-frisk policy."

"You look like a fucking abuse victim!" Carter yelled.

Rachel shrugged. "Nothing new. We were drunk and got carried away is all."

Christopher flashed her a sideways glance. "Carter, you know I'd never actually hurt her."

"It's true." Rachel nodded. "I usually have to do that myself."

"I'm aware," Carter muttered, eyes wide with irritation.

Rachel paused, studying his face.

"Why don't the two of you take a minute." Jesica looked back and forth between Rachel and Carter.

"Excellent idea, Jessica." Christopher was off the couch and following Jessica onto the front porch in a matter of seconds.

Rachel sighed, then got serious. "Carter, you're sad because you know it's really over. There's no more hope of me running back to you."

"You were never that happy with me. Not with anyone, ever," Carter yelled. He couldn't look at her. "Fuck, you slept! You never relax enough to sleep that long."

"I know," Rachel said. "You and I . . . We've hurt each other so much. So many times . . . just because we've always wanted different things. I could never be who you needed, and you couldn't be who I needed. We've always known that, but we tried to force it anyway," Rachel said.

"I've never stopped loving you, Rachel," Carter admitted. "But I wasn't loving *you*. I've never stopped loving who you were . . . before everything . . . before my mom got sick, before so many tragedies impacted our lives, one after another with no breaks, no respite in between. Just tragedy and death."

"Before Emma died." Rachel nodded.

Carter turned to her with a look of realization on his face. "I think that's it. I've never thought about it. Not in that way, really. You were always hyper and impulsive and a bit nuts. But after Emma . . . Something changed in you. Maybe not right away. And then my mom got sick right after, then she died, then my dad lost his shit completely, then your grandpa . . . It was four years of tragedy after fucking tragedy. Then college, then war . . . It's not strange we're both a little fucked up." He paused, finally meeting her eyes. "I need to stop wishing you were different, wishing I could erase all the horrible things. You're perfect how you are. Just not perfect for me. And I'm not perfect for you. I never was. But you know who I think is?" Carter glanced towards the front door. "I've seen you two together a lot over the years. Back when you used to call home and tell me when you were deploying or when you got back, you were always with him. He was always in the background, telling you your phone time was up or asking you a question about something. You were always on leave together, running around all over the world on crazy adventures. It's not strange you ended up together."

"You know, people keep saying things like that. Apparently the whole world knew how we felt except us!"

"That's 'cause you're too in love with the Navy to think about anything else!" Carter teased.

"So, what do we do now? Do you want to hate me?" Rachel asked. "It's okay if you do, but we need to decide. We can't keep fighting like this."

"We said friends, remember?"

Chapter 20

NOVEMBER 2020

RACHEL AND CHRISTOPHER PACKED up the truck, mentally preparing for Thanksgiving with their parents at the Williams' family ranch in Texas. They'd shoved everything into their duffel bags and were doing one final sweep of Carter's house to make sure they hadn't left anything.

"Rachel, don't forget your phone!" Carter called from the kitchen.

"Fuck, where is it?" Rachel's eyes darted around the living room.

"Right here." Carter held it up for her.

"I plugged it in for you after you went to bed," Jessica explained.

Rachel took the phone from Carter. Twenty-three missed calls and fifty-nine text messages. "Uh-oh." She scrolled trough the texts. There were a few from her dad to confirm her parents' flight information, a few from Christopher's mom to confirm what time she and Christopher expected to get to the ranch, and then— "Oh my fucking god."

Carter and Christopher looked over at her simultaneously. She was white as a sheet.

"Breathe, baby," Christopher said gently.

"I . . . I need to get to Landstuhl." Landstuhl Regional Medical Center in Germany was the evacuation and treatment center for all injured U.S. service members.

"Fuck!" Christopher yelled. "Meridian is the closest air station. Get us on a flight. Who is it? Which team?" It didn't matter. If anyone in their squadron was injured, Rachel would insist on going.

"Paige."

"Paige?" Cristopher's brow furrowed. "Who the fuck is Paige?"

"Paige Larsson?" She saw his blank stare and rolled her eyes. "The hot blonde you kept trying to fuck the last time we were in Khost."

Christopher chuckled. "Baby, you know I don't try, I only succeed. If I'd put any effort into it—"

"Really not the point, Christopher!" she yelled. "I asked her to help Yashfa and Yamna, and now she's getting transported to Landstuhl . . . I don't know why—" Her phone rang. She pushed Christopher towards the front door and out to the truck, giving Carter and Jessica a half-hearted goodbye wave as she did. "Admiral Eastwood, sir," she answered.

"You had a CIA analyst helping your assets?" Eastwood yelled on the other end of the phone.

"Yes. I'm on my way to Meridian to catch a flight to Germany as we speak." She climbed into the passenger seat of Christoper's truck as he started the ignition.

"You will do no such thing," Eastwood argued. "Stand down."

"But— "

"Her mother has already been notified and is en route. There is no reason for you to be there other than to implicate yourself more. It'll make you look guilty if you go."

"I am guilty. It's my fault."

"Explain," Eastwood demanded.

"I asked her to help put a tracker on Khalid Khan's car," Rachel admitted.

"When was that?"

"I dunno, a couple weeks ago?"

"So what happened yesterday?"

"Yesterday I signed my divorce papers and got drunk as shit and lost my phone, which I've now found again, and I have all these messages and missed calls. I—"

"You got drunk and lost your phone?" Eastwood was even louder than before.

Fuck, what a dumb thing to say. "Yes, sir, but it wasn't really lost. It was inside Carter's house the entire time." She grimaced, knowing that losing her phone would be a major security breach. It had been a poor choice of words, to say the least. "It's more that my phone somehow, temporarily, detached itself from my hand and was replaced by copious amounts of sparkling wine. Then I was sleeping, and I therefore missed some calls . . ."

"You missed several calls," Eastwood noted. "At what point were you planning on returning any of those calls?"

"It's 0730, sir. I just saw your messages right before you called me."

"Director Cruze is pissed."

Rachel rolled her eyes. She didn't give a shit about the CIA station chief's feelings.

"You compromised one of his best analysts."

"She is not his best analyst," Rachel corrected him. "She's a decent analyst and the only woman I knew in Khost who would be able to help Yashfa and Yamna with the tracking device." After a painful silence, she continued, "Paige didn't have to help. She could have said no."

"What did you ask her to help with other than the tracking device? If that was weeks ago, why was she at your asset's home yesterday?"

"I honestly have no idea."

"Find out!" Eastwood yelled before hanging up.

Rachel let out a long exhale, puffing out her cheeks as she did. She called Yamna. No answer. She tried Yashfa next.

"Rachel?" Yashfa sounded panicked.

"What the hell is going on?" Rachel asked in Pashto.

"Paige came over for tea . . . we thought our father was gone—"

"He *is* gone. His car is in in mountains outside Jalalabad," Rachel grumbled.

"I don't know where his car is or where he is now, but he came home and her hair wasn't covered. He . . . she had a card in her pocket with a phone number. We called as soon as we could and then some Americans came . . ."

"Are you okay?"

"I'm better than Paige or Yamna."

"What happened to Yamna?" Rachel asked, although she had a pretty solid guess.

"Our father hit her. Not as much as Paige, but he was yelling. I didn't understand really because he started yelling in English. I don't know much English, but something about Skylark and whore and spy. Those words I knew."

Rachel froze. "He said *Skylark*?"

"Yes, and he yelled at Yamna for working with Skylark. I didn't know what it meant, but I tried to spell it. It's a bird."

"Yeah, a Skylark is a bird." Rachel sighed and glanced over at Christopher. His eyes went wide as he mouthed *what the fuck?* "Skylark is also the name of an American spy. Remember when y'all kept asking if I was a spy?" Rachel winced as she led her to the admission.

"Yeah, and you were pretending to be a researcher at the university."

"Yashfa, I'm Skylark. Your father thought Paige was me."

"How does he know about you, know your name?"

"Well . . . I'm pretty good at my job . . ." Rachel hated where this conversation was going. "You and Yamna need to be very careful, and if you want to cut contact with me, I completely understand."

"Are you kidding?" Yashfa yelled. "I want him dead even more now!"

"Well, I have a team headed there, so if you can figure out where he went—"

"Team?"

"Soldiers," Rachel clarified. "Think about where your father may have gone, and I'll tell my soldiers, and they'll go after him."

"Okay. I'll try to figure out where he went," Yashfa agreed.

"Is there anything else I can do? Anything you need? If there's something you need that my men can get for you—"

"Nothing, Rachel." Yashfa sounded dejected.

"Are you sure, because—"

"Just find Kamal." Yashfa ended the call.

"Fuck!" Rachel yelled.

Christopher took his eyes off the road for a mere second to glance over at her. "What's the plan?'

"Go to the ranch. I'm not allowed to go to Landstuhl."

"Like hell you aren't. If you aren't allowed on a military plane, then fly commercial and just don't tell Eastwood you're going. Google flights from Dallas Fort Worth," Christopher instructed.

Rachel typed frantically on her phone. "United has a direct flight . . . It's two thousand dollars."

Christopher must have sensed her hesitancy because he squeezed her knee and said, "You'll feel better if you go."

"Are you coming with me?" she asked hopefully.

"For two thousand dollars?" Christopher practically yelled, moving his hand back to the wheel.

Rachel scrolled further down the page. "Hang on, this one is one stop and it's seven hundred and twenty-six dollars, but it departs at 1830 tonight."

"Book it," Christopher ordered, flooring the accelerator. "Wait! Passports?"

"I have both of our passports in my bag."

"Why?"

"In case of an emergency such as this one. I saw you'd left yours in the safe, so I grabbed it when I got mine."

"Your paranoia sure does pay off, doesn't it?"

Rachel nodded. "What day do my parents get here?"

"Wednesday, 1500 ish. 1507 I think."

"Well, they might have to wait for us for a bit." She shrugged. "Whatever."

Christopher drove as quickly as he could to the Dallas Fort Worth airport, calling his mom on the way to let her know about the change in plans. She hadn't been happy about it, but she was used to it by now. They got to the airport at 1705, just barely enough time to make their 1830 flight. As soon as they found parking in the garage at the airport, they repacked their bags and made sure that they didn't have any weapons with them, and locked their handguns in the glove compartment.

"Flying commercial sure is a pain in the ass," Rachel complained. Passports in hand, they ran for the check-in counter, left their bags, and then made their way for the TSA PreCheck line.

NOVEMBER 2020

RACHEL WALKED DOWN THE halls of Landstuhl Regional Medical Center with Christopher by her side, heart racing. She didn't have much information, just that Paige was here. Getting sent here was always bad though. She finally found Paige's room, gently knocked on the door, then went in. Visiting people in the hospital wasn't new to Rachel. Far from it. But she was not prepared for what she saw. Paige's face was badly swollen. She was covered in bruises and cuts. Her arm was broken and in a sling. It was worse than Rachel had anticipated.

"Can I help you?" a voice said from the corner of the room.

Rachel turned to see a woman in a white coat—the doctor, she presumed. "How is she?" Rachel asked, flashing her military ID in the hopes that it would get her some information.

The doctor came around to the foot of the bed, hanging up a clipboard with Paige's medical notes. "We put her in a medically induced coma. She has some swelling."

"I see that."

"Brain swelling, head trauma," the doctor clarified. "Internal bleeding, broken bones. Nothing we can't fix, but it will take time."

"Her nose is broken," Rachel observed. Paige had a pretty nose. Delicate and straight, perfectly proportioned to her beautiful face.

"Once she's stable, our plastic surgeon will fix it," the doctor explained.

"Once she's stable . . ." Rachel repeated.

"We're optimistic that she'll make a full recovery. But it will take time." Rachel nodded, looking over at Paige.

"Her mother should be back soon. You can sit with her until then. The cafeteria is—"

Christopher gave the doctor a warm, half-hearted smile. "We've been here before and know where everything is. Thank you, though."

"Of course." The doctor nodded then left the room.

Christopher took a seat in the chair next to Paige. Rachel snatched up the clipboard with the medical notes and examined them, confirming everything the doctor had just told them.

A few moments later, the door opened again and a slender woman with red, puffy eyes came in. "Who are you?" she asked.

"Mrs. Larsson?" Rachel asked.

The woman nodded.

Rachel showed her ID again and explained who she was. "I work with your daughter. I heard what happened and needed to come see that she was okay."

Mrs. Larsson's eyes darted to Christopher.

"I used to work with both of them." He pointed to Paige then to Rachel. "Just retired."

Mrs. Larsson nodded. "They say she'll be okay, but . . . I don't know. I begged her not to take that assignment, but she assured me it was safe. Sitting at a desk . . . She was so excited to go see the world, make a difference. No one can even tell me what happened."

"She was meeting with an intelligence asset. They got caught together and the target, the man she was trying to get information about, found out the informant was helping her."

"So much for sitting at a desk." Mrs. Larsson sighed.

"Her job *was* to sit at a desk." Rachel looked down at her feet. "I asked

Paige to help me with something. To get something to my asset. She did. The operation went well. This—" she glanced over at Paige, "—I don't know why she made contact with my asset again." Rachel swallowed, trying to get rid of the bitter taste in her mouth. "I've spent a lot of time in Khost. It's a lonely place for a woman, even an American woman. I didn't think introducing her to my assets, my informants, would lead to them being friends, to socializing. I guess they were having tea when this happened."

"We thought the target was on the other side of the country," Christopher chimed in.

"His car is." Rachel gritted her teeth.

"They said she fought back. Has defensive wounds," Mrs. Larsson told them.

Rachel nodded. "Is there anything we can do for you? For Paige? Anything you need?"

"The doctors told me I could check into the hotel here, but I don't want her to be alone."

"We can stay with her while you sleep." Rachel gave Mrs. Larsson a kind smile.

Mrs. Larsson's brow furrowed as she looked around the room at the sparse, uncomfortable furnishings. "Are you sure?"

"Yes, ma'am." Rachel nodded. "It's what we do. Leave no man behind."

"I'm not sure what happens if she wakes up, or if she dies . . . I guess the State Department—"

Rachel saw Christopher's eyebrows shoot up on the other side of the room and was happy Mrs. Larsson had her back to him. It was a common cover—telling your family you worked at the State Department—for CIA analysts and officers stationed overseas. She had her own ID card somewhere indicating the very same thing, though she had never actually worked for them. "I can check in with Paige's boss and confirm what the next steps are, but usually the doctors here arrange everything." She turned to Christopher. "Why don't you take Mrs. Larsson over to the hotel, get her checked in—and us—and set up a watch schedule so Paige isn't ever alone. Make sure she eats something."

"Yes, ma'am. What will you be doing?"

"I'll be harassing doctors and nurses for more information."

"Good plan." Christopher picked up his bag and Mrs. Larsson's and led her down the hall towards the adjoining hotel.

Rachel watched them walk away, then went back into Paige's room and closed the door. She started opening cupboards and drawers, looking for Paige's laptop and phone. Hospital rooms were not great places to hide things. She found Paige's laptop and CIA credentials and tucked them into her own duffel bag between her clothes.

No phone.

Christopher was fast asleep in the chair next to Rachel. Mrs. Larsson was in her hotel room, hopefully sleeping. Rachel reached down and quietly pulled Paige's laptop out from her bag. Making sure not to make too much noise, she grabbed Paige's hand and pressed her index finger to the laptop to unlock it, then plugged in a card reader and inserted Paige's ID.

A box popped up in the center of the screen. *PIN REQUIRED,* it said.

Rachel thought back on everything she knew about Paige. The girl was obsessive about the CIA, proud of her service. Rachel pulled out Paige's ID replacing it with her own military ID and used her own credentials to log in before skimming Paige's personnel file. She knew the pin had to be between six and eight numbers long and figured that an analyst wouldn't be dumb enough to use their own birthday. On a hunch, she checked the date Paige had joined the CIA then logged out of her account and to reconnect to Paige's account hoping her suspicions about Paige's pin number were correct. She slid Paige's ID back into the card reader then typed in the date Paige had been hired by the CIA: 071715.

INCORRECT.

Fuck.

She tried 07172015 next.

INCORRECT.

Rachel had only one more attempt before she was locked out of the system.

Okay, Paige is an analyst. They're pedantic and obsessed with protocol. How would she do this?

Rachel contemplated for a minute then realized the correct format for dates on federal documents was yyyymmdd. As a paper pusher, it was unlikely Paige would deviate from that. She took a deep breath and typed in 20150717.

Then she was in. A window with a half-written email was still open. Rachel started reading it, curious what Paige had been working on.

I've met with the assets three times since the original meetup, each time at the younger one's home. The first time was to get my bearings, assess the situation, and build trust. The second time, I planted a recording device. The third time,

That was it. She hadn't finished writing the email. Rachel opened Paige's calendar and scrolled back to the day she'd helped Yashfa and Yamna put the tracker on Khalid Khan's car. Then she looked day by day at what Paige had been doing. Meetings, meetings, and more boring-as-shit meetings. Then, two weeks ago, on a seemingly random Tuesday: *Tea @ Y.*

Rachel rolled her eyes. Not the most discrete annotation in a calendar. She went forward and saw the same thing again the next Wednesday, and then again . . . The other day, the day she'd been attacked, had been her third time going to Yamna's house. She'd written her summary email prematurely. From what Rachel could piece together, she presumed Paige had gone back to retrieve the recording device, although who had told her to do any of this, she had no idea.

Skylark to Yashfa: *Can you talk?*

No answer. Not even three little dots indicating that Yashfa was typing. She needed to know if there was a recording device in Yamna's home, and if so, what was on it.

Skylark to Eastwood: *Has Onyx deployed?*

Eastwood to Skylark: *They're getting ready to.*

Skylark to Eastwood: *I need them in Khost.*

Eastwood to Skylark: *The coordinates you sent were for somewhere northwest of Jalalabad in the mountains. You aren't that bad at geography.*

Skylark to Eastwood: *Paige planted a recording device in my asset's home. No idea why. I sure as hell didn't tell her to or even ask. She was having tea with my assets almost weekly. Again, not my idea. I need to get that device back and see what's on it.*

Eastwood to Skylark: *Onyx will be thrilled.*

Rachel could sense the sarcasm even if it was over text.

Skylark to Eastwood: *I've been to the house several times even if it was a few years ago. Should be easy enough for Lux to get in and out. Unless by some miracle I'm allowed to go.*

Eastwood to Skylark: *This is a higher priority than getting boots on the ground where these coordinates are you got?*

Rachel considered for a moment. While Khalid Khan's car was parked up in the mountains, the recording device might have some pertinent information on it that could help Onyx later. She sensed there was something deeper going on here. Maybe she could stop whatever Khalid was up to, and in the process, it would lead her to Kamal.

Skylark to Eastwood: *Yes. Send them to Khost.*

Rachel turned her attention back to Paige's laptop and navigated to the main HR page to investigate, immediately sighing when she saw Paige's pay grade. She hadn't gotten promoted since Rachel was last in Khost. She checked Paige's performance reviews over the years. All stellar. All outstanding. Apparently, she was better at her job than Rachel gave her credit for. Paige had been like a giddy schoolgirl the last time Indigo had been in Khost, batting her eyelashes at Christopher to the point that Rachel had to ban him from being within a hundred feet of Paige.

Rachel rolled her eyes. IT was far from her specialty, and it had been quite a while since she'd needed to hack into any systems.

"What are you doing?" Christopher mumbled as his head lolled to the side.

"Nothing. Go back to sleep."

"Why are you on the computer? It's the middle of the night."

"I'm just doing my job."

"Uh-huh," Christopher mumbled. "You're up to something."

"I always am." Rachel smiled to herself. She closed the laptop and sent off a text to an old contact who worked in cybersecurity, asking her to change Paige's pay grade, backdate her promotion, and add a few training certifications to Paige's profile, ensuring neither of them would get in trouble—at least not as much trouble—for Paige having acted as an officer rather than as an analyst.

Chapter 22

NOVEMBER 2020

RACHEL AND CHRISTOPHER HAD been at Landstuhl for thirty-six hours. The doctors and nurses had given up on trying to force them out of Paige's room, and Paige's mother was happy her daughter wasn't alone. Rachel's belief in the concept of *leave no man behind* was as firm as steel. No one went home until everyone went home. It was a rule her squadron had established even before she'd become a SEAL.

The sound of combat boots on the linoleum floor woke her up. She shifted and opened one eye to peek at which doctor was running which test this time, then sat straight up when she saw it wasn't a doctor at all. "Hey, Lux," she said to Onyx's team leader.

"Chris isn't with you?" Luke asked by way of greeting.

"Yeah, he's here somewhere." Rachel looked to the empty chair beside hers.

"Eastwood told us what happened." Luke looked over at Paige and cringed.

Rachel blinked, then rubbed her eyes. "Why are you here and not on your way to Khost?"

"This is on our way to Khost. Just landed about an hour ago. The guys are doing inventory and loading the plane as we speak. Then we'll refuel and fly out. You good?"

"I'm fine."

"Yeah, you look fine." Luke chuckled and ran his hand through her hair, messing it up even more than it already was, before plopping down in the chair next to her. "You look better than Paige, in any case."

Rachel gave him a sideways glance. "How well do *you* know Paige?"

Luke chuckled. "I've spent a lot of time in Khost over the years."

Rachel rolled her eyes. "Are there any blondes left in the entire world that you haven't slept with? Other than me, that is."

"Maybe a few." Luke smirked.

"Lux?" Christopher asked as he came into the room, two paper mugs of coffee in hand.

Luke was out of his chair and across the room in an instant, pulling Christopher into a tight hug and patting him hard on the back. "Good to see you."

Christopher held out both hands to the sides so the coffee wouldn't spill. "Mrs. Larsson is finishing up with the doctor. Why are you here?"

"He wanted to check on his girlfriend," Rachel teased.

Luke winked at Christopher and took one of the coffees.

"Not me! I was under strict orders not to touch her." Christopher motioned at Paige then took a sip of his own coffee.

"Oh, so you *do* remember her?" Rachel grinned.

"Yes, I remember you being jealous I was flirting with her and ordering me to keep my dick in my pants."

Rachel wrinkled her nose. "You're both disgusting."

"Like you're one to judge?" Luke chuckled. "You use sex as a cure-all for every emotion you ever experience."

Rachel pursed her lips, unable to deny the truth of that statement.

Luke took a long sip of the coffee he'd stolen from Christopher. "Since when do you put milk in your coffee?"

"That one is Rachel's."

Luke nodded and took another sip.

"Christopher?" They all turned to look at Mrs. Larsson in the doorway. "The doctors asked me which hospital I wanted her transferred to." She handed Christopher a paper. "I don't know which to pick."

"Medical decisions are Rachel's job." Christopher passed the paper to Luke who passed it to Rachel.

She scanned the document. "Walter Reed got me back on my feet. But it's far from home for you, so if you go there, make sure you're getting your hotel paid for and compensation for missing work or anything like that. Northwestern is closer to you, right? They're good too."

"Ty and Brad have both done considerable time at Northwestern," Luke chimed in.

"Dude, it's not prison." Christopher jabbed Luke with his elbow.

"It sort of is." Luke chuckled.

"Sorry, who are you?" Mrs. Larsson asked.

"I'm the Navy SEAL who's going to get the asshole who did this to your daughter, ma'am." Luke shook her hand. "Paige is a great girl. I've had the pleasure of working with her a few times over the years. We were already headed to Afghanistan to work on something related, but when we heard what happened, I insisted we stop in to see her."

"Thank you," Mrs. Larsson said, tears welling in her eyes.

"Best get moving," Rachel told Luke.

"Yup. Walk with me." Luke motioned for Rachel to follow him into the hallway.

As soon as they were in the hallway alone and the door to Paige's room was shut behind him, Rachel switched to Arabic so that no one would understand them. "You got the latest from Eastwood?" Rachel asked, keeping her voice low.

Luke nodded. "A recording device at your asset's house in Khost?"

"Yes."

"Are you running the op, or do I need to deal with Eastwood?"

"I don't know. I'm not technically working yet," Rachel reminded him.

"You sure?" Luke pulled a box out of his pocket and handed it to her.

Rachel opened it and smiled at the shiny silver star. "I guess I'm officially promoted."

"New ID too." Luke handed it over. "Eastwood suspected you were here and wanted you to have them sooner rather than later. Something about surprising your dad for Thanksgiving, assuming you're still going to Thanksgiving."

Rachel chuckled. "Yes, apparently Christopher and I care about holidays all of a sudden. Our flight back to Dallas is tomorrow morning."

Luke burst out laughing. "I thought the only holidays you two celebrated were the deaths of certain terrorists?"

"Pretty much." Rachel's upper lip twitched into a mischievous smile. "He's trying to force peace with our parents, so he invited my parents to his parents' ranch."

"Try not to kill anyone," Luke said, only half joking.

"And try not to get yourself killed."

"Yes, ma'am." Luke gave her a quick hug, handed her the coffee, then sprinted out of the hospital back to his team and their waiting plane.

Part II

BEGINNINGS

Chapter 23

NOVEMBER 2020

RACHEL AND CHRISTOPHER RUSHED off the plane once they landed in Dallas. Christopher had his phone out, checking the flight information for Tom and Anna-Beth's flight as soon as his phone connected to the network. Rachel was dragging him by the sleeve of his jacket so he wouldn't run into anything while staring at his phone.

"Global entry is this way," she informed him.

"Your parents already landed."

"Shit!" Rachel exclaimed. It was 1505 and her parents weren't supposed to land until 1507. Not that two minutes made much difference.

"Do they know we were in Germany?" Christopher asked.

"Not to my knowledge. Care to break the news?" Her parents liked him better anyway.

Christopher chuckled and started texting.

Chris to Tom: *Rachel and I are just getting back from Landstuhl. We're in the global entry line. It's not too long, but if you and Anna-Beth can make your way over to the international terminal, that would be great.*

Tom to Chris: *WTF? I didn't see anything come through about the teams being at Landstuhl.*

Chris to Tom: *Teams are fine. Analyst friend of ours is not.*

Tom to Chris: *We'll meet you at international arrivals.*

"Problem solved." Christopher flashed Rachel a wide grin.

Rachel shook her head. "Thank god they like you. Maybe I won't get yelled at for making my mother hike through the airport."

"She wouldn't yell in public," Christopher pointed out.

"No, but she'll repress her anger until we're in the truck, driving, and then we'll get an earful."

They drudged through the line. It wasn't long, but it was slow. Finally, they were called to the window and handed over their military IDs, passports, and boarding passes.

"Ma'am. Sir," the border patrol agent greeted them. "Thank you for your service," he said, noting their military IDs tucked inside their passports. "Reason for your travels?"

"Visiting a friend at Landstuhl, then rushing back for Thanksgiving so our parents don't kill us," Rachel explained.

The border patrol agent winced. "Landstuhl? Sorry about your friend. My younger brother is a Marine, so I've unfortunately spent some time at Landstuhl myself. Welcome home."

"Thank you, and happy Thanksgiving," Christopher said, swiping their documents off the counter and nudging Rachel towards the baggage carousel.

Tom and Anna-Beth were waiting when they finally cleared customs. Tom was on his phone, and Anna-Beth looked rather put out.

"All good?" Tom barely glanced up from his phone to ask.

"Yeah. Full recovery is expected, but it's good we went to check," Rachel explained.

"What happened?"

"Assets meeting informants. Shit hit the fan." Rachel shrugged. It was the most she could say in a public place.

Tom raised an eyebrow. "You will fill me in later, Captain Ryker?"

"Not unless you address me properly." She flashed him her new ID, showing she'd been promoted to rear admiral.

"No shit!" Tom exclaimed. "Looks like you're catching up to me!" Tom showed the ID card to Anna-Beth. She wasn't nearly as impressed. "Congratulations, Rear Admiral Ryker! I guess you achieved your goal then."

"Which goal?" Rachel asked as she hiked her bag up on her shoulder.

"To make admiral before you turn forty."

"I'm not admiral yet. You think I can get two promotions in four years by sitting on my ass at Command?"

"A rear admiral is still an admiral," Tom pointed out. "When do you start at HQ?"

"December seventh."

"And what will you be working on?" Tom pried.

Rachel shrugged and kept her tone light so it would sound like a joke to anyone else in hearing range. "Top secret spy shit, Daddy. What do you think we do at Special Projects?"

Tom chuckled. "Nothing you can talk about in the middle of the arrivals terminal!"

Rachel pursed her lips, her eyes wide as she nodded at him. He knew very well her division was even classified from the other SEAL teams stationed at Dam Neck in Virginia and Coronado in California.

"How was the flight from San Diego?" Christopher changed the subject. He picked up Anna-Beth's bag and led the way towards the parking garage.

Christopher's parents were waiting on the front porch when they arrived. Rachel hurriedly ran to the guest house while Christopher introduced everyone to her parents. She wanted to check everything was in order and up to her mother's ridiculous standards. She fluffed pillows that had already been fluffed and refolded blankets that didn't need to be refolded. She'd just finished spot-checking the furniture for dust—there was none—when Christopher came through the front door carrying her parent's luggage.

"Is dinner ready?" Rachel asked as he came inside.

"Yup."

"Okay," she said, turning to Anna-Beth. "Mamma, take whatever time you need to freshen up then come back up to the house."

"I'll need to change," Anna-Beth stated.

"You do not need to dress for dinner." Rachel rolled her eyes.

Anna-Beth glanced down at her pressed trousers, sweater, and low heels. "This is hardly proper dinner attire."

Christopher gave Rachel a sideways glance.

"It's a ranch, Mamma. We tend to keep things pretty casual around here."

Anna-Beth blinked at her.

Rachel pinched the bridge of her nose and looked at her feet. "Please tell me you didn't bring an entire suitcase full of Chanel."

Tom chuckled. "Given that her entire wardrobe is Chanel."

"Whatever." Rachel rolled her eyes. "Wear what you want, do what you want, but don't take too long." She glanced down at her mother's feet. "Did you at least bring boots or sneakers or some sort of shoes that can get muddy, because they will."

"What exactly do you presume I'll be doing while I'm here? Mucking out horse stalls?" Anna-Beth asked.

"Um, no, unless you want to." Rachel was doing her best to be nice, but heels and Chanel suits were hardly appropriate attire for the ranch.

"I'm sure Jackie wouldn't mind the help," Christopher added.

"No, she'd be more than happy to have whatever help you wanted to give. Your shoes, however, will get ruined just from going outside. There aren't paved paths everywhere. It's mostly dirt and gravel, because, again, it's a working cattle ranch." She glared at her mother's heels. "What size shoes do you wear? Eight?"

"Yes," Anna-Beth replied.

"I will get you proper shoes and socks to borrow."

"That's not necessary, Rachel," Anna-Beth protested.

"It really, really is." Rachel shook her head. "Babe, can you give them the tour and I'll meet you back at the house?"

"Sure," Christopher agreed.

She gave him a peck on the cheek then sprinted out the door and up to the main house. She burst through the door to find Mary in the kitchen.

"Dinner is almost ready," Mary told her.

"Great." Rachel looked around the house. "None of you are a size eight shoe, are you?"

"I think Sara is. Why?"

"My mother thinks her overly expensive heels are going to get her around. She needs boots. I'm a size nine so that won't work. Jackie, I presume, has tiny feet, given that she's tiny."

Mary chuckled. "Sara should be headed up here. Give her a call."

Rachel popped her earbuds in and called Sara as she ran around the house, making sure it, too, would appease her mother.

Sara answered on the first ring. "What's so urgent it can't wait 'till I see you at dinner?"

Rachel explained the situation with her mother's shoes in one breath.

"I got you covered," Sara told her. "Any preference of color?"

"If you have one black and one brown pair . . . I have no idea what she brought with her, and she's very particular about things matching."

"I'm sure she's not that bad," Sara said.

"You ever watch Gilmore Girls?"

"Yes."

"My mother is Emily Gilmore, but Southern. So, it's worse."

Sara burst out laughing. "Should be a fun few days then! I'll bring her some options to pick from."

After dinner, Bob was cleaning his rifle on the front porch while the rest of the family cleaned the kitchen and packed up leftovers.

Rachel walked out onto the porch, whiskey in hand, and watched Bob for a moment. "May I help you with that?" she offered as politely as she could manage. She'd already been called obsessive and gotten kicked out of the kitchen for micromanaging people's cleaning.

"You want to clean my rifle for me?" Bob raised an eyebrow at her.

"Rachel, Bob is doing a fine job with his rifle." Tom's tone was stern as he looked over Rachel's shoulder at Bob.

"Fine?" Rachel winced.

"Ignore her, Bob. She's a perfectionist." Tom sighed.

Rachel pressed her lips together, willing herself to stay quiet and polite.

Christopher chuckled as he walked out onto the porch and saw what was going on.

"Have at it, Rachel." Bob shook his head. "Less work for me."

Rachel immediately took the rifle apart and started over, entirely unconvinced that Bob had done a thorough job. "Babe, go get me a refill. This is gonna take a while." Rachel nodded towards her glass.

"I got you, Rachel!" Jackie said happily as she came out and leaned up against the porch railing, whiskey bottle in hand. Sara, Mary, and Anna-Beth were right behind her.

"Chris, you wanna come out with me? We've got a coyote harassing the calves," Bob asked.

"Sure," Christopher said. "Anyone else want to come hunt a coyote?"

"As in, you're gonna kill it?" Rachel glanced up at them and stopped working on the rifle.

"Yes," Bob and Christopher both said.

"No," Rachel answered definitively. "I'm not going to murder an innocent little coyote, essentially a dog, just because it got hungry and wandered over by a cow."

"It didn't just wander over by a cow," Bob said. "It attacked a calf that we've now had to put down."

"Then I guess we're having veal for dinner," Rachel said.

Christopher laughed. "You seriously aren't coming?"

"Are you going to eat the coyote after you kill it?" Rachel asked.

"No," Christopher cringed.

"Then I'm not going to help you kill it."

Christopher stared at Rachel, shaking his head. "I'm surprised. You don't usually shy away from shooting things."

Rachel cocked her head to the side and stared at him with disbelief.

"Yeah, Chris, she won't kill any animal she isn't going to eat," Tom explained. "She could shoot a buck straight through the eye by the time she was nine years old, but then she'd have to go and pet it and thank it for providing her with food. It was a whole thing. Sure made hunting take a lot longer than it needed to."

"Well, you didn't really need to kill five deer in one day, Daddy," Rachel argued. "How much were we really gonna eat? It's a waste of life."

"It's hunting!" Tom countered.

"God gave humans dominion over nature. That means it's our responsibility to care for nature and protect it, not go around killing everything unnecessarily. Genesis 1:26, in case anyone wants to look it up. There's also Luke 12:6: 'Are not five sparrows sold for two pennies? And not one of them is forgotten before God.' So, if you're gonna kill something, you'd best be thanking that animal for its sacrifice because that's what Jesus would want you to do," Rachel pointed out.

Mary laughed. "Well, there you go. I'd say she wins again."

Rachel turned her attention back to Christopher. "Are you going to pray for the coyote when you kill it?"

"Sure, baby. I promise I definitely will. Any specific deity that's in charge of coyotes?" He smiled at her.

"Not that I know of off the top of my head, but the Aztecs or Native Americans probably have one, so I'll google it for you before you go."

"Don't feel obligated to indulge her," Tom told Christopher.

"No, she's right. We're taking a life. It's a serious thing."

"Do you pray every time you step on a bug?" Tom teased.

"As a matter of fact, yes, I do." Rachel glowered.

"I thought you didn't believe in God?" Anna-Beth glared at her daughter.

"I don't believe in church and organized religion. I believe in several gods, and karma and reincarnation," Rachel corrected. "Killing innocent people, innocent animals, is gonna fuck up your karma." She glared at Christopher.

"Don't a lot of cultures believe that feeding animals helps you accumulate good karma?" Christopher asked.

"Yes."

He shrugged. "Dad feeds the cattle every day, and I feed you, so I think we'll be okay."

Rachel rolled her eyes. "I do not count as an animal, thank you very much."

Christopher chuckled. "I think I'll be okay."

"Fine, I suppose you will be. I guess I'm the one who has to worry," Rachel mumbled as she took another sip of whiskey and got back to cleaning Bob's rifle.

"Seriously?" Christopher gave her a sideways glance. "All the self-sacrifice and doing things for the greater good, never letting yourself actually want anything? I'd say your karmic balance is leaning towards good too."

Rachel shrugged. "I dunno. I've got a lot of bad karma to make up for, even if some of it was allegedly done for the greater good . . . Well, that's a matter of opinion, really." She took a long sip of her whiskey then refilled her glass.

Christopher gave her a questioning look.

"History is written by the victors," Rachel explained. "They decide what is right and wrong, true and untrue. If you win a war, of course you're going to make your own cause out to be the righteous one. However, your enemy believes their cause is the righteous one too, or else there wouldn't be a war happening in the first place. It's just a matter of opinion." She shrugged and looked at Christopher. "You've listened to the shit on the radio when we're over there. It's the same shit they tell us over here. 'We're the good guys, we're right, kill the enemy.' It's all just propaganda." She shrugged and took another drink.

"Are you drunk?" Tom glared at her.

"Not yet." Rachel chuckled.

Tom moved the whiskey bottle and Rachel's glass out of her reach.

She shook her head and rolled her eyes at him and kept talking. "Humans are indoctrinated by the society they live in from day one. I don't think there's ever been a civilization that taught its people that what they were doing was wrong or bad. Humans can justify just about anything if they try hard enough, and our brains are hardwired for conformity and pattern recognition. So as soon as we see something different or something that conflicts with what we've been indoctrinated to believe is good or correct, then an alarm goes off in our heads and we think threat, evil, enemy."

"You signed up for the Navy to fight a war, even though you think it's all propaganda?" Sara wrinkled her nose.

"Here we go." Christopher muttered under his breath. They'd gotten Rachel going now, and she was intoxicated enough that there would be no filter on this monologue.

"No. I know which parts are propaganda and which parts are true. I also never claimed to be fighting the war they think I'm fighting, the one they want me to be fighting. I don't give a shit about oil or politics or which stupid old man is making dumb rules in what territory, or the petty squabbles of old men who disagree about minuscule details in some book they think is magic. And those books are only magic and give them power and influence because of indoctrination, by the way." Rachel glared at Anna-Beth. "You know I'm fighting the real war." She smiled, turning to Christopher.

"What the hell war is that?" Tom asked, shocked and appalled.

"The war to overthrow the patriarchy and end the global subjugation of women," Rachel said matter-of-factly, as though she couldn't believe he didn't already know.

"Yes, I'm well aware of that." Christopher's eyes went wide.

"Explain," Tom ordered.

"Explain what? Surely you understand what *patriarchy* means, as well as the words *subjugation* and *women*. Which part is confusing?"

"What you're doing to fight it." Tom enunciated every word.

"Oh. That. Well . . ." She pursed her lips and averted her eyes.

"Tom, I'm not really sure this is the right venue for *that* conversation," Christopher pointed out.

Tom raised his eyebrows and gave his daughter a disapproving look.

"What? Everything's in line with the Geneva Convention . . ." Rachel responded with a one-shouldered shrug, as though it were no big deal.

Christopher choked on his laughter and looked down at his feet.

"Jesus Christ, Rachel!" Tom chastised her, noting Christopher's amused expression. He and Bob stared at her, shocked, while Anna-Beth and Mary exchanged confused looks.

"What's the Geneva Convention?" Jackie asked innocently.

"It's like the rules for what you can do in war," Sara whispered.

"Don't forget," Tom continued. His index finger was inches away from Rachel's face. "I have access to your mission reports, even if they are partially redacted. I know what the SEAL teams report, and I can imagine just fine what y'all are doing that's getting left out of those reports."

"Then why did you ask?" Rachel was genuinely confused.

"Anyway," Mary interjected, trying to change the subject. "Any specific requests for Thanksgiving? What kind of pie does everyone want? Pumpkin or—"

"I mean, you know how it is, Daddy. Or maybe you don't, I don't know, but the rules of engagement can change in a heartbeat. That's not *my* fault," Rachel asserted, hand to heart.

"I think the rules of engagement are pretty clear, Rachel," Tom argued.

"They most definitely are not." Rachel stared at Tom for a minute, trying to figure out what he wasn't comprehending. "Daddy, how would you define a terrorist?" She locked eyes with him and relaxed back in her chair.

"You're really going to have this conversation right here in front of everyone?" Christopher asked, glancing over at Sara and Jackie. He knew the more relaxed Rachel's posture was, the more prepared she was to fight, the more confident she was that she'd already won. This was the calm before the storm.

"Yes, if he's gonna sit there and try to accuse me of war crimes, I sure as hell am," Rachel replied before looking at her father again. "Answer the question, Daddy."

"A terrorist is a person who employs terror or terrorism, especially as a political weapon," Tom answered, quoting the dictionary definition.

"Precisely." Rachel pointed at him. "Now you just need to figure out your interpretation of the words *terror*, *terrorism*, and *political weapon*, because

I'd guess that's where we disagree. For example, I'm guessing you wouldn't consider a rapist to be a terrorist based on that crime alone, would you?"

"No, because how is that terror or a political weapon? It's a crime, a very terrible crime that should be punished, but it isn't terrorism."

"Except for when it is." Rachel paused. "The Islamic State uses rape to terrorize the general population into submission all the time. You *do* know that women who accuse men of rape in some Muslim countries are punished for zina, which is unlawful sexual intercourse? The punishment for zina is traditionally one hundred lashes, although stoning happens too. The Western interpretation of Sharia Law makes a distinction between unlawful sexual intercourse, meaning sex outside the confines of marriage, and rape, and interprets the law to mean that the rapist would be punished for zina but not the victim, assuming of course she had enough evidence to prove it was rape, which let's face it, no one ever does. We have that same problem with evidence and testimony here too, I might add. But several governments, or terrorist factions, are interpreting Sharia Law differently and using it to gain power, maintain political influence, and keep women from being allowed to fight back, because I think they all know if women fought back, we'd win. So, tell me again how a rapist, in this sort of circumstance, isn't also a terrorist? Especially when he's friends with all the terrorists we're tracking. He is using a political weapon—in this case, a fucked up, in my opinion, interpretation of Sharia Law to inflict terror on a woman. All women, actually. It's terrorism, per your own definition. So occasionally, extra targets and side missions get added to our to-do list to deal with these sorts of situations. Or maybe you think a rape victim *should* be stoned because she can't get enough evidence to prove her case? Which really, how could she, when she's not allowed to do anything to get that evidence, and no one believes anything she says and the man who raped her just has to lie and say she consented and then it's fine?"

"Yeah, that happens kind of a lot actually." Christopher's jaw clenched. "And it seems like we're always the ones who get to deal with it."

"Well yeah, I'm sure it's more convenient for the Navy to just retraumatize us than to fuck everyone up," Rachel complained.

"Plus, you're so good at dealing with it!" Christopher laughed.

"I know. I'm perfectly comfortable playing by their rules. Fight sin with sin," Rachel said solemnly. "Me being stuck at Command and you retiring probably set the war back at least a decade . . . But it's fine. There are enough battles to be fought here too," she said to Christopher.

"You mean from Command?" Tom asked.

"Yeah, that too, I guess." Rachel shrugged.

"I'm afraid to ask . . ." Tom started.

"Then don't."

"Christopher," Tom tried to reason, "please tell me she understands that she can't go around exacting vigilante justice on people."

"Well, I would have to be more discreet," Rachel said absently.

"You're always discrete," Christopher told her. "Except when the whole point is to not be."

"Yeah, I do hate cleaning up." Rachel wrinkled her nose. "Besides, if we're gonna talk about people doing fucked up shit in times of war . . ." She glared at her father. "How many innocent civilians had to go without electricity for how many weeks and months because of all those fucked up cyber-ops you and your friends like so much? Shutting down nuclear reactors just to piss off a certain government? Really, how is that not against the Geneva Convention?"

"National security," Tom barked.

Rachel rolled her eyes. "My teams are still cleaning up that particular mess. In any case, allow me to illustrate my point." She pressed play on a video she had saved on her phone, which Samir Al-Abadi had recently disseminated as a warning to women everywhere.

"These women are trying to take the place of men," Samir said, sitting cross-legged on a scarlet red velvet cushion. *"If they do not stop, we will force them to submit. We will force their daughters and granddaughters to submit and force their fathers and husbands to watch."* He proceeded to rattle off a list of women in Afghanistan working at the radio and television stations, working as human rights or women's rights activists, working at universities. It was a long list. *"Mothers are the heart of society. They birth children, raise them, teach them. Unfortunately, not all mothers are good mothers. Not all mothers are pious and deserving of keeping their children. That is also being corrected."*

"Case in point." Rachel shoved her phone in her father's face.

Tom sighed. "I see your point, Rachel, but there is a correct way to go about things—"

"There's a correct way, and then there's an effective way," Rachel argued. "I need a plane because I know where this idiot is," she dipped her head towards her phone, "but no one will listen."

"No, you don't need a plane, and you don't know where he is either." Christopher shook his head.

"He's with Khalid Khan outside of Jalalabad." She looked at Christopher like he was an idiot. "You can come."

Christopher's eyebrows shot up, clearly liking that idea.

"Neither of you are going anywhere," Tom stated definitively. "Do not make me make a call to get the two of you grounded."

Rachel scrunched up her face, knowing her father absolutely had the ability to block them from getting on a plane—commercial or military. "How about to the bar? Can we go to the bar?" Rachel tried.

"Yes!" Jackie exclaimed excitedly, her head shooting out of the palm of her hand. Clearly she was more interested in getting drunk than listening to Rachel argue with her father.

"Who's driving?" Sara immediately looked at Christopher.

Christopher dropped his face into his palm. "Fine. I'll be your designated driver, but I'm not staying."

"Why not?" Rachel complained.

"Because too many people I don't want to talk to are in town for Thanksgiving."

"People or girls you already slept with?" Sara teased.

"It's obviously the second one." Rachel smirked.

"How is that different from always?" Jackie teased her brother.

"Be nice, or I'll change my mind," Christopher threatened.

Jackie instantly pulled her lips between her teeth and sat up straight. "Did I mention you're the best big brother ever?"

"Yeah, yeah." Christopher rolled his eyes. "Get in the truck."

Jackie happily bounced over to Christopher's truck and climbed in. Sara stood awkwardly, glancing at Mary, who was uncharacteristically tense. Rachel didn't miss anything. She motioned for Sara to go to the truck then asked, "Mary, do you have some sort of take away mug or water bottle? Just want to be prepared so we have water with us."

Mary nodded and led her inside to the kitchen, grabbing three large water bottles out of a cupboard.

"Are you okay?" Rachel asked once they were alone.

"I'm fine," Mary said, though her voice shook as she filled the bottles with tap water.

Rachel chuckled. "I may be drunk but I'm not stupid."

Mary tried to wave her off.

"We all know Josh was the best big brother, and the best little brother," Rachel said, referring to Jackie's comment. She gave Mary a kind smile. "I know you miss him. You all do. I can't imagine how difficult this must be, holidays and all that."

Mary nodded, her eyes fixed to the floor. "Losing a child . . . it doesn't get easier. They say time heals all wounds . . ."

Rachel glanced to the framed folded flag sitting on a shelf behind the kitchen table. "By all accounts, he was the best human being ever. I wish I'd gotten to meet him. I know you believe in heaven and all that." She scrunched up her face. "You think he's in heaven?"

Mary nodded again.

"That always seemed so final to me. So one and done. I dunno. Never made sense. It's not the natural cycle of things. Everything else in nature dies and regenerates as something new. Plants and animals decompose, their bodies become nourishment for new plants . . . Heaven and hell, I dunno." She shrugged. "Reincarnation always made more sense to me. Because where does the energy and the carbon and all the other shit we're made of go when we're done? Reincarnation, I think, makes more sense. Your soul goes and takes a rest somewhere, then comes back when it's needed. When it's called for another purpose. When the other souls you're most connected to are coming back again too. You'll see Josh again, regardless of which of us is right. Either in another life or in heaven."

"I wish I'd stopped him." Mary's words were barely audible.

"From enlisting?" Rachel asked.

Another nod from Mary.

"Based on what I've heard, there's no way you could've stopped any of your kids from doing anything. They're all determined, decided. They each have a sense of purpose, in their own way. You did a good job, Mary. You made four amazing humans who grew up and followed their dreams. Who felt safe enough, physically and emotionally, to be exactly who they wanted to be, needed to be, without fear of judgement or rejection from you and Bob. Not all of us get that."

"Christopher could have stopped him. He wanted to be like Chris." Mary shook her head.

"Christopher didn't know he was going to enlist, and he'd never recommend anyone enlist. Not after the things he's seen. Don't get me wrong, he loved every day of it. But he never would have encouraged Josh to sign up for that shit."

Mary glanced up at her, hesitating a moment. "Reincarnation, huh?"

Rachel smiled. "I like the idea of getting to see my friends again. Another chance to go on adventures together, make a difference together. I hope I'm right, because the idea of lounging around in heaven, or purgatory, for the rest of eternity sounds incredibly boring. Hell, on the other hand, might be fun."

Mary shook her head. "I—"

"Everything okay?"

Rachel turned at the sound of her father's voice. "All good, just . . ." She gave a subtle wave of the hand towards the flag.

Tom's eyes followed her hand. His brow furrowed.

"Josh was five years younger than Christopher. KIA," Rachel explained.

Tom nodded. "Why don't you go out to the truck, Rachel. I think Chris is about to lose it with Jackie and Sara's teasing."

Rachel rolled her eyes. "They wouldn't be teasing him if he hadn't fucked half the county!"

That elicited a laugh from Mary. "I think the going joke is two counties."

"It's a very long list, in any case," Rachel noted. "Not that I'm one to judge . . ."

"I really don't need to know, Rachel," Tom scolded. "Go save Chris and keep Jackie and Sara safe tonight."

"Yes, sir." She dipped her head and made a quiet exit, knowing her father would know exactly how to help Mary.

Chapter 24

NOVEMBER 2020

CHRISTOPHER KNEW GOING TO the bar in Emory the night before any holiday would be a social nightmare now that he wasn't single. He really didn't want to deal with that many drunk girls at once. Especially given that he wouldn't be taking any of them home with him. Not that he wanted to. He could hardly believe it himself, but he had no desire to be with anyone but Rachel. Besides, staying home presented him with the perfect opportunity to take care of something very important. Something he needed to do—was terrified of doing—but could finally do now that Rachel's divorce was official.

As soon as he was back from dropping the girls off, he went to find Tom.

Tom was sitting on a bench near the lake, watching the sunset over the water with a bottle of whiskey next to him on the ground. Christopher smiled to himself, thinking of all the times he'd found Rachel sitting in that exact spot, doing the exact same thing. She and Tom were so similar—dedicated, hardworking, and stubborn as hell—even if Rachel would never admit it.

Christopher was nervous. He'd never thought in a million years that he'd be doing what he was about to do. But Rachel had changed everything. Being with her felt like some sort of destiny. Fate. He felt complete when he was with her, like she had put him back together, like their love had healed them both. His heart was pounding in his chest, and he took a deep breath to steady himself before approaching Tom.

"Sir, could I speak with you for a moment?" Christopher asked.

"Sure! Come have a seat, Chris."

Christopher walked over but didn't sit. "I wanted to ask you . . . Your daughter means everything to me. She's my whole world. I know you disapproved at first, and given the circumstances, you were right to. But I love her more than life itself, and I'm confident she feels the same way. I plan to make it my mission in life to ensure that she's happy and safe and can feel grounded. I know it's only been a few months, and this may seem fast, but it's really been closer to twelve years. Eleven years and eleven months that I've spent supporting her and caring for her as best as I could, given the situation. I was hoping, sir," Christopher reached into his pocket and pulled out a small blue box, "I'd like your blessing to ask Rachel to marry me." He opened the box, exposing an elegant two carat, emerald cut diamond solitaire set in white gold.

Tom nodded. "Christopher, I have never seen Rachel happy—I mean truly happy—until I saw her with you. Not even when she was a little girl. It was obvious already when you came to San Diego how the two of you felt about each other. That's probably why I overreacted after she got injured and you put in your papers for retirement. Happiness is the only thing I've ever wanted for her. So yes, you have my blessing." He paused. "But I have one condition."

"Of course, sir."

"Would you, for the love of God, please make her wear an actual wedding dress when I walk her down the aisle and not her dress whites?"

Christopher couldn't help but laugh. "Yes, sir, I think I can manage that. I can probably even convince her to invite guests and make it a proper wedding. Probably won't be able to convince her to have a pastor though."

"Good enough for me." Tom chuckled. "Try to get her to slow down on work too."

"Oh, that's never gonna happen." Christopher shook his head. "I will make sure she eats though."

Tom smiled at the ground. "Yeah, she needs help with that too." He shook his head. "Christopher," Tom said, seriously. "I know I said some things when she was in the hospital that I most definitely should not have thought, let alone said out loud."

Christopher nodded.

"I owe you an apology."

"Thank you," Christopher said. "Honestly, though, you were just being a scared father. I mean, you did kind of accuse her of some crazy things, but that's between you and her. I've kind of understood. Or, well, Carter's alluded to some things over the years. She's not some crazy, out-of-control kid anymore though." Christopher thought back to the exchange of stories when they had been having lunch at the White House. Rachel taking her father's car off base when she was fourteen, telling him she had to go buy tampons as though there wasn't a store on base that she probably could have walked to. It had all be chocked up to Rachel being an unruly teenager rather than a sign that something serious was going on.

Tom tensed. "What's the deal there? Last I checked, she and Carter were married. What the two of them were thinking with *that*, I do *not* know."

"They're divorced as of a few days ago," Christopher explained. "She just needed a legal next of kin on her call sheet since . . ." He bit the inside of his cheek and looked away.

"Since she didn't want me to know she was in combat." Tom nodded. "I definitely would have gotten her reassigned if I'd known," he admitted with a sigh. "I need to stop worrying about her, don't I?" His eyes met Christopher's.

"Do parents ever stop worrying about their children? If so, maybe you can give my mom some tips." Christopher chuckled.

"Your mom." Tom shook his head and looked at the ground. "I didn't know about your brother. Parents always worry about their kids, especially when they join up. I've spoken with a lot of concerned parents over the years. I've been a concerned parent. But I had the power to put my kids—well, Jamie at least—into a role where he'd mostly be out of danger and the knowledge to know at what point I really needed to worry. When someone dies . . ."

Tom winced. "A KIA is never easy on a family, but when there's a sibling on active duty too, it always makes things more difficult. In my day, mothers had to give permission to have more than one son in Vietnam at a time. It was that dangerous. That bad of a situation. We've had so many wars going on, keeping siblings from being in-country or being in a conflict at the same time has been impossible."

Christopher nodded. "We were never in the same place at the same time. Josh went through basic training then he was stationed on a ship in the Persian Gulf. I was in Afghanistan at the time, not technically in the thick of things, but . . . Well, Afghanistan in 2008, as you may recall—"

"Holidays are hard. Extra hard when grief comes into play." Tom locked eyes with Christopher. "It'll be easier on your mom if you make an effort to be home for either Thanksgiving or Christmas, if you can't do both . . . It would mean a lot to her, I think. Anna-Beth and I have given up on Rachel ever being home. But coming here? It helps your mom a lot. Rachel's more relaxed here. Didn't know it was possible to get her to relax. She's wound so tight all the time. I appreciate you including us. I know it wasn't Rachel's idea for us to come out here for Thanksgiving."

"No, that was my idea," Christopher confirmed.

Tom looked at his feet. "I'm happy she has you. She's been on her own for too long."

Christopher smiled and shook his head. "No, she hasn't been alone for quite a while. Not since BUD/s. She's a SEAL. She needs anything, she's got at least a hundred people who would drop whatever they were doing to help her. Granted, that requires that she admits that she wants or needs help . . . But our whole team, our whole squadron really, is in contact with each other more or less constantly. We know when someone's not okay."

Tom nodded. "What about you, Chris? What's next?"

"Next?" Christopher's eyebrows knitted together.

"I realize taking care of Rachel may be a full-time job." Tom chuckled. "But you may want to come up with something to do while she's at work?"

"Right." Christopher pressed his lips into a tight line. He'd been avoiding this issue for months. "I have no idea. I guess I've never really had any idea.

High school football got me to college, and then a Navy recruiter made driving around the Middle East sound fun. I guess it's sort of back to 'what do you want to be when you grow up?'"

Tom smiled. "You'll figure it out. You're smart and talented. But I get it. Better to find something you enjoy. It's not the same, I know, but the day they told me I couldn't fly anymore . . . I still do sometimes, but not in combat. Perks of being an admiral, I guess. No one wants to tell me no, so some of the pilots let me co-pilot with them." He sighed. "When your job becomes such a part of your identity—being a fighter pilot, being a SEAL—you've got to reinvent yourself a bit. Somehow, I ended up working on cyber-ops. No idea how. I didn't know shit about computers when I got the assignment. You're in a position where you can take time to figure out what you want to do."

"Yeah, not really sure what jobs require map reading, running, and killing people as top skills," Christopher joked.

Tom burst out laughing. "Navy SEAL is just about all I can think of!" He shook his head. "Really, Chris, you don't regret retiring? You don't miss it?"

"Not for a second. I know Rachel's worried I will. That I'll resent that she can't tell me stuff." He winked. "She's not as good at keeping secrets as she thinks though."

"You'll figure it out. Just remember to take care of yourself first. Rachel can sort out her own shit, and you won't be able to help her if you haven't dealt with your own issues, right?"

"I guess."

"If you make Rachel your everything, your main project, you'll end up resenting her. You'll be sitting around, waiting for her to get home." Tom sighed. "I know neither of you really get along with Anna-Beth, but dealing with an active duty workaholic is something she has a lot of experience with. Before Jamie was born, she'd ask every morning what time I'd be home. I'd tell her whatever time I planned to be home, and every night, I was late. She'd be sitting at the dining table, food cold and pissed off." He paused. "You understand the job, obviously, but it still won't be easy. You've got to find something that doesn't involve Rachel to entertain yourself with, or it's not going to work."

"I'm helping Hunter with that refugee fundraiser."

Tom's brow furrowed.

"Trischa Verity was trying to get Rachel to help plan an event."

"How the hell'd you get roped into that?"

"The funds are going to a nonprofit run by a friend of a friend. Rachel doesn't trust Hunter, or Frank for that matter, and asked me to chaperone."

Tom sighed. "What the hell does she think Frank's gonna do? And Hunter's harmless. A bit annoying, sort of stupid." He smirked then shook his head. "Hunter . . . well, he had a thing for her and was very persistent for a while. She, of course, wasn't the least bit interested. The way Jamie tells it, Hunter asked her to marry him, and she kicked him in the balls."

"That sounds about right." Christopher grimaced. He'd been on the receiving end of Rachel's kicks enough times to know it must've hurt like hell, and he suddenly felt some sympathy for Hunter.

"Her issue with Frank? I don't get it. He's a good man."

Christopher chose his words carefully, knowing Frank was Tom's best friend. "Rachel has really high standards for people."

Tom locked eyes with him. "What aren't you saying?"

"When we had our planning meeting, Frank seemed dead set on getting Ashley alone with him. It was a bit—"

Tom sighed. "Frank's always been overly charismatic. He'd never actually *do* anything."

Christopher shrugged. "Rachel asked me to keep an eye on it, so I'm keeping an eye on it. And getting a bunch of kids from a refugee camp in Kabul to the White House since that seemed far beyond Hunter's skill set."

"Hunter has always excelled at getting other people to do things for him. It's gotten Jamie in plenty of trouble. Hence why Jamie is on a ship out at sea where he can't do anything too stupid."

A low chuckle escaped Christopher's lips. "Oh, you definitely would have pulled Rachel from combat if you'd known."

"I would've pulled her from BUD/s if I'd known! I had gotten her stationed on a ship too where she would be mostly safe, sitting around analyzing intel. Then she came home and told me she'd gotten off the ship and started running around like the arrogant idiot she is." He shook his head. "My daughter playing hero and coming home with bullet wounds is *not* what I had in mind. She wanted to go into intelligence, fine. Sitting in a windowless room, piecing together scraps of intel, sounded like a great job for Rachel, as long as they let her run around a bit to get her energy out." He shook his head. "Don't get me wrong, I'm proud of her. Of the things I know about, that is. Even I don't have access to her full service record. Too many joint ops with the CIA. But that's what Special Projects is for so . . ." He shrugged. "Damned impressive the things the two of you did over there."

"We only did what needed to be done. Nothing more, nothing less."

"It's okay to be proud, Chris. I know humility is sort of built into all of you. Fucking SEALs. You're a special breed, that's for sure. Tough as shit. Potentially insane." He chuckled. "Well, if that doesn't describe my daughter to a tee."

"We've all decided to call it calculated risk taking." Christopher winked.

Rachel and Jackie were dancing on the bar and singing, with Sara filming them on her phone, when Rachel caught sight of Christopher moving through the crowd. Once the song was over, Rachel locked eyes with him and started belting out Taylor Swift's "King of My Heart" and Jackie jumped in on backup vocals. Every single person had their full attention on Rachel, watching her sing and dance, her moves becoming more seductive as she made her way across the bar.

The rest of the bar disappeared. They had been apart for less than six hours, but it felt like an eternity. She had been having a great time with Sara and Jackie, but nothing compared to being near Christopher. She wanted to be with him constantly and hated when they were apart. He was everything to her, everything that really mattered anyway. The only person who had ever understood her, ever truly loved *her*.

Plenty of people, men mostly, had told her they loved her, were *in* love with her even, but she knew it had just been sex and some primal desire for possession and dominance on their part. They didn't see her, didn't know her, and probably didn't have any interest in really getting to know her either. Christopher, though. He *knew* her, maybe better than she knew herself. He had never tried to change her or control her. Maybe he'd recommended some alternative behaviors or tried to get her to slow down on occasion, mostly out of interest for her own safety, but he accepted and loved her just as she was. And she knew him, understood him, in a way most people never could. They were so deeply interconnected: emotionally, spiritually, physically. The whole world made sense when they were together, and every struggle, every hardship, melted away into oblivion. There was no problem they couldn't solve together and no trauma they couldn't overcome.

Christopher waited for her to finish the song before he reached up and put his hands on her hips to lift her down so that she was sitting on the bar. She wrapped her legs around him and had her tongue down his throat in seconds. The entire bar erupted in applause and cheers.

"Take me home," Rachel requested. Christopher helped her hop down from the bar and put his arm around her shoulders. She slid her arm around his waist, and he signaled to Sara that it was time to go.

"I lost Jackie," Sara said as she wandered over to Christopher.

"No, she's in the bathroom deciding something," Rachel said.

"Deciding what?" Christopher asked.

"Give her a few minutes. These sorts of decisions take time," Rachel said.

"Oh God, who's she in there with?" Sara asked, laughing.

Christopher sighed and looked at the ceiling.

"That guy with the restored '67 Mustang. I don't remember his name. But he's cute, and then obviously there's the car—"

"Ben Henley!" Sara exclaimed. Rachel shrugged.

Christopher rolled his eyes. "Does she have to sleep with *all* of my friends?"

"Babe, it's a small town. I think she'd have very limited options if she had to avoid anyone you are or ever had been friends with. Besides, I mean, just the car would be enough."

Christopher laughed, knowing where she was going. "What? A pickup truck isn't good enough for you anymore?" Christopher joked.

Rachel smiled mischievously. "No, no, pickup trucks are incredibly practical. I guess I'll have to show you just how practical sometime. I mean, there's a reason they call the back a bed," she said seductively.

Just then, Jackie came sauntering over to them, arm in arm with Ben Henley.

"Good, our ride's here!" Jackie exclaimed.

"And where is it I'm taking you, Jackie?" Christopher asked as they all headed out to his truck.

"Home," she said, as though it should have been obvious.

"Ben, really?" Christopher glared at him.

"We're just recycling!" Ben joked.

"Yeah, I never fucked your sister."

"Not due to a lack of trying!" Ben teased.

"I do not sleep with my friends' sisters!" Christopher insisted.

"You should really be used to this by now." Jackie smiled gleefully. "You know we've been hooking up on and off for, like, seven years or something."

Christopher's jaw clenched. Rachel tightened her arm around his waist, knowing it was time to change the subject. "Hey Ben? Can I drive your Mustang sometime?"

Ben looked at Christopher to get a hint on how he should answer.

"She's a good driver. Your car will be fine."

"Sure, you can drive my car," Ben answered.

"Can I drive it?" Jackie asked enthusiastically.

"No," Christopher and Ben said in unison.

"Why does Rachel get to?" Jackie complained.

"Jackie, once you've navigated a truck through an IED field at top speed while taking heavy machine gunfire and yelling at a bunch of people on a radio, then we'll consider letting you drive a car that costs over seventy thousand dollars and is almost impossible to find replacement parts for," Christopher explained.

"My horse trailer cost more than that!" Jackie protested.

"Yeah, but it doesn't go nearly as fast," Ben pointed out.

"Rachel, did you really drive a truck through an IED field at top speed while taking heavy fire?" Sara asked, clearly impressed. "I'm surprised Chris let anyone else drive."

"Christopher was incapacitated at the time," Rachel explained.

"Incapacitated how?" Sara asked.

"He had a bullet lodged in his right knee and a fairly severe concussion."

"Yeah, that wasn't the best day. It wasn't the time I was thinking of though . . ." Christopher said, watching Rachel's face carefully.

"I had fun. I mean, once you finally shut up about how I stole your car keys and was mean for not letting you drive!" Everyone started laughing. "Seriously! Our medic had to sedate him. He was being such a pain in the ass," Rachel said humorously. "And Aiden was riding next to me, on the sat phone with HQ and on the handheld radio with local command trying to get anyone to agree on where we could go . . ." She trailed off.

The humor in her voice was suddenly replaced by sadness and painful grief as her mind flashed back to the mission she had just been telling everyone about. Images of death, destruction, and blood competed for space in her mind with the sounds of explosions and distant voices on a shoddy radio as she asked repeatedly for Command to repeat what they were saying. Rachel never had figured out if she'd needed them to repeat themselves so many times because she actually couldn't hear or because she simply hadn't been able to comprehend what they'd been saying. She had been twenty-nine years old, months shy of her thirtieth birthday, and had been a SEAL for four and a half years, not including the year of training. She remembered the voice next to her telling her to turn, telling her to respond to Command on the radio. Aiden had been forced to take over as navigator, second in command, and do his job as communications expert while Matt had desperately tried to patch people up. Rachel had had to do everything else. There was too much loss involved in that story. Too much pain. She wanted to lock it back away. The driving part had been fun, momentarily at least, but the rest? She couldn't let herself think about the rest.

They got to the truck and Christopher opened the front passenger side door for Rachel. She climbed in and slid into the middle seat as he walked around to the driver's side. Sara slid in next to her while Jackie and Ben got in the backseat. Christopher started the truck and put on some music, desperate to elevate the mood again. Jackie either hadn't noticed the mood had taken a dip or she didn't care. She was happily making out with Ben in the back seat.

Christopher saw that Rachel was lost in thought and suspected where her mind had taken her. He knew it was going to be a bad night. He hadn't meant to bring up those memories for her, for either of them. She'd driven trucks through IED fields countless times. He hadn't thought mentioning that would trigger this. There had been plenty of times when he had been driving the lead vehicle and she'd been following close behind in the second. Mentioning her driving through an IED field while taking heavy fire could have triggered any number of memories, but as soon as she'd mentioned the bullet in his knee, he knew where she'd gone.

He made a right-hand turn into the main driveway of the ranch and then a left, heading down the path towards their cabins. He dropped Jackie and Ben off first, happy to not have to watch them in the back seat anymore, before continuing on to Sara's cabin. He pulled over and parked so that she could get out, then opened his door too, climbing out of the truck and pulling Rachel out with him.

"We'll be back for breakfast!" Christopher shouted to Sara. Then he squeezed Rachel's hand before they took off running up the hill and out into the dense oak forest surrounding the ranch.

They ran two miles before Rachel slowed down. "I'm too drunk to run this fast," she admitted.

Christopher laughed and pulled her into him for a hug. She tilted her head up and kissed him softly on the lips. "Have I told you lately how much I love you?" she asked.

"No, it's been at least six hours," Christopher said before kissing her again.

"Well, I do love you," Rachel continued. She looked deep into his eyes as the moonlight peeked through the tree branches, giving everything a soft iridescent glow. She couldn't believe it had taken them eleven years to get here. They had pretended for so long that they didn't feel this way, but she wouldn't have changed a second of it. Every glance, every accidental touch of the hand, every hug, every night sleeping out in the desert or sharing a room while on leave, every argument about how many Taylor Swift songs were acceptable to play in a row while on a road trip together. It should have been obvious the whole time. She remembered all the times they'd woken up together, a little closer to each other than they should have been and all the times she'd been sad or mad or scared, and he'd taken her in his arms and held her close, promising her everything would get better.

Christopher kissed Rachel on the forehead and led her over to a hollow in the woods. He knew every inch of this forest and sat down in the soft damp grass and pulled Rachel down to sit between his legs. She had her back against his chest, and he wrapped his arms tightly around her as they looked up at the stars.

"That was a rough mission," Rachel said. "The driving part was kinda fun, if you don't think about how dangerous it actually was."

Christopher nodded.

"I was happy we got Ryan on the team after that, so I didn't have to be the backup driver anymore. I love driving, but it's hard to drive and yell at command at the same time," Rachel noted.

"Yeah, that was the last mission before you officially took over the team, wasn't it?" Christopher remembered.

"Just another consolation prize. It's not a good way to take over. When you lose people or they get injured and can't come back. And now Matt has to deal with all that, now that I'm not going back." It was the first time Rachel had admitted out loud that she wasn't going back to a combat zone, that she was done fighting. "It could have been worse. At least I still get to watch from command, I could be . . ."

Christopher's eyes welled with tears. He didn't want to think about what could be, what would have happened if Matt hadn't acted so quickly, hadn't been able to think on his feet and improvise. Rachel would have died. That was for certain. Images of her bleeding in Matt's arms—bleeding on the floor of the helicopter, images of Matt pulling supplies out of a poorly stocked medic kit to set up a direct blood transfusion in the back of a helicopter—flashed through his mind, together with images from the mission when Rachel had been forced to take over leadership. It hadn't been under happy circumstances, that was for sure. She'd gotten a battlefield promotion to Commander and had been informed that she was team leader since their former team leader was dead. They'd both been awarded the Navy Cross after that, but neither of them had wanted to accept it.

"Christopher," Rachel interrupted his train of thought. "Can you make me forget? Just for a little while, I need to forget it all. It's too much."

Christopher kissed the back of her head and released his arms from around her so she could turn around to face him. She was on her knees looking at him, her eyes wild with panic and fear. He put his hand on the back of her head and kissed her with as much fervor as he could, all while reaching under her shirt with his other hand, moving it up along her back. She pulled up his shirt, sliding it off over his head, before pushing him to the ground and climbing on top of him. He pulled off her shirt, then she unbuttoned his pants. Within seconds, they were naked, and she was on her back. He hovered over her, kissing her everywhere and letting his carnal, primal instincts take over as he moved down her body. His tongue was on her, two fingers inside of her, forcing her to roll her hips and arch her back as he edged her towards climax.

CHAPTER 25:

NOVEMBER 2020

RACHEL WOKE UP ON the forest floor tightly entangled in Christopher's arms. He was running his fingers through her hair, trying to get her to wake up.

"What's going on?" Rachel asked.

"Are you sober?"

"Yes . . ." Rachel drew out the word, wondering why the hell it mattered.

"We're going for a ride," Christopher explained. "Get up." He nudged her off of him, stood, then pulled her up, giving her a light kiss on the forehead before clasping her hand and pulling her towards the barn at a jog.

Jackie was feeding the horses when they got there. "Are you here to help?"

"No. We're here to steal some horses," Christopher explained.

"Where are you taking my horses?"

"Cash is *my* horse, first of all, and we're going up to the ridge. We'll likely be late to breakfast."

"Fine. Take Tundra and Cash, but only if you do something to fix my headache," Jackie complained.

Christopher chuckled and got Cash and Tundra's tack out of the tack room. "Rache, can you start while I help Jackie?"

"Sure." Rachel's brow furrowed. She was a much better medic than Christopher was, so the division of tasks wasn't exactly logical. She hurriedly brushed Tundra while Christopher sat with Jackie in the tack room. They kept a medic kit in there in case of accidents or injuries, and she figured he was running Jackie a saline IV to combat her hangover.

A few minutes later, Christopher was by her side, grooming and tacking up Cash, clearly in a hurry for some reason.

They got to the top of the ridge as the sun was rising, and the sky was igniting into ribbons of orange and pink. Christopher took Rachel by the hand and led her over to the large old oak tree. He stood face-to-face with Rachel, looking down at her. She was absolutely stunning. He brushed the hair out of her face and stared deep into her eyes with his hands on her waist and her palms on his chest.

"Rachel, ever since the first day we met, I've been captivated by your strength, your intelligence, and your grace. Watching you act consistently with compassion and bravery has motivated me to be a better man so that I might one day get to stand here with you and have you look at me with the same amount of love, respect, and devotion that I have felt for you for longer than either of us really cares to admit." He paused as they each let out a tiny laugh. "I'm always happiest on the days I get to spend with you and think about you constantly when we're apart. I want to spend this day, and all the rest of my days with you as your best friend, your confidant, and if you'd grant me the honor, your husband." Christopher took a shiny two carat emerald cut diamond ring out of his pocket and dropped to one knee.

Rachel was stunned. She clasped both hands over her mouth to keep from squealing.

"Rachel Marie Ryker, will you marry me?"

"Yes! Oh my god! Yes, yes of course yes!" Rachel exclaimed, bouncing up and down. He slid the ring onto her finger and stood up, putting his hands on the sides of her face and giving her a long, tender kiss as she held her hands on his waist, pulling him in as close as she could.

Christopher couldn't help but laugh as Rachel tried to escalate things. "There is one stipulation to this."

"What?" Rachel asked, amused.

"I might have promised your father that I'd make you wear a wedding dress and let him walk you down the aisle rather than letting you wear your uniform."

Rachel burst out laughing. "I think I can do that. Wait? You talked to my dad?"

"Yeah."

Rachel rolled her eyes. "You are too perfect!"

"He also requested that I make you slow down at work . . . I told him that wasn't possible, but that I'd promise to feed you."

Rachel shook her head. "Can't slow down."

"I know." Christopher pulled her face to his and kissed her again, this time with a lot more heat. He slid his hands down her back, pulling her to him until his hands were on her waist, sliding up under her shirt, grazing her warm, soft skin. He slid it off over her head, then paused to stare at her in the rose-tinted sunlight. She was perfect. Her eyes sparkled with desire and her hair was flowing beautifully in the light breeze. She kissed him again, her hands on either side of his face before she sat down in the grass, holding his hand, coaxing him to sit with her. He happily complied. She climbed onto his lap, facing him, her knees on either side of him, and kissed him over and over until he laid down, drawing her down with him. He rolled them both over so that he was on top of her, kissing her lips, kissing her neck, with one hand on her waist and the other holding him over her. She slid one hand under his shirt, running it up his chest. Her other hand was on his belt, pulling him towards her. He took the hint and paused the kissing to take off his shirt and her bra before diving back into her. His lips grazed her lips, then her neck, then her breasts as he moved his way down to her stomach and back up, doing his best to kiss every inch of her body.

She laid in the cool grass with her hands over her head, letting Christopher explore her, kiss her everywhere. There was something magical about this spot under the oak tree—their spot. They could be free and take their time, really savor every second with each other, every touch, every sensation. His hands moved to her jeans, carefully unbuttoning, unzipping, sliding them down just enough so he could kiss her right hip and then her left. He tapped on her leg, urging her to bend it so he could take off her boot. One foot and then the other, pulling off her socks too and tossing them to the side. He tugged on her waistband and she raised her hips enough for him to slide her jeans down, and then all the way off. He kissed her calf, her knee, her thigh, and her hip before moving to her stomach and then back down the other leg as his hands brushed over her skin, sending sparks of electricity straight to her soul. Christopher was back over her, kissing her lips again, lightly and tenderly letting soft kisses proclaim his love for her.

His desire for her took over, and he slid his hand down her body, caressing every inch he could before sliding his fingers over her and then inside of her, feeling the wet warmth of her. She let out small hums and gasps of air as he worked slowly, taking his time to build her up, wanting to ignite as much passion and fervor in her as he could, wanting to make her feel as much pleasure as was possible for anyone to feel. He used his lips, his tongue, his fingers to work her into a heated excitement and looked up briefly. She was caressing her own breasts, gently grazing her nipples in rhythm to his movements. Smiling, he kept going, slowly increasing the intensity. Her muscles started contracting. She let herself go erupting in a burst of pleasure. He slid his hand along her inner thigh, his mouth on her, his fingers inside her as she called out and arched under him. He kept going, urging her to let go more, to give herself over to him. Her body obeyed, and she came again and again under him, melting into a delirious ecstasy until he couldn't ignore his own cravings any longer. He took off his jeans and dove into her, submerging himself in her sex, instantly reaping the rewards of his earlier efforts as she tightened around him, calling out his name, giving voice to her bliss. He eased his way in and out of her, slow and hard and deep, delighting in his own indulgence and the sounds of her enjoyment.

Rachel wrapped her legs around Christopher and pulled him into her, never wanting to go a second without him inside her. She wanted to kiss him, but she couldn't catch her breath, couldn't stop vocalizing her satisfaction. Her back arched again. She couldn't think, only feel. She locked eyes with him and took a deep breath in. Her body was on fire, every nerve activated and triggering sweet sensations throughout her entire body. He kissed her neck and let the power of her release take control. It was too much for him. Her body demanded that he surrender to her. Every muscle in her was contracting, sending small quivers of pleasure into him as he throbbed inside her, trying to wait, trying to prolong his arousal as he slid himself in and out, deep inside her. Her body was persistent, urging him with each movement, each tremble, to give himself over to her. He let out a loud groan, pushing into her as deeply as he could and finished before collapsing in the grass next to her.

Rachel rolled towards him, brushing her palm against his chest as she kissed him softly on the cheek. She curled into him, resting her head on his chest and pulling his arm around her. He tilted his head down to kiss her forehead, pulling her into a tight embrace. She slid her leg over his, trying to get as close as she could and have as much contact as possible. Then she saw the shiny ring on her hand and smiled.

"Is this for real?"

Christopher's brow knit together. "Yes, of course it's for real."

Rachel pursed her lips and reached for her phone. "Once I send this photo to the entire squadron, there will be no backsies."

"What?"

Rachel snapped a photo of her ring and sent it to the squadron's group chat with the caption *look what Hawk did*. Her message was met with several *WTFs*, multiple *lols*, and a long thread debating whether or not it was a prank. Christopher glared at the phone before taking it from Rachel and tossing it to the side. She giggled then looked deep into his eyes.

"This diamond is unnecessarily huge by the way. I don't know what you were thinking, but I love it! It's so shiny!" She was absolutely mesmerized by the diamond glittering in the morning light.

"Well . . . it had to be better than Charlene's!" Christopher laughed.

Everything has to be a competition, she thought. "When did you even buy this?"

"When you weren't paying attention."

"Well, that part was obvious! I mean when? How long have you been planning this?"

"A while."

She hit him playfully on the chest. "Christopher! Tell me!"

"I bought it when I was on the way to the airport to pick your parents up before your confirmation hearing. It's good you don't actually know how long it takes to get anywhere. Why do you think I didn't insist on you coming with me?"

"How did you know my ring size?"

Christopher raised an eyebrow. "You always wore your grandmother's ring when we were deployed." She wasn't catching on. "I knew it was the right size, so I borrowed it and took it to the jeweler with me."

"Oh my god!" She was stunned by how much thought he had put into this. "And when did you talk to my dad?"

"Last night while you were at the bar. Just another reason I didn't want to go with you."

Rachel smiled up at him. "Well, now I know to be very suspicious every time you don't want to go somewhere with me or every time you don't want me to go with you."

Christopher laughed. "As if you don't plan crazy surprises all the time."

"Not like this! Besides, I don't send you away to do it."

"No, you just wait for me to fall asleep," he teased.

"Well, you sleep so much!"

"I sleep a normal amount! You don't realize that because you don't sleep enough."

"Well, there's just so many things that I want to do, so there's no time for sleep," Rachel said, sliding her leg along his.

Christopher laughed and pulled her on top of him so the kissing could start all over again. "Can we stay here and skip Thanksgiving?"

Rachel paused the kissing, pulling away slightly. "You know I'm more than happy to skip any and all holidays, but you insisted on coming here and inviting my parents. We should probably make an appearance. A brief appearance, but still."

"I didn't realize my mom would be so on edge."

"You miss Josh," Rachel stated. "So does she."

Christopher nodded.

"I haven't celebrated Thanksgiving in forever, other than whatever the team made me partake in. Pumpkin pie in Khost with Yashfa and Yamna." Rachel's upper lip curled at the memory, but the sadness she felt didn't match. "I need to find Kamal. I need to kill, ugh, so many people." She shook her head. "Holidays suck."

"Too many memories, too much trauma." Christopher ran his fingers through her hair and looked away.

Rachel raised an eyebrow "Am I finally going to get to hear about the mysterious childhood trauma that's never discussed?" Rachel teased.

Christopher winced. "You're never going to let this go, are you?"

"Of course not." Rachel chuckled. "You may as well just tell me."

"Alright," Christopher nodded. "Here we go then. The missing piece of the puzzle. The thing that made me who I am." He smiled to himself, then looked away towards the forest.

"My mom had a really difficult time when I was a kid," Christopher started. "I guess probably before I was born too. I don't know. There's a reason my siblings and I are so far apart in age. She couldn't get pregnant. Or that's not true. She couldn't *stay* pregnant. She had so many miscarriages, and having kids was the most important thing to her. Each miscarriage brought a fresh wave of debilitating depression. She couldn't function, and then she'd get pregnant again and feel better, be elated. Everything was centered around that. My dad did his best to keep the ranch going. I did my best to keep my mom going, trying to cheer her up. I got as excited as she did every time she got pregnant, knowing that it would make her happy again, at least for a little while, and that I'd get my mom back. But then she'd miscarry, and it would start all over again." He paused, mentally bracing himself for the next part.

"I found her one time," Christopher continued. "She was passed out on the stairs, covered in blood. We had practiced at school. You know how they teach kids about calling 911 and make them memorize their address and all that?"

Rachel nodded.

"So, I called, and the ambulance came . . . She had been completely unconscious, from the blood loss, I guess. I think the paramedics did CPR on her. I don't know. I was too young to know what was happening, but I think that must have been what they were doing, and then they loaded her into the ambulance. My dad was off on the property somewhere and it was before cell phones really were common or worked well, so they took her to the hospital and a social worker stayed with me and Josh until they could track him down."

"Oh my god," Rachel said. "How old were you?"

"I was six the first time."

"The first time?" Rachel was shocked.

"Yeah, it happened again when I was nine. Sara was a baby and Josh was at preschool. I had been sick, so I was home from school for the day and I went looking for her. I'd been sleeping and woke up and went to find her and there she was, on the floor of their bedroom in a pool of blood, just like the time before. My grandmother had died a few days earlier. She had moved in with us, so my mom could care for her. Hell, my mom basically had to learn to be a hospice nurse for those two years, watching my grandmother slowly slip away mentally and physically. It was horrible to watch. I guess that's why I never minded if I died in combat or on a motorcycle or anything like that. At least that would be quick."

Rachel nodded, still holding his gaze, understanding completely what he meant, having been through the same thing with her grandfather.

"Anyway, I guess the stress of my grandmother's death may have triggered the miscarriage. If I hadn't been home from school, if I hadn't found her, she would have been dead. I know she had CPR that time because the 911 operator talked me through how to do it, which, let me tell you, was very challenging to do while holding the phone, but it was right before lunch so my dad came home in the middle of it all and heard me upstairs yelling into the phone and took over while we waited for the ambulance to come. He begged her to stop trying after that, but she refused, and then we got Jackie about a year after that, and she and Jackie both almost died. I don't know really, I was too young to understand all the medical stuff, and honestly, I've never asked her. But I remember she said something was wrong and my dad told me to stay with Josh and Sara, and then he rushed her to the hospital. They did an emergency C-section, and a few weeks later, they brought Jackie home."

"Wow," Rachel said, searching for the right words. "That's a lot." She took a moment to process, staring deep into Christopher's eyes, straight into his soul. This was definitely the missing piece. The thing he wanted to run from, the defining experience that had erased his fear of death and encouraged him to live in the moment.

"You know, I always wondered what your trauma was. Most of us who choose to risk our lives to save others do so because we know there's something more important than our own lives. We've already been through hell and back, so it doesn't scare us in the same way it does other people. You know, some sort of childhood trauma that made us who we are, made us resilient. Made it so that we can stare death in the eye and keep going. Someone we lost, or someone we saved, someone we tried to save. Luke has his sister dying of cancer, Ryan has his abusive father and his father's death, Matt has his mom overdosing."

Christopher nodded.

"And usually it's bloody and violent, like a second birth almost. Some sort of primitive rite of passage, soul death and rebirth, like the phoenix rising from the flames, except its blood that makes most of us, not fire. The id and the ego die, and all our delusions and illusions about ourselves and the world fall away. We can see things for what they are and can let go, stop contemplating the meaning of life. There's not much of a meaning or a purpose really, just a desperate, selfish clinging to some hope that somehow we can maintain balance and stability.

"But for us," she continued, "for anyone with this sort of trauma, we learn almost instantly, right in that moment, the true nature of reality. We suddenly understand, whether we want to or not, how transitory everything is. That seeking security or meaning for our life will inevitably lead to being let down and cause more suffering. The concept of self is destroyed in that flash of trauma. Wants, needs, fears, cravings. They become unimportant, and we come to the realization it's a sort of enlightenment or disillusion, depending on how you want to look at it, that allows us to focus on the greater good rather than ourselves. It allows us to sacrifice ourselves for others in a way that most people would never be able to. We become something new. Selfishness dissipates, and we happily put on our battle armor and face the world, knowing that we can and must survive even the most horrific of circumstances."

Christopher nodded, knowing she was completely right, and kissed her temple, happy that she understood, happy that she could make sense of it for him.

Rachel smiled. "I always wondered what yours was, what led to your soul death and rebirth, what made you *you*, and now I know. You were born in blood, just like me."

Chapter 26:

NOVEMBER 2020

CHRISTOPHER'S PHONE RANG AT 0800. They were still up on the ridge celebrating their engagement. He answered when he saw it was Jackie.

"Alright, I was able to get you two partly excused, but your presence is being demanded. Besides, my horses need to be fed, and you stole them away from their breakfast."

"*Your* horses are fine. We took *my* horse and *mom's* horse."

"They still need to eat, and so do you," Jackie argued.

"Chill, we're on our way." He rolled his eyes and nodded towards the horses, very unhappy to tell Rachel it was time to put her clothes back on.

Rachel got a disapproving look from her mother as soon as she was in the front door. "What?" Rachel asked her mother, confused. It was 0820 and Rachel couldn't imagine what she'd managed to do wrong so early in the day.

Jackie laughed and came up behind her, pulling leaves and twigs loose from Rachel's hair.

Rachel glared at Christopher, her look clearly asking him why he hadn't noticed this himself.

"I was definitely not looking at your hair." He laughed.

Tom let out a sigh and put his face in his hand while Bob tried to stifle his laughter.

"If we leave the pies in the oven while we're gone, can we trust you two to keep an eye on them and take them out when they're finished? Assuming you aren't joining us for church," Mary asked.

She was met with a resounding *no* from Rachel, Christopher, and Tom.

"I wouldn't leave a pie under Rachel's supervision. You'll have a brick of charcoal when you get back," Tom explained.

Mary and Anna-Beth looked at Christopher expectantly.

"No, he's too easily distracted," Jackie chimed in. "And I'm really looking forward to pie."

"Rachel, I'm sure you can sit in the kitchen for an hour and remember to take a pie out," Anna-Beth said. "You can keep track of time in all other kinds of situations. I really don't know why this is so difficult."

"I already have plans," Rachel said, sliding her hands into her back pockets.

Sara burst out laughing, and Rachel hit her playfully on the arm with her right hand, signaling her to stop.

"And what are your plans?" Anna-Beth demanded, her hands firmly on her hips.

"Umm." She glanced down at the shiny ring on her hand that no one seemed to notice.

"Rachel, surely you can keep your hands to yourself for an hour," Anna-Beth scolded.

"Excuse me, why am I the problem? How do you know Christopher isn't the instigator?" Clearly announcing their engagement would have to wait.

"Because I know you. You're always the instigator," Anna-Beth said.

"'Do not deprive one another, except perhaps by agreement for a limited time, that you may devote yourselves to prayer; but then come together again, so that Satan may not tempt you because of your lack of self-control.' 1 Corinthians 7:5," Rachel quoted.

"Exactly. You can stop in order to pray," Anna-Beth insisted.

"Yes, but not to watch a pie," Rachel pointed out comically.

"Oh, come on Anna-Beth, they spent eleven years keeping their hands to themselves! Give them a break," Jackie petitioned.

"Jacqueline Fae Williams!" Mary scolded Jackie.

"She has a point," Rachel insisted.

"Well, if you can go eleven years then you can go an hour," Anna-Beth decided.

"Fine, but when I fuck it up, you can't complain," Rachel shrugged.

"Rachel, you will dedicate all of your focus and attention to this pie. We will set a timer, and you will take the pie out when that timer goes off or so help me God—"

Rachel rolled her eyes. "So help you God, what? What are you gonna do?"

"Anna-Beth," Tom pleaded. "Leave the kids alone, would you? The rest of us don't want burnt pie, and you and I both know that Rachel's never succeeded at cooking anything in her entire life."

"That's not true!" Rachel protested.

"Raw fruits and vegetables don't count as cooking, babe, I keep telling you," Christopher said.

"I make the team breakfast all the time!" Rachel argued.

"Mixing protein powder with water is also not cooking," Christopher noted.

"Well, Christopher knows how to cook, so we'll put him in charge," Mary suggested.

"He'll be distracted watching football," Sara pointed out.

"No, he won't." Rachel giggled. "I mean, distracted, yes. Football, I'm not watching that."

"Why the hell not?" Christopher asked.

"I just watched football last Thursday."

"You did not. You sat on the floor watching our friend's road trip through the sand box."

"And a lot of good that did!" Rachel yelled. "What's the point of tracking someone's car if the person I'm looking for isn't in their damned car?"

"Are you supposed to be spying on terrorists while you're on leave?" Tom's tone implied the answer was a hard *no*.

"Why don't you leave the turkey in the oven while we're gone and pop in the pies when we get back?" Sara suggested. "They won't have to do anything to the turkey, and the pies are quick. Really, you can bake the pies while we're eating dinner."

"I think Doctor Williams makes an excellent suggestion," Rachel said.

"Fine, but you two need to stay here in the house while the oven is on," Mary told them.

"That we can definitely do," Christopher assured her. He glanced around the kitchen. "Is there still food for breakfast or are we too late?"

"Yes, sit." Bob motioned towards the table with the spatula he was holding and came over with a frying pan full of scrambled eggs.

Rachel sat next to Christopher, her left hand on Christopher's right thigh, and he put his right hand on her left thigh, keeping them securely in place throughout the entire meal, each eating with only one hand. Rachel picked up a piece of toast with her free hand, and Christopher picked up his knife to butter it while she held it. She took a bite and then held it out for him to do the same, unaware or just not caring that anyone, let alone their parents, were watching them. They continued like that, anticipating each other's needs, until Christopher tried to cut a thick slice of ham and dropped his knife on the floor. Rachel tried to help but was laughing so hard she dropped her knife too. Neither of them could reach their knives without letting go of the other's thigh. Christopher stared intently at his plate, as though he could convince the ham to cut itself somehow.

"I got it," Rachel said, pulling her tactical knife out of her boot with her free hand. The knife was ten inches long in total, with a six and a half-inch blade and three and a half-inch handle. The entire family watched in dismay as she expertly cut his ham one-handed while he held it still with his fork.

"Kind of overkill, don't you think?" Tom asked.

"What?" Rachel asked, as though she had just realized anyone else was there.

"You need a ten-inch tactical knife for breakfast?" Tom clarified.

"Yeah," Rachel said, as though it were completely normal.

"Do you always have that in your boot?" Jackie's jaw had gone slack, and her eyes were wider than they'd ever been.

Rachel looked around the table, confused by all the questions. "Of course, I always have it . . ." She didn't understand why everyone thought it was weird. "What do y'all do when you need a knife?"

"Chris, do you always carry a knife?" Sara asked, ignoring Rachel's absurd question.

"I don't have mine on me right now," Christopher answered, seemingly also confused by their questions.

"Do you still have your Navy issued tactical knife?" Tom asked.

"Umm." Christopher looked at Rachel, trying to figure out how he should answer.

"You're retired," Tom reminded him.

"No one really asked for anything back . . ." Christopher said hesitantly.

"So, you also carry a ridiculous knife around all the time?" Sara asked Christopher.

"No, he's more partial to guns," Rachel explained.

Christopher looked back and forth between his sisters. "What? You both have conceal and carry permits and have guns in your trucks."

"Yeah, but mine's for work in case I need to euthanize a cow," Sara answered.

"Same, but horses and self-defense," Jackie said.

"No, you shouldn't use a gun for self-defense. It's too likely your attacker could get it away from you and use it against you. I'll teach you proper self-defense, and some offense," Rachel offered, taking another bite of her toast, and then holding it out for Christopher to take a bite.

"How is that different from your knife?" Jackie asked.

"I don't do defense," Rachel answered as though that was enough explanation.

Tom laughed. "Rachel's more of an inflict-the-most-harm-as-possible-as-quickly-as-possible type of girl. Not a lot of time for anyone to attack her, therefore not too much defense needed. Besides, no one's gonna get a knife away from her," Tom clarified.

"Tom," Anna-Beth said, trying to get him to stop this topic of conversation rather than encourage it.

"What? You've seen her fight," Tom said, looking at Anna-Beth. "She used to box with the Marines and do PT with them when she was in high school, and we lived on base."

Christopher burst out laughing. "PT! That's a nice word for it," he teased Rachel.

"No! I would get up and run with them and box with them . . . and some other stuff, which, yeah, is also physical training . . ." She reached across Christopher, tactical knife in hand, to get more butter.

"Rachel, your knife must be filthy. Use a spoon or something," Anna-Beth instructed.

Rachel paused and inspected the blade carefully. "Looks clean to me," she said.

Sara rolled her eyes and got up to get Rachel a regular butter knife. "Here, use this. I know you two are practically superheroes, but I don't think either of you are able to see bacteria with the naked eye. Not to mention whatever else might be on there." Sara cringed.

Rachel reached her left hand out to take the butter knife from Sara.

"What the hell is on your hand?" Sara grabbed Rachel's wrist and held up her hand for everyone to see.

"Oh, that." Christopher grinned. "We're engaged. That's why we were late."

"You could've led with that!" Sara remarked.

Mary was out of her seat, pulling Rachel and Christopher into hugs.

"We'll need to start making arrangements, and I'll need information and photos for the announcement," Anna-Beth listed off tasks to be accomplished.

"Mamma, stay out of this." Rachel's tone was severe.

"Are we allowed to put photos of you two in the paper now that you're both out of combat?" Mary asked.

"No," Christopher and Rachel answered in unison, their tone implying it wasn't up for discussion.

Anna-Beth protested immediately. "There is a protocol to these things,

Rachel."

Rachel looked at Christopher and laughed. "Do I *ever* follow protocols?"

"No."

"Then why start now." She smirked. "Dad, no photos, no words, no announcement of any kind. It's an issue of national security and everyone's safety."

Tom nodded. "Understood."

"Rachel—" Anna-Beth protested.

"Mamma, if you do anything that makes it at all easier for a terrorist to find either of us, or anyone at this table, if your actions result in anyone here being taken hostage or anything like that, we will find that person, rescue them, and then I will kill you with my bare hands. Do you understand what I am saying?"

Anna-Beth rolled her eyes. "You're so dramatic."

"She's right." Tom glared at his wife.

"I don't get it." Jackie looked around at everyone.

Christopher dropped his face into his palm. "I swear we've had this conversation a thousand times."

"Right . . ." Jackie pursed her lips. "Secret superhero shit . . . can't tell anyone your real identities or where you are so the terrorists don't come get you."

"No, they're welcome to come get me," Rachel corrected. "What we don't want is for them to come get any of you."

Chapter 27

NOVEMBER 2020

MARY CAME OUT ONTO the front porch of the main house Saturday morning as Rachel and Christopher loaded their bags into the truck. They had decided to drive through Lexington, Kentucky on the way back to D.C., which would add an hour to their driving time but also offer a free place to spend the night and an excellent opportunity to see their friends, Matt and Charlene.

"You two could stay for breakfast," Mary told them. It wasn't even 0500.

"No, we need to get to Lexington before dinner. They have a baby, and we're not allowed to mess up their routine." Rachel turned to look at Christopher. "You know Charlene wants us to be godparents?"

"Yeah, I know," Christopher said as he tossed her duffel bag into the bed of his pickup truck. He was equally horrified at the suggestion. "We'll need to figure out what exactly she thinks that entails . . ."

Mary was staring at them, shocked. "How good of friends are they that they're asking the two of you to be godparents? Neither of you are religious."

Rachel laughed. "Good enough that they know exactly what they'll get from us if we say yes, and for some reason, they still asked us."

"Maybe they just mean it in the legal way. That you'd take their child if something happened to them?" Mary suggested.

"Yeah, we'd definitely do that," Christopher said.

Rachel looked at him, horrified. "What the hell are we gonna do with a baby?"

"You know you'd take her if something happened to Matt and Charlene," Christopher insisted.

Rachel's eyes got wide as she raised both eyebrows.

"It's a baby, Rachel, not a bomb," Christopher insisted.

"No, a bomb would be more predictable. They usually have timers on them. Plus, I can run really fast. But please, enlighten me. What sort of trauma is it that kills Matt and Charlene but the baby survives? That doesn't make any sense."

"You want me to speculate on ways two of our best friends could die?"

"Not particularly," Rachel answered. "Besides, nothing's gonna happen to Matt. He's the medic."

"What, medics don't get shot at?" Mary asked.

"Not if we can help it," Rachel answered.

"Yeah, we make him stay in the middle of everyone as much as we can," Christopher explained. "Although now he's team leader . . ."

"No, it's fine. He's still in the middle," Rachel assured him.

"Is it their first baby?" Mary asked, desperate to change the subject.

"Yes," Rachel answered.

"A girl," Christopher said, knowing that would be the next question. "She's about five months old."

"And absolutely adorable," Rachel said, handing her phone to Mary so she could see pictures. "This is Miss Kristina Ryker Johnson."

"They named her after you two?" Mary asked.

"Yup," Christopher said.

"To clarify, Ryker is her middle name, not part of her last name," Rachel explained. "She is not mine. I do not own her or have responsibility for her in any way. I checked."

"Well, she's gorgeous," Mary exclaimed. "I will add them to my prayers."

"You two drive too fast," Matt said as soon as he opened the door. He let Rachel and Christopher into his and Charlene's three-bedroom, two-bath ground floor apartment on the north side of Lexington.

"No, we don't," Rachel insisted.

"Let's agree to disagree. We've got you two in the living room on the pull out sofa, if that's okay," Matt said as he led them inside. "Kristina is finally getting settled in her own room, so we didn't want to change things up on her," Matt said, opening the door wide so they could come in.

Just then, Charlene came out of the bedroom carrying a tiny baby dressed in a lilac onesie, paired with lilac and white striped leggings and a matching hat. "Hey guys, meet Kristina," Charlene said.

"She's tiny!" Rachel squealed.

"I can assure you she didn't feel tiny when I was pushing her out of me," Charlene laughed.

Rachel reached out for Kristina right away. Charlene willingly handed her over and Rachel got snuggled up with her on the couch.

"Weren't you just saying that babies are more terrifying than bombs?" Christopher asked Rachel, eyes wide and brow creased.

"Yeah, but I meant if *I* had one. I'm fine borrowing them, and she's so tiny and cute! Don't worry, we're fine 'till she starts screaming about something." Kristina had captivated Rachel's full attention. She stared at the sweet tiny baby in her arms, talking to her and cooing as though they were the only two people in the room.

Christopher sat down next to her and put his arm around her shoulders before kissing her on the temple. He was as engrossed in Kristina as Rachel was. They were both mesmerized by her tiny fingers and toes and her scrunched-up face. Rachel started singing to her, and Christopher quickly joined in. They stayed like that for an hour before Kristina started crying. Rachel immediately handed her back to Charlene with a look of terror in her eyes.

"She's fine, Rachel. She's probably hungry," Charlene explained. She took Kristina and Matt got up to get a bottle of breast milk from the fridge.

Rachel got up and observed how Matt warmed up the bottle and how Charlene got Kristina to calm down and eat.

"So," Charlene started, looking back and forth between Rachel and Christopher, "you two are engaged!"

A bright smile took over Christopher's face as he looked at Rachel.

"You've been dating for four months," Matt pointed out. "You realize this is slightly impulsive."

"No! It's been eleven years! Almost twelve. Almost *exactly* twelve," Christopher reminded him.

Matt glanced at Charlene wide-eyed and tight lipped. They would never be able to convince Christopher or Rachel that they were acting impulsively.

"Well, congratulations!" Charlene exclaimed. "When should we expect the wedding to be? I'm sure you haven't started planning yet, but approximately. What are you two thinking, like a year from now?"

"I was gonna just go to the courthouse right after he asked, but someone made certain promises to my father." Rachel glared at Christopher.

Christopher laughed. "Yeah, I may have promised Tom she'd wear a wedding dress and have a proper ceremony."

"I still think we should have gone and done it and had the party later," Rachel explained.

"Nope, this way's gonna be better. You'll see," Christopher assured her.

"Fine, but it's going to be next to impossible to find a time when everyone can come. The teams are on a pretty intense schedule," Rachel complained.

"We're on leave," Matt reminded her. "And I expect to be on U.S. soil for at least six more months."

"Doubtful." Rachel chuckled.

Rachel, Christopher, and Matt went for a run with Kristina in the stroller after Charlene left for work the next day. She was working as a counselor at the inpatient clinic at the VA hospital, which meant a rotating schedule working twelve hours a day for three days, then having three days off. Christopher and Rachel convinced Matt that ten miles was necessary before they all returned to the apartment to shower, change, and eat. As soon as they were done putting their dishes in the dishwasher, Matt started rambling off a list of errands he needed to run, clearly wanting company. Rachel quickly volunteered Christopher to accompany him.

She spent the next hour reading books and singing to Kristina, keeping them both thoroughly entertained while Matt and Christopher were away. She was enthralled with her tiny friend and was having a great time figuring out all the ways to make her smile and giggle, secretly wishing that they lived closer to Matt and Charlene so that she could borrow Kristina more often. She had spent years babysitting her cousins' kids. Babies and children were nothing new. But that was also how she knew exactly how much work they were, how dependent they were, and she knew she wasn't nearly mentally stable enough to take one home with her full time. Too much of that burden would fall on Christopher, and that wouldn't be fair to him. Even if by some stroke of luck, she ended up with a baby as calm and sweet as Kristina, she knew she had no business being anyone's mother, even if Kristina sort of made her want to be. But it wasn't like adopting a puppy. You couldn't go to the shelter and see which baby you vibed with, which one was calm and cute and sweet. A lot of times the baby wasn't even born yet, a lot of times the adoption was closed and you didn't even meet the mother. Then there was the issue of what to do with the kid once you got it home. How to keep it safe and sane and alive without losing your own sanity in the process.

She put Kristina in her crib for her nap and headed for Matt's home office. She scanned her ID on the keypad to unlock the door and entered her pin, then when she was in, she started sifting through the drawers of Matt's desk, easily finding what she was looking for.

"What are you doing?"

Rachel's head snapped around, startled by Matt's whispered scolding.

"What does it look like?" she replied.

"You are not supposed to be reading those intel reports while you're on leave, and you certainly aren't supposed to be leaving me notes." Matt snatched the file out of her hand and looked at the stack of files sitting next to her on the floor.

"I'll have to read them when I start work anyway." Rachel shrugged. "Besides, Kristina is asleep, so I needed a quiet activity." She nodded towards the crib.

Matt picked up the stack of files and pulled Rachel by the arm out to the kitchen where Christopher was unpacking groceries. "First of all, you don't have to sit in there. We have a baby monitor with audio and video. Second, I do not need notes." He snatched a pink Post-it off one of the pages of the file and shoved it in Rachel's face.

"You don't like random half logical theories and tangents that you have to be inside Rachel's brain to understand?" Christopher smiled and snatched the Post-it away from Matt.

I will put a bullet between his eyes, Matt. As soon as you find him, let me know and I'll steal a plane if I have to. Khalid Khan too . . . Shit, I have a long list . . . How do I convince someone to send me back over there? Maybe you can sneak me into the cargo hold on the plane and I can come with you, and we don't tell anyone ;)

Christopher rolled his eyes when he was finished reading the note.

"Seriously, do I need to warn Admiral Eastwood about this?" Matt asked, glaring at Rachel.

"He already knows. As does her father." Christopher's jaw clenched. "We were expressly forbidden from getting on a plane."

"Yes, being grounded means something much different in the Ryker household," Rachel grumbled.

"Well, it sure will be fun having you at HQ." Matt's tone was lacking in sincerity and enthusiasm.

Rachel pouted and glared at him. "It will not be fun."

"No?" Matt raised an eyebrow.

"How, Matthew, am I supposed to dismantle the patriarchy from a desk in D.C.?"

"You'll tell the rest of us what to do, I presume?"

Rachel nodded and looked at the floor.

"Rache, you're going to have direct oversight of the entire squadron. If anything, you'll be more efficient," Matt told her. "You know we'll do whatever you tell us. Sort of our job to follow your orders. Always has been."

Tears filled her eyes as she looked at the floor. "You know I'd never have any of you . . ." Her voice was weak. "I couldn't ask any of you to do . . . those things . . ."

"Which things exactly?" Matt asked.

"All the things that need to be done that we aren't supposed to do but need to do anyway. All the things I do so the rest of you don't have to."

"Executing rapists and liberating women from global subjugation?" Matt summarized.

"I'm sure Ryan will help," Christopher offered.

Rachel shook her head vigorously. "No. Can't put any more shit on Ryan. He has enough to deal with, and he doesn't sleep as it is."

"We'll sort it out," Matt promised her.

"May be considered a war crime . . ." Rachel noted. That was exactly why she insisted on taking care of those sorts of things and rarely let anyone help her. She understood and could accept the consequences of her actions, but she would never ask any of her men to take that risk or take on the psychological burden that came with it.

"Sky, don't worry about it," Matt told her.

"You have a kid now, Matt," Rachel reminded him.

"I'll put Aaron on it. He and Michael can take turns."

Rachel shook her head.

"We can just hand them over to the CIA for questioning. Doesn't that usually result in a slow and painful death?" Matt seemed desperate to make her feel better. "Not sure we can put you in the cargo hold of the plane," Matt teased.

"It's gonna be okay," Christopher assured her as he pulled her tight into his arms. He tilted her face up to his and brushed her tears away with his thumbs before kissing her on the forehead.

"Look, we all know you two are more or less irreplaceable," Matt said.

"New guys are no good?" Rachel's head swiveled towards him, her voice steeped with concern.

"They're good, just new," Matt clarified. "They aren't you two. No one is. A lot of changes are happening. It's a big adjustment for everyone, but we're all still a team, a family, right?"

Rachel nodded slowly, her eyes wide with panic.

"Look at me," Christopher ordered calmly, gently turning her face back to his. "It's just you and me, okay? Matt's got Indigo, and Onyx is in-country doing what they do best. Everything's going to work itself out," Christopher assured her. Rachel was instantly calmer, staring into Christopher's eyes with his hands on either side of her face. Christopher had a way of being able to soothe people even in the most chaotic situations. He was just one of those people you knew you could trust implicitly, always calm, always in control.

"Rache?" Matt started. "We'll take care of your entire list, okay? Every single terrorist, we will wipe them out and you will be at HQ leading and watching. I know it's not the same, but you'll still be with us."

"What about Christopher?" Rachel asked sadly.

"You know what?" Christopher chuckled. "As much as I enjoy killing terrorists with you, I think I found something I like doing with you even more." He grinned.

"Ugh." Matt sighed, obviously disgusted by how cute they were being with each other. "Rache, where do you want us to put our focus?" he asked.

"Samir and Khalid," Rachel answered quickly.

Matt nodded. "Khalid Khan is moving to the top of the list then?"

"Yup," Rachel confirmed. "For Yamna's sake. And Yashfa's. They don't need to lose their husbands or their sons . . . or their daughters, for that matter. They're valuable assets and need to be protected as much as possible. If I'm right about things—"

She was cut off by her phone ringing and grabbed it out of her back pocket. She glanced at the screen, saw it was Luke, and answered. "Lux?" She grabbed Matt by the hand and pulled him into the bedroom, closing the door behind them. "Sorry!" she yelled over her shoulder to Christopher.

Luke didn't waste any time. "We made contact with Yashfa. I would have called sooner, but things are a bit chaotic here. The CIA is pissed at you and therefore reluctant to help us with tech or resources or intel." Luke was never one for wasted time or B.S.

"Let me know what you need that you aren't getting, and I'll make some calls." Rachel sighed.

"Cool. We'd like to get this over and done with ASAP, so we have some downtime before our regularly scheduled deployment in August."

Rachel pursed her lips, looking wide-eyed at Matt. "I dunno what you're off to do in August, but this takes precedent."

"Where are you going in August?" Matt asked Luke.

"We're installing some sort of code on Iran's refinement centrifuges to keep tabs on them and track what they're up to. Supposedly it will allow the U.S. to monitor whatever research and development Iran is doing in the nuclear space," Luke explained.

Rachel rolled her eyes. "That sounds like a waste of your skills."

"No, it's not," Matt said, cocking his head to the side and furrowing his brow. "Because Wood is a nuclear physicist . . ."

"Yeah, Wood is the only one who can credibly get into these places since he understands all the science shit," Luke explained. "Any of the rest of us try to get into an Iranian nuclear facility and we're dead. So Dr. Wood will be participating in some sort of official international inspection, the specifics of which are still being sorted, and the rest of us will be there to back him up and exfiltrate if needed."

Rachel pinched the bridge of her nose between her fingers. "I am so sick of this malware nonsense. Please tell me that's not the same fucking code that nearly got me killed?"

"It's related, I think . . ." Luke said.

"The CIA is involved?" Rachel checked.

"CIA, NSA, President Verity, agencies I've never even heard of."

"For fuck's sake," Rachel grumbled. "Regardless, Samir and Khalid seem to be doing something awful."

"As per usual," Matt chuckled.

"As per fucking usual, Samir is involved in this missing kids situation. Samir still has a copy of that code, for whatever reason *he* wants it."

"Is the code programmed to specifically look at what Iran is doing, or can it monitor whatever system or infrastructure you upload it to?" Matt asked.

"I honestly don't know," Luke answered. "I'm not fully read in, and probably won't be to that level."

Rachel sighed. Luke would probably get the official information about a week before Onyx deployed, if he got it at all. He would only get the information crucial to completing the task. "Lux, I know back-to-back deployments suck, but you're the only ones with the competence to deal with whatever the fuck is happening in Iran, it sounds like. I appreciate you volunteering to help with this."

"No problem." Luke chuckled. "Like I said, we've made contact. We're mostly talking to Yashfa, but she assures us Yamna is taking every opportunity she has when she's home alone to look for the recording device Paige planted. Since we don't know what sort of device it is, we could only give her a general idea of what she's looking for."

"Any chance you can get into the house and do a sweep?" Rachel asked.

"We're working on that."

"You're gonna need to go in while the family is asleep, Lux," Matt said what they were all thinking.

"Yamna thinks her husband is going out of town in a few days. The other option is to go in while they're at the mosque. Trying to keep this as low risk as possible for her and her kids."

"I appreciate that, Lux." Rachel let out a sigh. Luke could come off as unfeeling and cold, but she knew it was a defense mechanism, a way to protect himself from getting hurt and that he'd do everything in his power to protect anyone who needed his protection.

Christopher was sitting on the sofa in Matt's living room, already on his third beer. He'd spent a few minutes with his ear pressed up against the door, trying to hear what Matt and Rachel were talking about. It was no use. He was just getting up to get a fourth beer when Charlene got home from work.

"You're here by yourself?" Charlene's brow furrowed. "Where's Kristina?"

Christopher popped his beer bottle open on the countertop. "Kristina was invited to the strategy session. I was not."

Charlene nodded. "I see."

"I'm sorry, Charlie." Christopher looked at his feet.

"For what?"

"For all the shit you've had to put up with. For always coming second. It's not easy being on this side of things."

"You're feeling abandoned, neglected, and left out?" Charlene guessed.

"Yeah."

Charlene grimaced. "I'm sure it's not easy. I'm used to it, and I was never on the other side. I bet you miss being included in the planning and execution. Execution of the missions, not—"

Christopher burst out laughing. "Definitely miss the execution, Charlie!"

Charlene let out an audible sigh. "It's hard being a military spouse, and it's hard being a retired combat vet. Being both . . . It's a lot. Are you talking to anyone about it?"

"I'm talking to you." He took a sip of his beer, eyes locked on hers.

"Christopher Williams, you know damned well that is not what I mean." Her fist was planted firmly on her hip.

Christopher shrugged. "Who the hell am I supposed to talk to?"

"A therapist. You like therapy."

"Sure. When there's something to go to therapy about. This is just—" He glanced at the closed bedroom door. "I'm being childish."

"Are you?" Charlene raised an eyebrow.

Christopher paused. Nothing he was thinking was good. He'd spent over a decade standing up for Rachel, supporting her career, helping her fight to make the military a more equal playing field for women. He had always admired her drive, her dedication, and now— He never thought in a million years he'd be saying what he was about to say. "I just wish . . . I wish Rachel wasn't so good at her job. That she'd care less."

"Yeah . . ." Charlene paused. "I heard Matt on the phone the other day . . . something about missing kids?"

"Yup," Christopher muttered through gritted teeth.

"It's always worse when kids are involved, isn't it?" She sighed. "It's going to get easier. I can't say when, but I promise, it will get easier. Hang in there." She pursed her lips, thinking for a minute. "Maybe you need a project?"

His brow furrowed.

"Having hobbies that don't involve Rachel would also help. Friends, too. You're completely starting over, Chris. Have some patience and compassion for yourself."

"I know."

"Buuuutttt?" Charlene drug out the word.

"I don't know what to do."

"As I understand, you have a wedding to plan."

"I don't know shit about weddings, Charlene."

"I believe you have a mom and two sisters?" Charlene raised an eyebrow. "Well, planning your wedding is your new mission, and your mom and sisters are your team. Strategize, plan, prep, execute."

Christopher grimaced. "Fine. I'll work on it."

"Also work on getting a job because that would be a more long-term solution," Charlene noted.

"Right." Christopher bobbed his head. "How does one go about that exactly?"

"How does one apply for a job?" Charlene wrinkled her nose. "How old are you?"

Christopher sighed. Charlene knew exactly how old he was. "Other than talking to a Navy recruiter and taking a test, I've never applied for a job. When I switched from being a Surface Warfare Officer to being a SEAL, I more or less mentioned I wanted to go to BUD/s, and the Navy issued me a plane ticket to California."

"I see." Charlene pressed her lips into a tight line. "Well . . . what job do you want?"

Christopher shrugged. He had no idea.

Charlene hopped to the other side of the living room and started inspecting a bookshelf. "I'm not a career counselor but . . . I'm sure I have a book about it somewhere . . . Here!" She pulled a binder off the shelf and flipped it open before taking out a stack of questionnaires. "Fill these out."

"Okay . . ." Christopher knew better than to question Charlene. She'd been nothing but helpful over the years, and he trusted she knew what she was doing.

Charlene put the binder back on the shelf then found a pen.

Christoper sat on the sofa next to Charlene, filling out questionnaire after questionnaire, each one filled with questions to assess his skills, interests, personality traits, and how he approached problems. He handed each one back to her as he finished. "Now what?"

Charlene took the final questionnaire from him and looked it over. "Now you give me a minute to review these." She tallied up the score on each questionnaire and flipped through a book before looking up at him with a smile. "Alright, in terms of values, or your beliefs about what is important and worthy of pursuing, you scored highest on benevolence and universalism. That shows you value protecting, enhancing, and preserving the welfare of others. Shocking, I know!" she teased. "You also scored high on self-direction and stimulation. So, you shouldn't be doing anything too regimented. Nothing where you'll be micromanaged, but something where you'll be challenged, be able to make your own choices. Something exciting. Nothing routine where you're doing the same thing day after day."

"That makes sense," Christopher said.

"For career anchors, basically what motivates or drives you, you scored highest on dedication to a cause or sense of service and pure challenge. Not much of a surprise there either. You also scored very high on lifestyle, meaning that your career isn't the most important thing to you. It isn't what defines you."

Christopher's brow knit together. "Am I supposed to have some sort of epiphany now or something?"

Charlene chuckled. "Wouldn't that make things easy? No. But maybe think of it in terms of what cause you're most passionate about? Something involving protecting people or improving people's lives, I would guess, if we're looking at your values and motivation together. Basically, what problem do you want to solve?"

"I dunno." Christopher was stunned. "Where do I even start? What problems can I pick from?"

Charlene pursed her lips. "Literally anything, Chris."

"Such as?"

"Well, if having a cause is what motivates you, then you should think about what issues piss you off the most and are most complex, because then you'll be really driven and have plenty to do."

"What pisses me off the most?" Christopher's brow furrowed.

"Yeah. Out of everything you've seen and had to do, what stuck with you that you can't let go of? What is something you find so appalling that you can't accept that it happens?"

"That doesn't narrow it down much," he grumbled.

Charlene nodded. "Let's try this." She got her phone and googled *list of the world's problems* then handed her phone to Christopher for him to read.

Christopher took it and skimmed the list, looking for inspiration. "Okay, children, human rights violations . . ." Christopher clicked on a link for the topic *human security*. He continued reading and fell down a rabbit hole of political science theory, reading about personal security and ways to protect people from physical violence from the state, external states, and violent individuals. That led to examples of domestic violence and child abuse. From there, he clicked another embedded link and started reading about the difference between human security and human rights approaches to solving problems, then went to the next section on NGOs. As he scrolled down to the bottom of the page to a list of related issues, his eyes landed instantly on one. He clicked it and handed the phone back to Charlene.

"Human trafficking?"

He locked eyes with Charlene and nodded.

She gave him a soft smile. "That's what's bothering you so much." She glanced across the room at the still closed bedroom door. "Kids are missing, and you aren't allowed to fix it."

"I feel guilty I'm not helping," he admitted. "I know there's kids in danger, I know so much about what's happening over there, and I'm sitting on my ass watching ESPN all day." He shook his head. "Rachel's not wrong. If we were over there . . ." He bit the inside of his cheek. "At the risk of sounding like an arrogant jackass, I know I could find those kids faster than anyone else can. The other guys, and Rachel, they're good. But finding people, it's what I do."

"Well, what other jobs involve finding people?"

Christopher's jaw clenched. "That also allow you to kill the assholes who took the people in the first place?"

"Yeah . . . maybe don't share that part with other people." Charlene grimaced. "I'm sure it's satisfying to kill the people doing these horrible things. I know a lot of cops who wish they could, but that's not how things work in the real world."

"I know." Christopher chuckled. "I keep telling Rachel she needs to trust the teams to get this shit done. I guess I should take my own advice."

"Probably," Charlene agreed. "But more seriously, what are you going to do to stop human trafficking? What job would allow you to continue doing that? You could work with policy, changing laws, or for an NGO or law enforcement. Law enforcement would allow you to occasionally shoot people."

The corner of Christopher upper lip curled as he shook his head. "See, now I don't think any other therapist would have made that joke!"

"I'm not your therapist," Charlene reminded him. "And it was a serious question. At least try to narrow down what you *don't* want to do."

Christopher grimaced. "Rachel's friend, Ashley, lobbies politicians for policy changes. She runs a nonprofit. I definitely *do not* want to do that."

"Good! That's something at least."

"I don't want to sit at a desk all day either."

"Federal agent?" Charlene suggested. "I think the FBI finds missing people."

"Pretty sure they have to wear suits . . . I don't want to have to wear a suit."

Charlene tried to stifle her laughter. "I cannot see you in a suit at a desk all day!"

"God, I'd be as miserable as Rachel's about to be."

Chapter 28

DECEMBER 2020

RACHEL ARRIVED AT COMMAND HQ on Monday, December 7 at 0700. She showed her ID to the guard and went through the metal detector at the security check, putting her belongings, including her tactical knife, on the conveyor belt for the X-ray scanner. Once she was in the clear, she headed up the elevator to the eleventh floor. She knew where she was going since she had been there before for meetings, but now she'd be the one calling team leaders to meetings. Meetings neither she nor they wanted to attend.

When the elevator doors opened, she got off, swiped her ID again, and opened a large door to the U.S. Navy SEAL Middle East Special Projects Command Headquarters. This was where the top squadron—her squadron—operated from. The air felt stale, especially compared to the open air of the battlefield, any battlefield, and she already wanted to run. She fought her instincts and instead made her way down the hallway to her left, to Admiral Eastwood's office. His door was open, but she knocked twice anyway.

Eastwood looked up from his desk and gave a slight nod of his head in acknowledgement. "Do you know where your office is and what you're supposed to be doing?" he asked her.

"Reading boring reports, I presume?" She crossed her arms across her chest and leaned casually against the door frame.

"Yeah, I guess you would see it that way. Come with me. I'll show you around." Admiral Eastwood gave her the full tour of the building, then took her down the hallway to her office. The door opened to a spacious seating area with a small desk in the corner, and Eastwood explained it was for her chief of staff, whom she would need to select promptly. Rachel wasn't really sure what a chief of staff actually did or why she needed one.

"Do you have any idea who you want? You can pick anyone who's on active duty, and we'll see if we can make it happen," Eastwood explained.

"Umm." Rachel looked at him, still unsure and not wanting to admit that she didn't understand.

"You're going to need someone who is good at scheduling and time management. Basically someone who can assist you with administrative tasks, manage your calendar, drive you around—that sort of thing."

Rachel nodded. It was making more sense now. "How long until I have to pick someone?"

"The sooner the better," Eastwood said. He led her across the seating area and through another door into a room with a large desk and floor-to-ceiling glass that provided a gorgeous view of the Anacostia River. "This is for you." He pointed at the desk. "Put your stuff down and I'll show you the rest."

Rachel put her laptop bag on the enormous desk and followed him back out to the hallway. He introduced her to so many people, some whom she'd met before and several more whom she'd spoken to on the phone or radio during missions.

"This is Admiral Miller, our head of logistics. I'm sure you've spoken with him before," Eastwood stated. Rachel reached out to shake his hand. He was a tall man in his late fifties with a solid build and salt and pepper hair. "You'll need to consult with Miller's department when you're planning your missions to make sure you have all the necessary supplies and transportation for your teams," Eastwood explained.

Rachel nodded. She already knew what he was telling her but decided to keep her mouth shut and be polite. He took her to the tech and communications departments, showed her the conference rooms, and then finally took her into Mission Control. The gigantic wall was one huge screen. There were three levels of raised platforms with desks, laptops, headphones, microphones, and buttons everywhere.

"As I'm sure you know, this is where we run the missions from. This is where we get to watch, and the microphones and most of the buttons are how we communicate with the teams in the field. You'll get trained on how to use all the equipment later. Usually, mission commanders like yourself can only watch the missions they plan themselves, but your responsibility is so broad as squadron commander that you can more or less come in and out as you please."

Rachel nodded. This was where she wanted to be. If she couldn't be in the fight, she wanted to be in here watching it live on the big screen. "When's the next mission running?" she asked wistfully, staring at the oversized screen.

"Probably not for a few days. We tend to only watch when something interesting is happening, not when the teams are just driving around trying to get somewhere."

"But it's possible to watch?" Rachel asked.

"God, you really miss it, don't you?" Eastwood chuckled.

Rachel didn't find it nearly as amusing. She loved her life now, loved being with Christopher, but being in the field, being over there with her team—that was where she had always felt most at home. Her team was her family and being with them, fighting alongside them, felt like how she imagined most people felt about going home for holidays. At least happy, functional people. She looked down and saw the shiny diamond ring on her finger and couldn't help but smile. Eastwood was right. She would be good at this. They needed her here. She could help more of them from here. Maintaining her contacts in the Middle East, her underground network of female spies, would be more challenging if she had to do it from HQ, but she'd figure it out.

"Are you ready to learn how everything in here works?" Eastwood asked.

Rachel's eyes were wide and bright with excitement. Eastwood chuckled and went to get someone from the tech department to give her a thorough overview of how to operate everything in the Mission Control room. She normally wasn't a fan of technology but found these buttons to be exceedingly interesting and useful, knowing it was her only way to communicate with the teams, her only way to see what was happening, her only lifeline. There were buttons to switch communications channels, to answer satellite phone calls, to switch views between the SEALs' body cameras, to zoom in on the video, as well as buttons to make calls to various desks at Command HQ and the regional command centers all throughout the Middle East. She had been aware, of course, that all these actions could be performed somehow from HQ but had never cared how they were done before. She picked it up quickly, taking notes so that she could study and memorize which buttons did what later.

After their meeting, Rachel wandered around HQ, considering her options for who could be her chief of staff. It would have to be someone she could tolerate to be around for eight to twelve hours a day. Someone who wouldn't annoy her and who would be able to keep her on schedule but also make up believable excuses for why she had to skip meetings. She also knew this would be an opportunity for a junior officer to get fast-tracked for a promotion. She made her way to the logistics department and wandered into Lieutenant Stephanie Hertz's office. Stephanie had assisted Rachel a number of times, including when Rachel needed to get her team back from Khost the year she'd met Yashfa and Yamna. Stephanie stood at attention immediately.

"Oh, enough of that," Rachel said a bit absently as she closed the door and sat down across from Stephanie. "Lieutenant Hertz, what are your goals and dreams and future plans? In terms of your career development, I mean."

"Um, I'm not really sure, ma'am," Stephanie answered.

"Well, is your dream to sit here and book flights for people for the rest of your life?" Rachel asked, certain that Stephanie did more than that, but she wanted to make a point that she could be doing much more.

"I enjoy it, yes, but of course I'd like to eventually have the opportunity to contribute in a larger way."

Rachel nodded and looked at her for a moment, curiously. She turned to double check the door was closed all the way before continuing. "Stephanie, I believe women need to be helping other women. We need to lift each other up and not sit around bitching and whining and bickering with each other. I'm currently in a position where I can help someone grow, move up the ranks quicker, that sort of thing, and I'd like for that person to be you. I've worked with most of the people here at Command, and you happen to be the brightest, quickest, most detail-oriented person in this place, other than me."

"Thank you, ma'am." Stephanie smiled.

"How would you like to be my chief of staff? I know it's pretty boring work. Fixing my calendar, driving me places, sitting in god awful meetings with me. But it would fast-track you for a promotion and give you a chance to see how the rest of Command, the rest of the Navy, really works so you can identify what your dream job actually is. Then, once you've done that, I promise to help you get whatever training or promotions you need in order to get that job."

Stephanie stared at Rachel, her mouth agape and her eyes wide.

"I also couldn't care less about you saluting me or addressing me by my rank or any of that shit, as long as no one else is around to yell at us about it. This is really more of a mentorship than you working under me. I need someone who is comfortable being candid with me and calling me out on my bullshit when I'm out of line, which I will be. I really hate going to intelligence meetings, and I *will* do everything I can to get out of going to them."

Stephanie couldn't help but laugh. She'd been on enough phone calls with Rachel over the years to know exactly what she was talking about. "I think I can do that," Stephanie said.

"I know you can. My question is if you want to."

"Permission to speak freely?" Stephanie asked.

"Yes, always. In fact, I insist you speak openly and freely with me at all times, whether you accept this position or not. I mean, if other people are around, then follow protocol, obviously so you don't get your ass handed to you by someone else, but I would never discipline someone for stating their opinion."

Stephanie nodded and smiled. "Rear Admiral Ryker, ever since I started here at Command, ever since the first time I was on the phone with you, I've wanted to *be* you. I could never actually pass SEAL training. I don't mean that. I'm very happy to be on a desk and not in the field. The way you lead, the way you inspire people to act, the way you argue for what your team needs, that's what I want to learn. You're sort of my role model. That sounds childish and weird, I know, but—"

"But there aren't too many women for you to look up to." Rachel nodded slowly before continuing. "I didn't have any women to look up to. There wasn't anyone showing me how to make it in this stupid alpha male, testosterone driven culture we've chosen to work in. I had to pave my own way, and trust me, it was hard. I had to quite literally kick the shit out of people before they would even consider letting me into a room, let alone let me voice an opinion once I got inside. Because of that, I want to do everything in my power, now that I've gotten to the point where I actually *can* make a difference, to make things easier and more equal for women in the Navy. You've been here, what, five or six years, and you're still a lieutenant doing basic tasks, despite being the smartest person in your department? I've been working with you a long time Stephanie, and I checked your FITREPS. All of your performance evaluations are stellar. Unlike some people in your department who are . . . not." Rachel pressed her lips into a tight line, reminding herself to be professional and not shit talk anyone. "I know there have been men who are less competent who have gotten assigned special duties and projects. You've been passed over several times and not given the opportunity to really show what you can do. I know what you can do. I've seen how hard you work, how dedicated you are, how creative you can be. Always thinking on your feet, always pulling my team—me, specifically—out of some pretty tight spots. If you agree to be my chief of staff, I will listen to your ideas, and together we can change the culture of this place, maybe even dismantle the patriarchy altogether."

Stephanie grinned. "It would be an honor to be your chief of staff."

"Good, I'll go break the news to Admiral Miller and let him know I'm stealing you." Rachel winked before getting up to leave.

She found Admiral Eastwood and Admiral Miller drinking coffee and chatting. *Don't they have anything to do?* "I'm stealing Hertz," she announced. "What do I need to do to get her a promotion?"

"Um . . ." Eastwood stared at her dumbfounded. "We can talk about that . . ."

Rachel narrowed her eyes at him. He'd told her to pick a chief of staff, and she'd picked. What was the problem? Seriously, every time she did what he said, it was an issue. When she didn't do what he said, it was also an issue. This was precisely why she ignored his wants and just did what needed to get done. "Nothing to discuss. Make it happen," Rachel demanded as her phone beeped.

Lux to Skylark: *All good in Khost. Attempting device retrieval tonight. Talk after.*

Rachel smiled to herself then turned her screen so Eastwood could see. "Boys are ready to search Yamna's house. We should know what Paige was up to in a few hours."

CHAPTER 29:

DECEMBER 2020

YAMNA TUCKED THE SCARF snuggly around her head and crossed her living room for the front door, opening it a crack. It was the middle of the night, pitch black outside because of the new moon. They'd lucked out that her husband needed to travel for work on the darkest night of the month.

A tall man was staring down at her, thumbs hooked in his back pockets. He glanced over his shoulder then back at her. "Skylark says hello," he said in Pashto.

Yamna nodded and let him inside. Rachel had said she was sending some-one—a man. A man Yamna had never met. She wanted to help Rachel so that Rachel could find Kamal. If being alone with a strange man was the only way to help, she'd just have to be brave. Lux, Rachel had said his name was. "Rachel said you would come . . . I'm sorry. I could not find what Paige left."

"That's okay. I brought this." He held up a small black plastic triangle with three lights on it that fit in the palm of his hand. "It detects electronic frequencies." He held it near his cellphone, and she saw the front green light flash more rapidly the closer he held the device to his phone. "Shouldn't be more than a few minutes." He took several long strides around the kitchen and living room, calm and steady.

Yamna stood, frozen in place, her heart beating out of her chest. She'd never been alone with a man who wasn't her father or husband or brother. Sure, her children were asleep in their room, but what would they be able to do? She forced herself to breathe. *Rachel trusts this man*, she reminded herself. If Rachel trusted him, surely he wouldn't hurt her? But it was highly improper for her to be alone with him, with any man who wasn't her father or brother or son. She prayed the neighbors hadn't seen him come. Prayed there wouldn't be talk and gossip. If her husband found out, well, that she could endure. But if her father ever knew she'd been alone with a strange man, *that* beating would be brutal. If he knew the strange man was American, she'd probably end up dead.

After wandering around the living room, he moved on to the kitchen. He paused, staring quizzically at the countertop, then moved the device around a bit more before picking up the tea pot and holding the device to it, turning it, inspecting it. "Well, that's not where I would have put it." He sighed and shook his head as he pried something off the concave bottom of the silver teapot she used every day. "I hope it didn't get wet," he muttered. "What the hell was Paige thinking putting it on the teapot?"

Yamna realized he was more asking himself than her but was fairly confident she knew the answer. Her voice was unsteady, but she tried to answer him. "I-I think she knew I'm the only one who touches it, so no one would have found it but me."

Lux's eyebrows shot up. "Shit that's smart." His eyes darted around the house. "How did she know you're the only one who uses it?"

"The men don't exactly serve their own tea . . . And my oldest daughter, she is only nine. Too small for the big tea pot." She gestured with her hand towards the silver teapot still in Lux's hand. "Is it okay?" Yamna could barely get the words out. *Stay invisible. Stay small. Just stay out of his way and you'll stay safe.* She knew better than to question him and was hoping desperately he hadn't come all this way just to be disappointed.

"Let's see." He flashed her a kind smile and, seconds later, they heard voices coming out of the tiny contraption. "Is that your father's voice?" he asked.

Yamna nodded.

Another voice came though, also male. "Do you know who that is?"

Yamna shook her head then winced, expecting it to be the wrong answer. She was supposed to help this man—Lux. But she didn't know whose voice it was. Men were so tricky to read. She never knew what they wanted. With all the talking she'd been doing, she kept waiting for him to strike her, yell—something. But he was just calm and kind.

"Alright. We'll figure it out. Thanks for this." He made the voices stop and shoved the contraption and the device that had guided him to it into his pockets.

Yamna had never seen a pair of pants with so many pockets. She blushed as her eyes followed his hands. She shouldn't be looking at him. But she couldn't stop herself either. "Will you kill my father?" Her voice caught. She couldn't believe she'd dared to bring it up, but something about him had emboldened her.

"Maybe. Someone will. I might not do it myself. We'll see what happens, but someone on my team will, yes."

"Team?" Yamna's brow furrowed.

"Yes," Luke nodded. "There are twelve of us. We all work under Rachel. She's our boss."

The confusion must have been evident on her face because he kept talking, kept trying to explain.

"She's the chief. The one who makes decisions and tells us what to do."

Yamna nodded. "You said the right word. I understood the word, just . . . that a woman can be the boss of anything, let alone one man. Twelve men . . ."

What he said next shocked her to her core, but his face softened, as if he understood how impossible that felt to her. "Rachel currently is the boss of about eighty-four men. Seven teams of twelve."

It was utterly incomprehensible. "I've never known such a thing," Yamna admitted. "Here, such things do not happen. Zarah told me, once upon a time, when Afghanistan was a very different place . . ."

"Zarah?" Luke's brow furrowed.

"She was my friend. Rachel's too. She's dead now. Like Veeda. Dead friends are something women must grow accustomed to here," she explained.

"Soldiers grow accustomed to dead friends too," Luke nodded.

"Yes." Yamna's eyes darted to the floor. She was being too brazen, too open. The deaths of her friends were surely nothing compared to the deaths of soldiers, of men. They actually mattered. She looked up through her lashes and saw he was studying her.

"Would you like it if women could be the boss here too?" he asked calmly.

Yamna nodded. "I think my sister could do it. Not me. I can barely get my own children to listen to me. And now Kamal . . ." Her eyes welled with tears. Tears for her son and tears for the pain she was sure would come. She'd never spoken this many words to a man. Not without consequences anyway.

"You could do it too. You have a strength you don't even realize." He smiled kindly at her. "Yamna, we're going to listen to everything Paige recorded. Hopefully it will lead us to your son. If not, we'll keep looking. Do you need anything? Food, money?"

Yamna shook her head. There was no way she had any sort of strength. She couldn't stand up to her father. She couldn't save her son.

"Rachel told me to get you whatever you want in exchange for helping us."

Her voice came out in a whisper as she choked back her sobs. "All I need is my son."

"We'll do our best to bring him home," Luke promised seconds before he was out her front door.

Yamna stood alone in the kitchen. Praying no one had seen him come or go. Praying her children hadn't heard anything. Thanking Allah that he hadn't hurt her. She would do anything, risk everything, to keep her children safe.

Chapter 30:

DECEMBER 2020

CHRISTOPHER HAD DONE HIS best to finish planning the fundraiser without actually having to meet with anyone in person. One meeting at the White House really had been more than enough. He was sitting at the kitchen table, documents spread out, when Rachel got home from work.

"How's it going?" she asked, letting out a low chuckle.

His brow furrowed. "What's so funny?"

"You look really irritated. Did someone who doesn't know enough about maps draw on your map or something?" she teased.

Christopher shook his head and forced a smile onto his face. She knew him too well. "I just spent an hour explaining to Hunter that airplanes fly at the speed they fly, and no, we cannot pay the pilot to make it go faster."

"That does explain the look on your face." Rachel kissed his temple then sat in the chair next to him. "Is any of this secret?" she pointed at all the documents spread out on the kitchen table.

"No." It was Christopher's turn to laugh. The idea that documents *weren't* classified was somewhat new to both of them.

"This is the flight info?" Rachel snatched a document up off the table and studied it for mere seconds, her expression hardening as she did.

"What is it?" Christopher's brow furrowed.

"This is who you're working with?" Rachel pointed at the paper, the concern evident in her voice.

Christopher leaned over to see what she was pointing at. "Eros Aid, yes. I've never heard of them but—"

"They're . . ." Her eyes darted to his. "Be very careful."

"Why?"

"I—Just . . . Fuck. I guess I have to go to this now."

"Weren't you always coming to the fundraiser?" Christopher was confused. She clearly knew something she wasn't willing to share, and there wasn't much she kept from him. He cocked his head to the side. "What is it about this NGO that has you so freaked out?"

"They're a front for—" she blurted out. "Fuck!" She slammed her hand on the table and stormed out of the kitchen, paper in hand.

Christopher sat for a minute then winced as he heard the door to her home office slam shut.

Rachel locked the door to her office behind her and opened the gun safe in the corner of the room. She popped open the false bottom and pulled out a burner cellphone and new SIM card before dialing President Frank Verity. "What the actual fuck are you up to?" she muttered into the phone.

"Who is this?" Frank asked.

"Don't be stupid, you know who it is. Call me back on a secure line." Rachel hung up. The burner cell rang again moments later.

"Care to be more specific?" Frank got straight to the point.

"It's fucked up, first of all, to give government contracts to NGOs that you're a majority shareholder in. Second, what the fuck is your organization doing with these refugee kids?" What she hadn't been able to tell Christopher was that Eros Aid was a front for an off the books organization within the CIA.

"Rachel?" Frank asked.

Rachel rolled her eyes.

"I guess Chris is involving you—"

"I assure you, he has no idea what's going on or what he's gotten himself involved in. I, however, have a pretty good idea." She paused to let him defend himself but was met with silence. "I will burn the entire world to the ground to protect him."

"Yes, well, love makes us all do stupid things," Frank teased.

Rachel grit her teeth. She needed to control her temper. If she started yelling, Christopher would hear every word. The way she'd stormed out of the kitchen, she wouldn't be surprised to find him right outside her office, ear pressed against the door. "What are you up to, Frank?"

"Evacuating refugee children, Rachel."

"Be more specific regarding the who and why please."

"How come when you say please it sounds more like a threat?"

"Stop wasting my time and tell me what I want to know."

Frank let out an audible sigh, and Rachel knew he'd need a minute to formulate a response that would satisfy her curiosity, calm her down, and get her off his back. "There are so many children in the Middle East," Frank started. "They aren't always in safe situations, so we're bringing some of them here."

"Who is we?" Rachel prompted, though she already had her suspicions.

"Eros Aid . . ." Frank hedged.

"I already know that part, obviously, or else I wouldn't be calling you! Doesn't the State Department usually handle that sort of thing?"

"Yessss."

"So, someone at the State Department gave you a contract? Aren't you supposed to divulge your personal and financial interest in the matter before the contract is awarded?"

"I happen to be a silent partner," Frank insisted. "And Petchill thought—"

Rachel's jaw clenched, her suspicions confirmed. "Petchill thought what?"

"Well, if my name were on any documentation for the organization, it would appear to be a conflict of interest."

"It *is* a conflict of interest," Rachel noted. "And Petchill being involved is not good, Frank. And *also* a conflict of interest considering he's director of whatever the fuck you two decided to call it!"

Another audible sigh from Frank. "Director of Covert Strategy. You know, your insistence on hating Petchill has always baffled me."

"That's because you're an idiot," Rachel clipped out. "Just because he kisses your ass constantly doesn't mean he's acting in anyone's best interest but his own. Not once in that man's life has he done anything that wasn't self-serving, manipulative, corrupt, and in many cases, downright evil. I swear, he'd murder his own mother to get ahead."

Frank burst out laughing. "Wouldn't you?"

Rachel winced. It was a poorly chosen example. "I would not kill my mother."

"Uh-huh." Frank was still laughing. "Get off your high horse, Rachel. You're no better than the rest of us." He hung up.

Rachel's anger boiled to the surface, and she was consumed by feelings she'd been suppressing for decades. Her frustration came out in a ferocious growl as she threw the burner phone against the wall and watched it break into pieces. Her stomach lurched and the bile rose in her throat. This fundraiser was going to be the catalyst for something awful. She just knew it.

Christopher was about to follow Rachel to her office, or walk quietly down the hall and listen through the door to overhear something, when his phone rang. "Williams," he answered on the first ring, not bothering to see who it was.

"Hawk, it's Viper. I'm in-country so have to make this quick. I've gotten an update for you. There's a lot of land being purchased in Pakistan. Not sure if it's at all related to the other thing, but it's suspicious, so our intelligence department is keeping an eye on it. The going theory seems to be kids go missing in Afghanistan and they're transported across the border. We really don't have much to back that up, but your team might."

"Thanks. I'll pass it along."

"Pass it along?" Viper paused. "What aren't you telling me?"

"Umm." Christopher wasn't sure what to say.

"Hawk, why would you pass this along and not look into it yourself? I would if I had time, but I'm sort of focused on something else right now."

"I maybe sort of retired," Christopher admitted. "And I'm maybe sort of bored out of my mind."

"For fuck's sake," Viper grumbled.

"I've handed everything you gave me over to my former C.O.," Christopher assured him.

"Retired, bored, and manipulating people into sharing classified information with you."

Christopher chuckled.

"Sounds like you need a job. You medically retire, or can you still run and jump and do stuff?"

"Fell in love with a female officer. One of us had to retire."

"Interesting. I'm guessing since I sent that report to an address in D.C. that you're living in D.C.?"

"Yes."

"Huh . . . I might be able to help with the job thing. Keep your phone close."

Chapter 31

DECEMBER 2020

RACHEL WAS SITTING IN a conference room at HQ the next morning. She'd listened to the recording from Yamna's house and was going through the most important excerpts with Navy intelligence, Eastwood, and Onyx.

"That voice, that's Samir Al-Abadi," Rachel insisted.

"How can you be sure?" Captain Dixit from the intelligence department asked.

Rachel glared at him. "I'd recognize Samir's voice anywhere. Yamna identified the first man as Khalid Khan. He says 'welcome to my home' essentially. Then we have the second man. His Pashto is nearly perfect, but that slight Iraqi accent and the use of the opener *shako mako* confirm the speaker is Iraqi since the phrase *is* Iraqi. It's not used a lot, but it's more a funny way to say *what's up*. The sigh from the other men on the call confirm they were exasperated and likely not used to the casual use of the phrase. *Shako mako* more directly translates to 'what is everything and nothing,' and comes off as a joke," Rachel explained. She motioned for them to start the recording over and held a finger to her ear, urging everyone to listen.

They all heard Khalid Khan greet everyone, then listened as the second man clearly said "Shako mako bros?," which was followed by a low chuckle. She'd thought she'd imagined it all the times she'd listened to it before, but there it was, clear as day. Shako mako *bros*. Her mind flashed back to the spring of 2008, when she'd been an intelligence officer in Iraq. *Shako Mako bro?* had been the common greeting between the American and Iraqi coalition forces she'd been working with. She knew because she'd been the one to start the trend in an attempt to force them to bond and to put both the Iraqis and the Americans at ease since none of them had been used to working so closely with a woman.

Less than a hundred people in the entire world were likely to use *that* specific phrase. Of those, only about half would be Iraqi. The man speaking had definitely been in Iraq with Rachel, and his tone and cadence were exactly the same as Samir's—much more casual and lighthearted than how most people spoke. He could have a gun to your head, telling you he was going to shoot you in the face, and you'd be laughing, thinking it was a joke up until the moment the bullet hit you. There was no doubt in her mind it was him.

"*Shako mako bros* specifically dates back to a very specific Iraqi coalition unit that was in play in the spring of 2008. Samir was part of that unit," Rachel told everyone.

"How do you know that?" Dixit asked.

Eastwood gave her a sideways glance. "Because she was—"

"Shut the fuck up." Rachel cut him off before he could explain to everyone that Rachel had been in Iraq at the time.

"Excuse me?" Eastwood's voice sliced through the room.

Rachel ignored him and pushed her memories of Iraq to the back of her mind. "I know because I'm good at my job." She huffed. "The third man—" She took a breath to steady herself. Those damned memories seemed rather insistent on stealing her attention. "From all the intel we have, I'd presume the third man is Aquib Faizan."

"Intel meaning a report and some thirdhand comments you somehow got from the Army?" Dixit raised an eyebrow at her.

"Don't you have some sort of software you can run this through to confirm her theory?" Eastwood asked.

"We're working on it. These things take time," Dixit explained.

Rachel rolled her eyes. "Why am I both smarter and faster than all this fancy tech shit y'all have? I swear, the Navy should just pay me whatever amount we're spending on developing this shit that kind of, sort of works. None of it seems to work as well as my brain."

"Ryker, stop whining." Eastwood glared at her. "I'm fairly confident you're correct, but this, like most things, is a trust-but-verify sort of situation. I know patience is not your strength, but—"

A young woman burst through the door, out of breath with a file in hand. "Samir and Aquib—" She tried to collect herself and stood at attention, eyes darting around the room. "Sorry."

"At ease," Eastwood told her.

She nodded and relaxed a bit, holding up the file in her hand. "Software has identified the three voices heard most on the recording as Khalid Khan, Samir Al-Abadi, and Aquib Faizan."

"Told you," Rachel muttered.

"What's our degree of confidence?" Dixit asked.

"Ninety-five percent, sir, which really is about as confident as we ever can be."

"What else did your team come up with?" Dixit asked her.

"Most commonly heard words or phrases all have to do with children and schools. They seem to be discussing the educational system in Afghanistan compared to other countries. What age children are when they start school, subjects studied . . . It all seemed rather innocent—"

"It's not," Rachel insisted. "Are they speaking in some sort of code?"

"Not that we can tell, ma'am."

"Did your fancy computer check?" She didn't bother to hide her irritation as she mocked the computer.

"Yes, ma'am. We've analyzed their conversations with every bit of software we have, ran it through every program—"

"Did you personally listen to the full recording?" Rachel always trusted humans over technology.

"Yes, ma'am."

"And?" Rachel's eyes were like daggers.

The young woman blinked at her.

Rachel took a deep breath and relaxed her face. This girl was a newly commissioned officer, probably scared out of her mind to be in a room with this many senior officers at once. She realized her resting bitch face might be intimidating and decided to restart their interaction with a more pleasant tone. "What's your name?" She could read the name and insignia on the girl's uniform just fine, but figured she'd give her a question she could answer confidently to help ease her into the situation.

"Ensign Rebecca Wright, ma'am," Rebecca stood straighter.

Rachel nodded. "Wright, what is your personal opinion regarding the recordings?"

"Well . . . umm . . ." Her eyes darted around nervously.

"Speak freely," Rachel encouraged her.

"I think, given everything we know about these three men . . . Everything *I* know," she amended. "Well, at first listen, it sounds like they're debating how to improve the school system in Afghanistan. They're discussing child development, what children of various ages are capable of physically, cognitively. It's actually a fairly high-level academic discussion."

Rachel nodded in agreement.

"But none of these men are known for wanting to improve the lives of children . . . Umm, if you go to . . ." She did her best to flip through the file while not letting any documents fall to the floor.

Rachel rolled her eyes and motioned for Dixit to stand. "Ensign Wright, take a seat."

Wright's eyes were wide, but she did as instructed. Dixit stood behind her, clearly displeased to have been replaced by his subordinate. Wright flipped through the documents for a moment before she found what she was looking for in her notes. "If we fast-forward so we are three hours and fifty-seven minutes into the recording . . ."

Rachel did as requested and queued up the recording.

"There are more opportunities in America than in the UK, and we have

better connections," Samir explained.

"I don't know if I trust your connections." Khalid sounded critical.

"What about the girls?" Aquib Faizan asked.

"You are greedy, aren't you?" Samir teased, causing all three men to erupt with laughter. "It would be odd for them if we only sent the boys. You have to understand the culture—"

Khalid cut him off by shouting, "The girls should not be in school! I do not like this."

"It's only for a short time." Aquib seemed to assure him.

Samir, ever the voice of reason, ever the confident leader continued, "You are a man of principle. I respect that. However, this is the plan that will work. You must trust me. All of the children go, or none of them do."

Wright paused the recording and shook her head. "I don't know what kids or where they're sending them, but it doesn't seem like actually educating the children is their main goal . . . If it's only for a short time."

"I agree." Rachel nodded. "What else?"

"Well, there is the issue of the mystery phone calls. I'm assuming they are phone calls since I just hear Khalid Khan talking then pausing."

"There are definitely several phone calls," Dixit confirmed. "Obviously we don't know who he's speaking to or what the other person is saying."

"If there's a way to determine the exact date and time of those calls, I can try to get his call log off his cellphone," Rachel offered. "Then we just identify who he's calling, perhaps with the help of the NSA—"

Eastwood dropped his face into his hand. "Please tell me you aren't back to this!"

She turned her head to look at him and pursed her lips. "You know precisely what I think is going on, and when the rest of these people leave, I'll fill you in on some other stuff I've uncovered."

"What part of *drop it* do you not understand?" Eastwood's voice boomed through the room.

Rachel rolled her eyes. "If you'll allow my insubordination for a moment, I promise to do however many pushups you want and clean all the bathrooms in this entire fucking building, sir."

"Don't you do that anyway?" Eastwood grumbled.

"Yes, because this place is fucking disgusting, and everyone on the janitorial staff needs to be retrained!" Rachel yelled. "I'm right. You know I'm right because ninety-nine percent of the time I'm right. That's why I'm here, that's why you hired me. I'm sorry if my theory—which is really just good intelligence work and spy craft—is uncomfortable or inconvenient for you."

"You are completely out of line!" Eastwood yelled back.

"What else is new?" Rachel countered.

"Ryker—"

"Send me back to combat if you don't like the truth!"

Eastwood slammed his fist on the table. "The rest of you, get out!"

Dixon and Wright fled the room like it was on fire.

"Petchill and Verity are working with Samir, as is Leftwich." Rachel stated it as a fact.

"Didn't I tell you to drop this?" Eastwood glared at her.

"I have evidence." Rachel glared right back at Eastwood.

"What evidence?"

Rachel winced then cued up a recording of her last call with Frank, placed the document with the flight information for the refugee children on the table in front of Eastwood, and pressed play.

Eastwood listened to the call with Frank, wincing and cringing as he did. "Eros Aid? Are you fucking serious with this shit?"

"Call Christopher if you don't believe me. Although he's so sweet and innocent, he believes it's some do-gooder NGO."

Eastwood scrubbed both hands over his face and groaned. "I suppose you're going to this event?"

"I'd really rather not, but I suppose I have to. Partly because Christopher planned the damn thing—my fault—and partly because someone needs to be there when shit hits the fan, which it inevitably will."

"Since when do Frank and Petchill give a shit about refugee kids?" Eastwood was clearly trying to put the pieces together.

"He told me and Christopher that he wanted to raise awareness for the plight of refugee children to gain sympathy for them and spin it somehow into some sort of propaganda to get people excited about bombing the Middle East again. I'm paraphrasing of course, seeing as I'm not so disgustingly dexterous with my words as he is."

"Right." Eastwood sighed. "The event is at the White House."

"Correct," Rachel confirmed even though it hadn't really been a question.

"No weapons."

Rachel pressed her lips into a tight line and nodded to confirm.

Eastwood looked her in the eyes. "Give it to me straight, Ryker. Which of your insane theories has the most clout? What do you think they're up to?"

"Honestly, sir, there are so many people, so many moving parts to this, I have no fucking idea."

Eastwood motioned towards a rolling whiteboard in the corner of the room. "Outline it. Walk me through everything. I don't want you walking into that event unprepared."

Rachel walked around the table and started scribbling names on the whiteboard, and lines connecting the names, talking a mile a minute as she did. "Leftwich is working with Samir. I know you doubt my evidence but—"

"I want to know the worst-case scenario, so operate under the premise that you're right about all of it," Eastwood instructed.

"Okay. Leftwich is working with Samir. Petchill is meeting with Leftwich, which means Petchill is working with Samir. Frank is working with Petchill, so Frank, knowingly or not—because let's be honest here, how often does Frank really know what he's doing—is also working with Samir."

Eastwood burst out laughing. "Can't argue with that!"

"I have a recording of Leftwich and Petchill talking—arguing—something about *kids* and *Sam*. 'Sam has the kids,' then a question of whether Frank knows, or what specifically Frank knows." She tapped the respective names on the white board each time she said them out loud. "Let's not forget too, Samir still has a copy of that damned malware code. No clue if that's related or if that's a separate project of his."

Eastwood nodded, encouraging her to continue.

"Now, Eros Aid, of which Frank and Petchill are both major shareholders, seeing as they're top members of the Eros Group, is evacuating refugee kids for whatever purpose. We both know Frank has a thing for teenage girls . . . I dunno how old these kids are, and I don't know that Frank would fuck a girl from the Middle East. He's got a type, you know? But maybe he's branching out? Trying to be less racist?"

"He's the poster child for failing up. Move on," Eastwood continued.

"Right. So, Samir, Aquib, and Khalid are discussing children, education, and sending kids to be educated in either the U.S. or UK at the same time Frank and Petchill are bringing a group of kids here from Afghanistan . . ." She cocked her head to the side. "Is there just the one group of kids?"

"What do you mean?" Eastwood asked.

"I need dates of those damned conversations and phone calls Paige recorded so I can put together a timeline and see if the kids Samir is talking about are the same kids Frank and Petchill are bringing here."

"That seems a bit far-fetched," Eastwood noted.

"You said to just lay out my ideas!" Rachel threw her hands up in the air. "I can't help it if this is where my mind goes!"

"Fine!" Eastwood raised his hands defensively. "You need dates of those recorded conversations. Call Lux and see what he can do about that."

Rachel nodded and got Luke on a video call.

"Ma'am, sir?" Luke answered. "How may we be of assistance?"

"Lux, is there a way to determine when the conversations recorded on that device actually took place?" Eastwood asked.

"Umm." Luke's brow furrowed. "Not my department, sir. Give me a second." He ran off screen and appeared moments later with Petty Officer Second Class Jeremiah *Caesar* Holden, one of the two tech experts on team Onyx.

Jeremiah smiled when he saw Rachel and Eastwood were on the call then held up the recording device that had been in Yamna's home. "You want more information off of this?"

"Caesar, is there a way to determine the dates of the conversations recorded?" Rachel asked.

Jeremiah's brow furrowed. "From this?" He shook his head. "Not really. The device is activated by noise, records for ten seconds, then stops if there isn't more noise. It doesn't record continuously, so it's not like an hour of recording necessarily corresponds to an hour in real time."

Rachel pinched the bridge of her nose. "There are recordings of the kids playing, arguing, the family having every day normal conversations. Can we extrapolate, deduce, *guess?*"

"I suppose we could, but I can't guarantee the accuracy of any of that," Jeremiah said.

"We know what day Paige installed it. If we listen again and count what we think are mealtimes, three meals a day, we can at least get close," Rachel suggested.

"Same with instances of them talking about going to the mosque, I suppose." Jeremiah shrugged. "It's gonna take a while."

Rachel turned to Eastwood. "Surely the intelligence department has some sort of software that can do this?"

"*Now* you want a computer's help," Eastwood teased.

"I concede, the computer may be faster than me at this particular task."

"Run downstairs and ask them." Eastwood shrugged.

Rachel bolted out of the room before another word could be spoken.

Chapter 32:

DECEMBER 2020

RACHEL GOT DRESSED IN a black pantsuit and a white button-up shirt, then pulled on her black boots. She'd just finished pinning up her hair and was all ready to head to the White House for the child refugee fundraiser when Christopher walked into their bedroom.

"Is that what you're wearing?" His brow creased.

"Yes."

"Did you get a job with the FBI?" He grimaced.

"No." She rolled her eyes.

"We are going to a fundraiser at the White House. You know it's cocktail attire."

"I need to be able to run. I can run in this."

"Rache." Christopher dropped his head into his palm. "There won't be any running at this event. I know you hate dresses for some reason, and at the risk of sounding like your parents, can you please just follow the dress code?"

"This is what I'm wearing!" It came out in an uncharacteristic high-pitched squeak.

Christopher sighed and pulled out his phone. He needed backup.

Christopher to Kristen: *Did you already leave?*
Kristen to Christopher: *Just about to walk out the door.*

Christopher snapped a photo of Rachel and sent it to Kristen.

Kristen to Christopher: *. . . that's not cocktail attire.*
Christopher to Kristen: *I know! Please help!!!*

Kristen arrived at their house twenty minutes later with several dresses and pairs of shoes tucked neatly into an array of tote bags. She followed Christopher into the kitchen and found Rachel sipping a beer and reading something on her phone. "Back upstairs, Ryker, unless you're changing in the kitchen."

"What?" Rachel's brow furrowed as she glanced up from her phone.

"You can't wear that!" Kristen waved her hand up and down, gesturing at Rachel's suit.

Rachel glared at Christopher.

"Told you."

Kristen continued. "I brought you several options. Julie is on her way with several more. Ashley is already at the White House and has confirmed that people are dressed in an array of outfits ranging from cocktail to semi-formal. Your pantsuit will not do."

"But—"

"Four against one, babe. You lose." Christopher grabbed his own beer out of the fridge and pointed towards the stairs.

Rachel stomped up the stairs, closely followed by Kristen, and reluctantly sifted through dresses and shoes. "I need straps."

"On the dress or shoes?" Kristen asked.

"Definitely the dress so I can wear a bra. The shoes . . . it would be easier to run with straps, but then I can't pull them off if I need to hit someone."

Kristen rolled her eyes. "Why do you need to be able to run or hit someone?"

"Because, you never know, and we can't take any weapons in."

"You *are* a weapon," Kristen reminded her.

"As are these stilettos!" Rachel's eyes lit up at the tall slim heeled shoes Kristen had brought her.

"You cannot actually run in those."

Rachel pursed her lips. "Let's see!" She pulled a black sequined dress with long sleeves and a crewneck out of the pile and slid it on. It fit like a glove and hit at her mid-thigh. *Perfect!* She slid on the heels and sprinted out of her bedroom, down the hallway and downstairs to the second, then first floor. "Christopher! Attack me!" She rushed toward him.

He grabbed her with both arms, pulling her in tight to him so that her back was against his chest. "Why am I attacking—" He jerked his head back and to the side, just as the tip of her heel came for his eye.

"Yup, this will do!" She grinned.

"You look beautiful." Christopher pulled her tighter to him and kissed the back of her head. "Why did you need to try to gouge my eye out with your shoe?"

"It's Kristen's shoe."

Christopher waited for her to actually answer the question.

"I'm not allowed to bring weapons into the White House."

"The Secret Service has weapons and will neutralize any threats. You're off duty."

Rachel winced. She was never off duty. Women and children were in danger everywhere. "We'll see." The Secret Service could only handle the threats they knew about. The fact that the president himself was a threat wouldn't occur to them. She needed to be on high alert, ready for anything if Eros Aid was involved—which they were.

"Before you settle on your shoes," Christopher glanced from Rachel's feet to Kristen's, "you both realize there's like three feet of snow on the ground?"

"We're just going from the car to inside then back to the car," Kristen reminded him.

Julie arrived moments later in a town car and rushed inside, her own assortment of dresses and shoes in hand. She let out a sigh of relief when she saw Rachel. "You dressed her! Good!"

Rachel grinned and nodded enthusiastically. "I can run and everything!"

Julie looked at Kristen and Christopher. "Do I want to ask?"

"No." They both shook their heads.

"Okay, well, I have champagne in the car. If everyone's ready, let's go. We're already late!"

Chapter 33:

DECEMBER 2020

FIFTEEN CHILDREN SAT CROSS-LEGGED on the floor of the White House ballroom, antsy to dive into arts and crafts and carnival games, while Trischa Verity gave a speech. Rachel leaned against a wall and pretended to listen, but this, like all of Trischa's speeches, was long-winded and nonsensical. The woman had a skill for saying everything and nothing all at once. Odd that Frank was the politician and not her. Rachel let her eyes dart around, observing the kids. Seven boys and six girls, all about middle-school aged. Trischa ended her speech with the line, "Go play. Enjoy the freedom democracy grants you." As if the kids had any idea what that meant, or cared. It was highly likely they didn't even speak English and hadn't understood a single word of what Trischa had said.

The kids got up and rushed to play games, get snacks, and do arts and crafts projects. Rachel had to admit, there was a lot of fun to be had. The girls had their hair covered, smiles on their faces, eyes locked on the arts and crafts. She watched them dart past her in a whirl of bright colors and then felt Christopher's hand on the small of her back.

"Bar?" he asked.

Rachel nodded and waved to Ashley, Julie, and Kristen across the room so they would see her leave. She followed Christopher to an adjoining room where a bar had been set up with tables for the silent auction.

"Anything good?" Rachel nodded towards the silent auction table, assuming he'd been involved in selecting the items to be actioned off.

"Nothing we can afford or would want to do."

Rachel chuckled. She'd been to enough of these events with her parents to know that was more than likely the case.

Three heads swiveled as they approached the bar, and she could feel one set of eyes lingering much longer than necessary.

"Oh my god! She actually fucking came!" Rexton Wheeler, Jamie and Hunter's friend from college, exclaimed.

Jamie was standing next to him and promptly handed Rachel his drink. "Better catch up!"

"I think I'm better off getting a drink directly from the bartender rather than relying on your poor judgment," Rachel said, nudging the drink back to him and turning towards the bar. "I really don't need to fail a drug test because you decided to mix cocaine into your whiskey and share it with me again."

Jamie shrugged off her comment and took a sip from his glass as Rex leaned in next to her, grazing his finger along her forearm.

"Tequila shots!" Rex insisted.

"Absolutely not." Rachel removed his hand from her arm.

"Come on! It was so much fun last time!" Rex insisted.

"Didn't y'all bring dates? Maybe they can amuse you, and if not, then you may need to be choosier about who you're hanging out with."

"Come on, Rachel, you know no one's as much fun as you!" Rex teased.

"Fuck you, Wheeler."

Rex flashed her a knowing smile. "Just say where, when, and how."

"I will cut off your balls and feed them to Hunter," Rachel threatened.

Christopher couldn't help but laugh.

"Rachel, honey, don't make empty threats," Rex said.

"No, I'm pretty sure she meant that." Christopher smirked.

Rex stared at Rachel, not believing she would be capable of such a thing.

"Jamie, do they not know what she does for a living?" Christopher asked.

"She's in the Navy. She's some sort of secretary or something." Rex shrugged.

Christopher burst out laughing. "Babe, did you know they think you're a secretary?"

"According to my father, Rachel is definitely not a secretary," another man corrected as he made his way over to her.

"Bryant Verity," Rachel greeted the president's son. "And where's *your* wife this evening?"

Bryant shrugged.

"Why did any of you even bother getting married?" Rachel asked them.

"Looks better." Bryant sounded bored.

"Easier to get elected," Hunter added with a confident smile.

"Wait, why would Frank know what her job is?" Rex asked.

"Well, it's a little hard to give a presentation to the National Security Council and have the vice president and president not know your name and job title by the end of it," Rachel said.

Jamie was laughing so hard he had to lean on Rex to keep from falling over.

"Yeah, she's like a fucking Navy SEAL or some shit. Total badass, apparently. That shouldn't surprise you, Wheeler," Bryant teased.

Jamie and Hunter were in a fit of laughter at that.

"Chris, can't you make her sing us a song? This event is rather dull," Jamie complained.

"Are you kidding? No one can make her do anything," Christopher said.

"That's true," Rex said with a bit of amusement in his voice. "Although she is much more amenable to suggestions when there's tequila involved." He gave Rachel a wink.

She reached across the bar and picked up a small knife the bartender had been using to cut limes and tucked it into her sleeve, then pulled a hairpin out of her hair and used it to secure the knife in place. "You've all been warned," Rachel said, locking eyes with Rex.

"Well, you're no fun! He was just joking, Rache," Hunter insisted. He never seemed to understand that people actually said what they meant sometimes.

"Doesn't matter anyway," Jamie said. He picked up Rachel's left hand, showing her ring to Rex and Bryant. "This is Christopher."

"Huh," Rex said. "How do we know she's not just making it up?"

"They bought a house together." Jamie chuckled.

"She made him help plan this stupid event with me," Hunter added.

"Oh, shit," Rex said. "Well, Rachel, you've finally succeeded in breaking the heart of every man in this room."

Hunter hit Rex on the chest with the back of his hand. "Would you try to show some respect." He tipped his head towards Christopher.

Rachel rolled her eyes knowing it was the best she'd get out of any of them. Leave it to Hunter rather than her own fucking brother to stand up for her.

Christopher gave her shoulder a reassuring squeeze and leaned across the bar to order two whiskeys.

Rachel gripped his arm. "One. I'm not drinking."

Five pairs of eyes turned to her.

"Fuck, are you pregnant?" Hunter asked.

"No, I'm—" She saw movement across the room as several men in suits peeled their backs from the walls in perfect synchronization. The Secret Service was on the move. Something was happening. Instinct kicked in and Rachel started running. She didn't give a shit if the Secret Service wanted her help or not. She was certain her help would be needed.

Rachel skidded to a halt in the doorway of a ballroom on the opposite side of the hallway from where she'd been and scanned the room. There was Frank with one of the children—a boy of about thirteen whom she knew well. He was tall for his age, thin, and sweat was beading on his brow. His eyes were wild with panic, head on a swivel as he tried to keep track of everyone and everything around him. Several Secret Service agents were in the room, having already forced everyone else out, their eyes locked on Frank as they assessed the situation.

She took a breath and raised both hands, palms facing Kamal. "Kamal, do you remember me?" Rachel asked in Pashto. "I'm friends with your mom. I'm Rachel." She'd only met the boy in person a handful of times. He'd been at school most of the times she'd been at Yamna's house.

"Ma'am, you need to leave this room," one of the agents barked at her. He positioned himself between her and Kamal and tried to back her out into the hallway.

Rachel ignored him, her full attention on Kamal. "Your Aunt Yashfa called me. Your family is very worried about you."

Kamal shook his head with defiance, his eyes never leaving Frank.

"Did your grandfather tell you to come here, to do something?" Rachel tried.

Kamal nodded.

"What did he tell you?" Rachel shoved past the agent and knelt down in front of Kamal taking his hand in hers.

One of the Secret Service agents had his hands on her, pulling her off her knees and away from Kamal, away from Frank. She flicked the knife she'd stolen from the bartender out of her sleeve and thrust it over her shoulder towards his neck. "Get your fucking hands off me!"

"She's fine," Frank assured them.

The agent didn't release her, but he stopped dragging her towards the door at least. Another agent approached her and wrenched the knife out of her hand.

"Kamal." She switched back to Pashto and kept her voice calm. "What did your grandfather tell you to do?"

Kamal's eyes were on Frank when he said, "Kill."

"You don't have to do what he told you, Kamal. You don't have to kill anyone." She could see the tears welling in his eyes and her chest tightened. "Kill him how?" she asked. It was then she noticed the wire hanging out the bottom of his t-shirt.

"What else did he say?" Rachel asked.

"Grandfather said . . ." Kamal's voice was shaking. "H-he said I must kill the United States President. That I must do it for my family's honor. For Allah."

Rachel switched back to English and whispered to the agent restraining her. "Assuming you already know he's wearing a vest?"

"Bomb squad is on their way. Should be here any minute now," he whispered back.

"You didn't move Frank?"

"Kid panicked when we tried to move Frank. Too many people here. We're working on moving everyone to rooms that are farther away, then we'll move Frank. We have time."

Rachel nodded and looked back to Kamal. The poor kid was sobbing. She switched back to Pashto and tried to calm him down. "Your grandfather says a lot of dumb things. So did mine." Rachel smiled at him. "My mother's father was not a very nice man. Yours isn't either."

"He said he would hurt my sisters if I did not go with him and help him," Kamal murmured.

"Well, it happens to be my job to make sure that doesn't happen," Rachel told him as she nudged the agent with her elbow.

After a nod from Frank, the agent released her, realizing she was helping them keep Kamal calm.

"What, specifically, did he ask you to do?" Rachel knelt in front of Kamal again and motioned with her hand, out of Kamal's sight, for Frank to move back.

Kamal lifted his t-shirt, exposing a mess of wires.

"How did you get this past the metal detector?" Rachel asked. She spun him around carefully, then pointed at a timer, locking eyes with the agent. They had seven minutes. Enough time for the bomb squad to arrive on the scene, just like he'd said.

"A man gave it to me after I was inside," Kamal explained.

"Would you recognize this man if you saw him again?" Rachel's voice was calm and steady. Adrenaline had taken over.

Kamal nodded.

"Alright." Rachel gave him a weak smile. "We're going to get that off you and show you some photos to see if you can identify the man who gave it to you." She pulled him in for a gentle hug. "I spoke with your mother the other day. She misses you very much."

Kamal was shaking with fear, pressing his face into her neck and letting his tears fall freely. He wasn't doing this by choice. He'd been coerced. Fuck, he was just a kid.

"Care to translate?" Frank raised an eyebrow.

"We need handheld metal detectors. Everyone fan out, do a sweep," Rachel told the agents. "Someone at this event gave Kamal the bomb after he was inside the White House. I don't know who, not yet anyway, but there may be more."

"That won't be particularly discrete," Frank protested.

"I'm saving your life. Shut the fuck up, put a smile on your face, and let the Secret Service work." Rachel glared at Frank then checked the timer again.

Five minutes. In five fucking minutes, my life could be over. She could get up, walk out of the room. This really was the Secret Service's problem. But she knew Kamal, felt responsible for keeping him alive. She wanted to get him back home to Yamna. Besides, she had him so secure in her arms that there was no way he could wiggle free and detonate the bomb early. She'd made sure of it. She started singing a lullaby that she'd heard Yamna sing her children. Kamal's breathing steadied, his heart rate calmed. She didn't want to think about the seconds and minutes ticking down. She just stayed on her knees in a sparkly dress with Kamal pulled tight against her.

Time stood still until it was shattered by the stomping of boots and calm steady voices. "Everyone out. Ma'am, get up. Let's go!"

She felt more hands on her, men prying her and Kamal apart. She didn't want to leave him. Didn't want him dying alone. And if they diffused the bomb, didn't want him dealing with the consequences of his actions alone either.

"Rachel." Christopher's voice was calm in her ear. He placed a reassuring hand on her shoulder. "Baby, you have to let go and let the bomb squad work."

"They're here?" She hadn't realized she'd squeezed her eyes shut.

"Yup. They're here. They have just over three minutes, so you need to get out of the way."

Rachel let go of Kamal, and Christopher had her on the opposite side of the room in an instant. Commotion ensued as the Secret Service pushed everyone out of the room and back into the hallway.

"What the hell was that, Rachel?" Frank muttered under his breath.

"I'd ask you the same." She glared at him.

"That kid just tried to kill me, and you—" He hesitated. "What were you saying to him?" Frank asked.

"We'll discuss it later, but I suggest you get Eastwood here," Rachel grumbled as Christopher's arms tightened around her. She watched as Frank pulled his phone out of his pocket and placed a call before wandering down the hallway as casually as he could.

"You good?" Christopher asked the second Frank was out of hearing range.

"I'm fine."

"Please don't ever do that again."

Rachel couldn't help but chuckle. "You know me better than that!"

"I know." Christopher sighed.

"I should call Yamna."

"Why?"

"Umm, to let her know her son just tried to blow up the president?"

"What? That's Kamal?"

"Right, you've never met him." Rachel chewed on her bottom lip.

"And here I thought you were just being reckless and willing to die for some random kid."

"No. Although, I probably would have done that regardless of which kid it was." She turned to look at Christopher, his hands sliding down and resting on her waist, her hands on either side of his face. "I wasn't being reckless. We had seven minutes when I went in there, and I hugged him to pin his arms so he couldn't reach the detonator. I was singing to him to keep him calm so the idea of struggling to reach for the detonator hopefully wouldn't occur to him." She studied his face for a minute. "You've seen me do that before. You watched Tull do it plenty of times—"

Christopher tucked a loose strand of hair behind her ear. "And I've hated it every single time I've watched you do it."

"You don't trust me?" Her brow furrowed. "Or you doubt my abilities?"

He shook his head. "No, I'm just terrified of having to live without you."

A soft smile spread over her face, and she tilted her face up to his. "If that's what's meant to happen . . . you know I'll see you in the next life."

He kissed the top of her head then pressed his forehead to hers. "I'm afraid waiting for that would be unbearable."

"It *is* harder to die together doing something stupid when we're both out of combat," Rachel joked.

He chuckled then pulled her tighter into him, resting his chin on the top of her head. Kristen, Ashley, and Julie were headed their way. "Incoming. I hope you have your story prepared," he whispered.

"Where have you two been?" Ashley asked. "I haven't seen you since the First Lady gave her speech."

"We've been busy." Rachel smirked.

"Seriously, you two? At a fundraiser for children?" Julie chided them.

Christopher burst out laughing. "Nothing quite that fun!"

"What's going on?" Kristen asked, looking back and forth between them.

"I had to run," Rachel said seriously.

Kristen raised an eyebrow.

"No one's seen the president for a while either," Julie noted.

"He's fine," Rachel assured them.

"Well, Hunter's in a mood about it. Part of the whole draw of this thing was to have Frank smiling and shaking hands with all the rich doners," Ashley complained.

"Where is Hunter?" Rachel asked.

"He's at the bar talking to a very attractive gentleman." Ashely giggled, showing Rachel a photo she'd taken with her phone from across the room.

"That's Jamie." Rachel wrinkled her nose.

"Jamie . . ." Ashley clearly wanted more information.

"Jamison Ryker, my brother. If sleeping with Hunter was low on my list of recommendations . . ." She cringed. "Could one of you please go get Hunter and bring him over here, preferably with a whiskey. For me, not for him."

"*Now* you're off duty," Christopher teased.

"Let's fucking hope so," Rachel muttered.

"I'm on it!" Ashley scampered off.

"What's really going on?" Kristen asked.

"I can't really say." Rachel's eyes darted to Julie. "But I might need you to stick around for a bit. May be in need of some legal help."

"Both of us?" Julie's eyes lit up.

"I dunno," Rachel hedged. "Not really your area of expertise, I don't—"

One of the men from the bomb squad poked his head out of the room. "Good job on staying fifty feet back," he chided Rachel. "Where'd the president go?"

"I dunno," Rachel told him. She hadn't heard anyone say anything about staying fifty feet away from the door. She pried Christopher's arms off her and shoved past her friends and into the room. "Campbell, with me."

"Ma'am, you can't—" She had her hand around the agent's throat and backed him into the room with Kristen and Christopher right behind her.

"I am on your side," she told the agent. "Do not fuck with me and do not get in my way! This is Navy business."

Christopher's arms were around her, pulling her off the agent. "Would you fucking behave? You're gonna get arrested for fuck's sake."

"Everyone, take a beat." Kristen held up both hands. "Credentials out. Let's use our words." Rachel, Kristen, and Christopher pulled out their military IDs.

Kristen started again. "Agent?"

"Melgren," he answered.

"Agent Melgren, Rear Admiral Ryker apologizes. She's used to operating in combat zones where violence is more effective than words. She will compose herself and mind her manners from here on out." Kristen glared at Rachel.

"I sincerely apologize for choking you. I got carried away." That demure Southern charm sure came in handy when she wanted it to. "This boy is my intelligence asset's son. He was kidnapped, trafficked, and coerced into doing this," Rachel explained, pointing to Kamal. He was sitting on the floor in the corner of the room, ankles and wrists bound.

"He's a terrorist," Melgren insisted.

"He's a child!" Rachel yelled. So much for staying composed.

"I don't care how old he is. He was wearing a bomb and tried to assassinate the president!" the agent yelled back.

"A bomb *your* team allowed to get into the White House!"

Kristen pinched the bridge of her nose and looked at her feet. "God, I wish you'd just punched someone, Rachel," she muttered under her breath. "This is a much bigger incident than I was anticipating."

The door opened then slammed shut again, and they all turned. "Sitrep, Ryker," Eastwood bellowed.

Rachel took a deep breath then filled Eastwood in on everything that had happened, careful to include the most minuscule details, down to choking out the Secret Service agent to get back into the room with Kamal, and Kristen's frustration at the legal complexities of the situation. She was talking so fast she was out of breath by the time she was done.

Eastwood puffed out his cheeks. "Where the fuck is Frank?"

The Secret Service agent raised his wrist to his mouth, speaking quietly into a microphone. "The president will be here momentarily."

"I told you," Rachel muttered. "I told all of you. Good thing I practiced running in these damned shoes."

Eastwood's eyes darted to her feet. "You ran in those?"

"These assholes wouldn't let me wear a suit and boots." Rachel pointed to Christopher then Kristen.

"Well, you look very nice." Eastwood cringed as he said it, as though commenting on her appearance were painful.

They waited in uncomfortable silence for several minutes until Frank and Joe Petchill entered the room.

"The kid is still here," Frank noted.

"He's secure," Melgren assured him.

"What are you doing about this?"

"There seems to be an issue of jurisdiction." Melgren glared at Rachel.

"Frank, we've been looking for this kid on multiple continents. He's the son of one of our informants and can lead us to a high value target," Eastwood explained.

"He just tried to blow me up!" Frank yelled.

"Because he was told his sisters and mom would be sex trafficked if he didn't help," Rachel explained. "Wouldn't you kill someone to save Trischa from that?"

Frank's brow furrowed.

Maybe not.

"Hell, Ryker is practically your daughter. What wouldn't you do to protect her?" Eastwood added.

Rachel's stomach turned in knots. All three of them knew precisely what Frank would allow people to use her for. "Frank—"

"Mr. President," Melgren corrected.

"He's my godfather for fuck's sake. I've known him a hell of a lot longer than he's been president." Rachel rolled her eyes before turning her attention back to Frank. After taking a deep breath, she tried again. "Kamal is—"

"Who's Kamal?" Frank asked.

Rachel gestured towards Kamal, hunched over in the corner. "Kamal is the son of my intelligence asset. He and his mother can lead us to Khalid Khan, and Khalid Khan can lead us to Samir Al-Abadi and Aquib Faizan." Rachel noticed Petchill tense up at that revelation.

"Well, how the hell did he get here?" Frank shouted.

"You're on the board of directors for the NGO that brought the kids here. You tell me!" Rachel shouted back. "As are you, you stupid piece of shit," she growled at Petchill.

"Wait, what?" Christopher yelled too. "How are you on the board of directors for the NGO we're working with? That's a complete conflict of interest and—"

Rachel held up a hand to stop him. "These two lining their pockets with taxpayer dollars is the least of our problems, Christopher."

"You *knew* about this?"

"Really not the time," Rachel dismissed his anger.

"For fuck's sake, Rachel," Christopher muttered.

Kamal started sobbing loudly in the corner.

"Okay, everyone, calm!" Rachel steadied her voice then switched to Pashto, realizing how terrifying the situation must be for Kamal. "Kamal, you're safe, I promise. No one will hurt you."

"We need to see what information we can get from the kid," Melgren decided.

Frank and Eastwood looked to Rachel.

"You want me to interrogate a *child*?" Rachel was appalled.

"Maybe don't go about it your usual way." Eastwood cringed.

Christopher crossed his arms over his chest and took a wide stance. "Why would Rachel interrogate anyone?"

"Interesting . . ." Frank rubbed his chin.

Eastwood looked at Christopher, head cocked to the side. "Seriously, Williams?"

Christopher raised both hands, looking helpless and confused. "Since when is Rachel trained to interrogate anyone?" Christopher asked again.

"Since about—"

"Since right now." Rachel cut off Frank before he thoughtlessly divulged too much information. The man really was careless with secrets.

Frank looked at Christopher and burst out laughing. "Oh, you have no idea who you're about to marry!"

"Do you have a death wish?" Rachel gave Frank a scathing look.

"What the actual fuck?" Melgren looked like he was about to punch her.

"What would be the point in me interrogating him? Most of you can't verify what we're saying, and I get the sense I'll be accused of lying and that none of you believe me about what's happening anyway. Or some of you would believe me but would deny it since you know I'm correct about the fucked up shit you're doing." She glared at Petchill.

"Hang on," Kristen interjected. "Can he type?"

Christopher translated the question, and Kamal nodded.

"So have him and Rachel type into Google Translate, and we'll be able to see an English translation of what they're writing. It might not be one hundred percent accurate, but it'll be good enough to know if Rachel's being honest about what the kid's saying."

"Highly unconventional!" Petchill protested.

"It's an unconventional situation," Kristen pointed out. "I don't think we have a better option, unless you have another interrogator who's fluent in Pashto on hand."

A laptop was brought in, along with a large screen and keyboard with the Pashto alphabet, so everyone could see in real time what Rachel and Kamal were typing. Rachel found the entire notion utterly ridiculous. She heard Eastwood's voice in her head *Trust but verify.* This was definitely a situation that needed verification. She understood that. But it was going to be difficult to do with the guilty parties in the room. She started typing easy questions first—name, age, why are you in the U.S.—trying to establish rapport and prove that the translation software worked. Then they started getting to the interesting parts.

Rachel: *Kamal, if I'm going to help you, I need to know what your grandfather was going to do.*

Kamal: *My mother would be very ashamed of me if I spoke of such things.*

Rachel: *I promise, your mother will forgive you as soon as she knows you are alive and well. She knows it's your grandfather doing these bad things, not you. Please write down what he said would happen to your sisters.*

Kamal: *The bad man would take their honor. Sell them to other bad men.*

Rachel glanced over at Eastwood and raised an eyebrow. He nodded, encouraging her to continue.

Rachel: *Do you know the bad man's name? The one your grandfather would sell your sisters to?*

Kamal: *Aquib. He is not a nice man.*

Rachel: *Have you met Aquib?*

Kamal: *Yes. At the camp.*

Rachel: *Tell me more about the camp, please.*

Kamal: *Grandfather took me. Mamma was scared. She didn't want me to go but grandfather said I must. He took me and there were other children and they gave us guns and told us how to be soldiers, how to be men.*

Rachel: *What does that mean, how to be men?*

Kamal: *He made us hurt the girls. Hold them down and do things to them. He said it was our reward for fighting, for jihad. That the girls needed to learn.*

Rachel wanted to hurl. She could read between the lines. She hoped desperately she was misunderstanding but was fairly certain she wasn't.

Rachel: *Where was the camp?*

"Don't tell her that!" Petchill yelled in Pashto.

Everyone in the room turned to look at him.

"I thought you didn't speak Pashto?" Rachel raised an eyebrow at him.

"I-I don't." Petchill couldn't meet her eyes.

"You just did though." Christopher's brows knit together.

"Joe, shut the fuck up and stop interfering in Rachel's interrogation." Frank scolded him. "Rachel." Frank pointed at the computer indicating she should continue.

Rachel: *When I found you, you had a bomb.*

Kamal: *Yes.*

Rachel: *Why? What were you going to do with the bomb?*

Kamal: *My jihad was to kill the United States President.*

Rachel pointed at Frank and Kamal nodded.

Rachel: *What about the other children? Did they have a jihad?*

Kamal: *To put the code on the network.*

Rachel: *What code?*

Kamal shrugged.

Rachel: *What can you tell me about the code?*
Kamal: *They should plug the stick into a computer. That's all I know.*

Interesting, but Rachel believed him that he didn't know anything else about it.

Rachel: *How did you get the vest with the bomb into the White House?*
Kamal: *I didn't. I got it when I was already here.*
Rachel: *Who gave you the—*

Everyone covered their ears as the fire alarm started blaring. Organized chaos ensued as evacuation procedures were implemented. Before Rachel knew what was happening, the Secret Service swarmed Frank and had him on the move. Another group of agents had Kamal and were moving him in the opposite direction. Suddenly, Rachel was outside on the White House lawn with Christopher, Kristen, and Eastwood.

"What the fuck?" Rachel yelled. "I was just getting to the good part!"

An agent ran towards them. "You all need to wait here while we clear the building and secure everything."

"What's happening?" Eastwood demanded to know.

"Not sure yet," the agent answered. "We're usually pretty quick about this." His eyes darted to Kristen and Rachel's legs. "Sorry, ladies, for the inconvenience. I know it's cold out here."

"Yeah, we didn't really anticipate standing outside in the snow when we chose these outfits." Kristen wrinkled her nose.

"I feel like I said something about this before we left." Christopher's face was screaming *I told you so.*

The agent nodded and said something into his radio. A few minutes later, another agent came running, blankets in hand.

"Thank you." Kristen accepted one of the blankets and wrapped it around herself.

Rachel was pacing and muttering to herself, frustrated with the entire situation.

"Baby," Christopher interrupted. "Blanket?"

Rachel's eyes darted between the now two agents who were seeming to guard them. "Where's the president?"

"He's secure, ma'am. No need to worry," the first agent said.

Rachel rolled her eyes. "What about the kid?"

"Kid?" the second agent asked.

"The one I was just questioning."

Rachel's question hung in the air, both agents acting as though they had no clue what she was talking about. Maybe they didn't. Neither of them had been in the room, but she highly doubted they hadn't heard about the entire incident by now.

Thirty minutes later, they were finally allowed back inside. Rachel saw Frank down the hall and made a beeline for him. "Where's Kamal?" she yelled.

Frank turned towards her and shrugged. "Your guess is as good as mine."

"What?" Rachel shouted again, louder now.

Petchill came sauntering down the hall from the opposite direction Rachel was coming from. "Kid's gone, Ryker. I don't know what you told him—"

"What *I* told him?"

"You're clearly working together!"

"You're one to talk," Rachel muttered.

"Both of you, stop!" Frank held up both hands. "This entire place was on lock down. He couldn't have gotten far."

"Not unless someone was helping him," Petchill noted.

"I have no idea how to get in and out of the White House," Rachel pointed out. "He had to have had help from the Secret Service. They're the ones who would know all the exits and where a break in your security would be."

"Melgren." Frank waved him over. "Where's the kid?"

Melgren shook his head. "Mr. President, we have no idea. Security cameras cut out. I'm sorry, sir."

Rachel forced a cough. "Frank, may I speak to you in private?"

"No," Petchill answered for him.

"Right, sorry, can't leave out the puppet master," Rachel mocked.

"Knock it off, Ryker," Eastwood interjected. "Williams, take Campbell home. Neither of you have clearance for this level of fiasco. Keep what you already know to yourselves, obviously."

"Yes sir." Kristen pressed her lips into a tight line and glanced at Rachel.

"You good, babe?" Christopher checked.

"Yeah. Just get Kristen home and check in with Ashley and Julie. Make sure they're okay. I'll call or text when I can."

Rachel, Eastwood, Frank, Petchill, and Melgren filed into a conference room to further assess and debate the situation. Shockingly, Eastwood was even more pissed than Rachel was. He pinched the bridge of his nose and looked down. "How does the Secret Service allow a bomb to get into the White House, then have that bomb handed off to a child, the child get near the president, and then allow the child to escape?"

"How do terrorists do anything, Paul?" Frank asked.

"In this case, with help from someone on the inside," Rachel muttered.

"Ryker, I swear to fucking God," Eastwood grumbled.

"Which god?" She smirked.

"Which one will you listen to?" he chided her.

"Stop, both of you!" Frank scolded them. "The Secret Service will find the kid, detain him—"

"You want to detain a thirteen-year-old boy who did something he thought would prevent his younger sisters from being raped and abused?" Rachel raised an eyebrow. "I'd trade your life in a heartbeat to save those girls."

"He tried to assassinate the president!" Melgren interjected.

"He was coerced!" Rachel argued.

"Whose side are you on?" Petchill glared at her.

"I could ask you the same!" she countered.

Rachel turned her attention to Melgren. "If someone told you they were going to rape and abuse your wife and daughter until they were dead, unless you did what they told you, what would you do?"

"Not the point." Eastwood shook his head. "The kid is gone. How that happened is a problem for the Secret Service to investigate. How to get the kid back, however—"

"Ryker's insisting it's Navy business. Make her find him." Petchill shrugged.

"Or you could just tell me where he is." Rachel glared at him.

"How should I know?" Petchill was a pro at feigning innocence.

"Well, let's see. You and Frank awarded yourselves this contract to bring these kids over . . . kids who were being held by Khalid Khan, Samir Al-Abadi, and Aquib Faizan. Kamal somehow gets a bomb after he's inside the White House, so it had to be someone here, someone who was trusted. Right when I was about to ask him who gave him the bomb, the fire alarm goes off and the security cameras malfunction. Then, once we're back inside, we discover that he somehow escaped when the entire property was on lock down." She shook her head. "No one in here is dumb enough to believe any of those things were mere coincidence."

"You're accusing me of trying to get myself blown up?" Frank blinked at her.

"Nooooo," Rachel drug out the word, her eyes fixated on Petchill. "I'm not accusing *you*, Frank."

"Ryker will find the boy, then we'll determine what to do with him," Eastwood decided.

Rachel wrinkled her nose. "Umm, what happened to all this insistence that I'm not allowed to operate on U.S. soil?"

Frank burst out laughing. "Oh honey, that's just what we tell the public so they feel safer! You think we want everyone realizing the CIA and NSA are watching and recording everything they're doing? Interfering in corporate mergers, political campaigns, suppressing messages, people, groups we don't like?"

"I really wish I'd recorded that." Rachel sighed. It was far from new information, but getting Frank to actually say it out loud?

"Find the kid, Ryker," Eastwood reiterated.

"Do I have a team? Any resources?" she asked.

"Don't be stupid, Rachel," Frank scolded. "You're a CIA officer and Navy SEAL. You have two agencies at your disposal."

Rachel watched as realization flashed in Petchill's eyes. *Fuck.* He'd just figured something out.

Chapter 34:

DECEMBER 2020

RACHEL WAS PACING IN Eastwood's office back at HQ. The only words she could get out were "I told you so," in various tones ranging from anger to frustration to utter hopelessness and despair.

Eastwood sat, elbows on his desk and index fingers pressed to either side of his nose. "Ryker, can you please calm down so we can figure out what to do about this?"

"What to do about what, *Paul?*" she yelled. She wasn't in uniform, she really didn't give a shit, and this issue seemed to predate her joining the Navy, so *Paul* seemed like the best way to get through to him right now.

"My feet hurt just watching you stomp around in those heels."

Rachel flicked off one of her shoes, turned, and flung it at him. They both knew she'd missed his head on purpose, but she'd still made her point.

"I should have listened to you," Eastwood admitted.

"Listened to *me?*" Rachel's brows shot up, eyes wide. "Listened to what? Not even my fucked up brain could have concocted this! Petchill was working with Samir and Khalid to assassinate Frank!"

"That's sort of what it seems like." Eastwood sighed.

"Then, oh, my favorite fucking part of this, when Petchill's plan failed, he helped Kamal escape? Exfiltrates him from the White House right under the Secret Service's noses? I *highly* doubt Frank was involved in *that* part either!" She turned towards Eastwood's desk just in time to see him pull a bottle of whiskey out from his desk drawer along with two paper cups. She took one of them and shot the drink back before slamming the cup back on the desk, demanding a second round. "What I wouldn't give to get that piece of shit alone in a room with me at a black site."

Eastwood chuckled. "I'd pay good money to watch that!"

"I could burn him at the stake. That sure would be poetic, wouldn't it?" Rachel grinned.

"Okay, no more history books for you." Eastwood shook his head.

Rachel wasn't done. "Is there anyone around here I'm allowed to kill because, fuck, I really want to hurt someone right now."

"I feel like that's true most of the time." The corner of Eastwood's lips curled. "You'll get your revenge eventually. Just not now. Petchill's a piece of shit, but he's got Frank's protection."

"Frank's sort of on my list too . . ." Rachel gave her ear a nervous tug.

"I know he is, and I know *why* he is, and I'm aware that it's for a similar reason to the reason that I'm *not* on your list of targets."

Rachel shrugged, really not wanting to think about it.

"Reconciling the past is a problem for the future. Right now, we've got to find this kid."

"Kamal."

"Right, Kamal. How are you going to find Kamal? Keep in mind, Williams is not allowed to help you with this. He's a civilian and would be interfering in a federal investigation if he did. So, unless you want to be visiting him in prison—"

Rachel crossed her arms over her chest and looked at her feet. "If Petchill got Kamal out of the White House, he could be anywhere."

Eastwood nodded. "We would have heard a helicopter though, so it's most likely Kamal got put in a car or was evacuated on foot."

"True," Rachel agreed. "Any way to hack into all the traffic cameras or security cameras around the White House? I highly doubt the Secret Service is going to let me watch their cameras."

"You want to get into Metro PD's system?"

Rachel responded with a one-shouldered shrug, "Yeah, I'm pretty sure the police have the city well covered."

"I'm very certain someone at Langley is already hacked into their network," Eastwood pointed out.

Rachel shook her head. "I'm not going anywhere near Langley."

Eastwood raised an eyebrow. "Did you forget your access code again?"

"No." Rachel rolled her eyes. Entering CIA headquarters was mentally impossible. Not physically. "I'm not going to Langley because one, I can't enter that building without feeling like I'm going to die, either of a panic attack or someone just turning around and stabbing me in the back. The fucking place is feral, and I don't trust a single person in that building. And two," she took a breath, "I don't have a car. How the fuck would I get there?"

"How do you get anywhere?" Eastwood's confusion was evident on his face.

"I borrow Christopher's truck."

"Then borrow the truck." Eastwood looked at her like she was stupid.

She shook her head. "You don't understand. The man is OCD about the damned truck. He documents the mileage, tire pressure, checks and updates the addresses in the GPS for all the places I go most frequently to make sure there is zero chance of me getting lost. If I took his truck out to Langley, he'd know I went to Langley and that would open a black hole of other horrific questions I'd have to answer that I'm really not prepared to answer at this time, if ever."

Eastwood blinked twice. "He . . . checks the GPS to see where you're going?"

"Yes!" Rachel nodded her head vigorously. "Then he sits me down and explains that, for example, if I got my coffee on the way to therapy, I could avoid making several left turns, thereby saving miles, gas, and time. And don't worry, he's very specific with exactly how many miles, how much gas, and how much time would be saved by me running *my* errands in *his* order."

Eastwood burst out laughing. "That poor boy needs a job! He's got way too much free time!"

"I know!" Rachel yelled. "Why do you think I made him help plan this stupid fundraiser?"

Eastwood held up a hand, palm facing her, trying to get her to slow down and focus. "You're in therapy?"

"Don't worry about it."

"Alright . . . So you're not going out to Langley. Doesn't mean you can't call someone on the phone who's already there."

Rachel scrunched up her face into a pout, knowing she'd burned a lot of bridges at Langley and wasn't at all in a position to be asking favors, certainly not over the phone. "Indigo is home."

Eastwood raised an eyebrow.

"Raven can make a trip to Langley. He's much less hated than I am."

"How much are you gonna tell him?" Eastwood asked.

"Just that Kamal is missing, and I need surveillance of the city to try to find him."

"He's in New York currently?"

"I assume so." Rachel let out a deep exhale. "I'm still trying to get a timeline and dates for the conversations on the recording Paige made. The intelligence department is remarkably slow, so I've been trying to piece it together myself. I should probably call Kamal's mother and tell her I found him . . . sort of . . ."

"Where are we with Khalid Kahn?" Eastwood switched focus.

"Kamal confirmed he was being held at a camp in the mountains. I guess we get Onyx up to Jalalabad to check it out? See if there are more kids there, if Khalid Khan or Samir or anyone is still there. The tracker on his car was a good idea, in theory, but I think we've learned that he's not necessarily in his car, so we can't rely on that."

"Recon in the mountains near Jalalabad?" Eastwood furrowed his brow. "Sounds like a fun way to spend Christmas."

"Right . . . Christmas." Rachel grimaced. "Is your daughter in town?"

"Yup. We're doing the whole family thing."

Rachel nodded. "Get Raven on this CIA surveillance. They can update him, and he can update me so no one at Langley is reminded I exist. I can camp out here and oversee Onyx and their oh-so-exciting reconnaissance."

"You sure?"

"You don't actually believe Christopher and I decided to believe in Jesus all of a sudden? Neither of us could give a shit about Christmas."

"You're actually going to sit here and watch Onyx do recon?"

"I'm going to sit here and keep them entertained. It's a morale boost for them, and in the event something actually happens, I'll be able to tell them how to handle it without delay. Raven can just call the emergency line if he gets any hits on Kamal anywhere in the city. What else can I do? Wander around and look for him myself? I highly doubt the White House wants this publicized. We can't really put Kamal's picture in the media without having to answer questions, and I'm sure Petchill would squash that idea anyway. Assuming Petchill even lets Kamal out. Again, I'm assuming Petchill has him because that's really the only thing that makes sense."

"I agree." Eastwood nodded. "Petchill was definitely involved. He had access to the kid, knows the layout of the White House, has enough influence, and he was really quick to point fingers and divert blame from himself, trying to make *you* look guilty."

Rachel's eyes went wide. "Where are all the other children who were at the event?"

"I dunno." Eastwood's brow furrowed. "I didn't know that was an issue. How many kids were there?"

"Fifteen. I just . . . I didn't see any of them after Trischa gave her speech and Christopher made me go to the bar where I was harassed by Jamie and his stupid friends. Then I saw the Secret Service moving, and that was it. The other fourteen kids—"

"Do you have pictures of all of them?"

"*I* don't. Christopher might, or Hunter or Ashley . . . Ashley would have taken pictures of them. I'll get their photos to Raven to run though the city's video surveillance too."

Eastwood nodded and lifted the secure landline sitting on his desk. He dialed Ryan Rhodes and put the call on speaker. "Raven, we need you in D.C.

immediately. Langley to be more specific. We've got missing kids, probably trafficked, potentially armed and dangerous."

"Fuck," Ryan complained. "You know Sky is in D.C., sir—"

"He knows I'm here!" Rachel yelled. "No way in hell am I stepping foot inside of Langley though."

"Right." Ryan paused. "Email me what you need me to do and whose ass you need me to kiss, and I'll be at Langley as quick as I can. Sky, maybe send my mom a present to make up for me missing Christmas?"

Rachel chuckled. "Sure. Text me what she wants or needs, and I'll take care of it."

Chapter 35:

DECEMBER 2020

"I DON'T HAVE PTSD. You tested me, remember?"

Rachel was back in Catherine's office. She didn't know where to start but gave a semi-coherent summary of Thanksgiving, flashbacks included.

"No, as long as you were honest a few weeks ago, then you don't have PTSD. Or at least not enough symptoms to get diagnosed with it," Catherine agreed.

"Well, being around my family may have brought up a lot of stuff." *Biological family, Frank, CIA assholes . . .*

Catherine nodded but didn't say anything.

"Stress can make things worse, right?"

"Correct."

"And being around terrible, obnoxious, people . . . My mother, I mean. I love Christopher's family."

"Did you just have the one episode of flashbacks?" Catherine asked.

"Yes."

"While drunk and talking about the event the flashbacks were about?"

"Correct." Rachel nodded.

"Well, that's not so strange, Rachel. I'm sorry you experienced that, but if it was the only time—"

"Count my blessings." Rachel chuckled. Thankfully she'd buried everything associated with the CIA—the Eros Group—deep in the darkest, most remote corners of her mind. The day all of that shit decided to surface would not be fun.

"Do you have time to read a book before our next session? It's called *The Body Keeps the Score: Brain, Mind, and Body in the Healing of Trauma* by Bessel van der Kolk. You should be able to find it pretty easily."

"What's it about?" Rachel asked.

"You're going to read it and tell me." Catherine smiled.

"I'm working though. I have to entertain Onyx while they look for Khalid Khan, and I have to find Kamal because the Secret Service is stupid, or corrupt . . . maybe both." Rachel pursed her lips, considering which it was.

Catherine raised an eyebrow.

"I saved the president from getting blown up," Rachel stated plainly. She may as well have told Catherine she'd had soup for lunch.

"What?" Catherine's shock was more than evident.

"Yeah, Frank surrounds himself with corrupt, self-serving sycophants." Rachel grimaced as she proceeded to fill Catherine in on everything that had transpired, starting with the day she found out Eros Aid was involved in the fundraiser. "And so, you see, by burying my head in the sand and ignoring these things, I only allowed the problems to grow and fester and take root and now these *men* get to do whatever the hell they want."

"Well, at least you finally trust doctor-patient confidentiality," Catherine teased.

Rachel raised an eyebrow and considered what Catherine said. "You haven't fucked me over yet, Catherine. You're honest with me, tell me when I'm wrong, and tell me when I'm right. You don't judge my thoughts and feelings or call me crazy. Even when I can tell you wish I'd open up more and tell you things, you don't lie or try to manipulate me. You're patient and wait for me to be ready, but give me little nudges."

"How does that make you feel?"

"What a dumb question." Rachel rolled her eyes.

"I don't care how dumb you think it is. I want a verbal answer," Catherine pushed.

Rachel thought for a minute. "It makes me feel like how I feel when I talk to Christopher. It makes me feel safe."

"How many people do you have in your life that you trust?"

"Eighty-seven," Rachel said without thinking.

Catherine sat back in her chair, her jaw slack. "That's a specific and very high number."

"All of the SEALs in my squadron, my boss, Christopher, and you."

Catherine nodded. "What about yourself? Do you trust yourself?"

Rachel blinked twice, staring straight at Catherine. "Now I feel nauseous and need some whiskey."

"Need?" Catherine asked.

"Oh, I'm definitely *not* an alcoholic." Rachel shook her head.

"No, you're a combat vet who doesn't technically have PTSD and uses alcohol and sex to cope."

"I'm fairly certain that's not an official diagnosis, meaning I don't have a mental illness and am therefore perfectly fine."

"And that would also be a technicality." Catherine chuckled. "Why don't you trust yourself?"

"I don't like this line of questioning."

"I know you don't."

"I'd prefer we just do book club."

"What?" Catherine's brow creased.

"I'll get the book you mentioned, read it, and then we can talk about it. We don't really need to talk about me so much. We can just discuss books. I think that would be better."

"Too big of a nudge?" Catherine asked.

"Like jumping off a fucking cliff. Except that's usually fun, and this is not."

"Right." Catherine pressed her lips into a tight line. "Let's backtrack a little. After your rundown of everything that happened at the fundraiser, you said something like you buried your head in the sand and allowed the problem to fester and now men get to do whatever they want?"

Rachel pursed her lips and looked the floor. She'd said *way* too much this time.

"What did you mean by that?" Catherine pressed.

Silence.

"Rachel, I'm sure there are corrupt politicians in this country. There are bad people everywhere. What I'm struggling to understand is how that could possibly be *your* fault."

"Oh, Catherine." Rachel sighed. "That story requires multiple bottles of whiskey, I'm afraid."

"Fine, don't tell me the story." Catherine gave a nonchalant shrug. "Tell me this: why do you blame all the world's problems on yourself?"

"Because they're all my fault."

"How so?"

Rachel chewed on her bottom lip, took a deep breath, then started explaining. "Once upon a time, there was a little girl. She was told she could grow up to be anything she wanted . . . sort of. She fought and worked hard and clawed her way to the top, seeking power, success, approval. Trying to make her father proud. No amount of hard work got her to where she wanted to be though. Doors kept slamming in her face. People—men—repeatedly told her no, her dream would never come true. It was impossible. So that little girl made a deal with the devil, and suddenly, the world was awash with golden rays of sunlight. People laid at her feet, bowing to her like she was the empress of all. A goddess." Rachel huffed out a laugh through her smirk. "Goddess of war and destruction and death, but goddess, nonetheless. One day, the little girl learned she was getting sent on an adventure. Goddess or not, she still had to take orders from the devil and his lackeys. Evil men who used her, used her body for evil purposes, personal gain, to manipulate the world into being what *they* wanted it to be, all so they could line their pockets with gold. But she had to comply with their sinister wishes. She'd sold her soul, after all. Her body, mind, and soul that is, and the devil had the paperwork to prove it. So she went on her adventure. She saved lives, rescued innocents from destruction and chaos, made a friend too. She'd never really had too many friends, so maybe she was just too excited someone wanted to hang out with her, and she was blinded, couldn't see the evil standing right in front of her. Not until—" Rachel looked down to where her nails were digging into her thigh. Her jeans were thick, and she could barely feel the pain through the denim.

"Her friend betrayed her, tried to kill her, left her for dead, took all of her secrets—or most of them, anyway—and went on to terrorize the world. That could have been the end. It almost was, but she grit her teeth and fought the pain and rose from the darkness, stronger than she'd been before. It's amazing what betrayal does to the psyche. It's like fortification, armor. That little girl was pissed and out for revenge. Betrayal was bad enough, but when she saw what her friend—her former friend—was doing . . ." Rachel shook her head. "She was goddess of war and destruction and death no more. He'd taken that from her. Stripped her of her title and taken it for himself.

"She had to change. Become someone new. There was a bird she trusted. A mythical, magical phoenix. So, she ran to him and begged for help. She didn't tell him everything though. It was too horrific, too embarrassing, and she didn't want anyone to know the terror she'd caused by befriending a snake. The devil himself, he could be reasoned with. But these other evil creatures . . . The rift between that little girl and her friend left no common ground. No room for discussions or negotiations. No talks of peace. He was burning the world to the ground right in front of her, and she knew it was her fault. Her cross to bear, so to speak. She vowed to fight back, destroy him and every man who had used her for evil, every man who had hurt her. But the list kept getting longer, like every time she killed one of them, two more appeared. Like, by spilling their blood, she was spreading their hatred, their lies, their dark magic. She knew the best way to fight back would be to embrace dark magic too. Fight evil with evil, sin with sin, but her trusted phoenix kept telling her no, insisting the time wasn't right. 'Not yet,' he'd tell her, always promising *one day*."

A tear ran down Rachel's cheek. "She sits alone a lot, contemplating how to fix it. Lamenting the deaths that are on her hands, the new friends she's made who have all died because of that one original sin, the sin they never knew about. If they had, they probably wouldn't have signed up to help her. If they'd known about that deal with the devil and subsequent misplaced trust in the snake." Rachel shook her head.

"The moral of the story is actions and decisions have consequences, and we can rarely anticipate what those consequences are in advance. Especially when we're blinded by determination, convinced we know what's best. And when revenge is clouding everything . . . I'm no better than the people who made me what I am. I, like them, use my charisma and charm to get what I want, to convince other people that my way is right, just, best. But it can't be because I keep losing, and other people keep getting hurt. They keep dying." She brushed the tears from her eyes. "How long can I keep fighting before I break?"

"What I hear you saying is that you don't trust yourself," Catherine summarized. "You think you make the wrong decisions, made deals with the wrong people, let your emotions cloud your ability to make decisions."

Rachel nodded.

"And because of that, the people who are helping you, trusting you, die?"

Another nod. "Sometimes I think if I'd just given up when he shot me, if I'd died that day, that none of this would have happened. But . . . I-I had to live. To run back and tell command we had a problem—that *he* was a problem. They didn't want to listen, not at first. But then . . . I know so much about him because we were friends. I told him some of my secrets, but he told me his secrets too. No one else will be able to stop him but me. But I keep failing. And now I find out he's in cahoots with the other assholes. I suspected it before, that someone—someone who was supposed to be on my side—was feeding him information about where my team was, what we were doing . . . it seems I've underestimated the level of betrayal this time too."

"You aren't willing to name names and make this more clear, are you?" Catherine's tone implied she already knew the answer.

Rachel stared at the clock.

"It sounds like you not trusting yourself is coming from your inability to predict what other people are going to do, just how far they'll take something." She cocked her head to the side. "You aren't a terrorist, Rachel, so is it really reasonable to expect yourself to be able to think like one?"

"I need to get back to work." Rachel stood, swiping her phone off the end table and shoving it in her back pocket as she stomped out of Catherine's office.

The house was quiet when Christopher got home. He pulled his phone out of his pocket and checked the time. Rachel should be home from therapy by now. He sighed, hoping she wasn't lost again, and dialed her number. He heard her phone ring in the kitchen, but she wasn't there. Her phone was rarely out of her hand, let alone out of her sight. He hung up the call and wandered upstairs, looking for her.

Rachel was lying in bed under a mountain of blankets in the dark, on her side, clutching a half-empty bottle of whiskey. It looked like she'd collected every single blanket in the house and bunkered down. Christopher listened for a moment from the doorway and heard her sniffles. "Therapy wasn't much fun, I guess."

"I am *not* an alcoholic," she insisted, her back still turned to him.

His eyebrows shot up. "Did your therapist accuse you of being an alcoholic?"

"No," Rachel muttered. "She told me I'm not a terrorist."

Christopher coughed to stifle is laughter. "No, you most definitely are not a terrorist . . ." He took in her silence, realizing she didn't find it at all funny. Realizing she was hurt and hiding out in her version of a blanket fort. "Umm, why are you offended by that statement?"

"I'm not."

"Okay." He sat on the bed and combed his fingers through her hair. He knew she was lying. "Tell me more."

"She said I'm not a terrorist, so it's unreasonable for me to believe I can think like one."

"Oh." Christopher chuckled. "I see what happened." He tugged on her shoulder, getting her to roll onto her back and look at him. "You're mad because most of the time you *can* think like a terrorist and predict what they're going to do, and she either doesn't believe you or something happened that you couldn't predict, and you feel bad about it. Something like Kamal trying to blow up Frank and then escaping the White House."

Rachel gave him a blank stare then propped herself up on her elbow and took a long swig of whiskey. "People keep getting hurt, Christopher."

"From what I know, and thanks for kicking me out part way through the evening," he grumbled, not at all happy he hadn't been involved. "But from what I know, no one got hurt at the fundraiser."

"Kamal said they were hurting the girls. They were filling his head with lies. God knows where he is now or what they're doing to him."

"You're worried about him."

Rachel nodded.

"Scared."

She nodded again.

"You're going to find him."

"How?" she grumbled.

"Put your helmet on, pick up your rifle, and look in every single cave. Leave no stone unturned . . . metaphorically speaking, because there aren't too many actual caves in D.C."

"Eastwood told me if you helped, you'd be interfering in a federal investigation and go to prison."

"I know."

"This sucks."

Christopher gave her a warm smile. He couldn't agree more. It really did suck.

"Hypothetically . . . if you were me . . . how would you go about finding him?" Rachel asked.

"The same way we always find hostages. Figure out who has him and where that person feels safe."

"Right." Rachel took another swig of whiskey. "I can't get to the person who has him."

"Why not?"

"They're too protected, have too many resources."

"Fine, give up." Christopher shrugged, hoping she'd take it as a challenge.

"I'm so tired of fighting, Christopher. I can't do it anymore." She collapsed back against the pillows and pulled the mountain of blankets over her head as tears rolled down her cheeks.

"Of course you're tired. You never sleep!" He saw quickly that teasing was not the right approach. She was being serious. She was dejected and defeated and ready to quit. He'd never seen her like this before. "You'll feel better tomorrow if you actually get some sleep, Rache. Put the whiskey away and just rest."

"Will you sing me my song?"

A wide grin took over Christopher's face. It was the first time she'd asked him that since they'd moved in together. The first time she'd really asked for help, other than telling him to unpack a few moving boxes and delegating tasks she didn't want to do. This was Rachel being vulnerable, letting him take care of her, admitting she needed him, trusted him. "Of course, baby." He scooted down in the bed and under the covers with her, into her secure blanket fortress. She snuggled into his arms, then he started singing "American Pie."

PART III:

FOREVER

Chapter 36

DECEMBER 2020

RACHEL MARCHED INTO HQ the next morning full of determination. There was no way in hell she was quitting. Not until she was dead, and even then, she'd do everything in her power to come back as some sort of spirit and haunt her men, lead them to her targets, torment their targets. Eastwood was out for Christmas, as were most people, so she didn't have too many people between the front door and the control room expecting her to chitchat. Thank god. Laptop and protein bar in one hand, cup of coffee in the other, she kicked open the door to Mission Control, then took a few long paces to the center of the room and dropped her belongings on the desk. That shiny button, her lifeline, was right in front of her, so she pushed it, connecting herself to Luke immediately. "Lux, where are you?"

"Standing in the middle of nowhere." Luke spun around, giving her a three-sixty view of what he was looking at.

"Why?" She winkled her nose.

"These are the coordinates you gave us off the tracker you put on Khalid Khan's car."

"Oh." Rachel pursed her lips. She'd sent him a screenshot of the coordinates off the tracker, so it's not like she could have written them down wrong. "Well, that's where his car went, so . . ." She opened her laptop, logged on, and opened the tracking software. "Right now, his car is in Kabul."

"Then why the fuck are we out here in the snow instead of in Kabul?" Luke grumbled.

"Because, if you may recall, he wasn't *in* his car last time I was staring at the tracking app, so what's the point in following his car? Besides, we need to know what's at that location so we can rule it out as a potential place for him to hide out. Or if you do find a house or something, you can bug it, and we can listen in on what's going on there."

"Yeah, okay." Luke seemed unhappy but accepted her logic. Not that he had much of a choice. "We're checking it out. Strat's getting the drone up. Everyone else is looking around. We've only been here for about ten minutes."

"You need to drive faster!" Rachel chided him. If she'd been driving, they would have been there hours ago.

"Sure," Luke said dismissively. "Give us some time to look around and I'll call you back with an update."

"Fine," Rachel agreed. She disconnected the call and plopped down in a chair, hoping it wouldn't take them too long.

After sitting and waiting and tapping her fingers on the desk for thirty minutes, the emergency phone line rang. "Ryker," she answered.

"Sky, I'm at Langley. I have people working on your project," Ryan announced.

"Well, aren't you efficient!" At least someone had made progress.

"Yeah, sorry. There was a lot of traffic coming from New York, so it took me longer to get here than anticipated, but like you thought, they've already got a team monitoring more or less every security camera in D.C."

"And they're including you?"

"Yes, because unlike you, I know how to make friends."

"I know how to *make* friends. I'm just not great at keeping them," Rachel argued.

"Whatever. I have the picture of Kamal but haven't gotten pictures of the other fourteen kids yet."

"Right! Sorry." Crying in bed had not been particularly productive. She started clicking on her laptop until she found an email from Ashley with several attachments. "I have a group photo and some individual photos. Forwarding them to you now, and I'll double check with Christopher that he doesn't have anything else."

"Sounds good. I'll just be sitting here, staring at screens, watching computers compute things," Ryan told her.

Rachel thanked him then hung up and called Christopher.

"Hey, babe! Miss me already?" Christopher answered.

"Do you have the kids' names and ages and birthdays?"

"Yeah, I have a spreadsheet. I didn't know you needed it."

"I don't know that I don't need it," Rachel huffed.

"Sorry, I'll send it over now. How's it going?"

"People are in the locations they need to be in so that they can attempt to make progress on the things I want them to be doing."

"Right." Christopher paused. "Well, I have demographics and everything required for customs and border patrol."

"Yes, I need all of that. Anyone else I should be speaking to?"

"I'm assuming you only want to talk to people you can trust?'

Her silence was enough to imply he was correct.

"I get the sense you don't trust anyone from Eros Aid."

"Obviously not."

"I'll send you their info in case you decide you *do* want to talk to them."

"The only interaction I want to have with any of them is the illegal kind."

"What?"

"We aren't supposed to use enhanced interrogation tactics." *Even if we always do anyway.*

"For fuck's sake. I'm sorry I asked."

"Uh-huh. Can you plan the wedding please? Assuming we aren't just going to city hall or something, which would be my preference, as you know." Now that he was done with one project, she needed to get him busy with another, and she had zero interest in planning a wedding, even her own. Besides, the whole thing had been his idea.

"Yeah, I'll work on it. It would help if I had a date."

"A date? Why do you need a date, Christopher? Are you not understanding what a wedding is?"

"Not a *date*. Not a slutty girl in a hot dress. I have you for that! A calendar date. A day, time, location, that sort of thing."

"Oh!" Rachel burst out laughing. "Assuming you want all the teams there?"

"Indigo, certainly. Onyx, yes. As many of the teams as we can have . . . I know deployment schedules are always tricky. Any sort of all hands mandatory training coming up that everyone will have to be at? We can just get married the day before or after one of those."

"Um . . ." Rachel clicked through the squadron's calendar and just kept seeing *D* written on every fucking day. Too many critical situations were happening in the Middle East. "Indigo is deploying in July, Onyx . . . well . . . they're gone most of the year unless they manage to wrap up their current project quickly." She kept clicking, day by day, week by week, until . . . "Memorial Day weekend."

"What?"

"Yeah, assuming Onyx finishes what they're doing. If not, though, they'll need to come home before this other thing for a bit." She double checked, then triple checked. "Babe, not a single team will be deployed over Memorial Day weekend. All seven teams will be stateside." *How the fuck did that happen?*

"Alright, I'd say we have a date! Look at you making magic over there! Now we just need a location." God he was so enthusiastic about her ability to click through a calendar. She quickly realized most women would kill to have such a supportive partner and decided to take the compliment, even if it was slightly ridiculous.

"Couldn't care less where we get married, babe, as long as it's not a church."

"I already knew that." Christopher chuckled. "It would be easiest for my family if it were in Texas, so they don't have to travel and hire on people to run the ranch for them."

"Why don't we just do it at the ranch?" Rachel suggested. "Up on the ridge, everyone can camp out—"

"Love it! Done," Christopher agreed just as several systems started beeping with notifications.

"Babe, I gotta go. Onyx is calling me." Rachel started pressing buttons to connect to the call with Luke.

"Okay. Get back to saving the world. Love you!"

Rachel hung up the secure landline and shifted her attention to the giant screen in front of her.

"Lux to Skylark—"

"I'm here. What's up?" Rachel asked.

"Not a lot. Area is deserted. We'll wander a bit, see if we find anything. You know, looking for tire tracks, buildings, campsites, anything like that. But as you can see, we've got about a foot of snow at this elevation, so I'm not hopeful."

"Alright, well, you have until the week before Memorial Day to find Khalid Khan and take him out. Hawk and I just set our wedding date, and y'all are expected to be there."

Luke chuckled. "Copy that. Best get off the phone and get to hiking then."

Rachel smiled even though he couldn't see her. "Enjoy your hike. I'm here if you need me."

"You're just sitting at HQ?" Luke's brow furrowed. "You know you can just take a satellite phone home with you, and I can call you on that."

"Are you trying to tell me how to do my job?" Rachel's tone was sharp.

"No, ma'am." Luke pursed his lips. "Just a suggestion."

Rachel's eyes narrowed at the screen. "One, I am not so bad at technology that I didn't already know I could take a sat phone home with me. And two, there's basically no one here because of fucking Christmas, so someone has to be here in case of an actual emergency."

"Right . . . Christmas . . ."

Rachel couldn't help but laugh. If anyone cared less about Christmas than her and Christopher, it was hardcore atheist Luke. "Take a ten minute break and email me everyone's gift lists and I'll get it taken care of." She was already shopping for Ryan, so she may as well shop for everyone. "Also, make a note if it's something the person the gift is for specifically requested. If it's something y'all came up with yourselves and I think it's stupid, I'll pick something better. I do not want another fiasco of Rio getting his wife a *Best Neurosurgeon Ever* mug. Even if it's true, that is not an appropriate gift for one's wife, and she already has several."

Luke chuckled, clearly remembering the coffee mug in question. "Thank you, Sky. Can you pick out some hippy spiritualist stuff for my mom? If it's almost Christmas, I'm assuming I missed the Winter Solstice. Not that she expects presents but—"

"Yeah, I've got you covered," she assured him.

Rachel decided to go home at 1500. Ryan was at Langley kissing ass, Onyx had set up camp and settled in for the night. There was nothing else for her to do other than sit by the emergency phone just in case. Christopher was nowhere to be found when she got home, so she pulled a file out of her backpack and flipped it open on the kitchen island, then went searching for a snack. She was halfway through the information she'd gotten from Ashley on the refugee kids and was almost done eating an apple when Christopher came in the front door, dripping with sweat.

"Can you call Sara?" he asked, leaning in to kiss her cheek.

"Why would I call Sara?" Rachel's face crinkled with confusion.

"To get recommendations for wedding vendors."

Rachel cocked her head to the side and planted her fist on her hip. "At what point do you imagine I'd have time to do that? Besides, she's *your* sister and it's *your* wedding too. Plus, you have a lot more free time than I do." *Especially now that I volunteered to do all this damned Christmas shopping.* She hated shopping but didn't want anyone's family to think they'd been forgotten about either.

He had both hands on her hips pulling her into him. "You're the bride."

"You're the one who wanted a fancy party." She tapped her index finger on his nose.

Christopher let out an audible sigh and stared up at the ceiling. "I thought we were going to do this together?"

"Sure, babe. Just as soon as I rescue a bunch of kids from Aquib Faizan and Khalid Khan." Rachel rolled her eyes.

"I need help, Rache!" He threw his hands up. "I called my mom today. She told me to talk to Sara, and Sara says she won't help with anything until she talks to you." His tone was uncharacteristically distressed.

Rachel rolled her eyes. How hard could planning a party actually be? "You know how to plan and organize things just fine without me. At least do some preliminary research and let me know what our options are."

"Can we just call her quickly now?" His phone was already in his hand with his finger hovering over Sara's name, ready to call her.

"I need to go back to work after we eat." Rachel wrinkled her nose. She'd much rather sit at HQ by herself than plan a wedding. Besides, she had everyone's addresses and their family's addresses at HQ, so she couldn't sort out all their holiday shopping from home. "There's a lot going on. I know you *want* my help, but you don't *need* my help." It wasn't often she had to baby Christopher like this. He typically didn't shy away from a challenge and was used to jumping in and doing administrative tasks without even being asked.

He folded his arms over his chest and looked down at her. "So you just came home to eat?"

"No, I came home to see you and maybe squeeze in a few other activities." She smiled, hoping to diffuse the tension and distract him.

"Right. Food and stress relief."

"Christopher, I'm sorry you're feeling neglected, and I'm sure none of this is easy for you. It's not easy for me either, but you know I have to work."

He shoved a finger in her face. "You could delegate more to Stephanie."

She took his finger in her hand and pulled the inside of his wrist to her lips, kissing it softly. "Stephanie is gone for Christmas. More or less everyone is gone for Christmas, so I have to be at HQ to monitor things. You know I love you. You know I want to marry you. Please, just call your sister and start on the wedding stuff without me. I'm going back to work."

Rachel grabbed the file off the kitchen island and tossed it in her bag before ordering a rideshare on her phone and going outside. Navy rations out of the supply closet would be more than adequate for dinner if it meant avoiding an argument with Christopher.

Christopher sighed then kicked one of the chairs next to their kitchen table. He knew Rachel had to work and understood the demands of her job perfectly well. That didn't mean he had to like it. He also knew she was involving herself a lot more than she actually needed to. There was no reason for Rachel to be at HQ watching Onyx do recon. Mission first had been a way of life for both of them for over a decade, but it really was miserable to be on the other side of that, to be the family that always came second. They really needed to buckle down with the wedding planning though, especially if they were getting married Memorial Day weekend—in just five months.

He knew his call with Sara would be long and arduous, hence why he'd tried to pass it off to Rachel. Sara was a perfectionist. Overly detail oriented and overly invested in everything, like Rachel. He went to the fridge to get a beer, then decided whiskey would be more effective. After a few sips, he pressed Sara's name in his contact list. "Help me plan this wedding please."

"Hello to you, too." Sara chuckled. "Is Rachel with you?"

"No."

"How am I supposed to plan a wedding without the bride?" Sara asked.

"Hell if I know! She's busy saving the world from eminent danger."

"Of course she is." Sara sighed. "Have you picked a date?"

"Memorial Day Weekend." Christopher shot back his whiskey then poured himself another.

Sara's frustration came out in a loud huff. "In five months? You're giving me five months?"

"Yes."

"You realize most people take at least a year to plan their wedding?"

No, how the fuck would I know that? He dropped his head into his palm. "Sara, please just tell me what to do. I'm completely lost and have no help other than whatever you're willing to help with."

"Where are you getting married?"

"At the ranch, assuming Mom and Dad agree to that. Somewhere near Emory, in any case, so none of you have to take too much time off work."

"Well, lucky for you, I've been a bridesmaid five times, and Maid of Honor twice. Several of those weddings took place in or near Emory. I'm emailing you a spreadsheet with wedding vendors as we speak."

"Great!" Christopher got out his laptop, sat at the kitchen table, and opened the email from Sara. "Why are there a hundred different tabs on this thing?" he asked as soon as he'd opened the attachment. It was worse than he'd anticipated.

"There are not a hundred. Learn to count." Sara scolded him in a voice that made him think she may have missed her calling as a drill sergeant. "There is one for caterers, one for sound equipment, one for cover bands, another for classical musicians like a string quartet or something like that. There's a tab for DJs too. Then you have photographers, florists, bartenders, since not all caterers have a liquor license. There are also tabs for dress shops with information for shoes, accessories, hair and makeup . . ."

"Fucking hell," Christopher muttered as Sara continued rattling off her list of vendor categories. "Do we really need all this stuff?"

"Yes," Sara insisted.

"What in God's name have I gotten myself into?" He tugged on his hair.

"It's a wedding, Chris," Sara said sternly. "The only tab on there you can potentially ignore is the one for ministers, since I'm assuming you aren't having a religious ceremony. Although, there may be a Justice of the Peace listed on there. Not sure."

"Alright, this is a lot of information. There is no way in hell I'm getting Rachel to look at all of this."

"Why not?"

"Because tracking down terrorists is a lot more fun than looking at wedding shit, that's why."

"Just go through it tab by tab and see which things you think she'd like best, then show her your favorites for each category," Sara suggested.

He shook his head even though he knew Sara couldn't see him. "Absolutely not. There are way too many things on here. You have over fifty caterers listed on here, Sara!" *How the fuck are there fifty different caterers in Emory, Texas?*

"If you scroll to the right, you'll see several columns where I've rated each vendor on price, quality of service, ease of working with them, things like that."

"Fantastic." Christopher grinned. He filtered Sara's rating columns to show only vendors with five-star ratings on all of her rating scales. There were none. He switched it to four stars. Not much better.

"There's also a column for style. If you want something more elegant or more rustic, for example," Sara offered.

"What's the correct answer to that question?" Christopher's brows knit together. He had no idea what Sara was talking about.

"Are you being serious?" Sara sounded horrified as her voice went up to an octave Christopher had never heard before.

Please stop shrieking. "Usually when I go to weddings, Sara, I'm more concerned with the bridesmaids than the table decorations."

"How did you get Rachel to agree to marry you?"

He scrubbed his hand over his face. *How to explain this?* "Usually when Rachel goes to a wedding, she's more concerned with the bridesmaids than the table decorations!" He laughed.

"Oh my god. You two really are too similar, you know that?" Sara grumbled. "How are you two going to plan a wedding? You're both hopeless!"

I'm going to convince you to do it for me. "Maybe I should have called Jackie . . ." He hoped that would spark Sara's competitiveness and need to prove she was the best, so she'd just take over.

"Sure, if you want your wedding to be a disorganized mess," Sara chided him. "I'm sending you links to several wedding blogs and websites with information so you can learn all the terminology and get a better understanding of where to start and the different steps. There should be a link to a style quiz on one of them."

No luck. He tapped his fingers on the table for a second then poured himself another whiskey. "I think you're trying to make this more complicated than it needs to be. We're just getting married up on the ridge. Mom can cook, I'll get some beer—"

"How many people are coming to this wedding?" Sara cut him off.

"Eighty-four or so SEALs, plus wives and girlfriends and a few other friends."

"Yeah, mom's not cooking for that many people. You need a caterer. You will need tables and chairs and linens too."

"Linens?"

"Tablecloths."

"Why?" Christopher grimaced.

"You're an idiot. Just go through everything I sent you and call me when you're done and need more guidance."

Christopher hung up the call and filtered Sara's spreadsheet, clicking on links to various websites. He slammed his laptop closed the second he saw the price list for the first caterer he'd clicked on.

Chapter 37

JANUARY 2021

RACHEL HAD BEEN AT HQ for eleven days straight, watching Onyx hike through the snow, before enough people were back from their holiday travels that she could finally take a morning off.

"Do you have time to check out some wedding vendors?" Christopher asked as Rachel shoved a forkful of pancakes into her mouth.

Rachel wrinkled her nose. She knew she was trapped at the table at least until she was done eating. If there was ever a time for Ryan to call and say he'd spotted Kamal. "I guess."

Christopher chuckled. "You're trying so hard to come up with an excuse so you don't have to."

"What do you need me to do?" Rachel sighed. She'd have to participate in this frivolous nonsense eventually.

"Just help me narrow down some things." Christopher turned his laptop so she could see. "Just click the links, read through the vendor's websites, then in this blank column, write *yes* or *no*."

"Okay," Rachel agreed and started clicking through the spreadsheet. "Holy fuck. What is this?"

"Deep breath." Christopher raised both hands defensively. "This is less than a quarter of the vendors Sara sent me. I've already narrowed it down a lot."

Rachel raised both eyebrows. "Not enough!"

"I took off everything in the highest price category and everything below three-star ratings, per Sara's criteria, okay? Look here . . ." He pointed at the screen. "You can filter for what sort of style you want, what sort of food—things like that in order to narrow it down."

"You made this spreadsheet?" Rachel asked. She knew he was more than capable, just surprised he'd put this much effort into wedding planning.

"Absolutely not. This is a simplified version of what Sara sent me."

"Simplified?" Rachel's eyes widened as she scanned the information, immediately feeling bad for anyone who had worked with him when he'd been a surface warfare officer. If he considered this spreadsheet to be simplified, she could only imagine how detailed his spreadsheets on supplies, logistics, and transport would have been. "Okay, anything with this many dollar signs in the rating column is a no." Rachel determined four dollar signs were too many. "And what do all these words mean?" She drew a circle with the mouse around one of the columns.

"Right!" Christopher chuckled. "Scroll down . . . click this link." He pointed at the screen. "It's a style quiz."

Rachel blinked twice, already knowing she was going to hate whatever it was Christopher was about to have her do.

"According to Sara, if we do this style quiz, it will help us narrow down our vendors. This column with all the words we don't know indicates styles that align with this quiz."

Rachel rolled her eyes but completed the quiz anyway. "Boho chic."

Christopher glanced over at the screen. "I got rustic when I did it."

She stared at him. "What's the difference?"

"You're asking me?"

Rachel chuckled, realizing he understood about as much as she did about this stuff and filtered the spreadsheet for both *rustic* and *bohemian*. "That does narrow things down considerably. Which of these things do you want me to start with?"

Christopher rambled on about food and cake and a variety of other mind-numbingly boring things. She nodded along, agreeing with him until he stopped making sense.

"Apparently, we need tables and chairs," Christopher explained. "Do you want just plastic folding chairs or wood, or what?"

Rachel stared at him. They absolutely did not need to pay for tables and chairs. "Tell people to take a knee."

"Sara says we need tables and chairs. Your mom is not going to sit on the ground to eat."

"She doesn't *have* to come."

"Babe, be serious."

Rachel rolled her eyes. "Pick the cheapest ones you think my mom won't be offended by."

"Got it." Christopher chuckled. "Music?"

"I'll make a playlist." *Finally something interesting.*

Christopher gave her a skeptical look. "Do you have time to make a playlist?"

"Do you know how boring and slow watching people do recon is? They're just up in the mountains wandering around. I'm basically watching them go on the slowest hike ever since they wander a bit, then wait for Jared to fly the drone around, then they wander a bit more. I've spent most of my time googling various types of paw prints, trying to resolve arguments about what sort of animals are in the area. I may as well be a Boy Scout leader! I finally told them, unless they have eyes on a snow leopard, I don't want to hear about it."

Christopher's upper lip curled. "I guess Onyx will be helping you with the playlist while they hike through the snow."

Rachel gave him a terse nod, hoping the conversation was ending soon.

"Do you want a DJ then, or how are we playing your playlist?"

"Off my phone."

"I'll rent speakers that we can connect to your phone."

"Cool. So, we're done?"

"No."

"Yes . . . food, music, all good." Rachel listed off. They'd already discussed more things than she cared about.

Christopher turned his laptop so he could type and proceeded to get her opinion—not that she really had one other than *what* and *no* in combination with various pissed off and disgusted facial expressions. He forced her to discuss videography, photography, hair and makeup before she stood up to leave, thinking they were done. He grabbed her wrist and pulled her back down to sit on his lap. "We still have flowers, invitations, table linens, decorations."

Rachel picked up her phone and started typing. "There, invitation sent." She showed her message in the squadron's group chat to Christopher.

"And for the people *not* in that chat?"

Rachel shrugged.

He gave her a kiss on the cheek. "We've exceeded your level of patience for this topic, haven't we?"

"Yes, I think we have. If I never see that horrific spreadsheet again, that would be fine with me."

"One more thing, not spreadsheet related." He wrapped both arms around her before she could escape.

She pulled his arms tighter around her, happy for the hug even if she saw straight through it and knew it was a preemptive strike—a way of forcing her to stay put and focus.

"We need someone to marry us. A judge or someone," Christopher explained.

"Last I checked, anyone can get ordained on the internet." Rachel glared at the spreadsheet, noting a tab that was clearly labeled *officiant*.

"Sounds good." Christopher nodded. "Who were you thinking? It should be someone who knows us. Someone who will actually take it seriously and is comfortable standing in front of people."

"I'll ask Eastwood to do it. He knows us as well as anyone does. I mean, if you think about it, he's the reason we met in the first place." Rachel shrugged. Seemed like the perfect job for the old man. Besides, it would motivate him to grant everyone paid leave or classify it as some sort of mandatory training since he'd need leave for the weekend too.

"What do you mean?"

"I had applied to be a SEAL straight out of officer candidate school, of course, but they said no because I'm a girl. So I did my two years as an intelligence officer and applied again. Eastwood saw my test scores. He was at Command HQ by then, and he came to see me. You know he's known me for most of my life, right? He worked pretty closely with my father for a while. Something about planes . . . Anyway, he shows up on base to talk about these fantastic test scores. Then he went off and yelled at a bunch of people until they agreed to let me into BUD/s. So it's entirely his fault that we met."

Christopher burst out laughing. "I think you should explain it exactly like that when you ask him tomorrow! And no, I didn't realize he's known you since you were a kid! That explains why you get away with so much shit with him."

"Get away with what?" Rachel asked, incensed at his implication.

"Um, back-talking, your attitude, your eye rolling and complaining about things, your crazy demands for random items to be added to the supply order. I've been in meetings where you have literally told him to go fuck himself, and as far as I could tell, you've had no consequences."

Rachel rolled her eyes. "I will tell him tomorrow that we have assigned him the task of officiating our wedding."

"Oh, God!" Christopher laughed. "Can I please be on the phone with you when you tell him?"

"We can take him to lunch and ask him. I'll text him and let him know he's having lunch with us tomorrow!" Rachel squealed. She pulled out her phone, sent the text, and received a prompt thumbs up in response.

"Now about the dress, 'cause I promised your dad . . ." Christopher ran the back of his finger up her spine before kissing her neck.

So much for one last thing. He really knew how to trick her into staying put. "I don't know. I'll just go buy one. How hard could it be?"

"Okay, but you have to invite your mom to go dress shopping with you. It's like a thing, right?" Christopher pointed out.

"Ugh, she's terrible though. I don't want to deal with her!" Rachel protested.

"We'll need to go to Texas to do some of the planning, so just stay in

Dallas and go dress shopping there. We can just fly in for the weekend, Friday night to Sunday, with one day to shop and straighten things out with caterers and photographers and whatever else. Surely you can buy a dress in a day!" Christopher's manipulation skills were off the charts today.

"Fine, but only if she brings my dad too."

"Yes, and my mom, Jackie, and Sara will go with you, so they can help mediate. It'll be fine. And I'll go with my dad to get everything else done. Just figure out which weekend you can go."

"Fine." She pulled away and stood before he could come up with any other items to discuss. "I'll be in the basement. Didn't get any gym time at work yesterday."

"Wait!" He tugged her back over to him. "Kiss."

Rachel smiled and bent down to kiss him just as her phone started ringing.

"What?" she answered then gave Christopher a peck on the lips.

"Um, Rear Admiral Ryker, ma'am?"

"Speaking."

"Ma'am, this is Ensign Wright. I have the dates of those phone calls . . . approximate dates, that is. I did my best."

"You did it or a computer did it?" Rachel checked. Rebecca sounded positively terrified to be on the phone with her.

"Both, ma'am."

"Good. What did you come up with?"

Rebecca rattled off a list of dates and approximate times—morning, afternoon, evening. Rachel listened, her head cocked to the side. She repeated the list of dates back and watched Christopher's brow furrow. She pursed her lips and turned his laptop to face her, clicking to open his calendar.

"Can you read me that list again please?"

"Yes, ma'am." Rebecca listed off dates, slower this time.

Rachel clicked through Christopher's calendar. She knew those dates rang a bell. Each of these phone calls had occurred within twenty-four hours of his meetings to plan that damned fundraiser. It was circumstantial evidence at best, and Rebecca had said her dates were estimates, but it was just one more coincidence to add to the list.

"Thank you, Wright. Can you email me that list too, please, and your report."

"Yes, ma'am, I'll include our report."

"*Our* report?" Rachel asked. "I have the official report with Dixit's signature. What I want is any other thoughts *you* have on that recording. Anything new *you* thought of since we discussed it last."

"You want . . . *my* thoughts?" Rebecca asked.

"Yes . . ." Clearly this situation was going to require a bit of coaching. "You seemed intelligent the last time we spoke, and you were able to look at the information from several different angles, use critical thinking, and incorporate what you already know about the targets. I want to know what else you, Rebecca, have come up with since we last spoke."

"Yes, ma'am. I'll send everything right over!"

"You know what?" Rachel looked at her watch. "Let's discuss this in person. I can head in now. Are you at HQ?"

"Yes, ma'am."

"Meet me in my office in one hour. Just you, me, and Hertz."

Christopher waited for her to hang up the call. His brow furrowed. "I thought you were taking the morning off?"

"So did I." Rachel grimaced.

"Rache, you promised."

Rachel looked down, pinching the bridge of her nose. "I'm sorry, Christopher. You know I want to spend the morning with you, but this can't wait!"

"I dunno, sort of sounded like whoever you were talking to could use more than an hour to throw their presentation together."

"Missing kids, Christopher. Gotta find these missing kids."

Rebecca and Stephanie were already in her office by the time Rachel got to HQ. They had laptops open and a slide deck cued up. "Huh." Rachel frowned. "I didn't even need to tell you to make that."

She didn't miss the wink Stephanie gave Rebecca. If only everyone showed up to meetings as prepared as Rebecca did. The girl couldn't be much older than twenty-three but was already more professional than several more senior officers she'd worked with. The only thing Rebecca was missing was a bit more confidence.

"Are you ready for Wright to start, or do you need to do something else first? We're a bit early," Stephanie said.

"Did you check in with Onyx this morning?" Rachel asked.

"Yup. They're freezing their asses off in the mountains north of Jalalabad, but all good."

"They have supplies?"

"Yes ma'am. For at least another week, then they'll need to go back to base. They said they can get a helicopter and drop in close to where they are now, or wherever they are when supplies get low, instead of hiking up."

"Good." Rachel nodded. "You don't actually need me, do you?"

"Of course I do!" Stephanie insisted.

"Stop kissing ass and have some self-confidence for fuck's sake. You absolutely do not need me to check supply levels or organize transport or explain to Onyx that they need to hike faster."

"No, ma'am. I suppose I don't need you for those things," Stephanie agreed.

"We only play dumb and helpless with men when we've exhausted all other options and need to manipulate them into doing what we want. Understood?" Rachel looked back and forth between Stephanie and Rebecca.

"Yes ma'am. Understood." They both nodded.

"Good." Rachel looked at Stephanie. "Christopher is going to start bothering you about wedding stuff."

"Fun!" Stephanie lit up.

"No, not fun," Rachel disagreed. "Just a heads up, he's more manipulative than I am so I'm guessing he'll send you stuff and expect you to trick me into having an opinion, so . . ." She shrugged.

"I will filter everything he sends me and only show you essentials."

"Thank you." Rachel grinned. "Wright, what do you have for me?"

"Um . . ." Rebecca looked at her laptop, then at Stephanie.

Stephanie gave her an encouraging nod of the head, apparently doing some mentoring of her own. *Good for her!*

Rebecca looked at her feet then back at her laptop. "Ma'am, you read the report?"

"Yes, several times." Rachel nodded.

"Well . . . I've been thinking . . . I listened to that recording over and over, trying to work out the timeline for the phone calls. It doesn't really add up. I mean, the timeline does, just, I feel like I'm missing something. We have several meetings between Samir, Khalid, and Aquib discussing education. Those conversations are interspersed with phone calls between Khalid and . . . someone." Rebecca shrugged. "The first one." She clicked to the next slide. "He says something about deciding targets. He thinks the UK, Europe in general, has a better system. Just system, not what kind of system. School system, maybe? Then he goes on to say that he understands America has a larger impact. He also says 'fuck Aquib' about a hundred times. Not sure what *that's* about, but it sounds like they aren't getting along."

"I agree." Rachel nodded. "I've also heard Aquib is a pain in the ass to work with."

Rebecca clicked to the next slide. "The second call that's recorded is about a week later. Seven to ten days, I would say. I think," Rebecca glanced over at Stephanie.

"You're good, Becks. We're all about fucking the patriarchy and going against what the official party line is in this office."

Rachel raised an eyebrow, instantly intrigued.

"Ma'am, Captain Dixit doesn't agree, but I think Khalid is speaking to someone in the second phone call who maybe isn't great at Pashto. There are several cases where what he says is quite clear. Not a lot of room for interpretation, but he slows down and overexplains. Now, I'm not a linguistics expert by any means," Rebecca held up both hands, palms facing Rachel, "but there seems to especially be confusion with prepositions. As with most languages, as I'm sure you know, ma'am, several prepositions can be used to mean a variety of things. They're difficult to translate, and you need the context to really understand."

"Pashto is grammatically complex," Rachel agreed.

Rebecca nodded. "So, I don't think we're dealing with someone who has Pashto as their native language."

"Neither Samir nor Aquib have Pashto as their native language," Rachel pointed out, knowing both men spoke it more or less flawlessly. She wanted to test Rebecca a bit though.

"But they converse just fine in person, so it can't be one of them," Rebecca noted.

Well done. "What else?" Rachel asked.

"The third phone call, Khalid seems to be giving someone driving directions from Jalalabad to Kabul, or somewhere near Jalalabad in the mountains. He says, 'you just go down the mountain,' then more specific directions from Jalalabad."

"That makes sense. That's where we think the kids are . . . or were." Rachel pursed her lips.

"Could the person on the phone calls, the one who's not great at Pashto, be someone from the NGO?" Stephanie asked.

"Could be. Let's find out. Cue up the recording to the phone call—the part where the person we can't hear seems to not understand and Khalid is explaining."

Rebecca nodded and skipped forward to that section of the recording while Rachel called Christopher. She put the call on speaker.

"How's work?" Christopher answered after three rings.

"Took you long enough to answer," Rachel complained.

"What's up, babe?"

"The people from Eros Aid, you said some of them spoke Pashto?"

"Yes."

"Like really spoke Pashto or spoke it well enough to deal with kids?"

"Umm, mixed, I would say. Why?"

"Listen to this and tell me if they would have been confused."

Rebecca played the recording for Christopher.

"Um, no I think you'd need to be an idiot to not understand that. It wasn't that complicated," Christopher noted. "Sounds like the guy—I'm pretending I don't have a guess as to who I'm listening to—is either really frustrated and impatient, or the person on the other end of the call is terrible at Pashto. The people from Eros Aid who I dealt with either spoke Pashto or they didn't. Mixed ranges of vocabulary, not everyone could get through a university level course taught in Pashto, but they were fluent to at least an eighth-grade reading level I would say. No one was like, beginner level, which is sort of what that sounds like."

"Thank you! That was very helpful!" Rachel hung up and smiled at Rebecca.

"If it wasn't someone from Eros Aid, who the fuck was Khalid Khan calling?" Stephanie asked.

"No idea," Rachel admitted. "If we could just get his call log or phone records or something."

"The European Union has a much better system for refugee children traveling without a parent," Rebecca commented out of nowhere. "Or did he mean the school system?"

Rachel cocked her head to the side. "Keep talking."

"Well, they mention the girls will have to be in school too, that it would look weird if they weren't, having to understand the culture . . . In both the UK and U.S., boys and girls attend school for the same amount of time."

"Yeah . . ." Stephanie's brows knit together.

"Rebecca, are you thinking those kids they sent here . . ." Rachel paused, trying to organize her thoughts. "There were fifteen kids from Afghanistan transported here by Eros Aid. Likely abducted by Samir and Aquib and Khalid, it seems. Now that they're here, they'd be in the refugee system, however that works. I'm not calling Christopher right now to ask because he'd ramble on about it forever, but at some point, they'd need to be enrolled in school."

"Yup." Rebecca nodded. "And they have access to explosives, apparently."

"Fuck." Rachel's eyes darted to Stephanie. "Get Rhodes on the phone."

Ryan answered immediately. "Hey, Sky," he said. "I don't really have an update. We're grasping at straws over here, but we have names, birthdates. I got fingerprints from border patrol . . ."

"I—Ryan, these kids . . . What do we normally do with asylum seeking refugee children?" Rachel asked. She already knew he didn't have an update.

If he did, he would have called.

"Yeah, I didn't know either, so I googled it. Typically, they're placed with the Department of Health and Human Services in the care of the Office of Refugee Resettlement. Typically, people seeking asylum have to wait forty-five days on average for an interview after their asylum application was filed. These kids, are they refugees or asylum seekers though, because according to the internet, there's a difference."

"Hang on," Rachel told him. She opened her laptop and started researching the difference. "Asylees seek and obtain protection from persecution once they're already inside the U.S. or at the border. Refugees are people outside the country of his or her nationality who are unable or unwilling to return to that country because of persecution or a well-founded fear of persecution based on race, religion, nationality, membership in a particular social group, or political opinion. They typically apply for protection before arriving in the U.S. The kids were at a refugee camp in Kabul, so I guess they're refugees, but that's not exactly outside their country of origin, is it? Didn't you just tell me you were researching this?" Rachel huffed.

"Yeah, but apparently I didn't know the difference between asylees and refugees or which we were actually dealing with."

"Fair." Rachel sighed. She didn't have a damned clue either, so she kept reading. "Looks like the process is that they get released to sponsors—adults who are suitable to provide for the child's physical and mental well-being. Going through the foster care system is a way to facilitate that."

"In all fifty states?" Ryan did not sound pleased.

Rachel frowned at her laptop. "I think so."

"Check all fifty states. Got it," Ryan replied.

"This is weird, Ryan. The kids aren't refugees. Kamal, at least, was forcibly removed from his home."

"By his grandfather though," Ryan reminded her.

"No, something's wrong with this. I—*we* have that report from Army intelligence about all the kids going missing. Did that have names in it or just statistics of how many kids went missing?"

"I have no idea what report you're talking about, Sky."

"Shit." Rachel slammed her palm on her desk. She'd forgotten to give Ryan all the background information on this. "Someone called one of their Delta navigator buddies and manipulated him to get some intel. Something like ten thousand boys disappeared from schools in Afghanistan over the past year." Rachel dug though documents on her desk until she found the report. She started flipping through the pages, looking for more detailed information. "Okay, there's a breakdown by region with how many kids went missing by age and gender. No names or names of schools." She logged onto her laptop and opened the email from Ashley with information about each kid, as well as the spreadsheet she'd gotten from Christopher trying to cross-reference them with the intel report from the Army. She'd thought she had everything more or less memorized but wanted to be sure. "Okay, most of these kids say they went to a camp sometime last summer, July and August," she specified. "Most of them are middle school aged. Eleven to fourteen, which is the highest demographic of missing boys, according to the Army's report. Nothing in here about whether they went to the camp willingly. I guess Ashley wouldn't have thought to ask them that."

"What do you want me to do?" Ryan asked.

"Well, we pieced together something terrifying today." Rachel glanced at Rebecca. "Lieutenant Commander Rhodes, speak with Ensign Wright, please."

"Hello, sir," Rebecca started. "It seems we have fifteen kids from Afghanistan somewhere in the U.S. Khalid Khan, Samir Al-Abadi, and Aquib Faizan have been discussing the U.S. school system, and given what happened at the White House, we know someone is able to supply these kids with explosives."

Ryan was dead silent on the other end of the call.

"Rhodes?" Rachel asked. "You still there?"

"I-I," Ryan stammered. "I think I need to work faster."

"I think we all do," Rachel agreed.

Chapter 38:

JANUARY 2021

RACHEL WAS JUST WALKING into HQ the next morning when the satellite phone that had practically become an extra appendage started ringing. "Skylark," she answered.

"Hey, Sky," Luke said. "We see a building on the drone and are headed to investigate. Are you at HQ?"

"Just walked in the door and the petty officer manning security is glaring at me. I guess I can't be on the phone while I go through the metal detector."

Luke chuckled. "Considering the phone is metal . . ."

"Thanks for the clarification." Rachel rolled her eyes. Luke was one of her favorite people ever, but also just such a pain in the ass. More like a brother than a friend. "How far is the building from where you are?"

"Best estimate, half a day's hike."

"I love that you know to tell me things in time rather than distance." Rachel smiled.

"Well, Hawk isn't there to translate for you!" Luke burst out laughing.

"Lux, move your ass up that fucking mountain and call me later."

"Yes, ma'am!"

Rachel hung up and made her way through security and up to her office.

Christopher met Rachel and Admiral Eastwood in the lobby of Command HQ at 1145 for lunch. They had decided on a local Asian fusion restaurant a few blocks away.

"Hey Williams," Admiral Eastwood said, shaking his hand and giving him a pat on the shoulder. "Don't tell me you're sick of this one already and want to reverse your retirement," he joked, pointing at Rachel.

"Hilarious, Paul," Rachel said sarcastically.

"Watch it! You're in uniform," Eastwood scolded her.

"See Rache, this is what I was saying last night, that you get away with all sorts of shit," Christopher pointed out.

"Yeah, well, I'd take her up on disciplinary action, but what am I gonna do? Make her work more? Force her to do some pushups? Have her clean something? She'd like that too much," Eastwood stated matter-of-factly.

"I think pulling me from combat was discipline enough," Rachel complained.

"Oh, you're still on that, are you?" Eastwood asked. "Well, buck up buttercup 'cause you're here for the long haul."

Rachel rolled her eyes.

They walked to the restaurant, sat down and ordered, making small talk the entire time. Once their food arrived, Rachel got down to business.

"So, as you may know, Christopher and I are getting married," Rachel started.

"Yeah, I kinda noticed the ring and was wondering when you were gonna actually mention it," Eastwood said.

"Babe, you haven't even actually told people we're engaged?" Christopher was shocked.

"I have an enormous diamond ring on my finger. I think it's fairly obvious." Rachel rolled her eyes.

"You *did* tell your parents, right?" Eastwood asked Rachel.

"Yes, she did," Christopher assured him.

"Good, 'cause this would be one of those sorts of things she conveniently forgets to call home about." Eastwood laughed.

"Anyway," Rachel interrupted, "there is one specific date that all of our teams will be stateside. Memorial Day weekend. So that's when we're getting married, and it will be at Christopher's family's ranch in Texas, and you're going to officiate."

"Stop. I'm what?" Eastwood asked, surprised.

Rachel pursed her lips, eyes wide with irritation, and pulled out her phone to show him a website. "Here, you just go on this site and read this information and then there's a quiz and then you can legally officiate a wedding in Texas. Look, it even tells you everything you have to do and say. It's super easy."

He chuckled again. "So you've decided that this is what I'm doing? You aren't asking, you're telling?" Eastwood clarified.

"Well, it's entirely your fault that we met, so yes," Rachel explained.

Christopher choked on his water. "See, and this is why I wanted to be here when she talked to you! Sir, we would really appreciate it if you would agree to officiate. It would mean a lot to us. No one knows us as well as you do."

Eastwood looked at Christopher. "It would be an honor, Williams."

They were all just leaving the restaurant when Christopher's phone rang. He looked down to see who it was, didn't recognize the number, but decided to answer anyway.

"Hello, this is Christopher," he answered.

"Hi, my name is Mitch McAllister. I got your information from a former colleague, Devin Hollister. He told me you might be in need of a job. I run a nonprofit in D.C. called Delta Project. We contract with the FBI on missing persons and human trafficking cases. We're mostly ex-Delta Force. You'd be our first SEAL, but I thought I'd reach out and see if you would be interested in coming by for a job interview later this week?"

Thank you, Viper!

"Absolutely!" Christopher exclaimed excitedly.

Mitch gave him the office address and a few times he was available.

"Can you give me one second, Mitch?" Christopher covered his phone with his hand. "Rache, are you coming home tonight or staying at work?"

"I don't know yet. Onyx just found a building they want to investigate."

Christopher nodded and turned his attention back to his phone call. "Mitch, I'm actually a few blocks from you right now. Not to come off as completely desperate and like I don't have a life, but I can come by now if that works for you?"

"Give me half an hour," Mitch told him before hanging up.

Christopher excitedly explained to Rachel and Eastwood about the job.

"Sounds perfect for you, Williams! If they need a recommendation or anything, have them call me." Eastwood smiled.

"You'll call me after?" Rachel asked.

"Of course." He nodded. Just as Rachel and Eastwood turned to head back to HQ, he called after them. "Either of you have any idea what happens in a job interview? What the hell are they gonna ask me?"

"No idea." Rachel shrugged.

"Probably about your work history, your skills, strengths and weaknesses, how you get along with other people, things like that," Eastwood told him. "You have a phone and thirty minutes. Google it."

"Shit." Christopher looked at his phone and started typing so he could do just that.

Christopher walked into a small warehouse that had been converted into offices and conference rooms and was greeted by a man in his late fifties with salt and pepper hair and dark brown eyes.

"Christopher? Hey, I'm Mitch," the man said, extending his arm for a handshake.

"Hey, Mitch. Thanks for meeting with me." Christopher shook his hand.

Mitch led Christopher into a small office. There was a large stack of case files on the desk and modest furnishings, almost spartan, almost like being on a military base. Mitch sat behind his desk and motioned for Christopher to sit across from him.

"Well, here's the deal, Christopher. Hollister has given me a rundown of your resume, so I already know you can do this job and do it well. You're an expert tracker and navigator. This should be child's play compared to what you were doing before. I mostly want to see if it would be a good fit for both of us. Right now, we're six guys. You would make seven. Everyone is retired Delta Force. We get cases from the FBI, missing persons and human trafficking mostly. Some adults, some kids, cold cases, active cases. It's a pretty mixed bag. Basically, anything the FBI doesn't have the time or resources to work on, they pass off to us. You'd have one, maybe two, active cases at a time, depending on what they are. You'd work with a partner on each one, and you can take as many cold cases as you want," Mitch said, gesturing to the high stack of case files sitting on his desk.

"Sounds fun," Christopher said. "Less getting shot at, I presume?"

"Yeah, typically," Mitch chuckled. "We do go into the field with the FBI sometimes, so there may be a little shooting."

"No problem," Christopher said, trying to hide his enthusiasm at the prospect of getting to shoot someone.

"Great! Well, here's what I can do. I can offer you a salary of seventy thousand dollars per year. You're worth a lot more than that, I know, but we are a nonprofit, so we don't have the resources to pay any more than that, unfortunately."

"That's plenty. I have my pension, and honestly, I'd just be happy to have something to do all day while my fiancée's at work. If that something helps put an end to human trafficking, then even better!" Christopher admitted.

"Yeah, I'm sure!" Mitch laughed. "What does she do?"

"She's Navy. Just got transferred to a desk here in D.C."

"I guess that explains why you retired then."

"Yup!" Christopher laughed.

"Well, you'll find we're pretty laid back around here. Not too many rules, no uniforms or hierarchy, really. I'll assign you a case and a partner, then it's up to the two of you to solve it and coordinate with the FBI. You'll have an office here and access to the conference rooms, but you can work from home or wherever works best for you. The only thing that's really mandatory is our monthly meetings. Just a quick check in and status report on everyone's open cases, but you all know what you're doing, and you can just reach out to the rest of the team if you need support or need to brainstorm ideas, anything like that. Come with me. I'll show you around and introduce you to everyone. We had our monthly check in this morning, so they should all still be here."

Mitch showed Christopher to an office in the back of the building with two desks. There was a man about Christopher's age standing in front of a bulletin board, examining a map with a thick case file in his hand.

"Austin, this is Christopher. He's gonna be your new office mate," Mitch said, introducing them.

Austin Bishop reached to shake Christopher's hand. "Welcome to the team. Delta Force?" he asked.

"SEAL," Christopher corrected.

"Well good, then we know who to call if the traffickers decided to hide under water!" Austin teased, and they all laughed. "When do you start?" Austin asked.

Christopher looked at Mitch. "I can start right now. It's not like I have much else to do. Besides, Rachel's office is just down the street, so I may as well hang around and give her a ride home." *Assuming she's ever leaving work.*

"Works for me," Mitch said. "Austin, where's everyone else?" he asked.

"Oh, Troy and Zach are having a pushup contest out back," Austin said.

"Clearly they need more work." Mitch chuckled as he led Christopher out to the back side of the warehouse where two men in their early forties were in fact on the ground doing pushups.

"Troy Harris and Zach Sol," Mitch said, pointing at the respective men.

An older man in his early sixties walked over to Christopher and Mitch. "Hey, Carlos Hernandez," he introduced himself to Christopher. "I guess you'll be joining the team?"

"Yup. Happy to be here," Christopher replied.

"Great! And this is Ethan O'Connor," Carlos said, pointing at a young man who was clearly timing the two doing pushups.

Christopher smiled and looked at Mitch. "Yeah, I think this is going to be a good fit." He pulled out his phone and called the emergency line at HQ, knowing they'd be able to connect him to Rachel.

"Hey, you're going to have to help plan this wedding because I have a job now too," Christopher told her as soon as she picked up.

"You got the job?" She didn't sound the least bit surprised.

"Yeah, I'll tell you all about it later. When are you done, and I'll come get you?"

"I don't know. I have one more meeting at 1500 so I can brief everyone on the day's progress. Should be quick. Maybe an hour?" Rachel explained.

"Okay, well, I'll just hang here with the guys and see if I can help out with a case."

"Hey, invite them all over for drinks or dinner on Saturday. Not dinner. I don't know how to do that . . ."

"You aren't working Saturday?"

"Nope. Not unless something awful happens. Eastwood will be here covering."

"Alright. I'll plan Saturday. You call me when you're done at work, and I'll come get you." He hung up and turned his attention back to his new colleagues. "So, I've just been instructed to invite all of you over for drinks on Saturday, if you all want."

"Sounds good," everyone said. They decided a time, and Christopher gave them their address and detailed driving directions before going back inside to help Austin with his case.

Rachel sat in a conference room at HQ on a video call with Luke. Admirals Eastwood and Miller were in the room along with Captain Dixit from Intelligence, Stephanie, Rebecca, and a mess of people from various other departments. Rachel pulled up a slide deck and gave everyone an overview of the situation before turning the call over to Luke.

"Hi everyone, from the freezing cold mountains north of Jalalabad." Luke smiled. "Approximately a quarter mile from where I'm standing, on the other side of the ridge line you can see behind me, is a compound. We don't know who's there. No cars or vehicles of any kind, but we do see lights flicking on and off, so someone, or several people, are inside the house moving around. We're camping here for the night but have a camera set up so we can monitor the front of the house. Lights going on and off, anyone coming or going."

"How are you on supplies, Lux?" Admiral Miller asked.

"Not great. Food and water are both low. We can be up here maybe two more days, comfortably. Longer if it's really necessary."

"No, we'll get you back to base," Rachel told him. "Anywhere good to land a helicopter?"

"Yes ma'am." Luke nodded. "Let me just share my screen real quick . . ." A few seconds later, they could all see his screen. "So, as you can see on this map we created, the star is the front of the house. We are the green dot. It's a quarter of a mile, like I said, but we've got this ridge line as cover so we're monitoring with cameras and the drone. This blue dot over here," Luke moved his mouse to circle the blue dot on the map, "is our extraction point. It's a mile away from our camp, but a helicopter should be able to land no problem. It's also a good spot to drop in when we come back."

Admiral Miller nodded. Logistics was his domain after all. "What's the plan? When do you want us to get you?"

"Sooner would be better," Luke told him.

"Alright. I'll confirm with the base in Jalalabad and get back to you. Send me those coordinates."

"Already done, sir," Luke confirmed. "You should have an email."

"If you don't, I have the coordinates as well," Rachel added.

"Is the camera you set up recording?" Eastwood asked.

"Yes, sir," Luke confirmed.

"Alright. We'll get you back to base for a few days. Anything else?" Eastwood's question was met with silence. "Meeting adjourned then."

CHAPTER 39:
JANUARY 2021

ALL THE GUYS FROM the Delta Project were set to arrive at the house at 1800 that Saturday for drinks and food. Christopher had gotten the food ready, of course, not trusting Rachel to respond to the oven timer. Rachel was running around, fluffing pillows and making sure the house was spotless. Her training as a Southern woman had kicked in. She had opted to play the role of fiancée rather than rear admiral. She had her hair down in loose curls and was wearing an emerald green short sleeve t-shirt dress that matched her eyes perfectly. She had even put on makeup. Not much, but just enough to show she had put in some extra effort. She knew Christopher had told his colleagues that they had met in the Navy but not what she did in the Navy. That would have to be a surprise. She wanted to see just how quick these guys were. Their house was covered in photos of Rachel and Christopher on missions and on leave, just the two of them, but also with their team. It should be pretty easy to deduce. She gave Christopher an excited look as the doorbell rang.

Mitch was the first to arrive, together with his wife Abby. Christopher quickly introduced them, and Rachel led the way into the library where she had the drink cart set up with everything needed to make basic cocktails, plus wine and a lot of beer. Mitch opted for a beer, Abby a vodka soda.

"How long have you two been living in D.C.?" Abby asked.

"Since September," Rachel said. "I got transferred here for work."

"Yeah, Chris said you're in the Navy," Mitch said.

"Yup," Rachel answered, taking a sip of her beer. "What about you two? How long have you lived here?"

"About fifteen years," Abby answered. "Our daughter went to Georgetown and then just sort of settled in, so when Mitch retired, we figured it was better to be near her. Then he got bored and decided to start the Delta Project."

"Oh! My dad went to Georgetown. How did your daughter like it?" Rachel asked.

"She loved it!" Mitch said. "She majored in anthropology and is working for the Smithsonian Institute now."

"That's cool," Christopher said.

The doorbell rang again, and Christopher went to open the door to find Ethan O'Connor together with Carlos Hernandez and his wife Reya. He greeted them and pointed them towards the library, seeing that another car had pulled up with Austin and Troy. He brought them into the library and introduced them to Rachel, who promptly ensured they had drinks. Five minutes later, Zach arrived with his girlfriend, Jenna.

Once everyone arrived, Rachel gave them a tour of the house. She was full of charisma and charm, with her thick Southern drawl coming out in full force. Christopher could tell some sort of training Anna-Beth had forced upon her was kicking in. They had never hosted new people before, so he had never seen her like this. She was bubbly, sociable, and intently focused on their guests.

When they were all back in the library, Mitch started checking out one of the bookcases, which was littered with books on philosophy, religion, cultural studies and a whole host of other topics. Rachel had memorized most of the books already, but she kept them around just in case she needed to refer someone to something in order to make a point. Mitch picked up one of the photos of Christopher and Rachel, looking it over, then turned to Rachel.

"What is it you do for the Navy?" Mitch raised an eyebrow.

Rachel smiled slyly. "You're looking at the photo. You tell me."

Carlos came over to join them, and Mitch showed him the photo in his hand. Rachel was dressed in her camouflage utility pants, a white tank top, and aviator sunglasses, her hair in a high ponytail. She was somewhere in the desert, standing in front of a helicopter with Ryan. She had her elbow propped up on Ryan's shoulder and was flashing a peace sign, her lips in an ironic, if somewhat flirtatious pout, and her assault rifle slung over her shoulder. There was a pile of helmets, bulletproof vests, backpacks, and extra ammunition on the ground beside them.

Mitch picked up another photo. Rachel was standing by the open door of a helicopter, checking Christopher's gear and clearly bossing around a group of men in line behind him, getting ready to jump. Mitch laughed and handed the photo to Carlos. Carlos studied the photos and then looked Rachel up and down before laughing and shaking his head.

Just then, Rachel's cell phone rang. "Rear Admiral Ryker speaking," she stated clearly, making sure everyone heard, as she walked out of the library.

Rachel scampered off to her home office as soon as she saw the caller ID on her phone. It was Ryan.

"Sky, I know you're not working today, but Eastwood said you're just sitting on your ass at home."

"I'm hosting Hawk's new colleagues . . . but same thing, I guess." Rachel chuckled. "What's the problem?"

"Um, I've been running the names of all those kids through every database I can think of, and a few of them just popped in the Virginia foster care system."

"What the fuck?" Rachel was beyond confused.

"Yeah . . . I dunno. I have three boys coming up now as seeking foster families and are eligible for adoption in the state of Virginia."

"Do a deep dive into any prospective foster parents. We'll need to keep tabs on where they go, who the kids have contact with . . ."

"I'm checking all fifty states. These are just the first three I've gotten hits on."

"What's the Office of Refugee Resettlement saying?" Rachel asked.

"Um, that's the weird thing. They have no idea what kids I'm talking about."

"What?" Rachel yelled.

"Yeah, I know. I've got some people there looking into it, seeing if their files just got misplaced or something, but like, how do you let fifteen kids fall through the cracks?"

"You don't. That's an epic fuck up," Rachel stated. "Unless someone there is in on it."

"Background checks on everyone at the Office of Refugee Resettlement." Ryan sighed.

"Look for connections to Frank Verity and Joe Petchill."

"I'm on it," Ryan assured her before hanging up.

Rachel wandered back to the library after she hung up with Ryan.

"Sorry. Work," she apologized to everyone.

"Well, they figured it out," Christopher told her.

Rachel looked at the clock on her phone. "Thirty minutes. Not bad considering y'all are Army," she joked.

"Hey, we happen to be the most highly trained elite force in the U.S. military," Carlos argued.

"Yeah, we're way better than you lazy SEALs who just hang by the pool all day!" Zach chimed in.

Rachel laughed. "I assure you, Delta is the second highest trained elite force in the U.S. military, right behind us," Rachel stated definitively as she pointed back and forth between herself and Christopher. "Would you like a list of high value targets that the SEALs were chosen to take out over Delta?" Rachel raised an eyebrow. "I can also give you the specific reasons why SEAL teams were chosen specifically for those ops. That really important one in

Afghanistan back in 2011?"

"If it's the one I'm thinking of, the country was divided up regionally between SEALs and Delta and we were all looking for him . . ." Carlos chimed in.

"No, I assure you, we would have been sent regardless."

"We?" Mitch cut her off, looking back and forth between Rachel and Christopher.

"She means the SEAL teams, not us specifically." Christopher flashed her a scathing look. The mission she was referring to had been one of the highest classified, top secret missions. Very few people knew how it had actually gone down or who was involved, and the story shared with the public was definitely not entirely factual.

Rachel smirked and winked at Mitch and Carlos before walking away.

"Babe?" Christopher called across the room to her. "Are we losing you for the rest of the day?"

"Relax, I'm just talking to Austin," she gestured to him. "Everything at work is as under control as it can be. Someone just called with a question is all."

Christopher let out a long exhale and gave her at thumbs up.

"Okay, well, she's terrifying," Carlos said to Christopher.

"Oh, you have no idea." Christopher laughed.

"You said she was on a desk," Mitch said. "On a desk doing what, exactly?"

Christopher couldn't stop laughing. "Planning and coordinating SEAL missions and yelling at people in between whining that she's missing all the fun!"

Chapter 40:

MARCH 2021

ONYX SPENT A WEEK at the base near Jalalabad. They stocked up on supplies then took a helicopter and dropped in a mile from the house rather than hiking back up through the mountains.

They'd been at their campsite for three weeks watching lights flick on and off in the house they were monitoring, just like they'd been doing since Christmas. No one had gone in or out of the building, but someone—several someones—had been home the entire time. No one went outside, no one looked out the windows. How they were surviving inside without having food or supplies brought to them was a mystery. At least the snow was melting.

Rachel was sitting in Mission Control with her feet up on the desk, careful not to accidentally press any buttons, impatiently tapping a pen on the desk. Watching reconnaissance was boring. Even more boring than *doing* recon. There was no reason for her to sit and watch, really. Luke was running point. He had everything under control, just like always. She was entirely superfluous to the situation. But *if* they saw something, she wanted to see it too, not just hear about it later.

"Can't you guys make something happen already?" Rachel complained.

It had been nearly two months. Whoever was living in the house had to be running low on food and supplies.

"Not really how recon works, Sky," Tyler teased.

"Ugh. I'm fucking bored out of my mind here," Rachel complained. "Lux, what the fuck is that smirk about?" Rachel chided Luke.

"What smirk? How can you see me?" Luke asked.

"Ty's camera is pointed right at you," Rachel explained.

"Ty, move so she can't spy on me," Luke demanded. Tyler shifted slightly and let out a low chuckle.

"Aren't you guys bored?" Rachel asked.

"We're fairly used to this, seeing how it's our jobs . . ." Luke reminded her.

Rachel groaned again and sunk down in her chair. Despite the fact that Luke was one of her best friends, his obsession with silently staring at a screen, waiting for something to happen, was annoying. Even if it was his job, and even if he was the best reconnaissance specialist in the entire Navy.

Rachel sighed and tapped her fingers on the desk for a minute. "How about some music?"

"No more Taylor Swift!" several voices responded in unison.

"Fine." She huffed. "Do you guys want me to read you a book or something?" She couldn't fathom how they were able to sit still for so long.

"What kind of book?" Luke asked hesitantly.

"A novel."

"Sure," he agreed.

Rachel picked up a book off the desk beside her, flipped to the middle section, and started reading out loud.

"'*Cassandra looked him up and down. She wasn't sure he wanted her, wasn't sure he'd even noticed her. His gaze was always hard and cool. Not cold. Not devoid of emotion. Just indiscernible somehow. But now, after a few drinks, she saw a slight twinkle in his eye as he flashed her a sidelong glance. 'Will you walk me home?' she asked. 'I'm a little drunk.' He nodded and secured his arm around her waist, his palm warm on the small of her back. Her breath caught in her throat at his touch as they made their way through the winding allies back to her apartment. She didn't have to ask. Didn't have to say anything. He followed her inside, walking a half pace behind her through the door and into her living room, following her until her face was pressed up against the wall, palm flat against it with his hand on hers. His other hand reached down between her legs, sliding her dress up, caressing as he kissed the side of her neck. He knew what he wanted and knew she wanted it too . . .'"*

Rachel kept reading, glancing up periodically to watch the faces of the men as she conveyed the details of the very graphic sex scene.

"What the fuck is happening?" Rachel's reading was interrupted by Derik's voice, full of confusion and something else. Not disgust but shock maybe?

"Good morning, Rio," Rachel teased.

"I popped in my earpiece, and the first thing I heard was *she licked his balls*. What the fuck?" Brad complained.

"And good morning, New York," Rachel chuckled. The guys were on a rotating sleep schedule, so someone was always watching the cameras and drone.

"Sky is reading to us," Tyler explained.

"What the fuck are you reading, Sky?" Brad demanded.

"A novel that was highly recommended by several of the other women here at HQ."

"That's the shit women read?" Derik asked.

"Yeah, your wife is reading this, Rio," Rachel told him.

"Women just, like, all read that shit?" Tyler asked.

"Yes, we sit on park benches reading smut with perfect poker faces so no one knows just how dirty and fucked in the head we are," Rachel said seriously.

"Jesus fucking Christ," Derik complained again.

"Oh, this is nothing. You should hear this weird fairy sex in this other book. Apparently, fantasy romance is a huge thing. Just magic and fairies and witches and all sorts of shit. I'm learning a lot by hanging out with women instead of you idiots."

"I'm afraid to ask." Luke sighed.

"But I *really* want to know!" Tyler finished.

Rachel picked up a second book from off the desk and started reading.

"'*The magic bound her wrists above her head, and she looked at him, a long look through fluttering lashes. That look contained a thousand words. He stared back at her, inching towards her until his hard body was pressed against her soft curves, his breath hot as she tipped her face up to his. That look said everything. She was ready to submit to him . . ."'*

Rachel kept reading, keeping her voice light and sultry as she purred her way through the magic laced bondage and dominance.

"That might be the hottest thing I've ever heard," Tyler stated firmly once she had finished.

"Sort of ruined by *you* reading it though," Derik noted.

"Yeah, sort of like having my sister read it to me," Brad commented.

"I wish my sister would read that to me . . ." Luke sighed, and Rachel watched as all the eyes on the screens in front of her darted to the ground. Luke's sister had died when he was in high school, and they all knew he'd give just about anything for one more day with her.

"Why is everyone being so weird?" Luke asked, as if he didn't know.

"Cause you're over there saying you want to read porn with your sister," Tyler teased, trying to make light of it as best he could.

"No, I—"

"We've got movement," Jared, the team's drone operator, interrupted just as a truck sped up to the compound and parked out front. Two young men got out and, suddenly, the front door to the compound slammed wide open.

"Sky, are you seeing this?" Luke asked.

"You mean the twelve or so kids getting loaded into a truck?" Rachel asked. "I see them. Follow that truck with your drone and run facial recognition on everyone else you get eyes on."

"Copy that," Luke muttered.

Rachel rolled her eyes. "I know you want to intervene, but—" She paused as more trucks pulled up to the compound and more kids came out of the house. "Holy shit." She stared, eyes wide, at the screen. Several of the children were refusing to leave the compound, pulling away and running back towards the house—yelling, screaming, kicking—to get away from the men trying to restrain them. The men, barley older than eighteen by the looks of them, got out of the trucks and started beating the kids who weren't cooperating.

"Permission to engage?" Luke's voice was tense.

"Denied. Stand down. I repeat, Onyx, stand down." Rachel's voice was sharp and stern.

"Sky," Luke protested.

"You are outnumbered, and those kids will panic as soon as you start shooting, and you'll have nothing but chaos. Your aim is good, but I will not be responsible for dead kids," Rachel explained. Not that she needed to defend her orders, but she respected her men enough to tell them how she was reasoning.

"Copy that," Luke grunted.

"Lux, you know I'm right."

"I said copy," Luke clipped out. His frustration was evident.

"Sky, my drone doesn't have as long of a range as their truck," Jared pointed out. "Permission to coordinate with the Army so we can track them?"

"Yeah, do it." Rachel nodded to herself. "I want to know exactly where those kids are going. Once they've cleared out, go in and do what y'all do best."

"Fucking hell," Tyler muttered as a young girl was beaten to the ground. One of the older boys picked up her body and tossed it into the back of his pickup truck.

"Guys, no shame in looking away," Rachel told them. "I'm watching. I've got you."

"We need to watch," Derik grunted. "That way we know exactly what type of retribution to come back with."

"Understood." Rachel chuckled.

"Sky? I'm having a very difficult time just sitting here," Brad admitted.

"Someone sit on New York's lap so he can't move," Rachel teased. "I know it's a shit situation, guys. You'll get your revenge. I promise."

Fifteen minutes later, all the trucks had pulled away from the compound.

"I'm turning on the infrared scanner on the drone to see if anyone is left inside," Jared announced. There was no sense in following the trucks too closely. They were headed down the mountain, and Jared could easily find them later. Several moments later, he added, "Looks clear to me. Circling back to catch up with the trucks."

"Breach when ready," Rachel ordered.

An hour of cardio and an hour of strength training later, Rachel was just about to head into the locker room to shower and change when her phone beeped.

Hertz to Skylark: *Army confirms they are maintaining eyes on the trucks. They seem to be headed for Kabul. The guys are cataloging the intel and have enough that you can start reading.*

Rachel sprinted for the elevator still dressed in yoga pants and a sports bra, making a beeline for Mission Control. Stephanie was still sitting at the desk in the middle of the room, chatting with the guys on a video call.

"What's happening?" Rachel asked, cracking open a plastic water bottle that was sitting on the desk.

Stephanie glanced over at her and pressed a button on the desk. "Lux, you're on with Skylark."

"Welcome back," Luke teased.

"Cut the crap. Sitrep, please." The only thing polite about Rachel's request for an update was the addition of the word *please*.

"I'm not liking what I'm reading, Sky," Luke said as he carefully flipped through a file that had been left out.

"Anything indicating an imminent threat, or can you keep documenting everything and read it later?" Rachel asked.

"Doesn't look like anyone's dying today, if that's what you mean," Luke joked.

"You want us to copy these hard drives, not take the laptops, right?" Jeremiah, one of the team's technical experts, interrupted to ask.

"Do not remove anything. They can't know we've been there," Rachel reminded them.

"Too bad. I really want to blow this place up." Brad chuckled.

Rachel rolled her eyes. That was usually Brad's solution. Nuclear physicist turned SEAL, he tended to get creative with the explosives.

"Sky, we might not have an attack happening today, but I think you're going to want to start reading this shit sooner rather than later," Lewis told her. "I'm sending the first batch of documents to you now. Something about targeting schools?"

"Fucking hell." Rachel thought back to the recording Paige had gotten them of Samir, Khalid, and Aquib discussing children's education and her subsequent discussion with Stephanie and Rebecca. She started pushing the refresh button on her laptop repeatedly, patient as always, until a new document appeared in their shared folder. She started skimming it immediately. "Allowing children to complete *jihad* . . . hitting the West where it hurts most . . . Guys, this sounds terrible, and why is it all so vague? There are no actual details. No dates, no list of targets. Please tell me you are finding more information about this!"

"Yeah, still uploading things to you and trying to skim as we go," Lewis assured her.

Once Rachel got through the first batch of documents, she moved onto the second and third. Lewis was uploading them faster than she could read.

"You all hiking back down the mountain, or how are you planning on getting out of there?" Stephanie asked the guys as she handed Rachel a cup of coffee.

"Affirmative, Hertz. We're wrapping up here," Luke told her.

"Ma'am?" Stephanie looked to Rachel.

"I know you know how to get a helicopter or a truck or whatever they need, Stephanie." Rachel sighed, irritated that her reading had been interrupted. "Just handle it."

"She's reading, isn't she?" Luke chuckled.

The corners of Stephanie's upper lip curled. "Yes, sir, she's very engrossed in her reading material. What's your preferred mode of transportation?"

"Whatever gets us to a hot shower and a hot meal the fastest!" Tyler told her.

"I have financial records for some energy company . . ." Luke's brow furrowed. "Mirage, what the fuck are you doing?"

Rachel glanced up. Shane was barely visible on screen, partially behind a wall, but he was kicking something. She pressed a button to zoom in on Shane's camera just as he yelled, "Shit ton of explosives, haul ass!"

Each of the guys grabbed their most essential gear and what intel they could and sprinted for the front door of the compound. Seconds later, the entire screen went white as an explosion erupted from a back room with a deafening boom.

"I sure hope they all had their ear protection on for that one," Rachel commented.

"They didn't." Stephanie's jaw clenched.

"Give them a minute to reset, Steph," Rachel assured her. "None of them were that close to the blast, and they were all running before it detonated. I think they're all fine."

"Fine doesn't mean uninjured," Stephanie noted.

"Sky?" Luke's voice came over the speakers then there was a blur of color on the screen. Someone was adjusting their camera. "We're all good, but we lost most of the intel, so whatever you already got and whatever's in our hands . . . Sorry."

"I checked for explosives." Brad's voice came over the speakers next, then his face took up the entire screen. He was clearly holding his body camera up to his face. "I swear, I checked."

"I believe you. It's your favorite thing to do, and I know you're always thorough," Rachel assured him. "Mirage, you saw the bomb. Where was it?"

"In that back room . . ." Shane panted. "Sorry, can't breathe."

"Extra cardio for you then," Rachel teased, trying to lighten the mood.

"Fuck. No, I inhaled a bunch of dust while running," Shane wheezed.

"Always good when the medic gets injured." Stephanie chuckled.

Shane coughed out a laugh. "I heard a ticking in the corner of that room.

It was weird, I couldn't find it." He coughed again. Tyler handed him a canteen of water. After several large gulps, Shane started again. "I couldn't figure out where the ticking was. It was so quiet. I moved to the corner, pressed my ear against the wall, and it got louder. I kicked the wall . . . it crumbled enough—" He coughed again and took another sip of water. "Enough that I could see the bomb. It was built into the wall . . . like how you put insulation or pipes between the drywall."

"Lovely," Rachel muttered.

"Genius," Brad corrected. He glanced over his shoulder at the building. "Umm, maybe we should move farther away in case there are more wall bombs?"

"Back behind the ridge line, in that ditch we were hiding in earlier," Luke directed.

"Please move faster." Stephanie's voice was pleading. "I don't want to watch any of you get blown up."

The guys all started jogging.

"Any injuries?" Stephanie asked.

"No," all twelve voices insisted.

Stephanie rolled her eyes. "Dust inhalation, burns, shrapnel?"

"We're fine," Luke insisted, his tone implying Stephanie was correct. "Just get us the fuck out of here."

Rachel read document after document, taking notes as she did, while Stephanie arranged for a helicopter to pick up Onyx and transport them back to the base in Jalalabad. Even if the guys insisted they were fine, they needed to get checked out by a doctor just to be sure, and hiking back down the mountain to their truck was not the best option now that most of them were injured.

An hour later, her pile of reading materials became so extensive that she needed to move to the floor. Stephanie was running in and out, bringing documents fresh off the printer since Rachel insisted on having paper copies that she could organize and reorganize to get a visual representation of how they were connected. Rachel's eyes darted up to Stephanie's as she reached for the next stack of documents.

"Onyx is back at base. They've showered and are happily fed and are going to sleep for a bit while you read. Doctors confirmed no major injuries. Thank God they're all so fast," Stephanie told her.

"Good," Rachel said absently. She was too preoccupied with what she was reading.

"Williams called too," Stephanie added.

"Christopher?" Rachel's brows knitted together as she glanced up at Stephanie.

"Yeah, your fiancé. He wanted to know if you were coming home or if you had everything with you.'"

"Tell him I'll be home tomorrow," Rachel said looking back at her papers.

Stephanie paused. "You haven't been home in a few days. I think he misses you."

"And I'm sure Yamna misses her son, as do the mothers of the fourteen other missing children," Rachel said irritably.

Stephanie narrowed her eyes at Rachel. "You've been here twenty-four seven for the past week! Do you have any idea what day it is?"

"March," Rachel answered absently.

"Yes, March fifth. Friday, March fifth. Do you remember what's happening on March fifth?"

"Sounds familiar . . ." Rachel flipped the paper she'd been reading over to read what was printed on the back.

"You're flying to Dallas to meet with your wedding vendors?"

"When?"

"Tonight. Chris needs to know if you've packed."

"Packed what?"

"Rachel!" Stephanie yelled.

Rachel looked up at her, shocked by Stephanie's tone. "What? What's wrong?"

"Ma'am." Stephanie calmed her voice. "I know you're very engrossed in what you're reading, but Christopher called to check that you are in fact ready for your flight to Dallas tonight. Specifically, have you packed? Assuming you have, where is your bag? If not, what would you like him to pack for you? Are you going home first, or should he pick you up here on the way to the airport?"

Rachel's eyes went wide. "That's tonight?"

"Yes, ma'am."

"Fuck, I haven't packed!" Her voice was steeped with panic.

"Are you going home to pack, or would you like Christopher to pack for you?"

"I—" Rachel looked around at the mess of documents surrounding her. "I have so much to read!"

"I know." Stephanie sighed. "Chris can pack for you. I'll tell him to be here in three hours to pick you up."

Luke pinched the bridge of his nose, staring over the shoulder of the Army drone pilot. A helicopter back to base, hot shower, and quick bite to eat had clearly taken too long. The Army had followed those trucks—the trucks full of kids—to an area on the north side of Kabul. "Why are you just circling?"

"Sir," the Army private piloting the drone started. "This is as far as I can fly."

"I don't understand." Luke shook his head. "Is the battery dead?"

"No, sir."

"Then make the drone go forward! You need to find those trucks!"

"It's a no-fly zone, sir."

"What?" Luke was pissed.

"We're too close to Kabul International Airport. Can't fly the drone here, sir."

"For fuck's sake," Luke grumbled just as his phone beeped with a text notification.

Yamna to Lux: *Come by the house tomorrow. My husband will be out of town.*
Lux to Yamna: *What is it?*

Yamna sent a photo. Luke zoomed in and saw it was a stack of documents all in English, but the photo was too blurry for him to make out what the top document said.

Yamna to Lux: *My father left these. I don't want to move them.*
Lux to Yamna: *What time is safe to come?*
Yamna to Lux: *Tomorrow night after the children are asleep.*

Chapter 41:

MARCH 2021

IT HAD TAKEN EASTWOOD and Stephanie, along with several reassurances from Onyx, to get Rachel out of Mission Control, then several more reassurances from everyone to get her down the elevator and into Christopher's truck. They'd barely made their flight, and she'd barely slept, but they needed to meet their families and get to their appointments.

Everyone was waiting for them in the hotel lobby at 0740. Jackie had a mocha in hand, ready to bribe Rachel into cooperating.

"Rachel, it's one weekend. Put your phone away," Tom scolded her.

"I need to read all this stuff—"

"Stephanie is reading through it, organizing it, and then Eastwood will go through it, and they'll fill you in on Monday. They are more than capable of working without you for two days!" Christopher reminded her.

"I just need to check my messages, then we can go," Rachel said after taking a sip of her mocha.

"No." Christopher grabbed her phone out of her hand and slid it into his pocket. "You promised no work and even took a vacation day. That means no checking messages, no phone calls, no texting."

"How am I supposed to call *you?*" Rachel glared at him.

Christopher smirked and handed her a prepaid burner phone. "This has my number, that's it. No data, lots of parental controls. The only person you can call or text on this phone is me, so try not to get separated from Jackie or else you'll be lost."

Rachel stared at him, dumbfounded. "For real?"

"Yup." Christopher nodded.

"But, like, just for today, right? Just for dress shopping?" She was completely baffled by the concept of not having her phone, not having a connection to work, to her teams, and was equally shocked that it was possible to limit who someone could call on a phone.

"Have fun." Christopher gave Rachel a quick kiss and left to spend the day with Bob, organizing everything with the caterers, photographer, and music.

As soon as Christopher was out of sight, Rachel unlocked the phone and dialed away. Christopher was an idiot if he didn't think she had phone numbers memorized. She called her father since he was standing next to her, phone in hand, texting someone. Nothing happened. "What the actual fuck?" Rachel muttered. She tried Jackie and Sara's numbers next. The calls wouldn't go through. She dialed Christopher just to check that the phone actually worked.

"Miss me already?" Christopher picked up on the first ring.

"What the fuck?" Rachel complained again.

"You didn't believe me about the phone, did you?" Christopher chuckled.

"This is cruel and unusual punishment."

"You typically enjoy that," he teased.

"Yeah, I'll show you just how much I enjoy this later," Rachel threatened.

"Like you can keep your hands off me." Christopher laughed.

Rachel let out an audible huff of frustration before hanging up.

"You seriously can't call anyone but Chris?" Jackie's brow furrowed.

"If someone dies because of this prank—" Rachel grumbled.

Tom rolled his eyes. "If someone dies, it won't be because you took a vacation day. It will be because someone shot them or something."

"Thank you for that, Tom," Anna-Beth scolded him.

"Rachel, Paul knows you're with me. If something happens and they actually need you, he'll call me," Tom assured her.

"I hate all of you," Rachel muttered.

"Do you want a cookie?" Jackie asked, handing her a large chocolate chip cookie.

Rachel wrinkled her nose before determining a sugar rush might make the day more bearable, or make her too sick to participate. "Okay, I hate *you* less," Rachel conceded and followed Jackie out of the hotel and to the first dress shop.

Rachel had done her research, or at least she'd thought she had. Stephanie had sat a stack of wedding magazines in front of her and forced her to pick what she liked with Post-its. It had taken hours. Stephanie had then compiled a cheat sheet for Christopher and Sara to work from, using the photos Rachel had liked from the magazines. Christopher had been grateful for the help—until Sara informed him that Rachel's cheat sheet was directionless and lacking vision. She'd liked too many dissimilar things, it seemed, but she *had* managed to narrow down ideas for her dress.

The first boutique was cute, small, and a bit laid back, as far as bridal shops go.

"Okay," the salesgirl said. "I need to know what styles you're interested in. Is this your first time trying on wedding dresses? And I'll need to know your budget as well."

"We're getting married outside at the ranch, so nothing over the top. Budget as low as possible. Can we keep it under a thousand dollars? Closer to five hundred would be better . . ."

"Rachel—" Anna-Beth protested.

"I don't need to spend thousands of dollars on a dress that I'm going to wear once! It's wasteful!"

"Well, you have the option to, so don't rule something out just because—"

"Mamma, it's fine," Rachel insisted. She turned back to the salesgirl.

"Something boho-chic. Lace, fit, and flare," Rachel started, happy she'd learned some of the terminology. She pulled up photos on her phone to show examples of what she liked.

"Alright, and when is the wedding?"

"Memorial Day weekend."

"Oh, so you have just over a year. That's perfect!" the salesgirl said.

"No, Memorial Day weekend of this year. In two months."

"Okay, that will limit your options a bit. But you should fit in a sample size, so that helps. I'll pull you some options to try, and then we can go from there." She walked away to select a few dresses.

"Rachel, I told you that you were doing this too last minute," Anna-Beth scolded.

"It's the only weekend that works for the wedding. I'm not going to get married when my friends can't be there. It's a once in a lifetime accident that no one will be deployed then, and I don't think y'all want to deploy with them to the Middle East, 'cause we'd happily do that if you'd prefer, then all my friends in whichever country we pick could come too! I will happily move the wedding to Afghanistan, for example."

"No," Tom, Mary, and Sara all echoed.

"I have a passport. I'll go anywhere!" Jackie, at least, was enthusiastic and supportive.

"You know, I was gonna just go down to the courthouse, but Dad insisted . . ."

"Anna-Beth, it's Rachel's wedding. Let her do what she wants," Tom said. "Other than making us all go to a combat zone because *that* is not happening."

"Daddy, I'm not crazy. I wouldn't take everyone to a combat zone." Rachel rolled her eyes. "There are plenty of places in Afghanistan and Iraq and Syria and other places in the Middle East that are not technically classified as combat zones. Khost, for example."

Tom gave her a stern look to shut down that train of thought before she got too carried away.

"Really, Anna-Beth, it's gonna be great! Rachel can just get one of the sample dresses. Everything should fit her fine, and it'll save money too!"

Jackie pointed out, not understanding that making things more affordable was never Anna-Beth's goal.

The salesgirl came back with three selections, all similar to the photos Rachel had shown her. She helped Rachel into the first dress. It was a lace fit and flare with thin straps that crossed over an open back and had a low V-neck. She went out to show everyone.

"Rachel, really? It's a wedding, not a nightclub," Anna-Beth insisted.

"It's beautiful!" Rachel protested. "And I would never wear this to a nightclub!"

"Okay, too revealing for Mom," the salesgirl said. "Let's try the next one." She ushered Rachel back into the dressing room.

Dress number two was a strapless fit and flare made of shimmering tulle with a layer of lace over it. "I think this will be hard to run in. I probably should have straps."

"We can add straps," the salesgirl explained. "That's a quick and easy alteration."

"Why do you need to be able to run in it?" Sara asked.

Tom laughed. "Honey, you aren't going to be running a marathon on your wedding day."

"Are you sure?" Rachel asked.

"What are you gonna do? Say I do and then go for a run?" Tom asked.

"Depends on how long I have to stand still for the ceremony," Rachel stated. "You know how long Paul can talk for."

"Paul who?" Tom asked.

"Admiral Paul Eastwood." Rachel stared at him, unsure why he wasn't keeping up. They'd just been talking about Paul a few hours earlier.

"Paul Eastwood is officiating your wedding ceremony?" Tom sounded skeptical.

"Yes . . ."

"Your boss?"

"Yes."

"How'd you get him to do that?" Tom asked.

"I told him he had to." She shrugged.

Tom laughed and shook his head as Anna-Beth let out another sigh. Jackie and Sara tried to stifle their laughter as best they could.

"Rachel, why don't you try the next dress?" Mary suggested. She was so much like Christopher, always trying to keep the peace.

Rachel tried dress after dress for three hours before they left to find lunch and head to the second shop. She texted Christopher as they walked.

Skylark to Hawk: *I'm in hell.*

Hawk to Skylark: *Hang in there! Did you find anything you like?*

Skylark to Hawk: *I have some ideas, but someone is being difficult.*

Hawk to Skylark: *Just breathe!*

Skylark to Hawk: *I almost got the wedding moved to Afghanistan. My dad said no.*

Hawk to Skylark: *DO NOT CHANGE ANY PLANS!!! I'm putting deposits on things as we speak!*

Rachel rolled her eyes and shoved the burner phone into her back pocket. "Daddy, do you have any messages for me?"

"No."

"Nothing from work?"

"No, Rachel. Like I told you, Paul knows you're on vacation. Why would he bother you?"

Rachel winced. "Can you call him and get me an update on what's happening?'

"No." Tom shook his head.

"Daddy, please!" Rachel whined.

Tom burst out laughing. "Never heard a rear admiral use that tone before."

"That's because your son is too dumb to get promoted, or else you'd hear it all the time." Rachel couldn't resist the opportunity to get a jab in at her brother.

"And my daughter, who *is* smart enough to get promoted, isn't smart enough to realize I can't be manipulated that easily."

"It was worth a shot," Rachel grumbled.

The second shop was a bit more upscale but not over the top. Rachel described what she was looking for, revising her answers to include straps as a requirement. Anna-Beth added that it couldn't be too revealing. The salesgirl brought her a few options to try and helped Rachel into her first selection. It was perfect! It was a floor-length ivory lace dress with a mix of crystal beaded floral appliqués and medallion lace, a structured sweetheart bodice, a hip-hugging fit and flare skirt, a sheer train that wasn't too long, and crystal beaded straps.

"I want this one!" Rachel exclaimed as she walked out of the dressing room.

"Wow," Tom gasped.

"You look beautiful!" Mary said.

Anna-Beth nodded her approval. "What shoes are you going to wear with it?" she asked.

"My boots," Rachel stated.

"Honey, you aren't going to wear combat boots with your wedding dress," Tom protested.

"No! My brown cowgirl boots," Rachel clarified, suddenly realizing that combat boots and her assault rifle *would* look great with this dress too.

"That will be perfect!" Jackie exclaimed.

"Now you just need a veil," Anna-Beth said.

"I do not need a veil," Rachel cringed.

"Rachel, it's a wedding dress. You need a veil," Anna-Beth insisted.

"How are you going to have your hair?" Jackie asked.

Rachel shrugged, and Jackie just stared at her for a moment before getting up. She pulled the hair tie out of Rachel's messy bun and twisted her hair into a loose bun at the nape of her neck, allowing a few strands of hair to frame her face. "Something like this, I think."

The salesgirl nodded and scampered off. She returned with a long simple veil that was the same length as the train of Rachel's dress and expertly slid the comb into the top of Rachel's bun.

"Good," Anna-Beth said. "That looks lovely."

"Fine, I'll have the veil," Rachel said. She had caught a glimpse of herself in the mirror and had to admit, the veil really was great.

"Okay! Now bridesmaids' dresses!" Sara exclaimed, clapping her hands together.

"Oh my god, do we have to pick those today too?" Rachel asked.

"Yes, we have to get as much done as possible! You're only here for the weekend," Sara said.

"Wait, how much is this dress? Now that I love it so much . . ." Rachel paused.

"Rachel, don't worry about it. You're not the one buying it," Anna-Beth stated.

"Excuse me, what?" Rachel asked.

Tom stepped in. "Rachel, just let your mother buy the dress. You like it, right? I think you even said you love it, so just let it go."

The salesgirl looked at her and whispered, "Don't worry, it's in line with the number you gave me."

Rachel mouthed a quick *thank you* to her and went to the dressing room to take it off. When she came back out, Jackie and Sara had already collected a pile of bridesmaid dresses that would go well with her dress.

Skylark to Hawk: *Can you please ask Charlene to call one of your sisters? I'm sure she'll have an opinion on bridesmaid dresses.*

Hawk to Skylark: *LOL! I'm sure Charlie will have several opinions about everything!*

Jackie's phone rang a few minutes later.

"Hey Charlie, which of these dresses do you want?" Rachel asked her, holding up Jackie's phone to the dresses so that Charlene could see.

Charlene started asking detailed questions about the fabric, the feel, and what colors they came in. Rachel had no interest and handed the phone over to Jackie.

"Y'all can pick whatever you want," Rachel said. "You're the ones who have to wear them, not me." She turned her attention to her phone, then remembered the phone in her hand didn't do anything. She looked around, trying to find her father. He was nowhere to be seen—shocking—so she went out to the parking lot. He was texting vigorously on his phone.

"Daddy, I am losing my mind," she said, interrupted Tom's texting. "I know you wouldn't be able to go this long without checking in at work."

"Rachel, I told you—"

"Dad, I have a critical situation going on with a team and kids missing and being trafficked and shit escalating left and right. I am here under duress, doing my best to act interested in this wedding because I know it's important to the rest of you. I don't care what I wear or where the wedding is. I *do* care if my team is safe."

Tom studied her for a moment before finally giving in and calling Paul Eastwood. "Paul, Rachel needs a sitrep." He clicked on the speaker so Rachel could hear.

"She definitely does not," Eastwood disagreed.

"Would you just tell me what they're doing?" Rachel pleaded.

"I thought you were planning a wedding?" Eastwood checked.

"You don't actually think I care what dresses Charlene, Jackie, and Sara wear, do you?"

Eastwood chuckled. "I suppose not."

"Okay, so, sitrep."

"Onyx is on their way back to Khost to meet your asset. I don't think they need *your* help navigating."

"No, they do not," Rachel agreed. "What about the other issue? Any updates from Raven?"

"No. Cameras aren't showing anything. Your target is in hiding, it seems. Haven't gotten a hit on any more names other than those first few."

"He's not a target, he's a hostage," Rachel corrected.

"Whatever. No sightings of anyone we've been looking for. Are you done bothering me?" Eastwood asked.

"Yes, she is," Tom answered for her.

"Good. How's it really going?"

"Well, she tried to convince me to move the wedding to Khost of all god forsaken places," Tom complained.

"Yeah, 'cause her target and her team are both currently in Khost, or driving from Jalalabad to Khost." Eastwood chuckled.

"Seriously, Rachel?" Tom chided her.

Rachel put both hands on her hips. "Two of my best friends happen to live there."

"Assets or friends?"

"Never mind!" Rachel huffed. She threw her hands in the air and turned on her heel, marching back into the dress shop. Somehow her father could always get her to act like she was six.

Jackie was on her the second she was back inside. "Can you at least pick a color for the dresses?"

"I don't know . . ."

"Well, what are the guys wearing?" Charlene asked through the video call.

"Blue?" Rachel guessed.

Charlene rolled her eyes and called over to Matt, who must've been in the background, to find out what suits the guys had picked. She confirmed that, yes, the guys would be in dark blue suits.

Sara held up a beautiful sky-blue V-neck, spaghetti strap, chiffon A-line dress. Everyone agreed that it was perfect. Charlene insisted that Rachel try on her wedding dress again and stand next to Sara and Jackie in the bridesmaids' dresses they were considering so that she could get the full picture before finally deciding the blue dress really was the perfect choice.

Once the girls finished ordering their dresses, they all headed out of the shop and back towards the hotel to meet up with Christopher and Bob. Rachel was exhausted and hungry.

"Can we go eat now?" Rachel asked once they had finally left the bridal shop. She saw a food truck and started walking towards it.

"Stop!" Tom called after her. "Restaurant."

Rachel turned and looked at him. "But—"

"Call Christopher and see where he and Bob are, and we can meet them somewhere," Tom suggested.

Rachel got out her phone and sent a text.

Skylark to Hawk: *Done! Dinner?*
Hawk to Skylark: *Where are you?*
Skylark to Hawk: *You think I know?*

Her phone rang a second later. "Hey, babe!" she answered. "You know I have no idea where we are. Why would you ask that?"

"Well, what do you want to eat?" Christopher asked.

"I tried to go to a food truck across the street from the dress shop, but apparently that was unacceptable."

Christopher laughed. "Put Jackie on." Rachel handed the burner phone to Jackie and listened as she discussed directions and restaurant options until they finally landed on a nice Italian restaurant that was a few blocks from their hotel. Jackie hung up and then called the restaurant to confirm that there were tables available.

Bob and Christopher were waiting outside of the restaurant when everyone else arrived. Rachel immediately went to Christopher for a hug. He pulled her in close and kissed the top of her head.

"How'd it go? Did you find a dress?" Christopher asked her quietly.

Rachel nodded. "We did my dress and bridesmaids' dresses. It took forever!"

Christopher laughed and kissed her head again. "But you survived, and now we can eat. You'll feel better after you get some food."

Rachel tipped her face up to his and gave him a soft kiss. "I missed you all day."

He smiled and brushed her hair off her face. "Let's go in and eat."

Their families had already gone into the restaurant and were seated at the table. Rachel saw that Anna-Beth was perusing the wine list and immediately snatched it out of her mother's hand. "I'll take care of that!" Rachel told Anna-Beth. "And I'm paying for dinner too," she whispered discreetly.

Anna-Beth gave her a critical look.

Rachel looked around the table, assessing who all was there before switching to French. "I am paying for dinner, and I am paying for the wedding, whether you like it or not. I'm not taking your money," she explained to Anna-Beth.

"You could have such a nice wedding. You could have it at—" Anna-Beth responded in French as well.

Rachel laughed and cut her off. "I think you need to take a trip to Paris soon, mother. Your accent is terrible. And to be clear, no, I'm not having anything to do with any of that. No insane, over the top things. I'm not inviting your family either. Now get on board or uninvite yourself," Rachel said as she sat down next to Christopher.

Tom flashed Rachel a look, pleading with her to not argue with her mother at dinner. Rachel ignored him.

"So, who wants wine?" Rachel asked, switching back to English and looking around at everyone as though everything were fine. They ordered and ate, having a very pleasant meal with good conversation and no arguments. Just as they were finishing up, Rachel handed her credit card to the server, glaring at her mother as she did.

Anna-Beth followed Rachel and Christopher into their hotel room once they had gotten back. Tom was right behind her.

"Rachel, it is completely improper not to invite your extended family to your wedding." Anna-Beth switched to French, clearly having deduced that Christopher wouldn't understand.

"Why? I don't speak to them," Rachel countered, also switching back to French.

"I also think that you need proper music. You can't just play music off your phone! And what are you doing about flowers? You haven't even thought about this at all. You know your father and I will pay for everything. I'll even plan for you!"

"You aren't paying for the wedding, and I fully intend on finding out how much you spent today on the dress and transferring the money back to your account."

Tom stepped in. "Anna-Beth, you know very well that Rachel has her own money. She can take care of everything and have the wedding she and Christopher want to have."

"Thank you, Daddy. Your French is flawless, by the way," Rachel said, giving her mother a spiteful look. "Are we done?"

"We are most definitely not," Anna-Beth said.

"I'm not going to let you, or anyone else, control me with money. I don't care about all that materialistic shit, and you know that. Nor do I care about your idea of what is and isn't proper. You can decide if you want to come or not, but it's my wedding and my life."

Anna-Beth turned and left, allowing the door to slam shut behind her.

Once she had gone, Christopher looked at Rachel. "You wanna fill me in?"

"Nope," Rachel answered.

Tom sighed. "They're just disagreeing on correct wedding etiquette. Nothing important."

Christopher nodded and looked at Rachel. "Explain."

"She wants to spend a bunch of money on things that no one but her cares about, and she keeps trying to pay for things so that she can get her own way. It's ridiculous."

"You really aren't inviting your cousins?" Tom asked.

"I'm inviting Jamie, isn't that enough? Besides, I'm sure they've all forgotten I exist by now, and if I'm such an embarrassment to Mom, she can just tell everyone I died. It'd be a perfectly believable story. I could even write it for her. Hell, I'll even let her pick *how* I died. Combat, suicide, drug overdose, car accident—you know, whatever's in vogue at the moment. Then we could stop having this problem all together," Rachel suggested.

Christopher looked at her, confused. "What the hell are you talking about?"

"She's trying to compete with her friends to see who can be the biggest snob, and she's mad that she's not winning. She'd spend a hundred thousand dollars on a wedding if I'd let her."

Christopher reared back. "How could a wedding possibly cost a hundred thousand dollars?"

"You'd be surprised by all the dumb shit people buy for their weddings," Tom said.

Rachel looked at her father, pleading with him. "Can we please just go to the courthouse? I'll wear the dress, and you can come, and we can just not tell Mom."

"No, you may not. You've already planned this wedding and invited people. Your mother will get on board with everything, eventually."

"Ugh, do I really have to invite Jamie?"

"Yes, you have to invite Jamie," Tom said. "You don't have to invite your cousins or your aunt and uncle or anyone. I agree with you, it would just be a pain in the ass to deal with, but you have to invite your brother."

"Fine, I'll just see if I can get his ship sent somewhere or something," Rachel said.

"Don't even try it. His leave is already confirmed," Tom informed her.

Rachel pouted and sat on the bed.

"Fix your fucking face, Rachel, and get it together," Tom instructed.

"Fine." Rachel forced her face into a sweet smile.

"Good, see you at breakfast."

The second her father was out the door, Rachel fell back on the bed and let out a frustrated scream.

"Your family is that bad?" Christopher asked, sitting on the bed next to her.

"Yes. They are truly awful, and I have spent my entire life trying to avoid them."

"What is your mom trying to buy that you don't want?"

"Oh, I don't even know. I just know it's in everyone's best interest to say no to whatever dumb idea she comes up with. Jamie proposed to his college girlfriend. She said no, but he'd told my mom he was proposing, and she planned the most ridiculous wedding before he'd even asked Maryanne! I think just the flowers she'd picked cost fifteen thousand dollars because she just had to import orchids out of season, just because she could. She had no understanding or care that either Jamie or Maryanne might have an opinion, and she was so sure Maryanne was going to say yes that she put down non-refundable deposits on things."

"Okay, that's completely insane," Christopher agreed.

"Seriously, do not ever let her buy you anything. She will hold it over you and try to control you for the rest of your life. And never ever let her pick a restaurant or order wine because she has no concept of what things should actually cost. I went to dinner with her and Jamie one time, and they ordered a bottle of wine that cost a hundred and fifty dollars just for the hell of it, even though there were much better bottles of wine they could have gotten for, like, forty dollars, but they had to get the exclusive small production wine just cause. They're fucking idiots. And everything is for someone else's benefit, just so someone else can see what she has or what she does. She doesn't do anything because it's what she actually wants to do. It's all about keeping up some sort of image, and clearly, I get in the way of that."

Christopher laid down on his side next to her and took her hand in his, pulling it to his lips to kiss it. "Hey, look at me."

Rachel turned her head to the side.

"It's just you and me, okay?" Christopher said calmly. "Ignore your mom, your brother, and even your dad if you want to. Everything's going to be great. You don't need to worry. We have everything planned now: officiant, rings, dress, food, alcohol. The only thing left is flowers, and we're doing that tomorrow. We'll just go down to city hall a few days before the wedding and get the marriage license, and that's all we need to do. Then we get married and have a huge party with all of our friends for the whole weekend. I'll talk to your dad and make sure he keeps your brother and you mom in line as much as possible."

"I don't even know why we have to do all of this," Rachel said.

"What do you mean? You don't want to get married?" His brows knit together.

"No, I mean, don't you remember? We already did this."

Christopher looked at her, clearly not understanding.

"Don't you remember when we were in Florida?" Rachel asked. "When you came to my apartment with me. We've already said our vows. Already promised to belong to each other, promised to be each other's forever and always, promised to love, honor, and cherish each other until the day we die.

That was enough for me. I took you as my husband then and became your wife. This other stuff, it's just paperwork and a party. It's fun, but it's more for everyone else."

Christopher smiled. "You are completely amazing, Rachel Ryker. Tell me, though, if you already considered us to be married, why were you so excited when I proposed?"

"Because then I knew it was for real and not just in my head, in my heart. I knew you had really meant it too. Besides," Rachel said, looking at her ring. "You can't go waving diamonds around in front of a girl and think she's not gonna get excited."

Christopher laughed out loud. "I'll have to keep that in mind."

Rachel looked at him seriously. "I love you," she said. "I can't wait to make it officially official."

Chapter 42

MARCH 2021

IT HAD BEEN A long day with a bomb, a helicopter ride, a missing truck full of kids—thanks to a rule-following drone pilot—then another helicopter back to Khost so Luke could meet Yamna. He was at the safe house in Khost listening to the team argue about whose turn it was to cook dinner when his phone beeped with a text notification.

Yamna to Lux: *My husband is gone.*
Lux to Yamna: *Thank you for confirming. Let me know when the kids are asleep, and I'll come by.*

Luke chuckled at the irony of the text messages. Usually when women texted him their husbands were away, they were asking him to come over for something very different. His texting with Yamna was starting to read like the beginning of those awful romance novels Rachel had taken an interest in. He got another text at 2130.

Yamna to Luke: *The kids are all asleep.*

Luke made his way through back alleys all the way to Yamna's house, careful to be sure no one saw him. She must have been watching out the window because she had the front door to the house open the moment he arrived and led him inside.

"Where are the documents?" he whispered in Pashto.

"Over here."

Luke followed her to the far corner of the living room and snapped on a pair of latex gloves. He pulled a ruler out of his backpack so he could keep the documents lined up exactly as they had been when Khalid Khan left them. He took a photo of the document on top with his phone then carefully flipped through the stack, taking a photo of each document and skimming the information as he did. There was a list of towns, all in Texas, and a list of schools, all private Christian schools. Then in large capital letters, *NEW TARGET*, was written in red ink with a circle around it and a hand-drawn sketch of a bird.

Luke immediately popped one of his earbuds in and dialed Rachel, knowing she was currently in Texas. It went straight to voicemail. In the eleven years he'd known her, she'd never not answered her phone. Even when she was drunk, she answered and could have a full conversation about more or less anything. "Fucking hell, Rachel," he muttered.

"Is it a problem?" Yamna's brow furrowed.

"Was your father here? Did he have anyone with him? Did you hear them talking?" Luke tried to stay calm, but this was bad.

Yamna shook her head. "I had to take my son to the doctor. These papers were here when I got back. I just saw them when I was cleaning, then I waited to be alone and texted you . . . Something is wrong."

Luke nodded. "It's a list of schools in Texas, in the U.S. I think . . . Yamna, I think they're planning to bomb a school."

Her eyes went wide.

"Have you found anything else your father left?"

She shook her head, tears welling in her eyes.

"Shit." Luke scrubbed his hands over his face. "Where does your father sleep when he's here?"

Yamna pointed to a small bedroom.

"Is it okay if I look around?"

"The children are sleeping," she reminded him.

"I promise to be as silent as possible, and as quick as possible."

Yamna nodded.

Luke started in the bedroom, looking through the small closet. He pulled clothes hanging on the rack to the side and gulped for breath. "Fuck me."

Brad and Shane were at Yamna's house less than five minutes later. Yamna was making them tea, despite their protests that it was unnecessary, but she insisted it was only proper to make tea for her guests. Explaining that they weren't guests hadn't worked. Luke saw she was shaking and figured she needed something to do, so he let her make tea and showed the guys what he had found.

"It's a list of schools," Shane said, stating the obvious. He swiped through the photos Luke had taken of the documents Khalid Khan had left at the house.

"Yeah, but why is there a drawing of a bird? What kind of bird is this supposed to be?" Luke asked.

"What team are we on? Have I memorized any birds?" Brad's nose wrinkled. Indigo was birds. They were not team Indigo.

Shane zoomed in on the photo and smiled. "It's a cute little bird. Sky would know, but I guess she's not answering her phone . . ."

Luke rolled his eyes. Remarkably unhelpful. "Mirage, hang with Yamna while I show New York the other thing I found." He led Brad into the bedroom and showed him the closet full of explosives.

"Umm, her kids are here?" Brad's brow furrowed as he stared dumbfounded at the back corner of Khalid Khan's closet.

"They're all sleeping." Luke nodded.

Brad grimaced. "Might want to wake them up and move them." He carefully moved a few things out of his way so he could get a better look. "That's a lot of explosives."

Yamna came in carrying a cup of tea. "Lux." She tried to hand it to him.

"Yamna, I appreciate the tea, but I need you out of this room." Luke kept his voice calm and steady.

"What's on the other side of this wall?" Brad asked, pointing at the closet. His Farsi was better than his Pashto, but Yamna seemed to understand.

"My children's bedroom."

Brad motioned for her to move closer to him then pointed to the back corner of the closet. He was careful not to touch her though. "Do you know what that is?"

Yamna shook her head.

"It's a bomb, or at least everything needed to make a bomb."

"Bomb?" she asked.

"Explosion, big boom, and we all die," Brad tried.

"I understand the word, but I *don't* understand why there would be a bomb in my house!"

"Umm, because your father is a terrorist?" Brad's brows knit together.

Luke shook his head. For a former college professor, Brad sure didn't have pedagogy figured out. "Yamna, it's not safe. I need you to wake your children up and move them while we look at this more closely."

"Move them where?" Yamna's body tensed, and she pulled her bottom lip between her teeth.

"Out to the truck," Brad suggested as he took a step into the closet, closer to the explosives.

"I'll help you move them," Luke told her. "Wake up the older ones and the little ones we can just carry outside."

"It's too cold," Yamna protested.

"We have blankets in the truck. Snacks and water too," Shane told her. "We won't let anything happen to your children."

"Ehsan is sick. He cannot be out in the night," Yamna protested.

"Right, you were just at the doctor." Luke looked to Shane.

"I have medicine too. Did the doctor help you?"

Yamna shook his head. "I did not have money for the medicine he needed. He has an infection in his lungs. I have to wait for my husband or father to return."

"I have antibiotics," Shane told her.

Yamna frowned.

"Shane is a medic, sort of like a doctor," Luke explained. "He makes sure no one gets sick and bandages us up when we get hurt. He can get you whatever Ehsan needs, if he doesn't have it with him already."

"Alright." Yamna hesitated. "But . . . what do we do with *that*?" Her eyes were wide as she gestured to the mess of explosives in her father's closet.

"*That* is his job." Luke gestured with his thumb towards Brad. "He knows how to make sure they don't explode, but he's not going to touch anything until you and your kids are safe."

"You too, Lux," Brad added.

Luke nodded. "We'll move the kids and let you work. I need to keep trying to get a hold of Rachel. I know she's taking a vacation day, but I didn't know she actually knew what that meant!"

"Her phone's off?" Shane's jaw went slack.

Luke nodded. "Help me with these kids. I'll try to call her again once we're outside."

They left Brad alone in the small closet and helped Yamna and her kids out to the truck. Shane was in the back with Yamna and the kids while Luke was up front in the driver's seat on the phone with Brad. It didn't take long to start making sense of things.

"It's a vest, Lux," Brad explained. "Explosives are packed tight . . . a lot of explosives. The vest is small, like kid's size."

"Delightful," Luke muttered.

"Oh, hey, the detonator isn't attached! It's not live. We're good." Brad almost sounded disappointed it had been such an easy job.

"You're sure?" Luke asked.

"Of course, I'm sure. We need to take this with us."

"If we take it and Khalid Khan comes back, he'll see it's gone and that will be a huge problem for Yamna."

"If we leave it here and someone sets it off, that will be an even bigger problem for Yamna," Brad pointed out.

Luke pinched the bridge of his nose. *Impossible decisions.* Sometimes being team leader really sucked. This was definitely one of those times. Leave a suicide vest in a house with a woman and her six kids or take it with them and risk that woman's father discovering the vest is gone and inquire where it went? Luke was fairly certain Khalid's questioning would involve his fists making contact with Yamna's face. He sighed, wishing he were anywhere else, then realized if he were, someone less competent than he was would be here trying to make this decision instead.

He went around to the back of the truck and asked Yamna, "When is your father coming back?"

She shrugged. "He never tells me anything."

"What about your husband?"

Another shrug.

Luke sighed. He couldn't in good conscious leave a bunch of explosives in a house full of kids. They'd have to take the vest with them and hope Khalid Khan didn't come back and notice it was missing. "Yamna, if your father comes back and sees that vest is gone, tell him a man came by and said he needed something to take to your father and that you don't know who it was. Can you do that? Can you lie to him?"

Yamna nodded. "Yes, I can do that."

Luke pressed his phone to his ear. "New York, make sure it's safe to transport. We're taking that thing with us. Go ahead and search the rest of the house while you're at it."

Chapter 43

MARCH 2021

CHRISTOPHER DRUG RACHEL WITH him to the florist the next morning, insisting it was her bouquet and only she could decide what she wanted it to look like. Rachel was doing her best to act interested.

"Rachel, can you at least decide which style of bouquet you want?" Christopher motioned towards the hundreds of photos the florist had laid out in front of her.

"Not pink," Rachel stated. "Can I please have my phone back?"

"Why?" Christopher asked.

"I need to check in at work." Rachel fidgeted in her chair.

Christopher rolled his eyes. "Can you please focus for ten minutes, and we can get this done? This is the last wedding planning thing we need to do, and I'm not doing it. I dealt with the caterers, got the speakers, folding chairs and tables, everything. The only two things I've expected you to help with were your dress and the flowers."

"Do you have a favorite flower?" the florist asked.

"No." All her favorite flowers were poisonous and didn't belong in a wedding bouquet.

"Can you at least look at these photos and say which ones you don't like?" Christopher tried.

Rachel scrunched up her face, sifting through the photos, setting aside anything she didn't like. "These are too generic, these are too over the top, these are pink . . ." Rachel explained.

Christopher's phone started ringing, and he glanced down and declined the call. His phone rang again seconds later. "What?" he answered.

"I need Ryker." Rachel could hear Ryan's voice on the other side of the line.

"Let me talk to him," Rachel demanded, dropping the photos and reaching for the phone.

"She'll call you back in fifteen minutes," Christopher argued, angling the phone away from her.

"Hawk. Ryker, now!" Ryan demanded.

Christopher reluctantly handed his phone to Rachel. She took it and ran outside. He followed her.

"What?" she yelled into the phone, already knowing it must be something bad.

"NSA has been picking up chatter . . . Onyx found some stuff . . . You're in Texas, right?" Ryan sounded scattered.

"Correct."

"I'm sending you an address. I think it's Kamal. Haul ass!"

Rachel looked at Christopher. "I need the truck and my phone."

"Rache, whatever it is can wait ten minutes while we finish this."

Without warning, Rachel reached into his pocket, fished out his keys, and sprinted to his truck. Christopher was right behind her. She pulled the door on the driver's side open, but he was faster, slamming his hand against the car door to stop her from getting in the truck.

"Christopher," she said. "I don't want to hurt you, but I will if you stand in my way of doing my job."

"I'll always be your second priority, won't I?" He winced as he said it.

"In an emergency? Yes, you will be." She elbowed past him and climbed into the truck, throwing it into drive before she even had her seatbelt on, and peeled out of the parking lot. Christopher's phone connected to the truck's audio system and GPS. "Raven, what the fuck is happening?"

"Hang on," Ryan mumbled. "You took Hawk's phone?"

"Yes." Rachel glanced over her shoulder and changed lanes. "That address you sent loaded into the GPS when I plugged it into the charger thingy."

"Yeah, Sky, it's called Apple Car Play, and we all love it," Ryan teased. "I'm just getting this satellite attached to Hawk's phone so I can track your location."

"Where are you?"

"Langley . . . as ordered."

"Ugh. Sorry." She really did feel bad for Ryan.

"All good. I forgot how fun the office could be." Ryan chuckled.

"Gross, Ryan! Stop harassing the junior analysts!"

"*I'm* not harassing anyone. If anything, these analyst chicks are harassing me!"

"Sure they are," Rachel grumbled. "I'm getting on the highway?"

"Yeah, I guess, I don't know where you are yet. This thing is slow," Ryan complained. "Anyway, while this piece of shit tries to connect . . ." He let out an audible sigh. "You haven't spoken with Lux or Eastwood, have you?"

"No, my phone has been in detention all weekend."

"Well, some shit is going down right now in Khost." Ryan proceeded to fill her in on everything that had transpired at Yamna's house and how he'd gotten the list of schools in and around Dallas from Luke and Eastwood. "I got someone here, someone at Homeland, and someone at the NSA all working on this, not knowing they're all working on the same thing. Figured if all three agencies could agree then we were on the right track. Anyway, chatter coming out of Afghanistan and Pakistan both indicate an increase in terrorist activity on U.S. soil. The CIA station in Khost was able to get phone records from Yamna's house and got a list of phone numbers we're assuming that Khalid called because Yamna didn't know who they were. So, we've tapped those lines . . . some of them at least. It's a work in progress. We've only been on this for a few hours."

"That's a lot for a few hours! Send me those phone records. I have several questions about who Khalid Khan has been calling." Rachel was shocked that Ryan was able to get this many agencies to cooperate and act so quickly.

"Yeah, will do. Anyway, those wire taps have picked up more chatter and confirmed Dallas is a target, which lines up with what Lux found at Yamna's house. The list of schools . . . It's a Sunday, so school isn't in session, but there was a call placed from Khost to a number in Houston. We passed the Houston number off to the NSA and they picked up a call confirming something was happening near Dallas today. Sunday. So I got all these analysts looking at each of these schools. Other than regular church services, most of which are over by now, only one of the schools has an event today—The Trinity Christian Spring Fling. Local police are refusing to shut down the event, and the school is throwing a shit fit about it . . . Eastwood is trying to talk some sense into them now, but since you're close . . ."

Rachel glanced at the GPS. "I'm seventeen minutes out."

Chapter 44

MARCH 2021

RACHEL PARKED THE TRUCK and took a deep breath. She couldn't just go running around frantic. She needed to stay calm. She closed her eyes and breathed in through her nose and out through her mouth, then reached over and opened the glove compartment. So many illegal things were about to happen. She grabbed Christopher's pistol and slid out of the truck, being sure to keep the gun out of view as she tucked it into the back of her waistband then pulled her shirt over it. She wandered, one foot in front of the other, doing her best to act casual. No need to cause panic. There were carnival games set up, booths selling raffle tickets, and a stage with kids performing in what they were calling a talent show. There wasn't much talent as far as Rachel could tell. No sign of Kamal, either.

She kept going. The buildings were open, so she went into one of them. Children's artwork decked the hallways, and the classroom doors were open. Kids were running around, dragging their parents by their hands and insisting they come see their desk, their drawing, their short story. It was loud and chaotic. But Rachel had found people in more tumultuous situations than this. Or Christopher had . . . He really was better at finding people than she was.

She paused, leaning up against one of the few walls not covered in student's work and pulled out Christopher's phone, pretending to text.

Think Ryker. What would Christopher be yammering on about right now? Something with maps. So fucking obsessed with maps. Did schools *have* maps? Maybe she should have brought him with her? If only he hadn't been being such a wedding obsessed pain in the ass. The school campus was bigger than she'd expected, and she definitely could use a second set of eyes.

Rachel waved down the first adult she saw wearing a name tag. *Mr. Hudson.* "Excuse me, do you happen to know if there is a map of the school anywhere? My husband and I are thinking of sending our son here, so I came to check everything out. Want to make sure I don't miss anything."

"Yes, ma'am." Mr. Hudson smiled at her. His Texas accent was as thick as her North Carolina drawl. "I'll take you over to where the school receptionists have their booth set up. They'll get you a map and all the enrollment forms and other information you'll need. How old is your son?"

"Five," Rachel lied.

"Oh, so he'll be starting kindergarten!"

"Uh-huh." Thank God she'd listened to David ramble on about his kids all these years.

"Where is he attending preschool?"

Shit. "Iroquois Point Preschool." She gave the name of the preschool she'd attended. "It's on Hawaii. My husband is in the Navy, stationed at Pearl Harbor . . . or he was, I guess. He just retired and we wanted to move closer to his family." All the best lies were really the truth just slightly altered.

"Oh, wow! What did he do in the Navy?"

"Fighter pilot." Father, husband, fiancé . . . whatever. Fighter pilot and Pearl Harbor went together in her head. It had been the last post her father had before they told him he was too old to fly and transferred him to Cherry Point.

"Impressive." Mr. Hudson nodded. "Please do thank him for his service."

"Yes, I sure will." Rachel smiled.

Mr. Hudson stopped at a table right outside the building on the opposite side of the building Rachel had entered from. He gestured to the woman sitting at the table. "This is Sandy. She works in our admissions office. Sandy, this is . . . so sorry, I didn't get your name."

"Oh." Rachel giggled. "My bad. I'm Anna-Beth." Another almost truth, seeing as Anna-Beth Ryker was married to a Navy pilot who'd been stationed at Pearl harbor. She could be her mother for a few minutes.

"Pleasure, Anna-Beth." Mr. Hudson turned back to Sandy. "Anna-Beth has just moved here from Hawaii with her husband, and they'd like to enroll their son in kindergarten to start in the fall."

"Hawaii!" Sandy's eyes lit up. "Well, doesn't that sound like a dream?"

"I dunno, Sandy," Rachel laughed. "If you think getting woken up at five a.m. and having to follow all the rules that come with living on a military base as busy and crowded as Pearl Harbor sounds like a dream, well, I know a lot of single sailors!"

"Anna-Beth's husband just retired from the Navy. He's a pilot," Mr. Hudson explained.

"Wow!" Sandy's eyes lit up. "Well, let me get you an admissions packet. It has all the forms you'll need, tuition information—everything you could ever want to know about the school."

"Anna-Beth, I'll leave you in Sandy's capable hands." Mr. Hudson shook her hand and walked away to join a group of parents conversing close by.

Rachel took the folder from Sandy and carefully opened it, sifting through the papers as though she were actually interested. "Sandy, is there by chance a map of the school and church? I promised my husband I'd take pictures of everything. He couldn't come with me today."

"Of course!" Sandy reached to the far end of the table and grabbed a map that had been printed on basic eight and a half by eleven-inch paper then grabbed a pen and started jotting down notes. "This is where the kindergarten is." She drew a big *K* so Rachel couldn't miss it. And the playground and church and gardens . . ."

Rachel smiled and nodded along, eyes scanning the crowd around her as best she could while still feigning interest in whatever Sandy was babbling on about.

"Any other questions?" Sandy asked with a bright smile.

"I don't think so. You've been remarkably helpful, Sandy. I do appreciate it."

"Well, enjoy today and come back by the table if you have any more questions."

"Thank you, I will." Rachel smiled at the map and wandered off. She scanned the paper. Now she at least had an overview of what all the buildings were and how spaced out they were. Next step: think like a terrorist. What buildings would be the most crowded? What would have the most impact? The buildings with classrooms were overflowing with people. Each of them would be an excellent target. But it would be hard to get inside wearing a suicide vest without being noticed. Not impossible, but Kamal was thirteen and not very well practiced at this, as far as she knew. Whoever had brought him here and given him the vest or bomb, or whatever he had, would be long gone by now so they wouldn't be injured or implicated. *He's thirteen. Thirteen and away from home and probably scared. Don't think like a terrorist. Think like a kid.*

Most kids would be scared. Indoctrination only worked so well. Kamal was probably off someplace by himself getting ready. Checking the bomb, praying, getting mentally ready.

Praying.

She glanced down at the map in her hand then made a beeline for the church. The map helped, as did the tall steeple that could be seen from just about anywhere on the school's campus. Churches were quiet—places of solitude, places where people would leave you alone and not look too closely at what you were doing.

The doors to the church were wide open, letting all the visitors come and go without the doors banging shut to disrupt the peace inside. Rachel looked around. Stained glass windows, an area for the choir to sing, piano, drums, guitars . . . and stairs. There was a balcony area. She didn't see anyone up there, but it would give her a good view of everyone on the lower level of the church. She advanced up the stairs, careful not to draw too much attention to herself. When she got to the top, she stopped and looked around. People were milling about below her. A few excited kids pointing out where they typically sat, people inspecting the stained-glass windows and paintings on the walls, and a few people kneeling, sitting, praying. None of them were Kamal.

She kept going. There were twelve rows of chairs on the balcony level. She walked up the center aisle looking down each row of chairs, left then right, as she passed, until she got to the last row. There, huddled in the back corner, behind the last row of chairs next to a gorgeous stained glass window, was Kamal. She raised both hands, palms facing him, and approached slowly, speaking to him quietly in Pashto. "Kamal, do you remember me?"

His eyes snapped to hers.

"Kamal, I'm your mom's friend, Rachel, remember? I'm here to help you, to take you home."

He shook his head. "I'm not going home. I'm going to paradise."

"You don't have to."

Kamal nodded. "This is my *jihad*. I must fight in the way of God with those who fight me."

"Verse 2:190. 'Fight in the way of God with those who fight you,'" Rachel nodded and knelt beside him. He was paraphrasing the Quran. "But no one is fighting you, Kamal."

Kamal straightened, jutting his chin out with an air of confidence and certainty. "America has blown up our schools and mosques. So now we must do the same."

Rachel closed her eyes. She knew he was right. Someone had blown up a school in Khost. She'd been there when it had happened. Whether it had been on purpose, that didn't matter. "Isn't the full verse 'Fight in the way of God with those who fight you, but aggress not. God loves not the aggressors?'"

Kamal's brows knit together.

"You can read, right?" Rachel got out her phone, switched the keyboard to Pashto, and googled the verse in question so he could see for himself.

Kamal squinted his eyes at the screen and started scrolling. "You made this up! You changed it!"

"No." Rachel sighed. "I didn't." The idea of her being able to change anything on the internet was hilarious. But Khalid Khan changing scripture to manipulate children to violence? That was horrifying.

Kamal's lip quivered. "Grandfather said—"

"He lied to you, Kamal. He's a bad man who wanted to use you to do bad things."

Kamal shook his head. "No. He is giving us the opportunity to prove ourselves."

Kill yourselves.

"Me and the others—"

"How many kids, Kamal? Just you and the other kids who were at the White House, or are there more of you somewhere?"

"Grandfather has a training camp in the mountains. One in Kabul, one in Pakistan. You will see. You will see the wrath and fury of Allah. We will show you."

Three camps. Well, the one in the mountains near Jalalabad had been blown to bits. So, two camps.

"Do the other kids have a *jihad*, like you?"

Kamal shook his head. "Not like me. They have a different purpose."

"Oh. What are they supposed to do?" Rachel figured she'd get as much information out of him while he was calm.

"To put the code on the computers."

Rachel's brow furrowed. "Huh?"

"They take the stick with the code and plug it into any computer, then grandfather and his friends could watch."

"Watch what?" Rachel didn't get it.

Kamal shrugged. "Whatever they want. The stick puts a code on the computer, and then grandfather and his friends would have access to watch what America is doing."

"Like a software to spy on people?" Rachel cocked her head to the side. *Samir still has a copy of that damned malware code. Samir said he fixed the code, that there was a flaw.* What the fuck did this code do? Had any of the kids managed to install it on any computers in the U.S.?

Another shrug. "I think so. I don't know so much about it."

Rachel turned her attention back to the real issue at hand. "I can help you get that vest off and take you home to your mother, Kamal. You don't have to do this."

"I do," Kamal insisted.

"Can you stand up? Can I just see if there a timer or something?" Rachel asked.

Kamal nodded and stood. Rachel stood too and inspected the vest.

Fuck that's a lot of explosives. It had to weigh a ton.

Rachel's hands traced the wires, trying to get a sense of what she was dealing with, as she looked for the timer. She'd diffused bombs before, but she was no expert. "How do you set this off? Do you press a button, or does it just blow when the timer goes off?"

"It goes when I find my target."

"Oh yeah? Who's your target?"

"It changed. They changed it after—" Kamal shook his head. "I failed. I didn't kill the president."

"I don't think you really wanted to kill the president," Rachel noted. She had narrowed it down to three wires that were hooked up to the detonator—the detonator in Kamal's hand.

"May I see what's in your hand?" Rachel asked.

Kamal narrowed his eyes at her. "They told me you were a very bad person. My mother should not be friends with people like you. Working with American spies. She is a traitor."

"No, your grandfather and his friends shouldn't be convincing young men that they need to kill themselves to be saved," Rachel disagreed. "Your mother and I are just trying to keep you alive."

"Your life is more important than mine," Kamal stated firmly.

Rachel was taken aback. What the fuck did he mean by that? "Who is your target, Kamal?"

"You can't guess? You should be able to guess Sky—"

Some sort of force collided with Rachel, and her back was suddenly flat against the wall of the church's balcony. She winced, grunting with pain as her head slammed against the wall, forcing her eyes shut. The sound reverberated through the building—shockwaves, sound waves, shattered glass. Someone's hands were on her, holding her still, holding her tight. She opened her eyes and blinked, taking in the ocean blue of Christopher's gaze. Christopher had his palms on either side of her face, forcing her to look at him. Not at the window, not at Kamal. People were screaming and shrieking with terror inside the church, outside the church. Her heart was pounding out of her chest as she stared at Christopher, wide-eyed, still unable to comprehend what had happened.

"Rachel!" Her father's voice broke the silence. She and Christopher turned their heads towards the stairs. "You're okay?"

Rachel said nothing. She was shaking. Eyes wide and lip quivering, Christopher pulled her tight into his chest.

"You're safe. I've got you," he whispered against her temple.

"I-I," she stammered, looking to the side where the beautiful stained glass window had been, the remnants of which were shattered on the floor and the ground outside. Her eyes darted around, collecting clues. Kamal had gone out the window. She looked back at Christopher and saw the fear, the guilt on his face. *He had pushed Kamal out the window and slammed her against the wall.* "Why did you do that?"

"I saw him reach for the detonator switch. He was going to kill you."

"He was just going to tell me who his target was, and then . . . and then . . . Why did you do that? I wasn't done getting information from him!" she yelled.

"Baby, he was going to kill you. His thumb was on the switch."

"But—"

Tom's phone started ringing. He answered it and put it on speaker. "Yeah, Paul. We've got her. Threat is eliminated. We're gonna have quite a bit of fallout, I think."

"What happened?" Eastwood barked.

"Kid went out a second story window from what I can tell. I missed it," Tom answered. "Williams?" He looked at Christopher and held out the phone so Christopher could update Eastwood without letting go of Rachel.

"Sir, Rachel was with Kamal, working on disarming the bomb when I found them. I saw the kid's thumb move to the detonator switch and . . . It was instinct, sir."

"I'm supposed to fill in the blanks myself?" Eastwood's tone was sharp.

Christopher gulped then continued. "I pushed him out a second story window seconds before the bomb went off."

"He was with Ryker, no one else?" Eastwood checked.

"I mean, there's other people around, but yeah, they were huddled up in a corner."

They all heard an audible sigh through the phone.

"He was just about to tell me what the target was." Rachel's voice was unsteady and weak.

"What or who?" Christopher asked.

"Huh?" Rachel's brow furrowed.

"Before you said he was going to tell you *who* his target was. Which was it? Was the target a location or a person?"

"I don't know. He said 'when I find my target.' Then I asked who—" Her eyes snapped to Christopher's. "I'm . . . you saw him go for the detonator?"

Christopher nodded. "Yup."

"But I was trying to help. I was . . . I was going to take him home."

"I know, baby." Christopher hugged her tight to his chest and kissed the top of her head.

"He said my life was more important than his," Rachel murmured. "That they knew his mom was working with an American spy . . . Sky. I asked him who and he said Sky. H-how do they know—"

Two FBI agents, guns poised, ran up the stairs, interrupting Rachel's train of thought. They looked around then lowered their guns.

"Everyone okay?" the first agent asked.

"Yeah, we're fine," Christopher answered.

"Did any of you see what happened?" the second agent asked.

Rachel nodded, forehead still pressed into Christopher's chest. She reached into her back pocket and pulled out her ID, then stretched her hand out, not to anyone in particular. Christopher reached around to her back and pulled the pistol out of her waistband, holding that out as well.

Tom took a step towards them and took her ID and gun. He handed both to the agent and explained what had happened. He was still on the phone with Eastwood, who was able to fill in even more details.

"Ma'am. Sir." The second agent approached Christopher. "We've got paramedics downstairs. Need you both to get checked out."

"Of course." Christopher nodded.

Rachel shook her head. "I'm fine."

"Just a precaution, ma'am," the agent assured her. He led them downstairs and outside. "You're Austin's buddy?" the agent asked Christopher.

He nodded. "Yeah, I just started working with him a few weeks ago. Messaged him on the way here asking if he knew anyone in the Dallas FBI field office who could help. I'm glad he passed along my message."

"Yeah, well, when I hear there's credible intel from a SEAL team, I tend to take it pretty seriously. You ever get a tip like this again," the agent reached in his pocket and pulled out his card, "that's my direct line."

They spent the next two hours getting checked out by the paramedics and giving their statements to countless federal agents and local police. Finally, they were allowed to go home. Or leave the school at least. They'd missed their flight back to D.C. They'd missed check out time at their hotel. The one thing neither of them had missed was the sentence no one had said out loud. The one bit of information they'd all pieced together but didn't quite understand. *Rachel* had been Kamal's target, and somehow, someone knew *Rachel* was Skylark.

Chapter 45

MARCH 2021

RACHEL'S HAND WAS SHAKING as she pressed Yamna's name in her contacts. She didn't trust her voice, didn't trust her words, but this had to be done—sooner rather than later. Sitting on the floor of a supply closet at the Air Force base while waiting for a flight back to D.C. would have to be the right time and the right place for this. She hated doing it but knew she had to. She always called the family of anyone killed in action, anyone under her command. Usually these calls were for soldiers—adult men, occasionally women, who volunteered to serve their country. Not kids who'd been kidnapped and indoctrinated and handed a suicide vest.

She took a deep breath before she spoke. "I found Kamal."

"What?" Yamna's joy made Rachel wince.

"Umm, found maybe isn't the right word." Her voice caught. "Yamna, I . . . he . . ."

"Rachel, what is wrong? Where is Kamal?" Yamna demanded.

"He's dead. I tried—"

Rachel's explanation was cut off by Yamna's wailing sobs. If there was ever a time to use the word hysterical, this may be it. Rachel had never been pregnant, never given birth, didn't even have a uterus at this point, but Yamna's sadness was connected to her womb. The loss of a child, no matter how old the child was, was worse than Rachel's hysterectomy. Was worse than any other pain in the world.

She heard a bit of commotion on the other end of the call, then another voice. Yashfa's voice. "Hello?"

"Yashfa, it's Rachel." Her tears were hot on her face. "I was calling . . . I-I found Kamal wearing a suicide vest. You know, explosives . . . I tried to get it off of him, to talk him down but-but . . . Yashfa, he was intent on killing me and himself in the process. I don't know why. I-I—" Rachel was at a loss for words for probably the first time in her life.

"What are you saying, Rachel?" Yashfa asked. "Why is my sister—" She paused, and Rachel could hear Yamna sobbing. The call must be on speaker.

Rachel bit back her tears and forced her voice to steady. "Kamal is dead. He . . . Christopher pushed me away from him just as Kamal was detonating the vest. He went out a second story window . . . The bomb exploded midair. No one else was hurt."

"Kamal is . . . dead?" Yashfa repeated, her voice breathy and weak. "I-I don't understand, Rachel. I don't understand at all."

Rachel took a deep breath and started from the beginning. The White House fundraiser. The botched attempt to assassinate the president. How Kamal disappeared. Then everything she and Ryan had done, how the intel Luke had found helped them find Kamal. She repeated Kamal's last words as best she could, letting Yashfa and Yamna know their father was well aware they were helping the Americans. "I'm sorry I couldn't bring him home. I tried. I really did everything in my power—"

"Lux, your team . . . they found such a vest at Yamna's house."

Rachel's eyes went wide. She hadn't been filled in on that tidbit of information yet.

"That my father was using children as suicide bombers." Yashfa sighed. "This is not so surprising, I suppose. That he would use Kamal, his own grandson?" Yashfa was quiet for three solid minutes, and Rachel could hear Yamna's crying grow quieter. "Rachel, this cannot go unpunished. You must find my father. It's the only way. I-I fear he will not stop this madness."

"Lux is still in Khost," Rachel said, assuming it was true. Luke was in Afghanistan somewhere in any case. "Finding your father—killing your father—will be priority number one for his team."

Rachel's head dropped into her hands as soon as Yashfa ended the call. She'd done a lot of crisis calls, visited a lot of families to tell them their child, their spouse was dead. It was always awful. It was always exhausting. None of it could compare to this. Kamal's death was the culmination of all of her failures. Failure to kill Samir, to kill Khalid, to find Kamal and get him back home to his mother. All of it was her fault.

Once upon a time, there was a little girl who made friends with a snake.
She felt her nails dig into her wrist.

Together, they plunged the world into chaos. Her failure to kill the snake caused the entire world to be covered in a blanket of darkness. Her failure caused children to die.

They'd been home for three days and Rachel hadn't eaten or slept. She just paced back and forth, replaying everything over and over, muttering to herself about what she should have done differently. Christopher got it. They all got it. The kid she was trying to save had nearly killed her, and none of them had seen it coming. Christopher had finally convinced her to come to bed at least. Even if she insisted she couldn't sleep, he hoped lying down might convince her brain and body otherwise, and if not, he slept better when she was next to him.

Rachel couldn't sleep, but Christopher's grip was tight around her, and he was dead to the world. She shifted slightly, reaching for her phone and earbuds on the bedside table. She could barely reach. She popped her earbuds in, more for the noise cancellation than anything else. Sensory deprivation always helped. As soon as she unlocked the screen, she turned the brightness down as much as she could, hoping to not disturb Christopher. She opened an app, an online diary of sorts, and started typing. She hadn't used it for years, but this was the quickest way to get back up without anyone knowing she was requesting or receiving outside help.

It's been a while. I'm sure you've been watching though. Too much is going on. I'm not sure if it's all connected. My asset's son nearly killed me. Won't make the news, I'm sure. I feel like I'm drowning, failing. I've never felt like this before. I mean, really, how hard is it to find a kid? There's been some interference though. The past is catching up and trying to become the present. Can I just hide in a blanket fort and ignore everything? I don't know how to fix this, how to fix me. Sometimes, I wish I were dead.

She pressed save then let silent tears stream down her face.

Rachel's eyes popped open as "Change (Taylor's Version)" started playing in her earbuds. The perfect fight song. Breaking down walls, starting a revolution, even though you know you're outnumbered. She didn't know when she'd fallen asleep. Then she remembered she'd posted to the online diary she shared with her friends. Friends she couldn't mention or talk to. Friends from long ago, another life, back when the CIA had been her only life. Friends no one could know about since it would inevitably lead to the question "How did you meet?" Obviously, none of them would answer that—*could* answer that—since the answer was "In a top secret, off-the-books CIA training program." "Change" really was the most applicable song. The girls knew how to get her back on her feet, that was for sure. They were all waiting for the right opportunity to destroy the Eros Group, too, and one day they'd start that revolution, outnumbered or not, and tear the whole thing down.

She turned her head as best she could, still restrained by Christopher's firm grasp around her waist, and saw he was still fast asleep. She opened the app on her phone and saw she'd gotten a response.

The revolution is coming, but we'll never win if you die, so don't give up yet! Betrayal is a bitch, but you already know all about that. Wish I could be there, but the best I could do was a song. Stay strong. Stay fearless. Make change.

Rachel closed the app and locked her screen, letting her silent tears turn to sobs. That woke Christopher up. His arm tightened around her even more and his lips brushed her neck. "It's okay, Rache," he mumbled.

"I feel like such a failure," she admitted.

"You can't fail unless you give up," he reminded her. "Are you quitting, or are you going to get back up and keep looking for Khalid Khan?"

"I don't know. I don't think I'm as strong as I thought I was, as I need to be. Luke can do it. Let him figure it out."

"Yes, you are strong enough, and crying is just getting all the cortisol out of your body, helping with a biological reset. Everyone gets it. Just take a few more days. It's okay to take a break. Eastwood, Luke, and Ryan are on top of everything, I promise."

Chapter 46

MARCH 2021

RACHEL SAT IN THE truck, unwilling to move. Christopher got out and came around to her side, opening the door, staring her in the eyes. The latest incident with Kamal hadn't made the news. The entire thing had been covered up. Rachel didn't want to talk about it. She didn't want to think about it. But she couldn't stop thinking about it. Christopher's hands on her, his weight against her, forcing her out of the way and away from Kamal. Forcing her to look at him so she wouldn't see. But every time she closed her eyes, she saw. She'd seen enough people get blown up. Her brain could put the pieces together and paint an image, a movie really, in vivid color just fine.

"You are going into the office. You will tell Catherine what happened. I will sit in the waiting room, and we will not leave until you talk." It wasn't often Christopher was so stern and demanding, but it had been a week since she'd posted to her online diary, connected with her friends, and admitted that she'd failed and didn't know how to move forward. Christopher had told her to take a few days. A few had turned into seven. Eastwood wanted her back at work, and Christopher wanted her to stop beating herself up over what had happened with Kamal. Rachel wanted to hide from all of it and pretend it never happened. If she went back to HQ, she wouldn't be able to pretend. If she went into Catherine's office, she'd have to talk about it.

Rachel rolled her eyes. "I promise I can keep my mouth shut for fifty minutes."

"I know you can. That's why I called Catherine, told her there was a problem, and changed your appointment so it would be the last appointment of the day. I got her to agree to sit and stare at you until you talked."

"I hate you," Rachel seethed.

"I love you too." He kissed her forehead.

"I'm fine, Christopher."

"You haven't slept in a week."

"How is that different from always?"

"Usually, you're awake reading or writing reports, running on the treadmill. Not pacing, not crying, not curled up in a ball in the corner of the room begging God to kill you." He brushed a strand of hair behind her ear that had fallen loose from her ponytail. "Baby, you can walk up there willingly and keep your dignity, or I can carry you kicking and screaming. I'm fine either way."

"Fine. Move!" Rachel knew he really would carry her kicking and screaming. It wouldn't be the first time. The first time he carried her into a therapist's office, sure. But kicking and screaming? That was nothing new. She got out of the truck and shoved past him, making a beeline for Catherine's office. He was half a pace behind her.

Catherine was in the waiting area. "Hi, Rachel."

Rachel didn't acknowledge her and went straight into her office, slumping down in an armchair.

"You must be Christopher," Rachel heard Catherine say.

"Nice to meet you, Catherine. Thank you for agreeing to stay late if necessary. It's been . . . Well, like I said, something happened. Something work related, and she's not handling it well."

"Only sociopaths could sleep after that!" Rachel yelled.

"Or normal, healthy people who call their therapist right after to talk about it," Christopher shouted back.

"Fuck you!" Rachel yelled.

"Sure, babe. Right after you tell Catherine what happened, and she gives me the go-ahead."

"You're mean!"

"That used to be one of your favorite things about me!" Christopher laughed. "You only like it when I'm mean to other people, I guess."

Rachel folded her arms over her chest and slumped down in her chair. "Did you read my book on discipline as a kink?"

"Baby, you have so many books, I have no idea which one you're talking about. Just settle in, talk to Catherine, and I'm right out here if you need me. If you can't explain something or need a hug, I'm right here."

"I need to kill someone."

"I know you do, and I'm very certain you have a team working on that as we speak."

"They're slow," Rachel complained.

"Baby, short of stealing you a plane and a pilot, there's nothing I can do about that."

"People who kill children . . . I swear to fucking God if they don't kill those assholes correctly—"

"Correctly?" Catherine whispered to Christopher, but she wasn't so quiet that Rachel couldn't hear from the next room.

"Slowly and painfully," Christopher translated. "I swear she's a normal, functional human being."

"I know she is," Catherine assured him. "Someone killed a child?"

"Technically Christopher did it," Rachel grumbled from the other room.

"I did not! I prevented you from getting yourself blown up!"

"Wow." Catherine held up both hands. "Christopher, take a seat. Let me talk to Rachel."

"Yes, ma'am." Christopher dipped his head and plopped himself in a chair in her waiting room.

Rachel slouched down in her chair, arms crossed over her chest, and watched as Catherine came in and closed the door.

"That was a lot of information," Catherine said as she sat down across from Rachel.

"We don't normally argue like that."

"Okay."

"Normally we just hit each other," Rachel blurted out.

Catherine raised an eyebrow.

"Not like that." Rachel sighed. "Just taunting and teasing and sparring in the basement. No one really gets hurt."

"Right." Catherine pulled her bottom lip between her teeth. "So, something about a dead kid and you trying to get yourself blown up?"

"I don't get to leave until I tell you, do I?"

"My next patient is at nine a.m. tomorrow." Catherine smiled.

Rachel leaned forward, elbows on her thighs and face in her palms. "For fuck's sake. Here's what happened."

She started with the incident at the White House and talked her way through finding Kamal at the school in Texas. Jaw tight, fists clenched, she didn't hold back on the details. "I could have talked him down. He was just about to tell me who his target was. I was getting so much information, then Christopher went and pushed him out the window!"

"It doesn't sound like Kamal was cooperating though. It sounds like he was intent on killing himself and you," Catherine pointed out.

"That doesn't mean he would have gotten his way."

Catherine raised an eyebrow. "We've been talking about trust a lot. Trusting other people, trusting yourself. You're confident in your abilities."

"I've stopped several suicide bombers. I'm pretty good at it."

"I wonder, though . . . was it confidence that you could talk him down and save him, or were you letting your determination and emotions cloud your judgement?"

"What?"

"In our last session, you said that you convince others that your way is right, or best, but it can't be because you keep losing, and other people keep getting hurt."

"Christopher's actions got Kamal killed."

"Christopher's actions kept you from getting blown up."

"It's a matter of perspective, I guess." Rachel shrugged.

"Rachel, you're really good at telling stories."

"Thank you?"

Catherine held up a hand. "You're good at telling stories and leaving out details that would change the story in a significant way if they were included."

Rachel raised an eyebrow.

"You told me about Kamal at the White House, but you didn't tell me how he got out of the White House. Now, doctor-patient confidentiality and all that, but I've been working in this town a long time. Long enough to know that if there's an incident involving the president, the Secret Service does not let the person or people involved get away."

Rachel shrugged. "Not everyone's as competent as you may like them to be."

"Do you remember telling me about what happened at the White House in our last session?" Catherine asked.

Rachel gave her a blank stare.

"I take notes, Rachel. What you told me today and what you told me in our last session . . . The story has changed from an NGO and corrupt politicians to you supposedly not knowing how Kamal got out of the White House."

"I *don't* know how he got out of the White House."

"You know who helped him get out of the White House."

"Really not the same thing."

Catherine sighed. "Normally I'm happy to let you direct our sessions, talk about what you want or need to talk about. But I'm taking the reins on this one."

"Fine."

"You were very angry last time about some people surrounding the president. You called them *self-serving sycophants*."

Rachel nodded.

"Then you said it was all your fault for burying your head in the sand and allowing the problem to fester. You told me a story about a little girl. A girl I can only presume is you, but you wouldn't name any names." Catherine cocked her head to the side. "Is it your fault someone gave Kamal a suicide vest?"

"Partly . . ."

"How so?"

"Well, if I'd let him blow up Frank, he wouldn't have been in Texas."

"True."

"If I hadn't made Christopher help plan that stupid event, I wouldn't have been at it and wouldn't know anything about this. Hell, if I hadn't have listened to you and gone to that bar with Kristen and met Ashley and ran into Hunter, then I wouldn't have made Christopher help with the event!"

"So, it's my fault?" Catherine pushed.

"No, it's Petchill's fault. It's Frank's fault. It's a lot of people's fault, and it's my fault, because if I'd just killed Sammy, if I'd just shot back, fuck!" she yelled before the words continued rushing out of her mouth. "Frank's fucked in the head. I know he's the president, but he's also my godfather. I've known him my whole life, and believe me, he is in no way a good person, not even decent. He's awful and he's sort of stupid, which makes it worse. The only positive thing about Frank Verity is that he's easily manipulated, which is helpful to me sometimes, but other people—very, very bad people—manipulate him too, and he's too dumb to know Petchill is working with Sammy and plotting with Leftwich to kill him."

Catherine's eyes were wide. "Well, that was a lot of names . . ."

"Fuck. You heard none of that."

"Alright, well, I can't really do anything about the other people. But if you'd just killed Sammy, none of this would have happened? Who's Sammy?"

"My former friend." Rachel grit her teeth. "I guess I name dropped enough I may as well tell you the full story. No one but me knows this story, and I'm not even sure *I* have all the details. It's a long story."

"We have all night."

Rachel gave her a slight smile and laughed to herself. "Once upon a time, there was a little girl named Rachel Marie Ryker. She was told she could grow up to be anything she wanted, as long as it fit inside a nice pretty box with a bow. No glitter, though. Her mother hated glitter. Too messy. The boxes were all confining, constricting. Box one: wife, mother, staying at home, helping with charity events, fixing her hair and plastering on a smile no matter how much it hurt to have a man—a husband—tell her what to do with every second of her time, waiting for permission to breathe. Box two: Naval officer working in some sort of safe, gender appropriate role. Assistant, human resources, recruiter, something nice and soft that mom and dad could explain to the neighbors. Something that sounded cool but would never result in battle scars. Box three: high finance, running a hedge fund, maybe sitting on the board of a nonprofit. But a nice nonprofit. Nothing too liberal. Nothing that actually helped anyone. Box four: pilot, also Navy, following in Dad's footsteps, except that planes are also remarkably confining, and Dad would have made sure she was never stationed anywhere there was an actual conflict.

"Rachel didn't like any of those boxes, so she worked hard. She fought with generals, admirals, and politicians, trying to convince them that women could do anything men could do. That women could serve in combat. That women could work in special forces. See, Rachel was naïve and thought her father would be proud of her service. He kept encouraging her brother to serve, to be a fighter pilot. Too bad Jamie's incompetent in so many ways . . . Anyhow, no amount of hard work got her to where she wanted to be. Doors kept slamming in her face. People kept telling her women couldn't serve in combat, they never would, and she needed to get a new dream. There *was* no new dream. She knew what she wanted. She knew who she was, whether people liked it or not." Rachel sighed.

"When Rachel was seventeen, an opportunity presented itself. It sounded like a good idea at the time, and it was fun . . . for a while. See, Rachel was approached by the CIA. A secret organization within the CIA that focused on covert operations. The Eros Group was comprised of spies, assassins, intelligence officers. It was everything Rachel had ever hoped for, so she signed her name on the dotted line and moved into a farmhouse in Northern Virginia.

"Everyone was blown away by how competent Rachel was. She outperformed all of her classmates, and suddenly, Rachel was the golden child. She could do no wrong. The men in charge, her teachers, gave her everything she wanted, everything she asked for. Training was a breeze, her first assignments a piece of cake. Getting information from people and killing people was second nature for Rachel, and it never bothered her the way it does most people. She was resilient. Mentally tough. Built for the work."

"Goddess of war and destruction and death." Catherine nodded.

"Exactly!" Rachel lit up. "After training, four fucking years of part-time training during college, Rachel had her choice of assignments. She wanted to go overseas. More importantly, she still had that nagging desire to please her father, make him proud, make him see her. So she begged and pleaded and made her wish and asked to be stationed on a Navy aircraft carrier with the cover of being a Navy intelligence officer. Rachel got her wish." She smirked.

"After a brief stint in Afghanistan, Rachel was transferred to Iraq where she made friends with Sammy. Sammy was an Iraqi soldier who became her intelligence asset, her friend, her confidant, her one constant in the ever-changing landscape of war. They did everything together. He even bought her a scarf in her favorite color—purple. She tells everyone her favorite color is red, like blood, because it sounds cooler. But she trusted Sammy enough to tell him the truth. He knew her maybe better than she knew herself.

"Everything was great. Rachel was getting the intel she needed, getting promoted, getting recognition. Until one day, she came back to camp from meeting with an intelligence asset and watched as Sammy put a bullet in the head of everyone in Rachel's unit. Her men. The people she was responsible for training, for keeping alive, they were all dead. So, Rachel ran. She ran and she hid, and Sammy found her. He shot her in the leg. She didn't have a suture kit—she'd used her last one on him the day before—so she pulled her tactical knife out of her boot and used a lighter to heat the blade enough so that she could burn her flesh back together. Enough that she could make it back to a helicopter, back to her ship.

"Pure grit and determination." Rachel shook her head. "She almost made it too. She was in the helicopter when her ship was bombed. Rachel told her superiors, CIA and Navy, that Sammy was a problem, but no one listened. Suddenly, the golden child wasn't so golden anymore. She didn't know why, what had happened to discredit her, but she had one person, one last person who had always been on her side, so she ran to Phoenix and begged and pleaded, and he made her wish come true. He made phone call after phone call until Rachel was safe and sound and tucked into a bunk bed at Coronado, ready to train, to fight, to prove that she could be a Navy SEAL."

Catherine nodded. "I'll stick to my earlier statement. You're an excellent storyteller, and you really do excel at leaving out pertinent details."

Rachel furrowed her brow. She'd told the whole story, more of it than she'd ever told anyone. "Which detail do you feel is missing?"

"Who is Sammy?"

"Sammy is the man who stabbed me in the back while looking me in the eye. The man who stole my favorite scarf and left me for dead. The man who wears that very same purple and black keffiyeh scarf every time he makes a video telling the world—taunting the world—by saying that first al-Qaeda, then ISIS, and who knows what organization in the future, is coming for them. Sammy is responsible for Aiden's death. For Veeda and Zarah, and probably Henry's death too, but I can't prove that one. And he's the one who has been working with Khalid Khan and Joe Petchill and a bunch of other people to bring children here, calling them refugees, and handing them suicide vests."

Catherine pursed her lips, clearly displeased with Rachel's half-assed answer and attempts to evade her questions. "What is Sammy's full name?"

Rachel lifted her head and locked eyes with Catherine, realizing that Catherine had likely pieced it together, but was going to force Rachel to say his name out loud. "Samir Qasim Al-Abadi."

Catherine nodded and relaxed back in her chair.

"So, you see, if I'd just shot him, pulled my gun when I saw him killing my men, if I'd shot him then . . . But I didn't. I ran and hid like an idiot. If I'd killed him then, can you imagine? The amount of chaos and destruction he's caused since then . . ." Rachel shook her head. "It's all my fault."

"Is it though?" Catherine cocked her head to the side. "You didn't tell Samir to pull the trigger. You didn't force him to plan and commit acts of terror."

"No, not technically."

Catherine raised an eyebrow.

"I trusted him. I told him things . . . explained ways in which America was vulnerable . . . I was trying to teach him about American culture, bond with him. I trusted him with my life, with my secrets. It was a severe lapse in judgement." She shook her head. "The only person I've ever trusted as much as I trusted Samir is Christopher, and Christopher's pure sunshine. He really is the golden child. His optimism and humility and integrity . . . He is grace personified. Sure, he does fucked up things, like push children who are wearing suicide vests out of windows . . . and some other stuff you probably don't want to hear about . . . but at his core, Christopher's soul is pure. It's impossible *not* to trust someone with that much integrity."

Catherine nodded. "You said once that when you talked to me, you felt the same or similar to when you talked to Christopher."

"Emotionally safe." Rachel nodded. "You have integrity too."

"What about you? Do you have integrity?" Catherine asked.

Rachel cringed. "I-I've been taught to lie, to manipulate, to *hurt* people. Literally *hurt* people, Catherine. I will dig my knife into someone and cut off a pound of flesh at a time if I think it'll get me the intel I need."

"I think that's called persistence and determination and dedication. I'm not sure what any of that has to do with integrity."

Rachel shrugged.

"You have your phone. Google the definition of integrity and read it out loud," Catherine told her.

Rachel pulled out her phone and typed, then read the definition. "'Integrity: adherence to moral and ethical principles. Soundness of moral character, honesty.'"

"Which part of that doesn't describe you?"

"I dunno."

"Do you go around just killing anyone at random?"

"No, I only kill people who deserve it or are trying to kill me." *What a dumb question.*

"How do you know if someone deserves it?" Catherine asked. "What would a person have to do to deserve to be killed?"

"Killing innocent people, rape, sexual assault, domestic violence, terrorism, repeated abuse of power, government corruption, human trafficking."

"Have you ever killed anyone for a reason not on that list?"

Rachel winced. "Yes. If someone is dying anyway and suffering, and I'm sure they won't get better . . . We do it for dogs, end their suffering . . . So, sometimes, when I'm sure there's no life-saving action, I'll help speed things along."

"While that's maybe not the most traditional or common moral code, it is a moral code, and, it sounds like you stick to it."

"Always."

"Do you ever hurt someone just for fun?"

"No."

"What about to convince them to act in your own best interest?"

"Everything I do is for the greater good, always. People don't always agree with me about what the greater good is, but I do my best to look at problems from all different sides and assess potential consequences, and then I act however I think would benefit the most people."

"But you don't have integrity and can't be trusted?"

Rachel's brow furrowed. "I guess I do have more integrity than I give myself credit for."

"Not every decision can have a positive outcome, Rachel. Just like every person, no matter how much integrity they have, can make mistakes or make decisions that result in worse outcomes than anticipated. We're all just doing our best with the information we have and the skills and tools available to us at the time. Looking at the situation with Kamal, what would you have done differently?"

"I would have called in a bomb threat to the police and FBI and sent them all of my intel instead of carrying that burden myself. I would have told Christopher that Ryan could wait, that Ryan needed to follow the chain of command. Call my boss since I was on vacation, trust them to handle things themselves."

"How would that have gone, do you think? What would have been the result?"

"The FBI and police would have eventually been forced to look at our intel and respond, found Kamal. Hopefully diffused the bomb. Then Kamal would be in some federal holding cell somewhere. Maybe he would have told them Samir was working with Petchill . . . Or they would have been too late, and Kamal would be dead, just like he is now." Rachel shrugged. "I would have stayed at the florist, bored out of my mind, pretending to care about flowers and eventually picking something and spending a ridiculous amount of money on something that I don't care about."

"Why didn't you do that?"

"I promised Yamna I'd find her son."

"You did find her son," Catherine pointed out.

"I let my determination, my need to fix things, my need to assuage my guilt over Samir, cloud my judgement. Every time he's involved in something, I lose my head, make rash decisions . . . leave him notes taunting him with paper dipped in jasmine oil and kissing the paper with red lipstick, trying to trigger a memory for him, trying to make him feel the guilt and shame I feel. If I stayed calm, if I stayed focused on the mission—not finding Samir, not getting revenge, but whatever the actual mission is . . . I'll get him one day. I'll get all of them one day, but my boss is right. Today is not the day for vengeance."

"No?" Catherine asked.

"No." Rachel shook her head. "It is, however, the day to keep my other promise to Yamna. It's the day to finally find Khalid Khan and put a bullet in his fucking head before he can hurt any more children."

"How are you going to do that?"

"By letting my team do what they do best. Reconnaissance, gather intel, track him down. My job is to be patient." She chuckled. "Try to be patient and get them the support and supplies they need to get the job done."

"Good!" Catherine grinned. "Maybe sleep first."

Rachel burst out laughing. "Yes! I will sleep first! And maybe some other things. Apparently, I need a doctor's note . . ."

Catherine pulled her lips between her teeth, trying not to laugh. "You want me to write a note giving you medical permission to have sex?"

"Yes, ma'am." Rachel giggled. "I'm dying to see the look on Christopher's face when I hand it to him!"

Catherine chuckled and shook her head as she ripped a piece of paper out of her notebook and scrawled something on the page. She folded it in half and handed it to Rachel before nodding towards the door.

Rachel bounced out of the room, laughing the whole way. "New orders." She grinned as she handed Christopher the note.

He took it and unfolded it, giving her a sideways glance as he did. "Permission granted to fuck Miss Rachel Ryker in any manner she deems necessary." He chuckled. "Well, I should probably get you home quickly before you get any bright ideas about what we can do with this room."

"You know I assess every room I walk into for potential threats and opportunities!"

Christopher flashed her a crooked smile and stood, wrapping his arm around her shoulders. He turned to Catherine. "She's good?"

"I'm better than good." Rachel smirked.

"I meant mentally and emotionally, not that!" Christopher chided her.

Rachel shrugged.

"She told me everything that happened and has made excellent progress since our first session. She's all good."

"Alright then." Christoper tucked her into his side and led her out of the building.

"Did you know I have integrity?" Rachel asked as though it were brand new information.

"What the fuck? Rachel, you have more integrity than anyone I've ever met!"

"Really?"

"Yes, god, I haven't even fucked you senseless yet and you're already asking silly questions!"

Rachel stopped dead in her tracks and turned to him. "You think I have integrity."

"Yes."

"You trust me."

"Of course I do!"

"You love me."

"More than life itself." He kissed her forehead. "Would you for the love of God stop talking and get in the truck? I have medical orders to comply with!" He held up Catherine's note and they both burst out laughing.

CHAPTER 47:
APRIL 2021

RACHEL HAD MISSED NEARLY two weeks of work following Kamal's death, but no one at HQ had missed her, it seemed. Everything was completely under control. They'd made no progress on finding Khalid Khan, but, technically, everything was fine. She was pacing the control room while Eastwood sat in a chair in the corner, smirking and laughing while she brainstormed with Luke. She knew him well enough to know he was laughing at the irritated expression on her face and her obvious frustration, rather than her ideas on how to find Khalid Khan.

"Sky, we managed to get cameras and mics up in Yamna's house while you were out so we can keep tabs on things there. Khan hasn't been by though."

"His car is in Kabul still . . . or again . . ." She wasn't sure. She hadn't opened the tracking app to check in over a week since she'd been wallowing in bed like an idiot. "Kamal told me there is a camp there. I mean, the camp he was at right before he came to the U.S."

"Yeah." Luke nodded in agreement. "We followed the trucks from the house in the mountains to Kabul, but it was too close to the airport, so we lost them. No-fly zone."

"What the fuck kind of bullshit is that?" Rachel complained.

"The kind of bullshit that keeps commercial airlines from flying into drones," Eastwood noted.

Rachel gave an irritated wave of the hand, dismissing his point entirely.

"You want us to go up to Kabul and look for him?" Luke asked.

Rachel pursed her lips, considering the idea. "There is also a camp in Pakistan, apparently."

"But if his car is in Kabul—" Tyler pointed out.

"That camp in Kabul, assuming it's the one Kamal came from, the one Eros Aid picked those kids up from to bring to the White House . . ." She shook her head. "I don't want you guys anywhere near it."

"Why the hell not?" Tyler asked.

"Because," Rachel turned to Eastwood, unsure how much she could tell the guys.

"Because Eros Aid is a front for the CIA. Or is run by several CIA operatives and a few politicians of questionable morals. That's why," Eastwood explained.

"Above our pay grade." Luke nodded.

"Not safe," Rachel corrected. "I tried to intervene at the White House, and the next thing we know, I'm the target of Kamal's bomb. I'm not putting any of you in that situation."

"We can handle it," Luke insisted.

Rachel grit her teeth. "I'm not willing to risk it."

"Guys, you can breach and clear any compound, sure. But the ramifications of messing with this particular group . . ." Eastwood grimaced. "They have endless resources and won't stop until you're all dead."

"I mean, if you know who they are . . ." Luke shrugged, clearly more than happy to kill the individuals in question.

"It's being dealt with," Eastwood assured him.

"What do you want us to do?" Luke asked.

Rachel turned to Eastwood. "Do the idiots in question know I'm still alive?"

"One of them does. Not sure what he told the others . . ."

"Maybe I need to stir the pot a bit." Rachel smiled.

"What are you gonna do?" Eastwood asked.

"Well, certain people seem to want me dead, so . . . maybe we tell them where to find me?"

"What?" Luke wrinkled his nose. "How the fuck is that gonna help?"

"I'm not going to tell them where I *actually* am." Rachel rolled her eyes. "I've been to Khost enough times, have enough pictures of me wandering around there. All I need to do is find some that will work, given the current weather, and disseminate them through certain channels—"

"Which channels?" Eastwood asked, voice stern as could be.

"Do you really want to know how I'm doing this, or would you prefer to remain in the dark?"

"Am I entirely in the dark, or are you using one of your contacts I already know about?"

"If you don't know about it, then you're dumb."

Eastwood shook his head and smirked. "Do you need money?"

"Probably not. I think I can get this handled for free."

Eastwood chuckled. "Have at it."

"Okay, I have to go home though because I'm not the keeper of the photos."

"Say hi to Hawk from us." Luke smiled.

"Will do. Try to stay entertained. This may take a while. But don't stay entertained doing anything stupid or unsafe."

"Promise."

Rachel bust through the front door of the house screaming for Christopher at the top of her lungs. She must have sounded scared because he came charging for the front door, gun in hand.

"All good, just need help," she assured him.

"Are you sure because your eyes look panicked."

"I need pictures of me in Khost in March or something that could pass for whatever the weather is there currently." She was out of breath and talking way to fast. No wonder he looked concerned.

"Why?" Christopher raised an eyebrow.

"To trick people into thinking I'm there right now. Petchill clearly wants me dead. Kamal failed. If he thinks I'm in Khost, he'll send Khalid Khan back to Khost to find me and kill me. But I won't *actually* be there."

Christopher cocked his head to the side. "I have so many questions . . ."

"Just help me please." *Before I get impatient and tell my friend to hack into your computer and find pictures for me.*

"Sure." Christopher wandered towards the kitchen where his laptop was. "Why does Petchill want you dead?" He clicked on the safety on his pistol and laid it on the table.

"Because I know things he would prefer I don't know, and I think he just figured out I'm the one who knows those things when we were at the fundraiser because Frank opened his dumb mouth and said something he shouldn't have."

Christopher raised an eyebrow at her as he scrolled through his photos. "What did Frank say?"

"Not important."

"Okay . . . what do you know that Petchill doesn't want you to know?"

Rachel had both hands on her hips, staring at him like he was an idiot. "Christopher, do you know how many dumb boring cocktail parties with politicians and defense contractors and all those people I was forced to go to as a kid?"

"A lot, I would imagine."

"Tons, yes. Do you think I just sat there minding my own business like the sweet, demure, well-behaved daughter my parents wanted me to be, or do you think I was listening and remembering and following people off to dark corners to eavesdrop on their conversations?"

"Definitely the second one." Christopher chuckled.

Rachel nodded. "I took notes. I took pictures—"

"You took pictures?" Christopher seemed skeptical.

"Yes. I stole an old spy camera my grandpa had. It was tiny and didn't make any noise, so I could be discrete. I saved all the film then finally developed it when I took a photography class in high school and had access to a dark room and, you know, learned how to develop film."

"Are you being serious?"

"Of course."

Christopher just blinked at her.

"I could topple the entire government if I wanted to. Or most of it, at least."

"Seriously?"

"I know which escort service most of the senators use. I know which clinic they all send their mistresses to so they can abort their illegitimate children. I know which bank doesn't mind assisting with under-the-table deals and paying people off through offshore accounts." *I know several bodies are buried in Rock Creek Park because I put them there.*

"Okay, I believe you. You could definitely do some serious damage." Christopher puffed out his cheeks. "Why don't you?"

"Eastwood won't let me. Keeps saying the time isn't right. No one's done anything bad enough yet apparently." She shrugged.

"Since when do you follow orders?"

"It's complicated, Christopher. I can't very well destroy the government without having a plan in place to preserve democracy . . . or reinstate democracy, I guess." She grimaced. "What do you think I'm going to do? Assassinate all these assholes and assume the throne like some sort of dictator?"

"No. Just . . ." He winced. "It's not like you to hold back."

"I'm playing the long game."

"Huh. You're not usually patient either." He turned his laptop so she could see the screen. "Will these work?"

"Yes. Email those pictures to me please."

Rachel was so excited by her plan she practically bounced across the house to her home office. She pulled a burner phone and sim card out of her safe and snapped pictures of the photos Christopher had sent. These needed to be as untraceable as possible. Since she sucked at technology, she was doing it this way, already knowing she'd get yelled at. She posted the photos to her online diary along with the text:

Hi-ya love! Be a doll and disseminate these. The puppet master wants me dead, and I want his buddy in Khost. Anything else you can do to lure KK back to his daughter's house would be very much appreciated. More info on the laptop. I'm sure you know how to get in. Let me know if you require payment or if the satisfaction of fucking these assholes over is enough.

It didn't take long to get a response:

Darling, so happy to help. Glad you're feeling better. No payment required. Please, though, learn to encrypt things so you can send me photos with proper resolution. What you sent me is shit and will take time to correct. Or tell me the source of these and I'll just snag them.

Rachel burst out laughing.

LMAO! Love you doll! His laptop is on the same WIFI as mine, which I assume you're monitoring. Snag whatever you need. Just make it look like I'm currently in Khost!

It sure was nice to have a friend who knew everything there was to know about computers. Not that she'd ever reveal her contact to anyone. It didn't matter anyway. She was just another woman the Eros Group had tried to fuck over, and therefore, more than happy to get any sort of revenge possible. There was one final post:

Congrats and best wishes BTW. Sad we can't all be there. Couldn't be happier for you, though! Glad you found love and a bit of peace. This photo project will take a while, so you know. I'm traveling and I need my good computer to do this properly. I'll be home in three weeks.

Rachel knew no thanks were actually necessary. It was more than implied. She took the sim card out of her phone, broke it in half, and tossed it in the trash bin under her desk. Now they just had to wait.

Chapter 48

APRIL 2021

RACHEL WAS SITTING IN her office at HQ when Admiral Eastwood wandered in. It wasn't often he came to her office. Either he was bored or something was wrong.

"Ryker, the president and Secret Service want an update from you regarding the kids who went missing from the White House fundraiser."

"From me?" Rachel's brow furrowed.

"Yup."

"Why?"

"They told you to find the kids."

"No." Rachel shook her head. "They told me to find Kamal. I found Kamal."

"The president is under the impression you were supposed to find all of them. He wants you at the White House ASAP."

Rachel pursed her lips. "I can't go to the White House."

"Why the hell not?" Eastwood bellowed.

"Because, sir, Petchill wants me dead. Now, that's problematic for two separate but related reasons." She held up a finger. "One, if I go to the White

House, Petchill is likely to be there and has the means to kill me if he wants." Two fingers now. "Two, pictures are being disseminated of me in Khost as we speak in an attempt to get Petchill to send Khalid Khan after me. So, you see, if I go to the White House, they'll know I'm not in Khost, Onyx will continue to sit on their asses waiting for Khalid Khan to appear, and I might end up dead or arrested or detained, or whatever Petchill convinces Frank is necessary."

"I see." Eastwood frowned.

"Do you know what you should do? You should send Rhodes to the White House and have him explain I'm in Khost looking for Khalid Khan and Samir Al-Abadi, all on my own, without a team, without back up . . ." She nodded. "That might work. Besides, he's the one sitting at Langley actually looking for these kids."

"Do you know *why* Petchill wants you dead?"

"Because I'm a woman and I'm smarter than him and he's a misogynistic jackass?" *Because I can destroy him and Frank and all of their friends.*

"Right . . ." Eastwood glanced over at the wall and cringed. "You want to send Rhodes to the White House?"

"Yeah, why not?"

"He's a great soldier, great analyst, but his presentation skills . . . not so great."

Rachel tried to stifle her laughter. She couldn't argue with him about that. Ryan had a terrible habit of going off on tangents and answering people's questions with more questions until everyone involved was confused, including himself. "Maybe you should go to the White House, and Rhodes can keep his ass parked at a desk at Langley."

"For fuck's sake. You think *I* want to go to the fucking White House and deal with this shit?" Eastwood yelled.

"Below your pay grade?" Rachel gave him a sweet smile that they both knew was forced and fake and her lazy attempt at manipulating him.

"Get Rhodes on the phone."

Rachel pulled her lips between her teeth and dialed Ryan's number.

"Yes, ma'am?" He answered on the first ring.

"How's it going with locating those fourteen kids?"

"Umm, not great," Ryan started. "I've been trying to get someone from The Office of Refugee Resettlement on the phone, but they aren't calling me back."

"What happened?" Rachel knew instantly she wasn't going to like whatever he was about to say.

"Well, of the fifteen kids, there were seven boys and six girls. Kamal is dead, so that leaves us with six boys and six girls."

"Thanks for the math lesson, Rhodes. Get to the point," Eastwood grumbled.

"Umm . . . sir . . . all six boys . . . they're now registered in the foster care system in Virginia, Maryland, Massachusetts, or New York. I can't find the girls."

Rachel's stomach turned. "None of the girls are popping up in the foster care system?"

"Nope. That's why I've been trying to get a hold of someone at the Office of Refugee Resettlement to find out why that may be. But, like I said, no one will call me back. When I call them, I get transferred from desk to desk. Like I told you before, no one there has any idea what I'm talking about."

"Samir promised Khalid the girls would only be in school for a short time . . ." Rachel mumbled. "Aquib is involved."

"What are you saying, Sky?" Ryan asked.

"Could they have taken the girls somewhere? Are they being trafficked?"

"My assumption would be yes, if Aquib Faizan is involved," Ryan agreed.

Rachel dropped her face into her palms. "How did I let this happen?"

Then Catherine's voice popped into her head. *You aren't a terrorist, Rachel. It's unreasonable to expect yourself to think like one.* She'd been so focused on Kamal, diffusing the bomb, making sure they didn't arrest him, detain him at a black site—she knew all about those—that she hadn't considered what would happen to the other fourteen children. Hadn't given them a first thought, let alone a second thought, until after they were already missing. She dug her nails into her palm and bit the inside of her cheek. "Set up a conference call with the president. I'll dial in from my satellite phone."

Eastwood nodded and went back to his office to do just that.

Paul Eastwood joined the meeting from his laptop, ensuring both his camera and microphone were switched on. The president was already online, looking more pissed off than Paul had ever seen.

"Where's Rachel?" Frank asked.

"Ryker should be calling in any minute now." *Stay calm, cool, and collected.* Paul and Rachel had been lying to Frank for years. Paul just hadn't lied to him since he'd become president. He put the job title out of his mind and focused on Frank—the conniving, self-serving asshole on the other end of the video call.

"Paul, this is a shit show. What is that girl up to?"

"We haven't even started with our status update and you're already calling it a shit show?" Paul raised his eyebrows. "Do you know something I don't?"

"I don't know what you know!" Frank yelled. "Rachel was supposed to find these kids and now I have people telling me—"

Frank shut his stupid mouth the second Ryan joined the call. He was in uniform with his background blurred, looking like Ryan Rhodes always did when forced to present something to anyone with authority. Focused and determined, with a hint of anxiety. "Mr. President, Admiral Eastwood, thank you for granting me a few minutes of your time. Looks like we're still waiting on Ryker?" He didn't wait for confirmation, but his eyes darted around the screen, likely checking the participant list. "I can start while we wait for her. She might be in a tight spot. You never know with these things. Anyway, we've located all the missing boys. One, Kamal, is deceased, as I'm sure you've been informed, Mr. President. The other six are in the foster care system, waiting to be assigned to families, as far as I can tell. The six girls, however . . . no sign of them, hence why Ryker's in-country."

"Where is she?" Frank demanded.

"Chasing down leads in Afghanistan," Ryan explained. "Most of the key players in this were last seen there so—"

"Apologies for being late." Rachel's voice cut him off. "Mr. President, Admiral Eastwood."

Rachel leaned back in her chair, feet propped up on her desk and satellite phone pressed to her ear. The rest of them were on a video call but she knew Frank was at least smart enough to figure out she wasn't in Afghanistan if he could see her on camera. So she called into the meeting from her satellite phone to make the whole thing more believable. She had a wad of loose paper in her hand, crumpling it sporadically near the phone's microphone to make it sound like static interference, and a YouTube video playing in the background of people wandering around Khost, turned up loud enough that everyone on the call could hear it. "Can y'all hear me okay?"

"Rachel, why are you in Afghanistan?" Frank yelled.

"Because I've got six preteen or teenaged girls missing, and they all came from here. The people who took them to that refugee camp you and your buddies were working with. Great job vetting them, by the way. Maybe go through the United Nations next time like you're supposed to—"

"I don't need your attitude, young lady!" Frank yelled again.

"Frank, chill." Rachel rolled her eyes. "You fucked up. It's not like it's the first time. No one on this call is gonna say anything to anyone about it. Just give me some time to sort shit out over here, make sure these girls are safe, find Khalid Khan, Samir Al-Abadi, and Aquib Faizan, kill them, then I'll be home safe and sound. No need to worry."

"You're *in* Afghanistan?" Frank checked.

"Sorry, is the connection not clear? Can you hear me?" Rachel knew they could.

"Loud and clear, Ryker," Eastwood confirmed as though he didn't know she was right down the hall from him.

"Okay, good." Rachel nodded to herself. "Well, I may be here awhile trying to get this sorted since I'm on my own. All our teams are deployed, or are deploying soon, and we didn't have anyone to send here but me." *Lies*

"You're by yourself?" Frank sounded more intrigued than concerned.

"Yeah, but I'm okay. Like I said, no need to worry. I'm safe and I know what I'm doing."

"Where are you staying?" Frank asked.

"At a safe house we have." Rachel rattled off a general description of a building near Yamna's house and a few nearby landmarks so that anyone who had been to Khost would be able to find it. "I've got eyes on Khalid Khan's daughters. Figure that's my best bet of finding him once he climbs back out of his hiding spot. I can only be here for about six weeks, though . . . I'm getting married, you know? Memorial Day weekend."

"I know. Your dad told me. Thanks for the invite, by the way."

"I assumed you wouldn't be able to come and didn't really want to deal with all the Secret Service and stress of *the president* attending my wedding. If you could just be Frank . . . but you can't. You can still send me a gift though!"

"I'm sure Trischa is on top of that, or someone on her staff is . . . So, you're just sitting around, hoping Khalid Khan shows up at his daughter's house?" Frank checked.

"Yeah, unless anyone has any better suggestions?"

"You could always borrow a play from Samir's playbook and make a video threatening Khan's daughters, try to draw him out?" Ryan suggested.

"I thought his daughter was your asset?" Frank asked.

Fuck, the idiot does listen. "Yeah, she is, but *he* doesn't know that." *Unless you and Petchill told him, which I'm fairly confident you did.*

"You're sure those six girls are out of the U.S.?" Frank sounded like he was covering his ass more than anything.

"Yes, sir," Ryan answered. "Not sure how they got out of the country, but there's no sign of them in the foster care system in any state, and the Office of Refugee Resettlement doesn't seem to know who they are, so the only conclusion we can draw is that whoever gave Kamal those bombs also got the girls out of the country."

"I see. You're all . . . very thorough." Frank sounded remarkably irritated that Rachel and Ryan had done their jobs.

"Yes, sir. Thank you, sir," Ryan replied.

"Alright well . . . I guess that's that, then." Frank grumbled. "Rachel, be safe, sweetheart."

"Always! And you know, if I die, tell people I died doing something really cool, okay?"

"Sure, Rachel." Frank left the meeting.

Rachel hung up the call and laughed to herself for a minute before walking down the hall to Eastwood's office, falling into the chair across from him. "That was too easy!"

Eastwood turned his laptop so she could see Ryan on the screen, still on the call, smiling and shaking his head.

"Sky, is he always that transparent?" Ryan asked.

"Yes." Rachel and Eastwood said in unison.

"I mean, he clearly doesn't care about your wellbeing."

"Funny that he's my godfather, right?" Rachel laughed.

Ryan wrinkled his nose. "Why am I completely grossed out by that?"

"We all are, Rhodes." Eastwood sighed.

"Nice job with suggesting I abduct Yamna. Very subtle."

"Thanks, Sky. I learned from the best, you know."

"I *do* know!" Rachel grinned. Ryan had been plenty skilled when he'd joined Indigo, but she'd definitely taught him a thing or two to up his game.

"You two came up with that in under fifteen minutes?" Eastwood checked.

"Yes sir." Rachel nodded. "We're that good. It's almost like you should be paying us more."

"Nice try. I don't set salaries."

"No, but you could promote Rhodes," Rachel suggested.

"Yes, you could," Ryan agreed.

"Shut the fuck up, Rhodes. You were just promoted not that long ago," Eastwood grumbled.

"Yes, sir." Ryan winced. "Or was I supposed to not reply and just be quiet? I wasn't really sure—"

Rachel burst out laughing. "Quit while you're ahead, Raven!" This was exactly why they didn't let him have a meeting alone with the president. Ryan was smart and funny, witty and charming. Perfect for interacting with middle management and people below management, but leadership, the president? God, that would be a disaster.

"Why does he always get like this?" Eastwood pointed at Ryan on the screen.

"He gets nervous around authority figures, especially male authority figures, and there's too much information in his head. I don't think he can keep track of it all. He might have a touch of undiagnosed ADHD. Not sure."

"I do not!" Ryan whined.

Rachel shrugged. "Are we done, or do we have more people to fuck with?"

"Psy-ops are over for the day. Class dismissed." Eastwood grinned. "Well done, both of you."

Chapter 49:

MAY 2021

IT WAS EARLY MAY before Khalid Khan's car made its way from Kabul to Khost. He didn't make contact with Yamna though. Onyx had been following him as best they could, tracking his car—which he never seemed to be in—and following him with the drone but frequently losing him on the crowded streets of Khost. The guys had spread out throughout the city, but the only sightings they got of Khalid Khan were of him entering or exiting the mosque, always surrounded by a crowd of civilians. Now, they only had two weeks before they needed to be in Texas for Rachel's wedding.

"Sky, what do you want us to do? It's almost your wedding day. I know we need to be back for that. Any ideas for how to speed this along?" Luke asked.

"There will be no wedding until this mission is complete," Rachel corrected.

"That's what I thought, but Hawk gave me strict orders to wrap this up so I don't miss the wedding. There have been several emails about suits and shoes and socks and ties." Luke paused. "Do you, as the bride, have an opinion about what socks I wear?"

"You can be barefoot for all I care."

Luke chuckled.

Rachel sighed. "Lux, he can't give you orders, just ignore him."

"He outranks me."

"He's retired!" Rachel shouted. "He can't tell anyone to do anything . . . Other than me . . . but that's only applicable to certain situations."

"Don't need to know that, Sky!" Luke complained.

"Lux, he told me that your presence is mandatory and that I'm to pull you if necessary," Rachel added.

"Seriously?" Luke grumbled.

"According to him, the only acceptable excuses for you not being there are if you're dead or in a coma," Rachel clarified. "And honestly, I'm not sure death would get you out of coming."

"Lux, I've got it covered," Tyler insisted. "Your two best friends are getting married. Of course you have to be there. Plan A is to get this all wrapped up in time for all of us to make it. Worst case scenario, we send you ahead of us. Hawk and Sky need you, and we'll need an eyewitness that they actually legally tied the knot, 'cause I'm still not convinced it's actually happening."

Luke chuckled. "I believe they're legally getting married. What their definition of marriage is and what their commitment to monogamy looks like is yet to be determined."

"Hey!" Rachel protested.

"Who are you kidding, Sky?" Tyler teased.

"We are perfectly happy and entertained just the two of us, okay?"

"I'm not buying it." Tyler shook his head. "In any case, we'll get Lux to the wedding, and I'll wrap up the mission."

"*You'll* wrap up the mission?" Derik glared at him.

"Rio and I will wrap up the mission," Tyler amended.

"You *do* remember that Ty is an officer, and you aren't?" Luke asked Derik.

"I don't give a shit if the kid went to Officer Candidate School or not. I do half his work for him."

"It's called delegating." Tyler smirked. "One of those things you learn to do at OCS."

"It's called you can't fill out basic paperwork," Derik corrected.

"I'm dyslexic. It's hard!" Tyler shouted.

"We will wrap up the mission and all get to your wedding. None of us want to deal with this power struggle," Shane chimed in.

Rachel rolled her eyes. "I can understand Ty's fucked up spelling just fine. If Lux has to come back early, Ty has command of the team. Ty, that does not mean it's a dictatorship. You will not let the power go to your head, and you will listen to the people on your team with more experience rather than getting overly creative. Is that understood?"

"Yes, ma'am," the entire team echoed.

"Good. Knock it off with the weird sibling rivalry vibes and get back to work."

"Back to work? When did we *stop* working?" Tyler muttered.

Luke folded his arms over his chest and looked at his feet. "We're watching the cameras in Yamna's house, city surveillance cameras, we have the drone up. We're starting to see some patterns in his schedule, but there aren't any opportunities to take him out. Not without a high risk of civilian casualties, anyway, and I'm assuming—"

"Civilian casualties would be unacceptable, Lux," Rachel confirmed.

"We're open to suggestions," Luke reminded her.

Rachel thought for a minute. "Does Yamna have contact with her father at all, or Yashfa?"

"Don't think so." Luke shook his head.

"What about their husbands? If they could just invite Khalid over for dinner or something . . ."

Luke nodded. "We can ask Yashfa and Yamna and get back to you with options. Yamna hasn't been entirely cooperative since Kamal died. She's . . . I don't want to say she's not handling it well. She's handling it exactly how you'd expect any mother to handle it." He winced. "She's handling it a hell of a lot better than my mother . . ." Luke trailed off.

Rachel sighed, immediately feeling bad for putting Luke in this situation. "I'll call Yashfa, get more info, and see what our options are."

Luke nodded in agreement. "Copy that. Talk soon."

Rachel got off the call with Onyx and went back to her office. She checked the time, then picked up her cellphone and dialed Yashfa.

"What?" Yashfa answered in Pashto, already irritated.

"I need your help if you want your father dead," Rachel explained. "Yamna isn't talking to my guys. They're following your father but can't get him alone."

"Yamna is in mourning," Yashfa huffed out.

"I know." Rachel empathized. "Yashfa, I am truly so sorry for what happened to Kamal. I did everything I could to save him. I was disarming the bomb he had, getting the vest off of him when he reached for the detonator. It's a miracle I'm not dead too."

"I understand, Rachel." Yashfa's voice was so full of empathy and sadness that Rachel had to believe her.

"I'm assuming you still want your father dead?"

"Yes. Yamna does too, more than ever. She's just . . . struggling."

"Of course she is. Her son just died. I get it, and normally I'd give her more time to grieve. So would Lux. Especially Lux. But my team needs to come back to the U.S. in a couple of weeks, so we need to push forward."

"What do you mean especially Lux?" Yashfa asked.

Rachel winced. She hated spreading gossip or talking about other people's trauma without them knowing, but she knew Luke was deeply affected by this. That he, more than anyone, would understand the grief Yamna was feeling. He'd watched his sister suffer from leukemia for years and had watched his parents battle the grief that comes with losing a child ever since. She was sure this was bringing up a lot for him—grieving mothers always did—but being the good soldier that he was, the good man that he was, he was pushing on, fighting through the emotional turmoil that came along with childhood trauma. She knew him well enough to know he'd never admit it, never tell her the situation was too difficult. Not that a dead kid and grieving mother was easy for any of them.

"His sister died when they were teenagers. She was sick for a long time. Neither of his parents are over it, and it's been decades. He knows how hard this is for Yamna, and I know he isn't going to push her. So I'm pushing because I'm the boss and I'm the one who gets to step in and be a jerk and make the tough calls and tell people to do things they may not have the emotional capacity to do. It's my job to motivate and push, and when that doesn't work, give orders and make threats."

"What do you want me to do?" Yashfa sounded completely dejected, like she'd given up on her father dying, lost her faith in Rachel.

"I know it's a big ask," Rachel started. "Can one of you invite your father over for dinner or something? Then we'll know when he's coming. We can get him alone—"

"It's an idea." Yashfa paused. "I will speak with my sister and let you know."

"Thank you, Yashfa."

Chapter 50:

MAY 2021

IT TOOK A WEEK for Yashfa to convince her sister to reengage with the world again. Convincing Yamna to keep fighting to get revenge on their father for Kamal's death had become everyone's primary focus. Finally, Rachel was standing front and center in Mission Control. Luke had his laptop open on Yamna's kitchen counter so she could see Luke and Yamna on her screen. The wedding was five days away, and it took an entire day to travel from Afghanistan to Dallas. They were running out of time. "I am under strict orders to get this wrapped up," Rachel explained.

"We'd love to." Luke smiled into the camera.

"I never know when he's coming and going anymore." Yamna sighed. "He doesn't tell me things. Our father is being very careful, Rachel. I don't know what to do." Yamna's voice was shaky.

"I told you what to do!" Rachel heard Yashfa in the background seconds before she crowded her way in between Luke and Yamna so that she would be visible on the screen. Tenacious, pissed off, and full of rage, Yashfa was a force to be reckoned with, and everyone got out of her way. "Zarah had an extensive network . . . contacts around the city, the country . . . I don't know, probably the entire Middle East," Yashfa explained. "When she died, that sort of fell apart. But," she paused for dramatic effect, "those women didn't go anywhere. They're all right where Zarah left them."

Rachel raised an eyebrow, both intrigued and irritated that this was the first she was hearing of Zarah's secret underground network. She'd always suspected Zarah had such a network, but learning Yashfa knew the key players—that was a game changer. "You have a plan."

"An idea." Yashfa shrugged. Her lack of confidence was showing. "We ask these women for help to follow my father. Most people have cellphones and can text. We just need some sort of centralized chat or phone number or something."

"A coordinator." Rachel nodded. "Lux, I'm assuming you don't have enough earpieces to get everyone on comms?"

"We don't have any extras. We could potentially get some, but it would likely take longer than a week."

"Texting it is!" Rachel decided.

"I'll have Cosmo and Hollywood set up a group chat on whatever platform they think is best and is most accessible to the women here. Yashfa, you'll need to get these women on board and get them to join the group chat," Luke said.

"Figure out a schedule of who can monitor that chat at what times," Rachel added. "Yashfa, how many women do you have?"

"Maybe fifteen. I need to ask around a bit more, but I've already spoken with many of them, and I think I have at least fifteen."

"Fifteen plus you and Yamna and the guys is twenty-nine people. That's a big section of the city that can be easily covered," Rachel noted.

"We can divide the city into sections based on how many people we end up with and divide it up. We know what areas he frequents most, so we'll put our focus on those locations." Luke nodded.

"So, you ask him to dinner, and we get everyone in place to track that he's actually coming to your house." Rachel nodded. This could work.

"I can ask him." Yamna pulled out her phone and started texting.

"Lux, explain to me again why we can't just track his phone?"

"That will only tell us what cell tower he's near. We can't pinpoint his exact location, but it can potentially let us know what area of the city he's in. Narrow it down, send some of Yashfa's friends to wander and look for him and confirm his exact location."

"My father says he can maybe come to dinner tomorrow, but he will not say for sure. He's been like this ever since . . ." Yamna's eyes filled with tears.

"We can work with that." There were a lot of *maybes* being discussed, but following him from the mosque to Yamna's house would be a piece of cake with twenty-nine people, plus a drone, following him. "Yashfa, get your network activated. We'll need to monitor him and follow him tomorrow, so we know if he'll be at Yamna's for dinner or not."

"Okay, he comes to dinner. Then what?" Luke asked.

"Then you do your job." Rachel chuckled.

"How, specifically, are you wanting this done?" Luke clarified.

"Discretely, preferably," Rachel told him. "If he's at dinner tomorrow, and we get this done, then y'all can be on a plane on Thursday and make it here on time for my wedding. Lux would even be on time for the rehearsal."

"You should get *us* on a plane to your wedding!" Yashfa suggested.

"Would if I could, hun." Rachel smiled. She would love nothing more than to have Yashfa and Yamna at her wedding, but getting them in and out of the U.S. would be tricky.

"So back to planning, Sky," Luke redirected.

"Right." Rachel refocused. "If it's at dinner, your kids will be there."

"Yes," Yamna confirmed.

Rachel grimaced. "I'd rather not traumatize your children . . ."

"I have an idea!" It was Tyler's turn to nudge people out of the way and get some screen time. He switched to English and kept talking. "What if I told you I had access to belladonna?"

"Poison?" Rachel raised an eyebrow. It was one of her favorite strategies. "Where'd you get that from?"

"I'm not telling you my sources."

"Agency friend?"

"Fuck you," Tyler complained. Rachel knew she'd been right. Tyler's job was quite literally to coordinate with the CIA and other government agencies.

"I'm ninety-nine percent sure I can get some, then Yamna can put it in his tea or food or anything. I'll get the antidote too, so we can go in and get him, take him wherever we're going, and question him, you know?"

"Shit. Ty, sometimes you remind me too much of me." Rachel laughed then translated for Yashfa and Yamna. "We have something you can put in his tea or his food or anything, really. It's very toxic to animals and humans. It will make him very sick if he swallows it, but it won't kill him."

Tyler switched back to Pashto to elaborate. "It will make him vomit, at which point he'll go to the toilet, and you can send the kids to their room or something. Then we can come in and get him. If you wait to put it in his tea, it should be dark out and your neighbors would be less likely to notice. Otherwise, you, or your husband, I guess, can say he needs medical attention and drive him to us."

"That's a good plan," Yashfa and Yamna agreed.

"Do y'all need me for anything else at this stage?" Rachel asked.

"Nope. We can get everything organized," Luke assured her.

Chapter 51:

MAY 2021

"HE'S IN THE MARKET," Yashfa reported. She was on a group call with Rachel and Luke.

"You have eyes on him?" Luke asked.

"*I* don't. Shabana does," Yashfa clarified.

Rachel smiled, happy that Yashfa's friend Shabana had stepped up. Rachel had helped get Shabana's sister out of Afghanistan on an asylum visa a few years ago. "What's he doing?" Rachel asked.

"Walking around." Yashfa's tone implied it was the dumbest question she'd ever heard.

"Is he buying anything, talking to anyone?" Rachel clarified.

"Chatting with people, she says. Very casual." Yashfa replied.

"What time did you tell him dinner was?" Luke asked.

"After prayers." Both Rachel and Yashfa sighed.

"Sunset is around 1850, so after that," Tyler clarified.

"He should be at Yamna's house, assuming he's going, between 1930 and 2000," Rachel explained.

"It's 1830 now," Luke noted.

"And the market is near the mosque he attends, so . . . that's probably where he's going," Yashfa added. She continued to update the group with reports from her friends until Khalid Khan entered the mosque at exactly 1840.

"Who's waiting outside the mosque?" Rachel asked Luke.

"Cosmo went in to pray. New York is outside being a tourist. Bellagio and Strat are in a van. The drone is in the air, so they'll follow him."

"My friends Benesh and Esin are also inside the mosque praying, but separate from the men, of course," Yashfa added. "Marlize lives on my street, between Yamna's home and the mosque. Once we see him leave, if he's headed towards my house, she will wait at the window and watch for him."

"What is Yamna doing?" Rachel asked, concerned for her friend.

"She is cooking." Yashfa chuckled. "Panicking and cooking. It's what my little sister does best. She has an emotion, she cooks."

"Interesting. Skylark has an emotion, and she cleans," Luke teased.

"Both of you should live with me. Then I'd never have to do anything again!" Yashfa laughed.

"Excuse me, you clean as much as I do, Lux," Rachel argued.

"Because I like things clean. Not because I'm emotionally damaged." Luke chuckled.

"Liar!" Rachel laughed.

"He's coming out," Brad announced.

"Drone's in the air. I've got eyes on him," Jared confirmed. "He's headed south."

"Yamna's house is south," Rachel noted.

"Quick, someone call Indigo and tell them Sky read a map correctly!" Tyler teased.

"Remind me to punch you when I see you." Rachel smiled to herself. She'd missed the camaraderie, the teasing and bickering that came with sitting around bored as shit, waiting for other people to move. It was almost like being in the field with Onyx. *Almost.*

"He's getting in a car. Do you want us to follow him by driving or just with the drone?" Jared asked.

"Both. But stay farther back than you normally would. Just make sure your car is close enough to track him with the drone."

"Copy that," Jared and Andre answered before giving a detailed description of the car, including the make, model, and license plate.

Everyone was silent for the next ten minutes.

"Marlize just texted me. My father drove by her house . . . or at least the car we think he's in did," Yashfa reported.

"Confirming he just parked one block from Yamna's house and got out of the car. He's walking towards her house now," Jared reported. "He's not alone. Running facial recognition . . . might take a minute."

"Switch to internal team comms. Disconnecting the call with Yashfa," Rachel told everyone before hanging up the group call.

Moments later, Khalid Khan was inside Yamna's home. Rachel switched her video feed from the SEALs body cameras and drone to the cameras they'd set up inside Yamna's house. She had a clear view of Khalid Khan seated on a cushion in Yamna's living room, right next to a man who could only be Aquib Faizan. Yamna brought them each a cup of tea.

"You think I want that?" Khalid asked his daughter. "I will not eat or drink anything you prepared. I do not trust traitors."

"Father, I prepared the tea," Yashfa lied.

"This one," Khalid Khan gestured towards Yamna but was clearly addressing Aquib, "conspired with Americans. She is their asset. Telling them things, giving them my explosives when I'm away traveling."

"Yes, I heard all about that." Aquib looked Yamna up and down in a way that made Rachel's skin crawl.

"Who told you that?" Yamna asked timidly.

Khalid raised an eyebrow at his daughter. "Am I wrong?"

Yamna's voice came out in a whisper. "No, father. You are not wrong."

Yashfa tried again. "Father, Yamna loves you. She is trying to make up for her transgressions against you. She was worried about her son. She did what any mother would do in that situation."

"Is that so?" Khalid eyed his eldest daughter. "And how did she even know an American to contact?"

"I do not know, father," Yashfa lied again. "It is a woman's nature to protect her children."

"Protect them from their grandfather?" Khalid Khan's brows knit together.

"Father, she didn't know where he was or what he was doing. She was terrified, then found strange things in your closet—explosives and guns. She was afraid. You must understand that!" Yashfa tried to argue on her sister's behalf.

"Watch what you say to me, or you'll meet the same fate as her." He gestured towards Yamna again.

"Fuck," Rachel muttered to herself. She knew that it wasn't a good sign that Aquib Faizan was there.

"Father, just drink the tea and let's all get along, okay? Is not forgiveness part of the prophet's teachings?" Yashfa took a sip of her own tea.

"The only reason I came tonight was to exact punishment for her crimes. She is a traitor to her family, to her country, to her people. A poor excuse for a daughter or a wife." Khalid looked to Yamna. "Dearest daughter, do you not wonder where your husband is?"

"He is at the mosque. I'm sure he is on his way home now."

"No." Khalid smirked. "Your husband is dead. He could not control his wife, could he?"

"You killed him?" Yamna shrieked.

"Father—" Yashfa started.

Khalid held up a hand to silence her. "This man," he gestured politely towards Aquib Faizan, "will be taking possession of your children. They belong to him now, as their father is dead, and you are an unfit mother. He will sell your children as mercenaries, slaves, whores—whatever he thinks would fetch the best price."

Every muscle in Yamna's body tensed.

"Lux, what the fuck are we gonna do?" Rachel asked.

She wished desperately that she could be there, rush in, save the day, kill these assholes once and for all. Fuck, it was hard saving the world from a desk. Even if Luke was there, even if Onyx was more than capable of doing exactly what she would do. The adrenaline and rage coursing through her veins made her body feel like it was on fire. Every muscle in her body was pulsing, urging her to move, to act, to fight. *How do we take out Khalid and*

Aquib without traumatizing the kids? Without Yashfa or Yamna or any of the children getting hurt in the process?

"He's not leaving there with those kids, Sky."

"No shit." Rachel cringed.

"Father, you cannot mean this. You cannot take my children and *sell* them," Yamna protested.

"It is what you deserve," Khalid insisted.

"No. It is my crime. My transgression. Take me and leave my children with Yashfa. My husband is dead. I belong to no one." She paused and looked her father in the eye. "I belong to you," she amended.

"You want this treacherous bitch?" Khalid looked at Aquib and gestured towards his daughter.

"Stand," Aquib demanded.

Yamna did as she was told.

"Disrobe."

Yamna stared at him, horrified. "You want me to undress in front of everyone?"

Khalid motioned towards the other side of the living room then followed Aquib and Yamna into a bedroom.

Yashfa was frozen in place. The children were playing, seemingly having no idea what was going on.

"Sky, what do you want us to do?" Luke's voice was full of fear.

"I . . . He cannot take those kids," Rachel stated plainly. "One life for seven."

She listened as the men muttered their disapproval of her plan.

"Calm the fuck down!" Rachel yelled. "We need to protect the kids and keep all of you safe too."

"Fuck that," Brad grumbled.

Trust others. My job is to be patient. Rachel remembered what she'd told Catherine in her last therapy session. "Let them leave with her. We'll see how it plays out. We have to prioritize the kids. Yamna is an adult. She can make her own decisions, even if we don't agree with them."

"I am not letting them take her," Tyler argued.

"Stand down, Ty!" Rachel barked. "This is *exactly* what got Aiden killed. Caring too much about a girl when there was a greater purpose at stake."

"Sky—" Luke tried to intervene.

"I don't like it either, guys, but she's sacrificing herself for her children. She knows what she's doing."

"I don't like it," Luke repeated.

"Your thoughts and feelings are duly noted, Lux."

Suddenly, Aquib, Khalid, and Yamna came out of the bedroom.

"She will do nicely." Aquib nodded to himself. "Very beautiful. And willing, it seems." He chuckled.

Rachel's eyes darted around the screen in front of her. "How long were they in there?" she asked, noting Yamna's disheveled appearance.

"Long enough," Luke clipped out.

"Now we go," Khalid ordered.

Yamna gave Yashfa a hug goodbye and whispered something in her ear that Rachel and Onyx couldn't hear. Yashfa looked straight into the camera that was hidden behind a plant and winked.

"Sky, you have to let us stop this," Luke argued again. "You know I'd just turn off my earpiece and ignore you, but I have too much respect for you."

You have integrity. Trust yourself. Trust your instincts. "She's an asset, Lux. Trust her decision. You missed it while you were whining, but Yamna said something to Yashfa, and Yashfa looked straight into the camera and winked. They're up to something. Let this play out."

"You're the one who takes the fall when this goes to shit," Luke clarified.

"Yes, I am. So shut up, sit back, and watch your screen like you're watching a movie," Rachel scolded him. "Strat, is the drone up?"

"Yes ma'am. I'm watching their car," Jared confirmed.

"Good. Follow them with the drone and with your own vehicle—legs—whatever you've got. Be more discrete than you've ever been before. Just watch. Do *not* intervene."

"Copy that," Onyx echoed back with varying degrees of enthusiasm. Rachel switched her screens so she could see the footage from the drone and the SEALs' body cameras again.

They followed the car through the city for fifteen minutes before Aquib pulled over and they all got out. Khalid grabbed Yamna by the hair, dragging her to a parked car across the street. Yamna was kicking and screaming, resisting as best she could. Khalid landed a solid punch to her solar plexus. She coughed then started fighting back, clawing at his face, his eyes, his neck. He hit her again, dragging her with him as Aquib unlocked the second car and got into the driver's seat.

Khalid had just landed a punch to Yamna's face when Aquib turned the keys in the ignition and glanced over at him. "Not her face! I need her face!"

Khalid slapped Yamna across the face anyway.

Rachel watched the footage from the drone as the altercation escalated, hoping and praying that Yamna could get away. "How close are you guys?"

"Two blocks," Tyler answered. "Permission to move in?"

"Sky, I have a clear view. She's in bad shape and he's not stopping," Shane added. No medic was comfortable watching someone get hurt if they could intervene.

"The order was to stand down. Do not engage," Luke reminded him.

"Sky!" Shane shouted again.

Assets are expendable. Her father's voice was in her head. *Not every decision can have a positive outcome.* Catherine's too. *Get it together, Ryker. Do not let your emotions cloud your judgement.* Every memory of Yamna flashed through her mind. Sweet, kind, caring Yamna who always wanted to feed everyone. Who'd offered herself to save her children. She was just a girl. A girl desperate for her father's love. Just like Rachel.

"She's an asset," Rachel said, though she was second guessing herself. *Be patient but trust your instincts. Act with integrity.* "One of our best assets."

Before Rachel knew what was happening, Yamna was on top of her father, a knife in her hand and hatred in her eyes. The blade glinted in the moonlight, and she could hear a ferocious, primal growl over the SEALs microphones. The guys were close. She watched as Yamna's arms plunged downwards towards her father's throat, both hands gripping the knife.

"Move in! Save her!" Rachel ordered.

Pandemonium ensued. Rachel couldn't see what was happening as Onyx filled her screen, surrounding Yamna. The only thing she could see was Aquib Faizan speeding away.

"Khan is dead. Faizan is in the wind." Lux announced moments later.

"Yamna needs medical treatment, now!" Shane yelled.

"Pretty sure that's your job, Mirage," Rachel reminded him.

"I mean a hospital. Where do we take her?" Shane asked. Normally, everyone was transferred to a base hospital or Landstuhl. But Yamna wasn't military.

"Take her wherever you'd take yourself," Rachel ordered.

"We'll need approval—" Tyler started.

"Approved! Get her help, and make sure Yashfa and the kids are safe, then get Lux on a plane to Texas. If you need logistics help, call Hertz, but everything, *anything*, you need is approved. Once this is cleaned up, you have a mission complete." Rachel smiled to herself. "I'll see y'all at the wedding."

CHAPTER 52

MAY 2021

RACHEL WAS SITTING IN Admiral Eastwood's office at Command HQ, giving him an update on the situation in Khost. He was less than pleased. Sure, Khalid Khan was dead, but *how* that had come to be was a detail that seemed to be upsetting him.

"Your asset murdered her father?" Eastwood had his head in his hands, elbows on his desk, as he massaged his temples.

"I'm uncomfortable with the word *murder*," Rachel evaded. "Neutralized?" she suggested instead.

"Semantics," Eastwood grumbled. "Now what?"

"Well . . . Ty is cleaning up, Lux is allegedly on a plane, Aquib Faizan is once again in the wind . . ." She was interrupted by her phone ringing. She looked down, saw it was Tyler, and answered, placing the call on speaker immediately so Eastwood could hear too.

"Sitrep!" Eastwood bellowed.

"Oh, good . . . Ummm hi, sir. How are you?" Tyler seemed as excited to be talking to Eastwood as Rachel was.

"I'll be better when I get some actual information," Eastwood grumbled.

"Well, Yamna is getting medical treatment. They think she'll be okay. I called in a favor with the agency. They're going to relocate Yamna and Yashfa's families, get them new identities. It's a whole thing."

"Why?" Eastwood barked.

"Because their safety is at risk," Tyler explained. "Yamna is technically a criminal now. We want to protect them from accusations of collusion with us, hide them from whoever's left of their father's network, from Aquib Faizan. They've done a lot to help us over the years. I'm sure Skylark can give you a detailed run down—"

"How the hell did you pull this off? The CIA is not witness protection!" Eastwood kept getting louder.

"Just called in some favors . . ." Tyler hesitated. "Umm, I was told actually, Sky . . . you have no more favors or pull with them after this."

"Bullshit." Rachel laughed.

"Yeah, I dunno . . ." Tyler tried again. "They seemed pretty mad and put out by the whole thing. I was told to tell you that you're pushing your luck and testing their patience."

"Who specifically at the CIA said to tell me that?" Rachel asked.

"Umm, Eros? I dunno, Agent Eros or Mr. Eros. It wasn't anyone I spoke to personally, so I'm not sure who that is, exactly."

Rachel's eyes got wide as they locked with Eastwood's. They both knew it was the Eros Group, the faction of the CIA that had recruited Rachel so many years ago. They were pissed. She forced her voice to remain calm and steady. "Ty, what else did they say?"

"Something about you staying in D.C. and being on notice. That's all I know. I didn't really understand what they were getting at, but I promised to pass along their delightful words." Tyler's sarcasm was impossible to miss.

"Thanks, Ty. What else do we need to know?" Rachel sighed. She understood the message perfectly well.

"Oh, everything's just about wrapped up here. Lux is en route to D.C. to meet up with you. I'll send you his flight info. You'll need to get yourself and Lux, and I don't know who else, from D.C. to Texas because I couldn't get that sorted from here. Sorry."

"No worries. I'll figure it out," Rachel assured him.

"You should have his flight info now. Just sent it," Tyler said, seconds before Rachel's phone beeped with a notification.

Rachel opened the email on her phone and grimaced. "I think we have to push back the wedding rehearsal to Friday morning."

"That will give me more time to wrap things up." Eastwood nodded. He took Rachel's phone and read the email from Tyler. "Ryker, you and Lux head to Texas as soon as he gets here, and I'll finish things up with Onyx, get them all on a plane, and head there once their travel is confirmed. Ty, get back to whatever you were doing, and I'll check in on you later."

"Copy that, sir," Tyler said before hanging up.

Eastwood glared across the desk at Rachel. "You're out of favors, and they're out of patience."

Rachel rolled her eyes. "I'm not worried about the CIA."

"Maybe you should be. It's been a while since you've done anything they asked—the way they asked, that is."

"Well, I'm not going to worry about that now. I'm going to Texas, I'm getting married, and the CIA can go fuck themselves."

Eastwood raised an eyebrow. "Past decisions and past actions have consequences."

"I'll pay for all my sins when the time comes. For now, I'm choosing to be happy. Being happy requires me to ignore the past, ignore the Eros group and the CIA in general, ignore all the things I know I'll have to do in the future to atone for my past sins, my past decisions and mistakes. They really shouldn't let seventeen-year-olds make such permanent decisions . . ."

"I tried to talk you out of it," Eastwood reminded her.

Rachel shrugged. "I don't care. I don't regret any of it. I'm going to Texas. I'm marrying Christopher. Then, when the time is right, I will remind those assholes that I have so much dirt on them that they'd better not try to threaten me again."

"You're playing with fire," Eastwood noted. "If you don't get in line, just a little, what's stopping them from killing you? I know you could blackmail them for all eternity, but at some point, they'll get sick of that and take you out."

And the real reason Petchill wants me dead. Petchill needed certain people in office to maintain his own power. Frank's revelation that Rachel was not only a Navy SEAL but also CIA had been the final puzzle piece Petchill needed to identify the woman who could take them all down. "You think I don't have a contingency plan for that?" Rachel scoffed. "The day I die, someone, I won't say who, will gain access to certain files and will release them. Unredacted files with pictures, dates, names. Everything. They're stupid if they think killing me would erase their crimes."

"It would expose your crimes too," Eastwood pointed out.

"Yeah, but I'd be dead, so who gives a shit?" Rachel shrugged.

"Your future husband might care."

Rachel dismissed his concern with a wave of her hand. "Christopher knows exactly what I'm capable of. He wouldn't be shocked at all."

"Whatever you say, Ryker." Eastwood shook his head, clearly not agreeing with her.

Rachel responded with a one shouldered shrug. "I can always ask Frank to negotiate with them on my behalf. Buy me a little more time. He is the president. They sort of have to listen to him."

"Yeah, they listen to him about as well as you do." Eastwood changed the subject. "Are you packed and ready to head to Texas, or do you need to go home first?"

"That is a question for Stephanie. I have no idea, but I'll let her sort that out while I start looking for Aquib Faizan."

"For fuck's sake," Eastwood grumbled. He stood from his desk and went out into the hallway. "Hertz!" he yelled at the top of his lungs.

Stephanie came running from Rachel's office. "Yes, sir?" She stood at attention.

"Would you please get this lunatic out of my office and on a plane to Texas so she doesn't miss her wedding? Change her login and password to everything if you have to." He handed Rachel's phone to Stephanie with the details of Luke's flight pulled up.

"Yes, sir." Stephanie tried to suppress her smile but failed. "Ryker, let's go get some travel sorted."

"Fine. But *do not* change my password. I finally memorized the current one."

"Are you changing your last name after you get married?" Stephanie asked.

"No, why?"

"Because, if you were, then you'd be issued a new email and password and everything."

"Another reason not to do that then. Fuck the patriarchy and fuck the IT department." *And fuck the goddamned CIA,* Rachel thought to herself as she followed Stephanie down the hallway.

The elevator pinged and the doors opened. Stephanie pressed the button for the garage just as Rachel's phone buzzed with a notification. It was a text and a link to a video.

Unknown to Skylark: *I got your number off Yamna's phone. /Samir.*

Rachel clicked the link. There was Samir Al-Abadi seated on a cushion on the floor, together with six teenage or preteen girls.

"Fuck me." She angled her screen so Stephanie could see. "Why won't this shit load?" she yelled at her phone as the circle in the middle of the screen continued to swirl and swirl.

"WIFI sucks in the elevator," Stephanie reminded her.

Rachel focused on her breathing, her hand curling into a fist by her side as she stared intently at her phone, waiting for the video to load. The elevator doors opened and Stephanie nudged her towards the car. She followed Stephanie and got into the front passenger seat, buckling her seatbelt as Stephanie accelerated towards the garage exit, turned onto the main road, and hauled ass towards Joint Base Andrews where they would be meeting Luke and hopping a flight to Dallas, Texas.

"Finally!" Rachel exclaimed as the video loaded.

"Skylark, *how* surprised I was to see your name in sweet Yamna's phone!" Samir started in English, his posh London accent coming through loud and clear. "I hope this message finds you well. Or, well enough, at least. Such a tragedy that Kamal did not fulfill his *jihad*. If he had, you'd be dead. The other children—" Samir shook his head. "I seem to have overestimated their competence. Or Khalid Khan's ability to train them. I suppose he won't be an issue anymore!" Samir roared with laughter. "Who knew Yamna had it in her to kill someone? Well, I guess she did." He shrugged. "As you can see," he shifted the camera so she could see six girls seated behind him, "I have the rest of my special helpers here with me." A few of them looked scared. Several others looked drugged. No visible signs of abuse, but all Rachel could really see was their faces. They wore loose clothes and their hair was covered. "Apparently installing malware on a computer was too difficult. It's fine. I have other plans for them now. You see, this business is all about relationships. Building relationships, networking . . . These girls are all virtuous, pious, dutiful girls who aim to please Allah. Their dream is to provide their husband with children, because children are the future. The light and innocence and hope that inspires us all."

"Where the fuck is he going with this?" Stephanie took her eyes off the road and glanced at Rachel's phone.

"Nowhere good. I can assure you, this is leading to something disgusting," Rachel continued.

"Allah encourages us to populate the earth," Samir continued. "Children are a gift from Allah and reproduction is the responsibility of all mankind. With fertility rates declining across the globe, we must take into account biology. Women are educating themselves, staying unmarried and childless longer and longer. As they age, it becomes more difficult for them to reproduce. As such, I have taken it upon myself to pair such pious young women with deserving, virtuous men whose first wives cannot bear them any more children. These girls," Samir glanced over his shoulder at the girls sitting behind him, "have been chosen by Allah to fulfill their sacred duty. As such, they will be married upon their sixteenth birthday in keeping with Pakistani law. I have given this much consideration, and while the Pakistani Council of Islamic Ideology has declared that laws prohibiting child-marriage are un-Islamic, I am a politician and therefore must follow and encourage others to follow the local laws wherever I am. These girls will be the first six to show the way, to inspire other girls to join us, to choose their sacred duty of motherhood and devotion to their husband and family."

The video continued with each girl stating her name, birthday, where she was from, and the phrase "I choose my duty to Allah. I vow to devote myself to the task of bearing children for my husband."

Rachel's eye twitched as she listened to the girls. Something was nagging at her. She pulled up the spreadsheet she'd gotten from Ashley with the information on each of the missing children. The names and birthdays matched.

"Those are the six girls we've been looking for. They're in Pakistan," Rachel told Stephanie, as if she hadn't been listening to the video while she drove. "That's them, right on the screen. All six girls, and we have four months to find them before the first girl turns sixteen."

Epilogue:

MAY 2021

STEPHANIE HAD DROPPED RACHEL off at Joint Base Andrews where she would be meeting up with Luke to head to Dallas for the wedding. Rachel was still in uniform, duffel bag on the ground next to one of the buildings. She wandered around, aimlessly weaving between the planes. Samir's video was playing on repeat in her head.

Four months. In four months, Samir will marry off the first girl to someone.

She didn't know who these intended husbands were, but they had to be awful if Samir had chosen them, if Samir was trying to network and build relationships with them.

She wasn't really paying attention to where she was going. She'd spent her entire childhood on Naval Air Stations, after all, which meant countless hours staring at planes, listening to people talk about planes, and staying out of the way of the people working on the planes—all to her father's dismay since she wasn't supposed to be anywhere near the planes.

"Ma'am, are you supposed to be over here?"

Rachel's head swiveled in the direction of the voice.

"Petty Officer Landon." Her eyes quickly scanned his insignia and name badge. "Where are you headed?" Rachel asked. No, she was not supposed to be over there.

"Islamabad, ma'am."

"Islamabad." Rachel nodded. *Pakistan.* She glanced down the row of planes, instantly spotting the tail number of the one she was supposed to get on, the one headed for Dallas. This might be her one shot—her best shot—at finding Samir.

But Christopher? The wedding?

Her head swiveled back and forth between the two planes. Duty versus honor. Anger versus love. Samir versus Christopher.

Rachel reached down to grab her bag. "Any chance you have room for one more?"